Praise for the novels of
#1 *New York Times* bestselling author

P.C. CAST

"Cast once again challenges readers to look beyond
outward appearances and, simultaneously,
crafts an exciting adventure that will appeal both to
romance and traditional fantasy fans."
—*RT Book Reviews* on *Brighid's Quest*

"The action becomes both intense
and thoroughly entertaining."
—*Kirkus Reviews* on *Destined*

"P.C. Cast is a stellar talent."
—*New York Times* bestselling author Karen Marie Moning

Praise for the novels of
***New York Times* bestselling author**

GENA SHOWALTER

"One of the premier authors of paranormal romance."
—#1 *New York Times* bestselling author Kresley Cole

"Gena Showalter knows how to keep readers
glued to the pages and smiling the whole time."
—*New York Times* bestselling author Lara Adrian
on *The Darkest Surrender*

"The Showalter name on a book
means guaranteed entertainment."
—*RT Book Reviews* on *Twice as Hot*

P.C. CAST

GENA SHOWALTER

AFTER MOONRISE

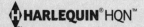

ISBN-13: 978-0-373-77822-5

AFTER MOONRISE

Copyright © 2012 by Harlequin Books S.A.

The publisher acknowledges the copyright holders of the individual works as follows:

POSSESSED
Copyright © 2012 by P.C. Cast

HAUNTED
Copyright © 2012 by Gena Showalter

Recycling programs for this product may not exist in your area.

Printed in U.S.A.

www.Harlequin.com

CONTENTS

POSSESSED

P.C. Cast

Acknowledgments

I want to send hugs and kisses
to Gena Showalter! It is beyond awesome to be
able to work on cool projects with my girlfriend.
Ms. Snowwater, I totally heart you!

A big thank-you to my wonderful longtime editor
Mary-Theresa Hussey. It is soooo nice
to be working with you again!

Katie Rowland—
THANK YOU FOR THE TU DETAILS.
Now go get ready for finals. Seriously.

As always, I appreciate, respect
and adore my agent, Meredith Bernstein.

This one is for my man, the Rose. Thank you for reminding me about hope. I love you.

1

THE BULLY'S DAD caused Raef to discover his Gift. It happened twenty-five years ago, but to Raef the memory was as fresh as this morning's coffee. You just don't forget your first time. Not your first orgasm, your first drunk, your first kill and, not for damn sure, your first experience of being able to Track violent emotions.

The bully's name was Brandon. He'd been a big kid; at thirteen he'd looked thirty-five—and a rough thirty-five at that. At least, that's what he'd looked like through nine-year-old Raef's eyes. Not that Brandon picked on Raef. He hadn't—not especially. Brandon mostly liked to pick on girls. He didn't hit 'em. What he did was worse. He found out what scared them, and then he tortured them with fear.

Raef discovered why the day Brandon went after Christina Kambic with the dead bird. Christina wasn't hot. Christina wasn't ugly. She was just a girl who had seemed like every other teenage girl to young Raef: she had boobs and she talked a lot, two things that, even at nine, Raef had understood were part of the pleasure and the pain of females.

Brandon didn't target Christina because of her boobs or her mouth. He targeted her because somehow he had found out she was utterly, completely terrified of birds.

The part of the day that was burned into Raef's memory began after school. Brandon had been walking home on the opposite side of the street from Raef and his best friend, Kevin. On Brandon's side of the street was a group of girls. They were giggling and talking at about a zillion miles per hour. Brandon was ahead of them and, as usual, by himself. Brandon didn't really have any friends. Raef had barely noticed him and only kinda remembered that he'd been kicking around something near the curb.

Raef and Kevin had been talking about baseball try-outs. He'd wanted to be shortstop. Kev had wanted to be the pitcher. Raef had been saying, "Yeah, you got a better arm than Tommy. No way would Coach pick—"

That's when Christina's bawling had started.

"No, please no, stop!" She was pleading while she cried. Two of her friends had screamed and run off down the street. Two more had stayed and were yelling at Brandon to stop.

Brandon ignored all of them. He'd backed Christina against the fence to Mr. Fulton's front yard, taken the smashed body of what was obviously a road-killed crow and was holding it up, real close to Christina, and making stupid cawing noises while he laughed.

"Please!" Christina sobbed, her face in her hands, pressing herself against the wooden fence so hard that Raef had thought she might smash through it. "I can't stand it! Please stop!"

Raef had thought about how big Brandon was, and how much older Brandon was, and he'd stood there *across the street, ignoring Kevin and doing nothing. Then Brandon pushed the dead bird into Christina's hair and the girl started screaming like she was being murdered.*

"Hey, this isn't your business," Kevin had said when Raef sighed heavily and started crossing the street.

"Doesn't have to be my business. It just has to be mean," Raef had shot back over his shoulder at his friend.

"Bein' a hero's gonna get you in a lot of trouble someday," Kevin had said.

Raef remembered silently agreeing with him. But still he kept crossing the street. He got to Brandon from behind. Quickly, like he was fielding a ball, he snatched the bird out of Christina's hair, and threw it down the street. Way down the street.

"What the fuck is your problem, asshole?" Brandon shouted, looming over Raef like a crappy version of the Incredible Hulk.

"Nothin'. I just think making a girl cry is stupid." Raef had looked around Brandon's beefy body at Christina. Her feet musta been frozen because she was still standing there, bawling and shaking, and hugging herself like she was trying to keep from falling apart. "Go on home, Christina," Raef urged. "He ain't gonna bother you anymore."

It was about two point five seconds later that Brandon's fist slammed into Raef's face, breaking his nose and knocking him right on his butt.

Raef remembered he was holding his bleeding nose and looking up at the big kid through tears of pain and he'd thought, Why the hell are you so mean?

That's when it happened. The instant Raef had won-

dered about Brandon, a weird ropelike thing had appeared around the boy. It was smoky and dark, and Raef had thought it looked like it must stink. It was snaking from Brandon up, into the air.

It fascinated Raef.

He stared at it, forgetting about his nose. Forgetting about Christina and Kevin, and even Brandon. All he wanted was to know what the smoky rope was.

"Fucking look at me when I'm talking to you! It's sickening how easy it is to kick your ass!" Brandon's anger and disgust fed the rope. It pulsed and darkened, and with a whoosh! it exploded down and into Raef. Suddenly Raef could feel Brandon's anger. He could feel his disgust.

Completely freaked out, Raef had closed his eyes and yelled, not at Brandon, at the creepy rope, "Go away!" Then the most bizarre thing happened. The rope-thing had gone away, but in Raef's mind he went with it. It was like the thing had turned into a telescope and all of a sudden Raef saw Brandon's home—inside it. Brandon was there. So were his dad and mom. His dad, an older, fatter version of Brandon, was towering over his mom, who was curled up on the couch, holding herself while she cried and shook like Christina had just been doing. Brandon's dad was yelling at his mom, calling her an ugly, stupid bitch. Brandon watched. He looked disgusted, but not at his dad. His look was focused on his mom. And he was pissed. Really, really pissed.

It made Raef want to puke. The instant he felt sick, actually felt his own feelings again, it was like turning off a light switch. The rope disappeared, along with the telescope and the vision of Brandon's house, leav-

ing Raef back in the very painful, very embarrassing present.

Raef opened his eyes and said the first thing that popped into his head. "How can you blame your mom for your dad being so mean?"

Brandon's body got real still. It was like he quit breathing. Then his face turned beet-red and he shouted down at Raef, spit raining from his mouth. "What did you just say about my mom?"

Raef often wondered why the hell he hadn't just shut up. Got up. And run away. Instead, like a moron, he'd said, "Your dad picks on your mom like you pick on girls. I know 'cause I just saw it. Inside my head. Somehow. I don't know how, though." Raef had paused, thought for a second and then added, trying to figure it out aloud, "Your dad was calling your mom an ugly, stupid bitch last night. You watched him."

Then the weird got, like, weird squared because Brandon reacted as if Raef had all of a sudden grown two feet, gained a hundred pounds and punched him in the gut. The big kid looked sick, scared even, and started backing away, but before he turned and sprinted down the street, he yelled the words that would cling to Raef for the rest of his life. "I know what you are! You're worse than a nigger, worse than a creeper. You're a Psy—a fucking freak. Stay the hell away from me!"

Oh, shit. It was true. No way…no way…

Raef had sat there, bloody, confused and—embarrassingly enough—bawling, while his best friend called his name over and over, trying to get him to snap out of it. "Raef! Raef! Raef…"

"Mr. Raef? Raef? Are you there, sir?"

Coming back to the present, Raef shook himself,

mentally and physically, and picked up the phone, punching the intercom button off. "Yeah, Preston, what is it?"

"Mr. Raef, your zero-nine-hundred appointment is here, thirty minutes early."

Raef cleared his throat and said, "You know, Preston, it's a damn shame my Gift doesn't include predicting the future, or I'd have known that and been ready for her."

"Yes, sir, but then I would probably be out of a job," Preston retorted with his usual dry humor.

Raef chuckled. "Nah, there'd still be all that filing to do."

"It's what I live for, sir."

"Glad to hear it. Okay, give me five and send her in."

"Of course, Mr. Raef. Then I'll get back to my filing."

Raef blew out a breath, grabbed his half-empty coffee mug and stalked over to the long credenza that sat against the far wall of his spacious office. He topped off the coffee and then stood there, unmoving, staring out the window. Not that he was actually seeing the excellent view of Tulsa's skyline on this crisp fall day. Kent Raef was trying to scratch the weird itch that had been tickling his mind all morning.

What the hell was wrong with him? Why the walk down memory lane this morning? God, he hated the thought of that day—hated remembering that scared, crying kid he'd been. He'd just wanted to be shortstop for his team, and try to fit in with everyone else. Instead, he'd been a psychic. The only one in his class. Norms didn't react so well to a Psy—especially not a nine-year-old Psy that could Track violent emotions, no matter how supportive his parents had been—no matter how cool it had been when the USAF Special Forces had recruited him. Raef hated remembering those years and the pain in the ass it had been learning to deal with his Gift and the way asshole Norms reacted to it.

It made him feel like shit to go back there—to revisit those memories. Today it also made him feel kinda shaky, kinda strange. If he didn't know better he'd think he was picking up emotions from someone—soft emotions, like yearning and desire, overshadowed by a deep melancholy.

"Shit, Raef, get it together," he grunted to himself. He did know better. Soft emotions? He snorted. *His* psychic powers didn't work that way—didn't ever work that way. A pissed-off jerk who took out his problems by kicking his dog was the softest Psy Tracking he'd ever picked up. "I need to get a life," he muttered as he returned to his desk and sat down, just in time for the single knock on the door. "Yeah, come in," he snapped.

The door opened, and his secretary, Preston, announced, "Mrs. Wilcox to see you, Mr. Raef."

Raef automatically stood as the tall blonde entered his office. He held out his hand to her, and ignored the fact that she hesitated well into the realm of rudeness before she shook it. A lot of Norms didn't like to be touched by his kind, but *she* had come to *him,* not the other way around, and so she was going to have to play by his rules. On his team, a handshake was non-negotiable.

Of course, her hesitation might be due to the fact that his skin was too brown for her liking—she did have the look of one of those fiftysomething, old-oil-money cougars who were convinced that their shit didn't stink, and that the only reason God made anyone with skin a darker shade than lily-white was because of the unfortunate but unavoidable need for menial laborers.

"Constance Wilcox," she said, finally taking his hand in a grip that was surprisingly firm. He recognized the name as belonging to one of Tulsa society's elite, though he definitely didn't move in those circles.

"Kent Raef. Coffee, Mrs. Wilcox?"

She shook her head with a curt motion. "No, thank you, Mr. Raef."

"All right. Please have a seat." Raef waited for her to settle into one of the straight-backed leather chairs in front of his wide desk before he sat. He didn't particularly like the fact that he'd had old-world gentleman programmed into his genes, but some habits were just not worth the effort it took to break them.

"What can I do for you, Mrs. Wilcox?"

"Don't you already know that?"

He tried not to let his annoyance show. "Mrs. Wilcox, I'm sure my secretary explained that I wouldn't be Reading you. That's now how my Gift works. So, relax. There's no reason for you to be nervous around me."

"If you can't read my mind, how do you know that I need to relax and that I'm nervous?"

"Mrs. Wilcox, you're sitting ramrod straight and you've got your hands so tightly laced together that your fingers are white. It doesn't take a psychic to tell that you're tense and that your nerves are on edge. Anyone with half a brain and moderate powers of observation could deduce that. Besides that, my Gift deals with the darker side of the paranormal. People don't come to me to find lost puppies or communicate with the ghost of Elvis. People come to me because bad things have happened to them or around them, and bad things hap-

pening in a person's life tend to make him or her—"
he tipped his head to her in a slight nod "—nervous
and tense."

She glanced down at her clasped hands and made
a visible effort to relax them. Then she looked back
at him. "I'm sorry. It's just that I'm not comfortable
with this."

"This?" No, hell, no. He wasn't going to make it
any easier for her. Not this morning. Not when it felt
like something was trying to crawl under his skin. He
was fucking sick and tired of dealing with people who
hired psychics from After Moonrise, but acted as if
they'd find it more desirable to work side by side with
someone who was unclogging their backed-up septic
tank—by hand.

"Death." She said the word so softly Raef almost
didn't hear her.

He blinked in surprise. So, it wasn't the psychic part
that had her acting like an ice queen—it was the dead
part. That was easier for him to understand. Death,
specifically murder, was his job. But that didn't mean
he liked it, either.

"Death is rarely a comfortable subject." He paused
and, realizing there was a distinct possibility he had
come off like a prick, attempted to look understanding.
"All right, Mrs. Wilcox, how about we start over. You
do your best to relax, and I'll do my best to help you."

Her smile was tight-lipped, but at least it was a smile.
"That sounds reasonable, Mr. Raef."

"So, you're here because of a death."

"Yes. I am also here because I don't have anywhere
else left to go," she said.

He'd definitely heard that before, and it didn't make

him feel all warm and cuddly and saviorlike, as it would have made some of After Moonrise's other psychics like Claire or Ami or even Stephen feel. Which made sense. They could sometimes save people. Raef only dealt with the aftermath of violence and murder. There was no damn salvation there.

"Then let's get to it, Mrs. Wilcox." He knew he sounded gruff, intimidating even. He meant to. It usually made things move faster.

"My daughter Lauren needs your help. She's why I'm here."

"Lauren was murdered?" Raef dropped the gruffness from his voice. Now he simply sounded clinical and detached, as if he was a lab technician discussing ways to deal with a diagnosis of terminal cancer. He picked up his pen, wrote and underlined *Lauren* at the top of a fresh legal pad, and then glanced back at Mrs. Wilcox, waiting semipatiently for the rest of the story.

She pressed her lips together into a tight line, clearly trying to hold in words too painful to speak. Then she drew a deep breath. "No, Lauren was not murdered. She is alive, but she's not whole anymore. She's only partially here. I need your help to restore her spirit."

"Mrs. Wilcox, I think there has been a mistake made in scheduling. It sounds to me like you need to meet with another member of the After Moonrise team—one of our shamans who specialize in shattered souls. My powers only manifest if there is a murder involved." He started to lift the phone to buzz Preston, but her next words made him hesitate.

"My daughter *was* murdered."

"Mrs. Wilcox, you just said that Lauren is alive."

"Lauren is alive. It's her twin, Aubrey, who was murdered."

Raef put down the phone. "One twin was murdered, and the other's alive?"

"If you can call it that." Her face was pale, her expression strained, but she was keeping herself from crying.

Despite his bad mood his interest stirred. A living twin and a murdered twin? He'd never encountered a murder case like that before.

"Mr. Raef, the situation is that one of my daughters was murdered three months ago. Since then my other daughter has become only a shell of herself. Lauren is haunted by Aubrey."

Raef nodded. "It happens fairly often. When two people are very close—siblings, husband and wife, parent and child—and one of them dies or is murdered, the deceased's spirit lingers."

"Yes, I know," she said impatiently. "Especially when the murder is unsolved."

Raef sat up straighter. This was more like it. "Then you *have* come to the right psychic. I'll need to be taken to the murder scene, and will also need to speak with Lauren. If her twin is haunting her, then I can probably make direct contact with Aubrey through Lauren and piece together what happened. Once the murder is solved, Aubrey should be able to rest peacefully." He rubbed his forehead, wishing the uncomfortable feeling of yearning would get the hell out from under his skin. He was *not* that nine-year-old kid anymore. He was tough, competent, and he knew how to handle his shit.

"Yes, peace. That's what I'm here to find. For both of my girls."

"I'm going to try to help you, Mrs. Wilcox. You said Aubrey was killed three months ago? And the murder hasn't been solved yet? It's unusual that the forensic psychic wasn't able to close this file."

Her blue eyes iced over and the sadness that had been shadowing them was frozen out. "Is solving my daughter's murder what you mean by closing this file?"

Damn! He'd actually said that aloud. What the hell was wrong with him? He might not have the graveside manner of someone like touchy-feely Stephen, but Raef usually showed more tact than offhandedly insulting an already upset client.

"Yes, ma'am. I'm sorry that my wording seemed callous. I assure you that I am cognizant of, and sorry for, your loss."

She continued as if he hadn't spoken. "The reason Aubrey's file wasn't closed is because the police psychic couldn't communicate with my daughter about the murder. Either one of them."

Raef frowned. "That's highly unusual, Mrs. Wilcox. Did you give legal permission for your daughter's spirit to be questioned?"

"Of course," she snapped. "But it's not that simple with Aubrey and Lauren. It never has been."

"I'm sorry, ma'am. I don't understand what—"

Her imperiously raised hand cut him off. "Perhaps it would be easier if I showed you." Without waiting for Raef's response or permission, she stood and walked quickly to the office door. Opening it she said, "You can come in now, Lauren."

The woman who entered his office looked like a younger version of her mother—a leggy, twentysomething blonde with waves of platinum hair so light it was almost white. Her body was lusher than her mother's, who had the appearance of too many carb-free years and maintenance liposuction. Lauren, on the other hand, looked like she might enjoy a burger and a beer once in a while. Scratch that—the expensive silk knit sweater and the designer slacks and shoes said she might enjoy a fillet, a fancied-up potato and some expensive red wine once in a while.

His gaze traveled from her curvy body to her gray-blue eyes, and he felt his own narrow in response to what he saw—emptiness. Her smoky eyes were as expressionless as her face.

Lauren stopped in front of his desk and stared blankly over his shoulder. Then there was a shimmering in the air around her, and a transparent duplicate of her materialized.

It was as Raef got to his feet to face this new apparition that it hit him like a punch in the gut. The ghost radiated waves of emotion—yearning, desire, loneliness, longing—emotions Raef had never picked up from another human being, dead or alive, since his psychic talent first manifested that day so many years ago.

He tried to throw up his mental barriers, the ones he used at murder scenes to successfully block out the lingering spirits and their terror and pain and anger, the only emotions he had, until now, ever been able to Read. But his barriers weren't working. All he could do was stand there and be battered by the desire and longing that emanated from the ghost.

"Kent Raef?" The spirit's voice drifted through his mind.

He cleared his throat before he answered, but his voice still sounded scratchy. "Yes. I'm Kent Raef."

The spirit sighed with relief. *"Finally!"* She glanced at her twin. Lauren blinked, as if coming awake after a long sleep, and the ghost and the girl exchanged smiles. *"Good job, sis."*

"You knew I'd figure it out eventually," Lauren said.

"And you know it bothers me terribly when you speak to the air like that," said Mrs. Wilcox.

"I can tell that corncob is still firmly inserted up your butt, Mother," said the ghost.

Lauren coughed to cover a giggle, which was echoed by the ghost, who laughed out loud.

The laughter in the room raced across his body like static electricity, tingling and bringing all the nerve endings in his skin alive, totally disconcerting him.

Raef pulled his thoughts together. *Ignore the emotions. You can figure out what the hell is going on with that later.* Right now he just needed to do his job—solve the murder, put the spirit to rest, close the case file.

"Aubrey, why don't you tell me about your death and from there I can—"

Raef was interrupted by a shriek that moved across his skin with the force of a blow. Aubrey's mouth was wrenched open as she screamed in agony, a sound that was echoed eerily by her living sister, then her spirit wavered, like heat waves off a furnace, and she disappeared.

2

"So you saw, or at least heard something?" Mrs. Wilcox's words were clipped, and in the silence that followed Aubrey's disappearance her voice sounded
unnaturally loud.

"Aubrey manifested and spoke to me. Briefly."
Raef answered her, although he didn't look at the older
woman. Instead, he was watching Lauren carefully, noting that her empty expression hadn't returned, and even
though her face couldn't be called animated, she at least
didn't look zombielike anymore. And also noting that
the torrent of emotions that had poured from Aubrey
had been abruptly cut off. He cleared his throat, wishing like hell his coffee had a shot of Jack in it. "Please
have a seat, Miss Wilcox. There are several things I
need to go over with both you and your—"

"Why don't you go home, Mother?" Lauren surprised him by interrupting in a brisk, no-nonsense voice
as she sat in the chair beside her mother's. "It would
probably be better if I answered his questions alone."

"What if it returns, Lauren?"

"Mother, I've told you before that I see Aubrey a

lot. She's dead. That doesn't make her an it. She's still Aubrey."

"I wasn't speaking of your sister's ghost," Mrs. Wilcox said coolly. "I'm referring to the horrid fugue state that sometimes comes over you."

"Mother, I've tried to explain this to you before, too. It doesn't just 'come over' me. There's a reason for it." Mrs. Wilcox's face remained implacable and Lauren sighed. "I'm not going to be driving. If I zone out again I'm sure Mr. Raef can babysit me long enough to get me home."

"Lauren, I…" her mother began, and then seemed to check herself. She stood and inclined her head formally to Raef. "I assume you will be certain my daughter returns home safely?"

"I will," Raef said, not liking the family drama he'd stepped into.

"Then I will speak to you later, Lauren. It was a pleasure to meet you, Mr. Raef."

After the door closed behind her mother, Lauren sat and met Raef's gaze. "She's not as cold and uncaring as she comes off as being. But all of this is just too much for her."

"Define *this*," he said.

"*This* would be my sister's death and the fact the police have been unable to solve it. Add a dash of Aubrey haunting me with a sprinkle of possession and stir in a big blob of my soul being drained and you get a recipe that would freak out anyone's mom." Lauren's voice was calm, her body appeared relaxed. It was only in her blue eyes that her desperation showed.

Raef got up and walked to the credenza. He topped off his coffee and then poured a generous cup for Lauren. "Cream or sugar, Miss Wilcox?" he asked over his shoulder.

"Both, and if we're going to work together I wish you'd call me Lauren."

He fixed the coffee and then handed it to her. "Lauren it is. My friends call me Raef." He resumed his seat and gave her a brief smile. "Actually, my enemies call me Raef, too."

"Do you have many enemies, Raef?"

"Some," he said. "Do you?"

She shook her head. "No."

"How about your sister?"

"No. That's just one of the reasons this whole thing is so awful. None of it makes sense."

"Tell me what you know about your sister's death, and I'll see if I can begin making some sense out of it."

"I don't know where to start." Lauren's impassive expression tensed and when she sipped her coffee Raef noticed her hands were trembling.

"Start at the beginning. When was she killed?"

"July 15. She was alone, even though she shouldn't have been. I'm almost always with her on jobs—" She paused, flinched in obvious pain. "I mean, I *used to* almost always be with her." Lauren corrected herself and regained her composure, then continued in a steadier voice. "July is in the middle of our busy season for maintenance, so we often had to split up to finish jobs on time."

"Maintenance? What type of work did you and your sister do?"

"Landscaping. July can be a rough month on plants if we don't get enough rain and the Oklahoma heat turns up early, like it did this past July. Plants burn up if they're not maintained properly through the heat. Aub and I own Two Sisters Landscaping. Or at least we did." She faltered again, and took another sip of her coffee. "I'm sole owner now."

"Of the company? As in you are the biggest stockholder?"

"Own the company as in Aubrey and I started it, ran it and were its first two employees." She met his eyes. "Yes, we actually got our hands dirty. A lot." She held up one hand and Raef's brows lifted in surprise when he saw that instead of being well manicured and delicately white, Lauren had short, bluntly clipped nails and obvious calluses on her work-hardened palm. He would have never guessed that the daughters of a rich Tulsa socialite would be into something as blue-collar as landscaping.

"I would have thought a psychic would be better at hiding his thoughts," Lauren said.

Raef looked from her hand to her eyes. Then, much to his own surprise, he heard himself admitting, "I usually am."

"Dirt-digging girls from rich families must seem pretty unusual to you," Lauren said.

Raef gave her a lopsided smile. "Sounds like it's a reaction you're used to."

"Let's just say our family wasn't thrilled when Aubrey and I opened the business six years ago. We were lucky they couldn't stop us."

"Explain that," Raef said. He didn't feel the prickle of foreboding he usually did when he stumbled on what would eventually become a lead for solving a murder, so he really didn't need to question Lauren about her family's attitude about her business, but he realized he *wanted* to question her—wanted to know more.

And that was odd as hell.

"Aubrey and I received an inheritance from our grandfather when we turned twenty-one. It was ours to do whatever we wanted with—so we started our own business, but instead of buying a chic little boutique in Utica Square someone else could run, or following family tradition and investing in real estate, we bought plants and dirt. At least, that's how our mother put it. Our decision wasn't popular, but it was ours to make."

"So, how was business?"

"Excellent. It still is. We have five employees and have had to actually turn away jobs. That's why Aubrey was alone that day—we'd overextended and she was the expert in aquatic plants. So she went by herself to Swan Lake."

Raef felt a shock of recognition, and couldn't believe he hadn't put two and two together before then. "Aubrey Wilcox, middle of July, electrocuted to death while she was working with the water plants on the Swan Lake island." Then he realized why he hadn't recognized the name on his appointment book. It wasn't a murder investigation. The death had been ruled accidental. What the hell?

"It wasn't an accident," Lauren said firmly, as if she was the mind reader.

"But if I pulled the police report it would say your sister's death was accidental, wouldn't it?"

"Yes. Does that mean you won't take the case?"

"No, I'll take the case." Which was nothing unusual. Sometimes families needed his services for closure. Hell, not just *his* services, but psychics in general. The

police could tell the bereaved over and over that it was
suicide, or an accident, and they would still hold on to
the hope that there was a bad guy, a reason, a focus for
their rage and despair. That's where a Psy came in—
and it was one of the reasons they'd become big business, even in a world that was mostly filled with Norms
who were uncomfortable with psychic Gifts. By communicating with the spirit of the dead person directly,
a psychic could help families come to terms with the
truth, move on, find closure. Of course, Raef person-
ally usually preferred a good, old-fashioned murder
case—hatred and anger he could deal with. Despair
was another story.

"Aubrey told me she was killed."

Raef shook himself mentally. "I thought your sister's
spirit was having a hard time communicating about
her death." He'd witnessed that. He'd asked her about
her murder and she definitely *hadn't* communicated
with him.

"She *is* having a hard time communicating. When I
say she *told me* I don't mean that she actually said, 'Hey,
sis, I was murdered.' I mean she told me in here." Lauren closed her fist over her heart. "There are things she's
not allowed to put into words, but I can *feel* them. She
and I have always been two halves of the same whole. I
don't know how else to explain it because if you're not
us, it might be impossible to comprehend. Add to the
whole confusing mix that whatever is going on after
Aub's death is affecting me, and you have some serious
weirdness. Raef, the truth is, even I don't understand
what's really happening. I was hoping you could help
me—help us. Please help us, Raef."

Raef paused, studied Lauren and collected his

thoughts. When he finally spoke it was slowly, as if he was processing information aloud. "The police ruled her death an accident, but your twin has made it clear to you, and only you, that she was murdered. Is that correct?"

"Yes."

"And even though she manifests to you, which I've witnessed, there still seems to be some barrier between the two of you, as if she's being blocked or controlled by another force?"

"Yes, especially when she tries to communicate with me directly about her murder." She sounded incredibly relieved. "You can't know what a relief it is to talk to someone who doesn't call me a freak and who will actually listen to me!"

His smile was authentic, but grim. "Try being a nine-year-old who can Track negative emotions, and only negative emotions. I understand what it's like to be discounted and called a freak."

Lauren expelled a long breath in a relieved sigh. Her shoulders relaxed and she finally took a sip of her coffee. "Good. Then we talk the same language."

"So your sister is actually possessing you," he said, looking up from the notes he was taking. That was unusual. Possession by a spirit wasn't unheard of, of course, but spirits didn't usually possess family members. He couldn't remember ever hearing of one twin possessing another.

"Well, I don't know if you'd call it real possession. She manifests, like she did earlier, and we can talk." She paused, blinking hard as if trying to keep herself from crying. "I miss her. A lot. I don't feel normal without her." Lauren shook her head and wiped at her eyes. "But that's not what's important. What's important is that when she does try to communicate with me about her death, she gets ripped away from here and I can feel what's happening to her, and it's like…" Lauren's words trailed off. She shuddered. "It's like I'm being killed, too."

"Hang on. Your sister's already dead. Maybe what you're feeling is her struggle to stay attached to you while her spirit is being drawn to the Otherworld. Lauren, the truth is that for most spirits it is difficult for them to remain on this plane of existence. They should be moving on." He tried to speak soothingly, but he wasn't good at the touchy-feely stuff. Plus, it was looking more and more as if he should just refer Lauren and her family, dead and alive, to the After Moonrise medium.

"You're not getting it," Lauren said, looking more and more animated. "Aubrey isn't moving on. She can't. He's not done killing her."

"Come again?"

Lauren sighed. "This is what Aubrey has been able to tell me: her killer has bound her spirit. He's bound all of their spirits. Physical death was just the beginning of their murders. He doesn't stop until he drains their souls of life, too. You have to find him. He's not done killing."

3

"And you know that this psychic serial killer is draining spirits because your sister told you in there." Raef pointed to where Lauren still clenched her fist over her heart.

Her spine stiffened and her chin went up. "Don't patronize me, Raef. I know it the same way you know you're talking to ghosts of the dead instead of your own overactive imagination, even though no one else can see and feel what you do."

"All right." He nodded his head slowly. "You got me there." He stood up and took his keys from his desk drawer. "Then let's go."

"Go?"

"To the scene of Aubrey's accident."

"You mean to the place she was murdered," Lauren said firmly.

"Either way, I need to check it out." He raised a dark brow at her when she didn't move. "You did know that it is my standard procedure to go to the site of the death, didn't you?"

"Yes—yes, I knew," she stuttered. "It's just that, well, I haven't been back there since."

"Not once? Not even when your sister has been manifesting to you?"

Lauren shook her head. "No." The word was a whisper.

"I can take you home first," he said, walking around his desk to her. "We can talk afterward and—"

"Would it be better if I come with you?" she interrupted, her voice sounding firmer. "I mean, for you and the investigation."

"It probably would be, especially because your situation is so unique."

Lauren stood. "Then I'll go."

THE TRIP FROM THE After Moonrise downtown offices to Midtown's Swan Lake was short and silent. Not that Raef minded. He was naturally quiet and never had understood the need most people felt to chatter uncomfortably to fill a peaceful lull. He also had to ready himself for what would happen when he visited the site of a death and opened himself to the psychic images left there. Accident or murder, it wasn't exactly a walk in the damn park, and it was always better to take a quiet moment to center himself first.

As he drove down Utica Street, he glanced at Lauren. Her face was pale and set. She was staring straight ahead. He thought she looked like a marble sculpture of herself.

"It's not going to be that bad," he said, turning right at the entrance to the lake and parking his car along the curb that ringed the area. "I'm the psychic, remember?" Raef tried to add some lightness to the moment.

She turned cold blue eyes on him. "She was my sister. My twin. We've been together since we were conceived. Psychic or not, going to the place where she was killed scares me."

Before he could even try to come up with something comforting to say, her gaze moved from his to Swan Lake. She shook her head and gave a little humorless laugh, saying, "It's stupid to call this place a lake. It's tiny. Except for having water, there's nothing 'lake' about it."

"They call it Swan Lake because Swan Pond doesn't sound right," he said.

She looked back at him. "I hate this place."

He nodded. "That's a normal reaction, Lauren. Your sister died here—of course you have a strong negative reaction to it."

"There's more to it than that."

He wanted to tell her that the relatives of the dead always felt like there was more to it than simple death, even if it took their loved one peacefully, in the middle of the night, during the winter of life. Instead, he swallowed back the condescension and said, "Are you ready? You can wait here if you need to."

"I'm ready, and I'm going with you."

She sounded one hundred percent sure, but her face was still unnaturally pale as they walked slowly to the sidewalk that circled the oblong-shaped body of water. Raef thought that Lauren had been right—the place was no damn lake, even if it was pretty and well tended. The sidewalk had only a fourth of a mile circumference, or at least that's what the helpful signpost said. It was the same signpost that talked about the different types of waterfowl that could be found in the area, in particular noting the mated pair of swans for which the lake had been named.

The sign also asked visitors not to feed the fowl, including the swans. And it insisted everyone except "authorized personnel" remain outside the fence that ringed the area.

"The entrance to the dock that takes you to the island is over there." Lauren pointed down the sidewalk to their right.

Raef nodded and they continued walking. He glanced around them. The October morning hadn't turned cold and cloudy yet, as Channel Six weather had predicted. Big surprise that they got it wrong. So it was a gorgeous morning, but an off hour, only just before 10:00 a.m. Too late for morning walkers and bird-watchers, and too early for those who liked to eat their lunch at the park. There was only a retired couple sitting on a bench on the opposite side of the lake, reading a paper together. *Good. Less gawkers,* he thought, while he followed the line of the sturdy green fence that ensured park visitors didn't disturb the waterfowl. A flurry of honking and splashing pulled his gaze to the lake. One of the swans was bullying a group of ducks that must have drifted too close to his personal space.

"They're mean," Lauren said. "Doesn't matter how pretty they are—they're mean and dirty. And the biggest reason my company has to come out here so often."

"You still have the contract to maintain the plants here?"

Lauren nodded, but she looked uncomfortable. "Aubrey wants it that way. She doesn't like to let a little thing like her death get in the way of good business."

"But you said you hadn't been here since her death."

"I haven't. I have five employees, remember?"

Then Lauren's use of the present tense about her sister's wishes caught up to his thoughts. "So she communicates with you about your business?"

"She communicates with me about lots of things, just not about her murder. Actually, I don't feel right unless she and I are talking. I don't feel whole without her…." Lauren's words trailed off as she came to an awkward silence. As if just realizing what she'd said, she shook her head and attempted a smile. "I'm repeating myself, but it's hard not to. My life isn't the same without her."

Raef started to comment, but Lauren's humorless laugh silenced him. "Yeah, I know. It's normal for me to feel her loss. Normal for things to be different. Normal to grieve." She shook her head, looking out at the small lake. "I've heard it all. Not one single person really gets it."

There didn't seem to be anything Raef could say to her that hadn't been said, obviously to no effect, by others. Plus, maybe Lauren was right. He'd never heard of a twin manifestation and possession before. Maybe there were unusual forces at work in this death. Who was he to scoff at the abnormal? Hell, he lived in Abnormalville; even the other psychics at After Moonrise kept him at a distance. You don't have to be a Greek god to know that if you invite Discord to a party, all hell is gonna break loose.

Shit, his life sucked.

They'd come to a locked gate in the fence, and Lauren stopped. Just inside the gate there was a small wooden dock and a slim, slatted walkway that led from it to the island of craggy stone, foliage and a waterfall-like fountain cascading down one side of it that sat in the middle of this end of the lake. "There." Lauren's voice was pitched low. "It's out there that it happened." The eyes she turned to him were haunted with sadness. "You'll need to go out there, won't you?"

"Yes."

She drew a deep breath. "Then let's go." Lauren flipped open the metal cap that held an elaborate keypad for the locking mechanism on the gate. Her hands shook only a little as she pressed the series of buttons that made the gate whir and click, and finally open. Without waiting for him, she strode through it and onto the dock. It was only then that she stopped, hands fisted at her sides, eyes looking at her feet, at the water, at the shore. Everywhere except out at the island.

"I'll be right behind you," Raef said.

"Okay. Yes. Okay. I can do this."

Lauren stepped onto the walkway. Raef stayed close to her, worried that she might pass out and fall into the damn water. That was something neither of them needed. They were halfway to the island when Raef steeled himself and then dropped the barriers he usually kept firmly locked around his mind.

Death, he whispered to himself, *come to me.*

He braced himself for the influx of terror and anger and hurt and pain that always flooded him so near the site of a death.

And there was nothing. Absolutely nothing.

The only thing he felt was the brush of the unseasonably warm October breeze and his own confusion.

"Here." Lauren had reached the island. Raef realized he'd stopped and quickly closed the distance between them. "This is where it happened." She pointed a shaky hand at the base of the rocky island where it met the water. There were several floating plants that looked to Raef like lily pads, along with some bushy clumps of underwater grasses. "Aubrey was replacing the water lilies, trimming the black bamboo and cleaning the algae from the spirogyra. She stepped down there—" Lauren motioned to a ledgelike edge of the island "—and was working with the plants, half in and half out of the water. The mechanism that powers the pump to the waterfall is under that ledge. The police say she cut the electrical line while she was working with the plants. The pump shorted out, sending an electrical current through the water and killing Aubrey. Technically, that's what happened. But it was no accident."

"Are you sure?"

Lauren's pale cheeks flushed. "I already told you. I am absolutely certain my sister was killed!"

"That's not what I'm asking. I want to know are you sure that this is where she died."

"Of course I am."

"Her death happened here and not at St. John's?" Raef made an impatient jerk of his chin at the hospital that was directly across the street from Swan Lake.

"Yes. She was dead when the joggers found her. They even came to her funeral. I talked to one of them myself. She was floating facedown in the water right there, tangled in the spirogyra grass." Lauren's hand was still a little shaky when she pointed to the spot below them where her sister's body had been discovered. "There—right there is where they pulled her from the pond."

Raef didn't say anything else. He just continued to stare at the water and the odd, curling grass that floated like Medusa's hair just beneath the surface.

Nothing. He felt nothing.

"Raef, what is it? What's happening?"

"Your sister couldn't have died here."

Lauren frowned at him. "Of course she did. That's the one part of the police report that was completely accurate."

"How about the coroner's report? Are you sure it concurred?"

"Yes. The coroner listed her time of death as more than an hour before the joggers called 9-1-1."

"You've read it? You've seen the report?"

"Yes and yes. I've scoured over it. I practically have it memorized, much to the TPD's irritation. Raef, what is it?"

"There's nothing here. No psychic Tracing of a death at all. And that is impossible."

Lauren opened her mouth, but instead of speaking, a strangled gasp wrenched from her. She swayed, her eyes fluttering, and Raef moved quickly to her side, steadying her by grasping her arm.

"Easy there. I'll figure this out and—" His words broke off abruptly as emotions rippled through him. But they weren't death scene emotions, familiar if numbing in their violence. Instead, joy and warmth and a poignant sense of longing filled him. He tried to throw up his mental barriers, but his traitorous Gift ignored it, leaving him naked and defenseless to the onslaught. Then the air beside Lauren rippled and her twin's ethereal body manifested.

"I knew you'd come. I knew you wouldn't let us down. I remembered you from that article in Oklahoma Today *magazine last year."* She grinned impishly. *"It said you were the best psychic detective in*

Oklahoma—that you were like an Old West sheriff. You always got your man."

Raef swallowed hard, trying to pull himself together. *I can feel her joy!* Never before. Never during the twenty-five years his Gift had manifested had he ever felt a positive emotion from any spirit.

Aubrey laughed and the sound washed through his body like magic, sensitizing his nerves and his skin so that the fine dark hair on his forearms prickled as if she had just run a teasing, caressing hand over them.

"Ah, come on, Kent, relax. You look like you've seen a ghost," she said, still smiling joyously.

"Raef." He ground the word out automatically, the usual gruffness of his voice intensified by the force of the emotions filling him. "People call me Raef."

"I'm not going to," Aubrey said. *"I like Kent better. Plus, you can't really call me a person anymore, can you?"*

Raef just stared at her. Had a spirit ever called him anything? No, hell, no, none of them had. He usually just Tracked the negative emotions left by the bad guys. He followed violence and hatred and fear until it led him to a living murderer. Ghosts didn't have shit to do with him.

Until *this* ghost.

Aubrey's gaze went from him to sweep around Swan Lake. *"It's beautiful here, don't you think? The trees are particularly lovely. So wise and strong, like soldiers standing guard."* She turned shimmering blue eyes back to him. *"They must take a lot of care."*

As soon as she'd spoken the words Raef felt it. The slicing pain hit him as Aubrey's semitransparent body doubled over. Lauren moaned, and her arm trembled violently under his grasp.

"Kent!" Aubrey gasped. *"Help us!"*

She disappeared as Lauren collapsed into his arms.

4

"OH, GOD," LAUREN groaned. "I think I'm going to be sick."

"No. Not here." Raef slid an arm around her waist and half carried, half dragged her from the dock and through the gate. He'd retraced their path and was almost to the car when Lauren spoke again.

"Wh-where are we going?"

"Don't know. Right now I'm just getting us the hell outta here," he said, wrenching open the door to the car and guiding her semicarefully into the passenger seat. He hesitated, watching her closely as she sat, face in hands, and trembled. "You still gonna be sick?"

"Maybe," she muttered into her hands.

Yeah, well, me, too, he thought, but instead said, "Try not to be," then closed her door and hurried around the car, putting it in gear and getting the hell outta there. Silent and on autopilot he drove, turned left on Lewis and was halfway to Fifteenth Street before he realized he was heading for his house. *What the fuck is wrong with me? I'm taking a client home?* Raef glanced at Lauren. She'd taken her face from her hands. Her arms were wrapped around her, as if she was literally trying to hold herself together. Her face had gone from dead pale to splotchy pink. She was still trembling.

Suddenly she reminded him of Christina Kambic all those years ago, and he had a terrifying urge to protect her. *Shit! Shit! Shit! What's wrong with me?*

"I'm not going to be sick. At least, not right now," Lauren said stiffly, definitely misunderstanding his sideways glances.

"Want me to take you home?" he asked inanely.

"No." Lauren made two quick shakes of her head.

"Your mother's place?"

"Hell, no." She looked straight at him then. "Anywhere but there."

He only met her blue-gray eyes for a moment before making his decision. Raef grunted and turned right on Fifteenth, catching the green light and taking a quick left on Columbia, entering the quaint little neighborhood that was hidden between busy Fifteenth Street and kinda dicey Eleventh Street. He drove down a couple side streets, took another left and then pulled into the cobblestone driveway of the 1920s-era brick house he called home.

Raef turned off the car and looked at Lauren, who was gazing at him, an obvious question mark on her flushed face. He blew out a long, frustrated breath, got out of the car and opened her door for her. "It's my place," he explained. "I don't take clients here."

"Yet here I am," she said as he closed the car door behind her.

"Yeah, well, that's just part of a list of *don'ts* that I've broken today." As they walked together up the curving sidewalk that led to his spacious front porch, he held up his hand and ticked off fingers like an umpire keeping count of strikes. "First, I *don't* usually feel as fucking bizarre as I did right before I met you." He paused when they were standing on the porch and added, "And your dead sister." Another finger went up. "Then I *don't* go to a murder scene—a documented scene of a death—and not pick up death emotions."

"Death emotions?" she interrupted.

He bit back his annoyance and answered her with a sharp nod and a sharper tone of voice while he dug in his pocket for his house key. "Yeah, death emotions. Bad ones. Like fear and panic and agony and hatred. Being able to Track negative emotions is my Gift."

"That sucks," she said.

He shrugged. "It's the way it is—the way it's been since I was nine."

"Yeah, don't take this the wrong way, but a Psy Gift is really pretty weird. I mean, it's not like anyone can predict it."

"You're telling me?" He snorted, and then opened the door for Lauren and motioned for her to go inside, following her closely, still explaining but also watching how her eyes opened in surprise as she took in the sheen of the hardwoods and his antiques that were comfortable as well as expensive and tasteful. "Which leads to don't number three." He put up the last finger. "I *don't* feel what I felt when your twin manifested—joy." Raef paused again and shook his head, remembering. "I even felt her laughter. *Her laughter.*"

Lauren's brow furrowed. "But you're a psychic. Feeling emotions is what you guys do."

"It's not that simple. No one just gets a blanket ESP stamp, like, *Hey, here ya go, buddy, now you're a psy-*

chic so you can read everyone's minds," he said sarcastically.

"Look, you don't have to sound like that. I don't know about this psychic stuff. No one really does—or at least I don't think anyone really does." She put her hands on her hips. "It's not like your people are super-open with how the Gift works."

"It's not like *your* people really give a shit," he countered.

"Well, I give a shit now!" Lauren shouted, surprising both of them. She sighed and ran her fingers through her hair. "Sorry. I'm not usually such a bitch."

He chuckled. "Yeah, well, I'm usually such a bastard."

The air around them shimmered, and then, in the middle of Raef's living room, Aubrey manifested, saying, *"No wonder you don't bring women home."*

This time her emotions were muted. Her sparkle wasn't totally gone, but it had definitely dimmed. Still, she smiled at him, and as she did Raef felt a flutter of pleasure wash against his skin as, once again, he picked up her emotions. *She's pleased to see me,* Raef realized. *That's what I'm feeling.*

"He didn't say he didn't bring *women* home." Lauren broke into his internal dialogue. She shook her head at her twin, speaking to her in a totally normal, if tired, voice. "He said he didn't bring *clients* home. I've been telling you for years, if you're gonna eavesdrop, get it right."

"Touché," Aubrey said, grinning at her sister.

Raef frowned at both women. "It's not just about me not bringing clients here. I also don't bring work home. Period."

"You mean this cool old house is a no-ghost zone?" Aubrey said impishly.

Raef didn't say anything because he was feeling her playful sense of humor, and that feeling had his voice lodged somewhere in his gut.

"I have to sit down," Lauren said, glancing at him and then the wide leather couch. "Do you mind?"

"Yeah, I mean, no. Hell, I mean, yes, you may sit," Raef stuttered like an idiot.

Aubrey giggled, obviously getting some of her sparkle back.

"You're freaking him out," Lauren said as she sat heavily. "And you're exhausting me."

Aubrey's sparkled dimmed. "Sorry, sis," she said. She didn't move to sit beside her sister, whose face was back in her hands, but Raef watched her lift a semitransparent hand toward her, like she wanted to touch her. He felt her sadness then, and realized he hated it and had a ridiculous urge to do something, anything, to erase her sadness and bring back her joy—her joy he could feel.

And that was just fucking not normal.

"Okay, that's enough," he said gruffly. Both women, alive and dead, turned their pretty faces to him. "I need to know what the hell is going on here." He pointed at the ghost. "Were you murdered or not?" Raef watched the twins exchange a look.

Lauren spoke first. "Tell him. He'll see, and it'll make the explanation easier."

"It'll hurt," Aubrey said.

"I know. Just do it fast and get it over with. I'll see you again soon," Lauren said.

Aubrey nodded and then faced him. She met his gaze for a long time—long enough for Raef to be struck by her beauty. Yeah, she looked a whole lot like her twin, that figured. But she was softer, curvier, shorter—and her hair was longer. Just then it was lifting around her in response to a nonexistent wind.

"I know you can help us. I believe in you, Kent."

He knew she was telling the truth. He could feel her belief. It was warm and strong and very, very disconcerting—which left him utterly unprepared for her next words, and the flood of agony that followed them.

"My body was murdered by a man who has trapped my soul and the souls of a lot of other people. He's feeding off our pain. His name is—" Aubrey's words were sliced off as her ghost was ripped in half and Lauren shrieked with her twin in agony—an agony Raef felt all too well, an agony so great that it had his vision narrowing and his heart racing. The torn pieces of Aubrey's ghost were burned away like morning mist before sunlight and she was gone. Again.

Raef realized he had staggered to the couch and was clutching the back of it to keep himself upright. He raised a shaking hand and wiped sweat from his brow. The sound of a body dropping to the floor had him struggling to refocus in time to see that Lauren had slumped, unconscious, from the couch.

"Shit!" Raef hurried to her, carefully lifting her back on the couch, laying her down and checking for a pulse. "Strong and steady," he muttered. "Good—good. Hey, come on. Wake up. You're fine. Everything's fine," he said, more for himself than for her.

Lauren's eyelids fluttered and then opened. He started to breathe a long, relieved sigh, but then he realized how vacant those blue-gray eyes looked. Not only was the light not on, but nofuckingbody was home.

And that scared the shit out of him, so much so that he automatically fell back into what he knew best about dealing with while scared. His voice deepened, hardened, and MSgt Raef barked at her like the Special Forces NCOIC he'd once been. "Lauren! Get your ass back here on the fucking double! You haven't been given permission to go any damn where!"

Lauren blinked, shook her head as if she'd just come in from the rain, and then her eyes animated and she focused on his face. "Raef."

Even though the name wasn't a question, he nodded. "You're back. Good."

"Feel bad, though," she said weakly.

He grunted and nodded. "Bet you do. Your soul's attached to Aubrey's, isn't it?"

"Yes. Always." The two words were whispers.

"All right. Well, that explains a lot about this cluster fuck." He stood.

"Are you leaving?"

"Sadly, no. You're in my house, remember?"

Lauren looked around, as if she hadn't remembered until then. "Oh, yeah, that's right. You don't bring clients here."

"I don't brew strong tea with honey for them, either. Which is what I'm going to do for you. Sit. Don't move. Don't faint. And don't fucking disappear on me again."

"Yes, sir," she said with what he already understood was uncharacteristic meekness.

He stopped halfway to the kitchen. "And for Christ's sake, don't call me sir. I was an NCO. I used to work for a living, unlike a fucking officer."

He didn't need to be psychic to feel Lauren's confusion all the way from the living room. "Civilians…" he grumbled as he clattered through his orderly cupboards and flipped on the electric kettle, tossing a bag of English breakfast tea, a dollop of local honey, a squeeze of fresh lemon *and* a healthy slosh of single-malt Scotch into each of the large mugs.

When he brought the brewed and spiked tea to the living room he was relieved to see that Lauren was sitting up and studying the art on his fireplace mantel. She turned and raised a brow at him. "Erté?"

"Yep," he said, handing her the mug of tea. She took the couch and he sat in a leather chair across from it.

"Your wife likes Erté?"

"Not married. Anymore. And no, she did not. I like Erté."

"Erté was gay."

"Yes, I'm aware of that."

She raised a brow at him. "You were military, weren't you?"

"Air force—OSI, that's Office of Special Investigations to civilians. Ten years—been out for almost five now," he said, sipped his tea and then added, "FYI—most military men don't give a shit whether the guy beside him is gay. They care more that the guy will stay beside him and cover his back. You shouldn't stereotype, Miss Wilcox, since you don't appreciate it when people assume you're just some stuck-up rich bitch who doesn't work for a living."

Her other brow raised at the word *bitch,* but she just sipped her tea, nodded and said, "Scotch and lemon and honey is my sister's favorite kind of tea."

"Was," Raef corrected her. "She's dead. Let's start right now with dealing with that, even though you can still see her and talk to her. That might help you start separating yourself from what's happening to her—at least long enough for me to try to figure out how to catch the guy who's doing it to her."

"She's not going to be able to help you do that."

"Because he's keeping her from helping me," Raef said.

"He's keeping her from helping anyone—even me. Any time Aubrey tries to talk about her murder, even tries to hint about it, it's like he has some kind of electric line into her soul." Lauren shook her head and Raef could see she was fighting back tears. "How the hell can he keep causing her such pain even after her body is dead?"

Raef didn't have one damn clue about how to answer that question, so he countered with one of his own. "It's not just Aubrey who feels pain caused by him. It's you, too."

"Yes, it's me, too. And that's not all. She's getting weaker. He's draining her, and the weaker she gets— the more she's drained—the weaker I get. Somehow he can use her, and apparently several other people, even though they are all dead." Lauren stared into his eyes. "How? How is he doing it?"

"I'm going to be straight with you, Lauren. I've never heard of anything like this. Even when I was in the air force and Tracked terrorists. I experienced some really bad stuff, and some really bizarre stuff, but nothing that was leeching a ghost's soul *and* the ghost's living twin. Sorry, but I just don't have the answers for you."

"So, basically, you don't know what you're doing."

"Basically, you're correct. With your case I do not."

"Well, then, what am I going to do? Just fade away with Aubrey where we'll exist forever somewhere be-

tween agony and darkness?" This time a tear escaped
Lauren's eye and rolled down her smooth cheek.

"Not if I can help it," Raef heard himself say.

Lauren threw up her hands and repeated, "How?"

"By doing something I hate like hell. I'm going to
call in the cavalry and ask for help, even though it's a
damn annoying cavalry and she's going to be obnox-
iously pleased that she's going to have to bail me out."

5

"SHE'S WAY TOO small to be the cavalry," Lauren whispered from beside Raef.

They were sitting at his huge old desk peering into the big-screen Mac as the redhead answered the video call. She raised a scarlet brow and turned clear green eyes on Lauren, saying, "I don't know what you mean by cavalry, but *she's* not deaf."

"Hey, I'm sorry," Lauren began. "I didn't mean to—"

"Yeah, yeah, stand down, tough girl," Raef interrupted. "Milana Buineviciute, this is Lauren Wilcox. She's a client of mine and *I* called you the cavalry, she didn't." Raef moved his gaze from the quick-tempered little redhead to Lauren. "Lana is the head medium for our Oklahoma City branch of After Moonrise. She's a pain in the ass, and even though she claims to be Lithuanian I suspect her of being a Russian spy, *but* she knows more shit about ghosts than anyone I've ever met. Not that that's a compliment."

"Atsiknisk," Lana told Raef blandly. "Which means 'fuck off'—in Lithuanian, *not* Russian. Try moving into the twenty-first century, Raef. The Cold War has

been over for longer than I've been alive." She looked at Lauren. "Good to meet you, Lauren." Lana glanced back at Raef. "Hey, *sudzius,* she's not a ghost."

"I've worked with you long enough to know you're calling me a shithead, and I know Lauren isn't a ghost, Nazi. It's her twin sister who is dead."

"Nazis were German, not Russian or Lithuanian," Lana told Raef smoothly before turning her attention back to Lauren. "A twin's death is always difficult. Her ghost, she is with you?"

Lauren nodded. "Yes, quite often, actually."

"What you are doing with this girl?" Lana snapped the question to Raef, her accent suddenly becoming more pronounced with her annoyance. "She should be working with a medium. If Vivian Peterson isn't the right choice there in Tulsa, bring her here to me."

"Her sister was murdered—that's why she's here with me, not because I'm into overtime or trying to poach someone's clients. You should know that," Raef said, not caring that he sounded as pissed as he felt.

Lana's expression softened and she brushed back a strand of bright red hair from her forehead. "Sorry, Raef. You are right. I've been going through my own *sudas* lately."

"Which makes you the shithead?" he said with a quick smile.

"*Taip.* Definitely. And now that we've established that, I am ready to listen." Lana picked up a legal pad and a pen. "Tell me what has happened."

Raef quickly recapped Aubrey's death and the events that had followed, reluctantly admitting everything, even the fact that he could feel her softer emotions, and ending with her latest manifestation in his living room. While he talked, Lana took notes, asked just a few pointed questions and looked grimmer and grimmer. When he was done she sighed and ran her hand through her fiery hair again.

"Do you know what he is? This murderer who steals souls?" Lauren asked into the silence.

"I do, but only through rumor and what amounts to fairy tales used to frighten children."

Lauren looked confused and Lana smiled. "I should clarify and say fairy tales used to frighten *psychic* children."

Raef felt a sliver of shock and sat up straighter. "The murderer is a psychic."

"Taip," Lana agreed. "But more specifically, the murderer is a psychic whose Gift has to be much like yours."

"Mine?" Raef shook his head. "What are you talking about?"

"You said you felt her emotions, and they were all softer, positive emotions. That's not the norm for you, Raef."

"To say the least," he snapped.

"And this ghost, she seems to be filled with positive emotions?" Lana said.

Lauren nodded. "Aubrey was full of joy and positive energy in life—she still is in death."

"When Aubrey tries to talk about her murder, when she gets anywhere close to darker, more negative emotions, like the fear and pain and even anger or hatred that remembering what happened to her evokes, that's when she dissipates, correct?" Lana asked.

"Yeah, it's like he has a hook into her that he can reel back whenever he wants," Raef said.

"Not *whenever*." Lana continued, "Lauren, if Aubrey manifests and says nothing about her murder, if she simply visits you, does the killer pull her back to him?"

"No, but we always end up trying to talk about her murder. She's being drained. Even when we don't say anything about her death at all. She's still being drained," Lauren said.

"Because he's feeding off her emotions—the negative ones—fear, pain, panic, hatred. He can't tap into the softer emotions. My guess is he can't even Trace her spirit when she's feeling them." Lana met Raef's gaze. "He's a psychic like you gone bad."

"Shit. I knew this was a cluster fuck of massive proportions," Raef said.

"Why? If he's like you, then it should be easier for you to find him," Lauren said. "Can't you use your—" she paused and made a vague gesture with her hand "—your Gift or whatever and Track him down?"

Raef jerked his chin at Lana. "Ask the cavalry. She's the ghost expert."

Lana's green eyes sparkled and her smile reminded Raef of a ginger cat who had just lapped a bowl of cream. "Oh, Raef can find him, but he cannot use his Gift like he usually does. The murderer has that way blocked. You already told me what happens whenever your sister tries to speak of her death."

"He knows it. He stops her," Lana said. "And he hurts her more."

"Which proves Aubrey does know who killed her

and could lead us to him—if he let her," Raef said. "Damn! It's frustrating as hell!"

"Aubrey can still lead you to her killer, she just has to do so through positive emotions. Use them to Track him."

"Positive emotions?" Raef snorted. "How the hell do I learn about Tracking with those? Joy isn't gonna lead me to a murder site and a serial killer."

"You don't have to learn about positive emotions, *sudzius*. I have told you before, if you let go of your attachment to negative emotions, your soul will naturally reset itself and begin to accept and understand their opposites."

"And I've told *you* before—I'm not like the rest of your touchy-feely gang," Raef said.

"Great, you mean *he* has to get happy to find my sister's killer?" Lauren said.

"What the fuck is this, a motivational speech? I don't have any attachments to negative emotions. Negative emotions are my damn job. I don't need to get happy. I just need to find a murderer," Raef told the two women.

Both women smiled knowingly back at him.

He considered pouring more Scotch into his tea. Instead, he faced Lana. "So, that's the bottom line? I have to move through positive emotions to find this killer?"

"That's the bottom line," Lana agreed. "Like you, the guy is a fish out of water when he's not attached to hate and fear and pain. Let Aubrey show you how to flank him through joy and love and happiness."

"Flank him, huh? I knew you were a Russian spy," Raef muttered.

Lana grinned. "Here's the good news. All human

souls are designed to accept love and happiness and joy, or at least they are if they can let go of their attachments to hate and fear and pain. And you're human, even though you are a man. Good luck. You'll need it." Lana waved a goodbye to Lauren and then disconnected the Skype call.

Raef and Lauren sat in silence, watching the screen saver come on—a series of pictures of a North Side beach house in Grand Cayman where he vacationed every year. At that moment Raef wished desperately he had his ass in the sand and a cold beer in his hand.

"Do you think that's true?"

Lauren's question seemed loud and out of place, but weirdly enough Raef thought he knew exactly what she was asking.

"You mean the part about all human souls being designed to accept love and happiness and joy?"

"Yes, that's what I mean," she said.

"No," he said. "I don't."

"I don't think I do, either, but I can promise you Aubrey would think it's true—even now. Even dead."

He looked at her and saw how tired she was and how dark and sunken her blue eyes were. "I guess it's a good thing Aubrey's leading this hunt, then."

"She won't be doing anything for a while. When he jerks her back like that, so hard and so painful, it takes a lot out of her and she doesn't manifest for hours, sometimes a whole day."

"It takes a lot out of you, too," Raef said.

Lauren shrugged. "I'm still alive."

"You need to rest. Let me take you home, or to your mom's. Whichever you'd rather," he said, disconcerted by how hollow the thought of Lauren being *not* alive made him feel.

"Thanks. You're right. I'm exhausted. You can take me to my home. Not my mother's. Never my mother's, no matter how out of it I am."

"You're not out of it. Actually, I think you're doing pretty damn well for someone who's being soul sucked by a serial killer."

Lauren smiled as they walked back to the car. "That shouldn't make me feel better, but it kinda does."

"Hey, that's me. Mr. Warm and Fuzzy."

Lauren laughed then, and Raef was taken aback by how much she suddenly reminded him of Aubrey— so taken aback that he didn't have much to say as he drove the short way to Lauren's house, which was in the Brookside area of Midtown Tulsa, just a few miles away.

When he pulled up in front of the neat little bungalow, Lauren said, "Thanks, Raef. I guess I'll see you soon."

"I'll call you tomorrow. Let me do some digging about this soul-sucking crap and then you and I will take another whack at working with Aubrey."

"Sounds like a good plan."

Raef went around and opened her car door for her, and when she hesitated, obviously gathering her energy to get out of the car, Raef took her arm and guided her to her feet.

"Thanks," she said. "I'll be fine from here."

"I'm going to make sure you stay that way," he said.

Lauren looked up at him, and as their eyes met and held, Raef felt a sensation deep inside him—one he hadn't felt in a very, very long time.

"I believe in you," Lauren said, eerily echoing her twin. Then she went up on her tiptoes and kissed his cheek softly before turning away from him and going into her dark house and leaving Raef to drive away rubbing his cheek and muttering, "Cluster fuck…a total goat-herding, cat-roping cluster fuck…"

6

RAEF DIDN'T GO home. Instead, still muttering to himself about *un*natural disasters, he stopped by his After Moonrise office and grabbed some Psy books from a very surprised Vivian Peterson, who was their resident expert on ghosts.

Raef didn't like her. Never had. She was just too damn ooie-ooie. Her hair was green, for God's sake.

On the way back to the house he stopped for takeout pizza at the Pie Hole and a six-pack of Blue Moon beer—both the liquor store and the pizza place were within walking distance of his house.

"Which is just one of reasons this place is so perfect for me." Raef sighed with contentment as he chugged the first bottle of beer between bites of the Everything Pie Hole Special. He didn't open the first research book until he'd worked his way through half of the pie *and* half of the six-pack. *Then* he started reading.

Within fifteen minutes he was shaking his head and opening another beer. He flipped through the chapters of the first book, *The Spirit Hunter's Guide,* reading quickly. "'Possession, succubus infestation, poltergeists, noxious aroma invasions…'" Raef read aloud. "This ghost stuff is some seriously not right shit." He swigged another beer and tossed that book aside, picking up a slimmer volume titled *Shamanic Retrieval.* Paging through it Raef found essays sectioned off with the titles "Soul Theft and Loss," "Souls Lost to Love" and finally "Retrieving a Stolen Soul."

"About damn time," he said under his breath and began to read.

Retrieving a stolen soul must be done with skill and care. Remember, we must act in harmony with the universe—harming others, even others who have stolen souls, puts us out of harmony.

Raef snorted. "Like I give a fuck?" He kept reading.

Soul thieves usually take spirits because they believe they need the power to live. This is rarely true. Only one psychic in thousands can actually feed from the energy of another's soul. The problem is some less than scrupulous psychics can convince themselves that they can use the power of another—therein you find a soul thief.

"The problem is the asshole I'm dealing with *can* feed from souls." Raef continued.

Because of the power attachment to the stolen soul, it is complicated to convince the thief to release it. There are two basic ways to attempt, with responsibility to universal order, to retrieve a stolen soul.

Then in bold writing Raef read:

1) Offer the thief a gift to replace the soul. Sometimes an animal spirit can be traded for the human soul.

"That sucks for the poor dog," Raef said.

2) Trick the thief by distracting him or her, and then pull the soul away yourself. Of course, this takes the well-honed skills of a shaman or a medium, and should not be attempted by a psychic with a different Gift. To do so may cause harm to the thief and, possibly, the stolen soul, as well as the inexperienced psychic.

Raef sat back, sipping his beer and thinking. Should he bring in another psychic like Lana? He didn't give a shit about the thief's safety—the guy was a killer. Even though he'd rather not get his own ass in a bind, he wasn't particularly worried about himself. Raef had been handling his own shit for decades. He did care about Aubrey, as well as her sister—which was almost as irritating as it was unusual.

It just wasn't normal for him to care.

"Hell, this isn't a normal case," he reasoned aloud. "And this isn't a normal soul stealing, either," Raef rationalized aloud. "It's a murder. The soul part is only secondary. So, the ooie-ooie crap needs to take second place to the murder. And I'm the right man to take care of the murder part." He reread number two. "'Trick the thief by distracting him or her, and then pull the soul away yourself.' How 'bout I do the distracting, like get this guy arrested and put away for life, and Aubrey just runs like hell—so to speak."

Nodding to himself, Raef paged through, skipping the sections on "Restoring a Soul's Light" and "Finding Shattered Souls," but stopping at the heading "Retrieving Souls from the Land of the Dead."

The Land of the Dead is not the equivalent of a Christian heaven or hell. It is not one of the three layers of the Otherworld. It is a place for lost and broken souls—be they dead or alive. It is a dangerous place, even for a trained shaman or medium. It's filled with hopelessness. Sometimes shattered souls can be found there. Sometimes soul thieves choose the Land of the Dead as a holding place for their victims. Whether you are healing a shattered soul or retrieving a stolen one, enter the Land of the Dead without protection and experience, and you risk becoming lost, too.

"Jackpot!" Raef said. "Definitely sounds like the place I need to go." He skipped the rest of the warnings and went straight to the heading titled "Entering the Land of the Dead."

Begin by lighting a candle. You are seeking shadow and smoke, death and darkness, you will need to keep a light close to you, both figuratively and literally.

Reluctantly, Raef got up and went to his bedroom where he always kept a vanilla candle ready to burn. He used to like the way the candlelight flickered off his wife's smooth skin. Kathy had been lush and sexy, and the warm light of a flame used to make her look like a love goddess come to earth. Of course, he hadn't actually burned the damn candle in years, not since his wife had decided she couldn't live with his job—or in her words, *I can't stand what your job does to you, Raef. It makes you sad, and nothing I do ever changes that.*

Raef paused halfway back to the living room, candle in hand. "Why the fuck am I thinking about that? Kathy's been gone five years. The candle only stayed because I like the way it smells." Raef stifled a sigh of annoyance. So, yeah, it would be nice to see another naked woman in candlelight, but that hadn't happened in a long time. "Too long," he said as he lit the vanilla candle and picked up the book and the beer again. "All right, what next?"

Shamanic battles of life and death can happen in the Land of the Dead. If you attempt to go there you must be skilled and courageous and well protected.

"Yeah, yeah, get to it," he mumbled.

The Land of the Dead can be found past the Otherworld boundary. Think of the Otherworld as if it were an ancient map when man believed the world was flat, and if you went too far you fell off into nothingness. That nothingness is the Land of the Dead.

To find it, keep the light of your candle strong in your mind's eye. Then begin to meditate upon the reason for your quest. A shaman or medium can Track a soul with the help of his or her Gift.

"Huh." Raef snorted. "I'm not an ooie-ooie shaman or a medium, but I can Track things. Usually murderers, but whatever. Nothing is normal about this case. Maybe I can Track more than I thought I could, or at least when it comes to Aubrey and Lauren maybe I can." He kept reading.

Know that once you have Tracked the soul to the Land of the Dead, your psychic Gift will cease to work. You must use mortal guile and your own wisdom to retrieve the lost one.

"First good news I've heard yet," he said, chuckling softly.

Raef closed the book and looked at the candle. He stared at the flame until it seemed as if the light was burned into his mind.

Then he began thinking of Aubrey.

She made him feel joy.

She laughed. She laughed a lot, especially for a dead girl.

She was blonde and beautiful and had a sparkle that even death couldn't dim.

She called him Kent. No one called him Kent.

Raef closed his eyes, held the light in his mind and Aubrey in his heart and, just as he did at a murder scene, began to feel around with his Gift…seeking…questing…searching…. Only this time he wasn't trying to Track rage and fear and pain. This time he was questing after a sparkling blonde whose laughter reminded him of champagne.

When he actually found her it jolted him with surprise. Murder victims he'd Tracked before had led him to their killers with dark, smoking trails—or rivers of pain and hatred like oil slicks. Aubrey's trail was a shimmering thread of joy that flickered bright and then dim. *Why?* he wondered. *What's going on with her?* Then he recognized the dimming—he'd seen it before; it was worry. Raef reached with his Gift to grab on and Track the illusive, glittering thread, but instead of Tracking he felt an already familiar sensation pass over his skin, and her voice, somewhere between annoyed and surprised, sounded in the air around him.

"Kent, what are you doing?"

He opened his eyes. Aubrey had materialized in front of him, between the couch and the old steamer trunk he used as a coffee table. It had gotten dark while he'd been reading, and the living room was dim—the only real light cast by the vanilla candle. The lack of light agreed with Aubrey. She looked almost substantial, and Raef noticed she was wearing only a slip of a dress, one of those silk things that laced up the front and hugged women's curves so well. And Aubrey had some serious curves to hug.

The joy that had been dimmed by worry sparkled alight as Aubrey cocked her head to the side, studied him and then began to laugh. Her laughter skittered across his skin, raising the hair on his forearms, and calling alive sensations that had been dead within him a lot longer than Aubrey had been.

"What?" he said, scrubbing a hand roughly across a forearm. "Why are you laughing?"

"'Cause I just realized what you're doing."

She grinned, but didn't continue until he prodded, "And what do you think I'm doing?"

"It's not think, Kent. It's know. I know you're checking me out."

Raef frowned, trying to ignore the crackle of humor that lifted around her and washed against him. "That's not what I was doing before you showed up, and why does that make you laugh?"

"Because it means your love life is even deader than me." She giggled.

"That's not funny," Raef said. "And before you showed up I was trying to Tr—"

"No!" For a moment she sounded frantic, and the humor that had been bubbling around him faded. Then, she reached up and took hold of one of the diaphanous laces that held the front of her dress together. Aubrey smiled teasingly at him. *"No, let's not go there. If we go there, then I'll have to leave, and neither of us wants that. How about we go here instead."* With one deft pull, she undid the tie and the lacing fell open, exposing her naked flesh.

"You're naked!" Raef blurted, and then mentally smacked himself. *Were boobs all it really took to make me forget she's dead?*

"No, I'm naked under this." Aubrey slowly ran her hands down the front of the silk dress, lingering over her breasts until her nipples began to harden. She gasped in pleasure. *"Wow—"* her voice was a breathy whisper *"—I feel amazing."* Still touching herself, Aubrey half walked, half floated closer to him. *"You can feel me, Kent. I know you can."*

She was only an arm's length from him, and she

was so fucking sexy there in the candlelight, all skin and lush curves and nipples that were tight and ripe and ready for his tongue. Raef reached for her, and felt a shock and a chill when his hand met with nothing but air.

Her laugher bubbled around them. *"Not like that, silly! Feel me in there."* Aubrey took one hand from her body, leaned forward and pressed her hand against his chest, over his heart.

He didn't feel the pressure from her hand. He didn't feel anything except her laughter and his raging hard-on. "I don't feel shit! You're a ghost. I don't know what the fuck I'm doing."

"I've made you feel before. I can do it again, and it's important that you do. It's the only way we can move forward. The only way we can fix what's wrong." She was standing right before him. Her hands went to one of the loosened laces of her dress. She tugged again, this time harder, and the silk slid through, opening the dress completely. With a teasing smile she shrugged her shoulders and it slid from her body to pool in a semi-substantial puddle at her feet.

"Oh, God. You are so damn beautiful," Raef couldn't stop himself from saying.

"Then feel me, Kent. Let go of all of that baggage you have because of the past, and allow yourself to feel pleasure again." Aubrey caressed her breasts. Then slowly, she moved one hand down her body, over the curve of her belly, and slid her fingers under the triangle of blond curls between her legs.

Raef couldn't take his gaze from her. His body was aching in hot, hard response. Automatically, he rubbed his hand over his jeans and down the long length of his swollen cock.

"Yes! Let me see you. Let me watch you."

"Then let me feel you!"

"Kent, baby, you can do that yourself. Just let it happen. Let go of the past and be willing to feel pleasure in the present."

"Yeah, okay. Anything," he said. "I let go of all that crap."

"Why? Tell me why," Aubrey whispered.

"Because I want to feel pleasure. With you!" He almost shouted the words.

As soon as he'd spoken it hit him—her emotions. He'd felt her laughter before. He'd even felt her joy. But what he was feeling now sliced through him like a sword: joy, laughter, lust, desire, pleasure, all wrapped together. The emotions entwined and implanted within him. Raef ripped open the front of his jeans and took his cock in his hand, stroking himself as he watched her blue eyes widen.

"You are incredible!" Aubrey said. *"And you do feel me."*

"I do feel you," he gasped. "I feel what you do to yourself. I feel what you do to me."

"Then feel this...." Aubrey's gaze never left his as her fingers moved more quickly over herself. Raef was staring into her eyes as they both came to orgasm— he was still staring at her when she whispered, *"This makes you closer to me, and the closer to me you get, the closer you'll be to finding him. But you can't do it through negative emotions. You have to Track him through the opposite—joy and pleasure, happiness and*

*hope. He can't fight that, and he won't be able to stop
you from—"*

This time the soul thief didn't rip Aubrey in half
when he jerked her back to him. This time he made her
explode into little pieces, so that her scream was cut off
like a snuffed candle, leaving Raef drained, confused
and alone in the darkness without her.

7

"I JUST JERKED off with a ghost. I am seriously fucked up."

Raef stared at the ceiling, lifted the bottle of single-malt Scotch he'd retrieved from the kitchen and took several long drinks. He meant to go back to reading the soul-retrieval stuff. Instead, he stared at nothing and thought about Aubrey. "She staged the whole thing," he mused aloud between gulps of Scotch. "She has to be guiding me. She's probably getting info from her connection with Lauren. And hell, she's the one trapped. She's gotta have something figured out about what would get her free. She obviously knows I can't Track this guy through negative emotions. He has them blocked. But he's not gonna pay attention to positive emotions because guys like him—and me—aren't good at the softer side of emotions. We're not used to 'em."

He blew out a long breath. How long had it been since he'd had sex, anyway? "More than a year since my *relationship* with Raven had crashed and burned. Christ, her name had been *Raven*. What the fuck had I expected?" He shook his head at his own stupidity, and at online dating in general, and realized the room was spinning a little around him.

Raef snorted and took another drink of Scotch. By now he hardly felt the burn. "Aubrey's good at positive emotions. Hell, Aubrey's good at a lot of things." He stared at the ceiling until his eyes blurred, blinked and finally closed.

Later he would remember that his last thought that night wasn't about Aubrey's hair or her boobs or how hard she'd made him or the way she touched herself— his last thoughts had been about her laughter and how the sound and feel of it had been better than all of the sex stuff…and the sex stuff had been really good.

THE BANGING ON RAEF'S front door woke him. It was loud and jarring, and only slightly less obnoxious than the pounding pain in his head. "Yeah, Jesus, yeah, I'm coming." He glanced at the clock before wrenching open the door—8:30 a.m.? Damn, he was going to be late for work. Which meant he should have opened the door with a thank-you-for-being-my-alarm-clock instead of a snarl, but life just wasn't fair. "What the hell do you—" His words broke off when he saw Lauren's raised brows.

"I'm a morning person. I figured you'd be on your way out the door for work. The cab dropped me off 'cause I thought I'd go with you," she said unapologetically, though she did raise her hands, which were holding two tall cups of QT coffee. "I come bearing offerings."

He opened the door, took one of the coffees, stepped back and, with a grunt, gestured for her to come in.

She walked past, giving him a Look. "You're not ready to go to work."

"No kidding." His voice sounded like there was gravel in his throat.

"You look bad. Real bad," she said.

"Scotch. A lot of it," he said.

She shuddered. "I did that once. Never again."

"I'm a slow learner," he said. "I got some Merritt's doughnuts in the kitchen. They're only two days old so they're not too much like bricks. Make yourself at home while I'm in the shower." He disappeared into the bathroom, closed the door, and as memories of the night before flooded his mind, Raef thought seriously about using the razor to slit his wrists. "Why can't I be one of those drunks who don't remember anything?" Raef asked his rough-looking reflection in the vanity mirror. He shook his head. Slightly. It still hurt like hell. "You had sex with a ghost, and that ghost's twin sister is in your kitchen." He sighed and started to lather up his face, muttering, "Might as well be a freshly shaven, clean perv."

When he got out of the shower and opened the door to the hall, Raef was confronted by two things—the smell of bacon and eggs, and Lauren. She had *Shamanic Retrieval* open in her hand and was carrying it back to the kitchen. Looking up from its pages she stopped to stare at him.

Color bloomed in her cheeks.

Raef tightened the towel that was around his waist, feeling even more naked than he was—and he was pretty damn naked.

"I made breakfast," she said, before turning away and hurrying the rest of the way to the kitchen.

"I'm hungover," he called, hurrying the rest of the way to the bedroom.

"I know. It's good for you, though. Trust me. I was a biology major in college," she called in return.

Raef pulled on jeans and an old air-force sweatshirt. As he walked into the kitchen he told his phone, "Call work." Feeling oddly like an obedient child, he sat at the breakfast-nook table, where Lauren had already placed a full plate of eggs, bacon and toast—along with a cup of fresh coffee and a shot of what smelled and looked suspiciously like single-malt Scotch. He raised a brow at her as he spoke. "Preston, reschedule my appointments for today. I'm still on the case I took yesterday and I'll be working in the field. Thank you." Raef hit the end-call button, forked up some eggs and bacon, and said to Lauren, "What does being a biology major in college have to do with hangovers?"

She sat across from him with her own plate of breakfast. "Simple. Hangovers are biological. Food helps. So does hair of the dog. Actually, I'm not sure if the hair-of-the-dog part is biological or psychological, but it works."

"Yeah, this isn't my first rodeo. I'm just surprised there was any Scotch left in that bottle." He gulped the shot and grimaced, reaching for the coffee.

"Well, there was barely a whole shot left. I'm assuming the bottle was mostly full when you started?"

"Yep," he said through bites of eggs and bacon that were really tasting damn good.

"Rough night?"

He swallowed and avoided her eyes. "Yeah."

"Okay, well, sorry about your rough night, and like I said yesterday, I'm not usually this bitchy, but hungover or not we have work to do. Aubrey should be able to manifest again by now, so as soon as we're done eating I'll focus my thoughts and she should—"

"Oh, go ahead and eat. I don't mind watching. I'm finding out that I kinda like it."

Aubrey's giggle washed around them as she materialized and Raef almost choked on a mouthful of eggs.

"Good morning, sis. Morning, Kent."

"Hey, Aub, you look good. All bright and happy," Lauren said.

"I had a verrrry interesting night."

The smile she sent Raef was brilliant and sparkling, and seemed to catch him in a spotlight. He felt it. He actually *felt* her happiness. It was like an endless Saturday, or having box seats at the World Series, or knowing you're going to have lots of sex. Lots of really good sex.

"Oh. My. God. You two did it. I don't know how it's possible, but you two *did it* last night," Lauren said, glaring from Raef to her sister.

"How the hell could you know that? You're a Norm! You're not psychic." Raef threw up his hands in exasperation.

Aubrey giggled some more, causing Raef's skin to prickle. *"She knows because Lauren and I have always been connected. I think you'd call it our own interpersonal psychic link, which means you really do have to stop lumping us with the Norms."*

"Which also means you two did do it last night."

"What we did was create pleasure, and pleasure is definitely a positive emotion. Right, Kent?" She grinned at Kent.

"Doesn't feel like it right now," he mumbled.

"Cheer up. It's not like she got you pregnant," Lauren said. Then raised her brow and, sounding so much like her mother that Raef even recognized it, announced, "You didn't masturbate, did you, Aubrey Lynn Wilcox? You know what I told you about that." And then Lauren Wilcox dissolved into giggles that included a very unladylike snort.

Aubrey laughed with her sister, full-throated, filling the breakfast nook with joy that washed through Raef. He couldn't help it. He couldn't stop it. Raef threw back his head and laughed along with the ghost and her twin sister. *Happy,* he thought. *I'm happy around her—around them. And I haven't been happy in a very long time.*

"That's right, Kent. Feel it. Feel it with me. Pleasure and humor, joy and happiness. Feel them and keep them close to you, like shields. Because when you stop looking at the forest and find the tree, you'll only get one piece of the puzzle. He has the rest of the pieces hidden where only you can find them when you follow me. You won't be able to use your Gift there, but you can use—"

"No, Aubrey! Don't!" Raef shouted, and came to his feet so fast the chair toppled over behind him. But he was too late. Aubrey's semitransparent body had already been ripped away.

"Oh, no!" Lauren gagged. Holding her hand over her mouth she staggered to the kitchen sink and puked up eggs and bacon and coffee.

"Here." Raef handed her a paper towel. "Just breathe."

She took the paper towel with a hand that trembled and wiped her mouth. Raef went to the fridge and grabbed a can of Sprite, popped the top and held it out for her. "This'll help. Rinse your mouth and then sip it."

Lauren didn't take the can. She just stood at the sink, wiping her mouth over and over again, staring blankly out the kitchen window to Raef's backyard.

"Lauren?"

She didn't even blink. He jerked the paper towel from her hands, threw it into the sink and then took her shoulders into his hands, turning her to face him.

"All right. That's enough. Come back now."

She stared straight ahead at his collarbone. He hadn't realized until then how short she was—petite, really. And those sharp blue-gray eyes of hers were still vacant and glazed. Raef gave her shoulders a shake. Not too rough, but hard enough it should bring her attention back to her body. He deepened his voice and took all the emotion out of it. "I said that's enough. Get back here, Lauren!"

Like throwing a switch, the light came into her eyes. Lauren blinked and looked up at him. "Raef? What—" Her whole body started to tremble and, feeling totally in over his head, he did the only thing he could think to do—he pulled her into a hug.

She buried her head in his chest and shook.

"Hey, it's okay. You're back. You're fine," he said inanely, thinking how small she was—God, would she even weigh a hundred pounds soaking wet?

"It's getting worse," she said against his chest.

"Where were you? Where do you go when that happens?" he asked.

She stepped back out of his arms and looked at him in surprise. "Ohmygod, Raef! I never even thought about where I go, just how I feel." She shook her head and went back to the breakfast table, pushed aside her half-eaten plate and sat heavily. Lauren wrapped her hands around her mug of coffee and took a sip. Raef righted his chair and did the same.

"So, describe it to me," he said.

She looked over her mug at him. "It's foggy there. And cold. Ugh, and it's wet, too."

"Wet? It's raining?"

Lauren shook her head. "I don't think so. Maybe it's not really wet, but that place makes me feel like I'm drowning," she said.

"Could be part of the spiritual draining. That must be how your body and mind are interpreting it."

"It's so hard to tell you anything for sure because everything is in black and white, but foggy or blurred, like one of those old silent movies." Her eyes narrowed contemplatively. "Actually, it's a lot like a silent movie. Things skip around, like movie frames freezing."

"Is anyone else there?"

"Yes," she said without hesitation, and then added more slowly, "Aubrey is there, and there are other people, too. But they're hard to see. They fade in and out. They're only vague images. I do know they're in pain. They're all in pain." She shook her head again. "I've known it all along and just refused to think about it because it's so, so terrible there. But it has to be where the murderer is keeping his victims' souls."

"The Land of the Dead," Raef said.

"What?"

He snagged the slim book from where Lauren had left it on the kitchen counter. "It's in here. It's also what

Aubrey's talking about when she gets ripped back there by him."

"Bread crumbs. She's trying to lead us to her with bread crumbs, but they keep getting eaten," Lauren said.

"Maybe not totally eaten." He got up, refilled their coffee and brought a legal pad and a pencil back to the table. "So, whenever Aubrey's emotions change—whenever she tries to talk about her death or her killer—he can sense it and he rips her away from here. Correct?"

"Correct. But it happens so fast that she never really gets to tell us anything."

"But she tries," Raef said. "Maybe we should listen better."

"Okay, well, I'm not going to be very good at that because I feel her pain and I get ripped away with her. Or at least part of me does—that part that's attached to Aub."

"I get that. So let me help, or at least help with what I've witnessed. The first time Aubrey disappeared was in my office when you hired me and I asked her to tell me about her murder."

Lauren nodded. "I hired you because she told me to, and that took her a while because she kept getting ripped away. She finally just described you and then said 'KooKoo Kitty.' I figured it out from there."

"KooKoo Kitty? How the hell did you find me from that?"

Lauren smiled. "It's twin speak. We had a cat when we were twelve. Someone had dumped her on our grandparents' ranch by one of our guest cabins. She was, of course, pregnant. She was a sweet, friendly little thing, so Mother let us keep her as one of the barn cats, but said we'd have to give away the kittens and get her spayed. We called her Cabin Kitty. Well, she had her kittens and then promptly lost her mind protecting them. She attacked every cat, dog, chicken and even horse at the ranch. We renamed her KooKoo Kitty."

"Nice story. Still don't know why the hell that led you to me."

"Oh, that's easy. After Moonrise and the whole Psy thing is seriously cuckoo, and you're the only tall, dark and handsome working there."

"Thank you. I think." Then he tried not to dwell on the fact that Aubrey described him as handsome. "So, that was time number one."

"Obviously the murderer doesn't want you involved in his case."

"Yeah, well, too late. Second time was at Swan Lake." Raef thought back, frowning. "I don't remember her saying anything even vaguely pertaining to her death, do you?"

"Actually, I do remember what she was saying because it seemed harmless." She moved her shoulders. "Sometimes I can tell she's getting ready to get ripped back. I mean, I know that she's trying to tell me something."

"Like today."

"Exactly. But yesterday she was totally happy. All she was doing was talking about the trees. She called them soldiers, wise and strong, and said they must need a lot of care. And that was it. He took her away."

Raef's eyes widened. "I'm an idiot. She wasn't talking about trees—at least, not just about them. She had to have been giving us a clue about the murderer for him to have jerked her away." He sat up straighter. "Ah, shit. She did it again today. She said when I stop looking at the forest and find the tree I'll get a piece of the puzzle."

"Raef! Whoever killed her must have been working on the trees at Swan Lake," Lauren said.

"Puzzle piece found," Raef said grimly. "And that tree-loving bastard better watch the hell out."

8

"So what you're saying is on July 15 there were no city tree trimmers at or around the area of Swan Lake?" Raef was talking into his cell as he paced across his home office.

"That's correct, Mr. Raef, I see no record of having sent our tree trimmers out to Midtown at all that day." The city worker's voice sounded like she was talking to him through a tin can. Hell, with the City of Tulsa Works Department and their crappy budget, that might be true. He glanced at Lauren where she sat at his computer. She looked up at him. He shook his head, and she went back to concentrating on the computer. "Could you double-check your records, ma'am?"

"Certainly. Hold please," she said.

"I'm on hold. Again." Raef growled and continued prowling around his office. Finally the tin-can voice returned.

"Sir, I have checked and rechecked our records for that day and the day before. All of our tree-trimming teams were in the Reservoir Hill neighborhood on the

fourteenth and the fifteenth of July. I am sorry I couldn't be of more help."

"Yeah, me, too, but thanks," Raef said, disconnecting. "Struck out," he told Lauren.

"Well, I think I just hit a home run," she said, excitement raising her voice.

"How so?" He went to look over her shoulder at the Swan Lake website she had up. She'd clicked into several of the pictures and was studying them intently.

"First, I've quit thinking like a grieving sister and started thinking like a landscaper. Those are elms." Lauren pointed at the picture. "Actually, almost all the larger trees lining the pond are elms."

"Okay, why is that important?"

"Because of our weather patterns elms are especially susceptible to Dutch elm disease. It can be devastating to them."

"And?" Raef prompted.

"And the pretty neighborhood around Swan Lake wouldn't stay pretty if its biggest shade trees withered and died from a nasty, highly contagious fungus. These trees are healthy—strong and soldierlike, as my sister would say. That tells me Midtown has an arborist."

"A what?"

"Tree doctor. This many elms, old and young, tell me they've been well cared for. Hang on, if I remember correctly…" Her fingers flew across the keyboard as she searched and clicked. "And I do! There's an innovative preventative treatment for Dutch elm disease that needs to be applied in the spring and early summer." She looked at him. "Mid-July would have been a perfect second-application time."

"I was calling the right department, but asking the

wrong question," Raef said, but before he punched the city number again, Lauren's words had him pausing. "He has more souls trapped than just Aubrey's. I can feel them."

"He's a serial killer," Raef said grimly. "I wonder how many more *accidents* have happened to people in Tulsa in the past year or so, and how many of them were close to other well-tended groves of trees." Raef hit the number to the After Moonrise office. "Preston, I need you to get into the database and do a search for me. Deaths ruled as accidental in the past year. I'll need specifics on the death sites. Pay special attention to details about the trees in the area—like, did the accident happen in Mohawk Park or did someone fall down the stairs at the BOK Arena. I'm interested in the trees, not the structures. Our killer has a connection to trees, might even be a tree doctor. Got it?…Good. Call me back ASAP." He disconnected and glanced at Lauren.

Even though she was completely focused on the computer she must have felt his look because Lauren said, "I'm already checking arborists in the area. Call the city back."

Raef did as he was told.

"So, THE CITY USES three arborists. Chris Melnore, out of Hardscape in Bixbie, Steve Elwood, who has his own tree-trimming business in Broken Arrow, and Dr. Raymond Braggs, who is a professor at TU." Raef read from the list the public-works director had given him. "All three have serviced Midtown. Murphy's Law is working well, which means the city had a major computer crash last week, so they don't have a record of which one of the three might have been to Swan Lake in July.

They're gonna check and see if anyone kept any physical notes, but it's doubtful that they'll find anything. It was back in July and this is October."

"Can't we just call the three men and ask if he was at Swan Lake that day? We could pretend like we're calling from the city for, uh, tax records or something like that," Lauren said.

"We could, but you see how jumpy the guy is already. He jerks Aubrey outta here if she so much as mentions a damn tree. I don't want him going rabbit on me."

"Then how do we figure out which one he is?" Lauren rubbed a hand over her face and brushed back a strand of long blond hair.

She looks tired, he thought. *Again. I have to remember that this is draining her along with Aubrey.*

"Well, we can't do much until we get the list of accidental deaths from my office. Then we'll check out the death scene and see if there is any link to a tree doc, and go from there."

"Or we could print off pictures of each of the three guys and when Aubrey manifests next see if she can point us to one of them."

"You mean before she screams and gets torn into pieces and part of you gets sucked away with her? No. How 'bout I try some old-fashioned detective work instead."

"Aubrey and I can handle it. We've been doing this for months."

"How much longer do you think you two have?" he asked bluntly, his voice a lot colder than he meant it to be.

Her face lost the little color it had had. "I don't know," she said listlessly. "I can't tell because I don't feel right—don't feel whole—without Aubrey. So a piece of me is missing whether I'm being drained by a serial killer or not."

"All right, then, let's not push it." He gentled his voice. "You're tired."

"I'm always tired."

"I'll take you home. You can rest and I'll call you as soon as I have something."

"Do you have to?"

Raef raised a brow at her. She looked away and he saw some color in her cheeks. Before he could say anything she seemed to collect herself and turned her eyes back to his. Their gazes met and held.

"I know you have a thing for Aubrey. That's fine." Lauren looked away.

"That's weird," he said, wishing she'd meet his gaze again. "She's dead."

"That's fine," she repeated as if he hadn't spoken. "I don't want to stay because I want to have sex with you or anything like that." When he just stared at her, she added, "Not that you're not an attractive man. You are. Really. Obviously my sister thinks so, and she and I have similar tastes in men." She pushed a thick strand of blond hair from her face, looked up at him. This time her cheeks were bright pink.

She was beautiful.

His throat felt dry. He cleared it. When she didn't continue speaking he prompted, "You and Aubrey liked the same guys?" Then he realized what he'd said and he hastily added, "Not that I'm into twin sex fantasies or anything too weird."

"Define *too weird*." Her eyes found his again.

And damned if *his* cheeks didn't suddenly feel hot.

"Well, after what happened last night between your sister and me, I think my definition of *too weird* is changing."

Lauren's smile was warm—so warm it made his skin tingle. She gave a little laugh. "Okay, before this gets too crazy, let me start over. Raef, I'd really appreciate it if you'd let me stay here until we find my sister's killer. I mean, if you don't mind too much."

"That might be days or weeks," Raef said.

"It can't be," she said, no longer smiling or blushing. "There's no way Aubrey and I have that long." She drew a long breath. "The truth is that every time Aubrey gets ripped out of here and takes part of me with her, I'm afraid I may never come back. For some reason you are able to get me back. I don't think you always will be able to, but for right now being around you makes me feel as safe as I'm able to feel."

Ah, shit, no! he thought. What he heard himself say was, "Fine. You can stay. But you get the couch."

"That's perfect. I like to go to sleep watching TV."

"That shows a lack in your upbringing," he said.

"To say the least."

"What, rough time with nannies?" he asked sarcastically.

"Mother doesn't believe in nannies. She didn't have any. Mother also doesn't believe in children, especially not girl children. Sadly, she had two of them. And our father never paid any attention because we weren't a son. Here's a news flash—you don't have to live in a trailer to be abused as a child."

"Hey, sorry. That was out of line of me," he said, feeling like a douche bag.

"Don't worry about it. Almost everyone assumes

Aub and I are spoiled rich girls." She shook her head wearily. "*Were,* I mean. She's dead. I have to start remembering that."

"All right, that's enough. Let's go." Raef gestured for her to come out from behind his desk.

"Are you making me leave?"

He hated the soft, scared tone of her voice. "No, I said you could stay. I may be an ass, but I don't break my word. What I'm making you do is take a nap."

She stopped halfway down the hall. "Seriously?"

"Naps are healthy. Again, this shows another lack in your upbringing."

"I can assure you that's only the second of many," she said, following him to the wide leather couch that was already loaded with soft pillows and a faux-fur throw. She plumped a pillow, kicked off her shoes and curled up on her side, pulling the throw up to her neck. "You know, it really does look like a girl lives here."

"I didn't realize pillows, a blanket and a few antiques and art were gender specific."

"Your pillows are baby-blue and cream, your throw is faux leopard and your art is Erté. I have two words for you, and they're hyphenated—girl-like."

She was looking at him through big blue eyes that were ringed with shadow, her hair was already rumpled and she was all curled up in a ball that he thought was so little he could almost pick her up and toss her into the other room—but she had an impish smile and a lifted chin that said she'd dare him to try.

Raef liked her. Really liked her.

He leaned down, clicked on the universal remote and handed it to her. "Girl-like or not, I also have all the cable channels—in HD."

"That's not girl-like. That's civilized."

He chuckled all the way back to his office.

RAEF TRIED TO WORK, but it was an exercise in frustration. He searched the internet for everything he could find about the three tree doctors, and then stared at their websites. Nothing stood out and screamed *psychic serial killer* about any of them. Melnore, a white guy in his mid-thirties, was divorced and had a part-time kid, or at least that's what his Facebook page said. Elwood, another white guy, didn't have a Facebook page. His website had a fish with a cross in it and by his Photoshopped picture he looked to be late thirties to early forties and in denial about balding. "Great, a church boy. He's gonna be fun to research." According to the TU faculty website, Braggs completed the white, middle-aged trifecta. He was single and newly tenured at the university. His faculty picture was standard conservative suit and tie. He looked professorially boring. His bio didn't mention any family. He needed a haircut, but besides that looked as harmless as the other two. "Could be any or all of them."

Raef pushed his chair back from his desk and rolled his shoulders. He felt like shit. Not hungover anymore, but tired and woolly-headed. He glanced at the computer clock—just after noon. Preston would be at lunch. He wouldn't call for at least the next hour or so.

"Combat nap time," he told the air around him, then he padded quietly down the hallway and stole a peek at Lauren. The TV was on, but turned way down. The day had become overcast, and the room was dim, but he could see by the light from the TV that her eyes were closed. *Good. We'll both be better off after forty winks.*

Raef reclined onto his wide bed, fully clothed, put his phone on Vibrate, slid it into his jeans pocket and closed his eyes. Sleep came to him like it had since his days in the military—fast and easy.

Which was exactly how he came awake, too, when the feeling intruded on an excellent dream he was having about playing shortstop during the World Series.

Hope! I know it's ridiculous, impossible, but I can feel hope. Raef lay there for a moment, just soaking in the emotion. God, it felt good. Better than pleasure. Better than joy.

And then he realized why he was feeling it.

Aubrey had to be here.

Quickly, quietly, he padded on sock feet to where he could look into the living room. He'd been right. She was there, sitting on the couch beside Lauren, who was awake. They were talking in low voices, their heads tilted toward each other, and Raef was struck by how alike they were. It wasn't just how they looked. It was the way they moved—the way they both talked with their hands. As he watched, Aubrey swept back a strand of diaphanous blond hair that had floated over her face, just like Lauren had been doing all morning. She said something Raef couldn't hear, but it had Lauren giggling and then pressing a hand over her mouth, as if she'd just laughed at something mischievous—*or raunchy,* Raef thought as he watched Lauren fan herself like her face was suddenly hot.

He didn't think he'd made a noise, though he was smiling, but Aubrey chose then to look around her sister and straight at him.

"Come on in, Kent. We have a proposition for you," she said, sounding both mischievous and raunchy.

9

"WHAT'S THE PROPOSITION?" he asked, wondering why even though he sounded reluctant his feet were propelling him quickly to join the two women.

"Aubrey wants to give you something," Lauren said, still looking flushed-cheeked and sounding a little breathless.

"But I need Lauren's help." Aubrey grinned at her twin. *"And she's agreed. Happily."*

Raef was almost as suspicious as he was curious. Almost. "All right, what do you want to give me?"

"We'll tell you—or rather, we'll show you—but first I want you to promise me you'll open your mind and your heart and be willing to just go with it."

A red flag went up for Raef, but it was hard to assess the warning when Aubrey and Lauren were both beaming full-wattage smiles at him. "I need to know what it is I'm being open about before I make that promise." Even he could hear the bullshit in his voice. Hell, he'd agree to be open to sprouting wings and jumping off the fucking garage if those two kept smiling at him like that.

"It's part of being open, Raef. You don't get to know what you're promising—you get to be *open* to all sorts of possibilities." Then Lauren giggled, and her cheeks got even pinker.

Raef went from being curious to intrigued, and that trumped suspicious. "All right. I promise. Now, what are you two cooking up?"

Aubrey stood. *"Just a little hope, and that plus pleasure and joy makes for a feast."* The ghost lifted her hand and Lauren stood beside her. The women smiled at each other. *"Are you ready?"* Aubrey asked her.

"As I'll ever be," Lauren said. Raef thought she sounded nervous.

"It'll be fine. I'll drive," Aubrey said teasingly.

"You always were better at *driving* than me," Lauren said. She shook back her hair and laughed. "Just do it. I'm ready to take one for the team."

Aubrey looked from her twin to Raef. She *really* looked at Raef—moving her gaze from his feet, all the way up, slowly, to meet his eyes. Raef felt himself start to harden. *What the hell? Just her look does that to me?*

Then Aubrey turned her gaze back to Lauren. *"Oh, please, sis! Take one for the team? This is going to be better than buttered popcorn and Raisinets!"*

Raef thought he heard Lauren whisper something that sounded like "Nothing's better than popcorn and Raisinets…" but he couldn't be sure, and what Aubrey did next blew his mind so totally and completely that he forgot everything except what was happening right before him.

Aubrey and Lauren were facing each other. Lauren opened her arms and Aubrey stepped into them, as if they were going to embrace. But their joining didn't end with a hug. Aubrey seemed to melt into Lauren. Slowly and without any of the ripping or tearing or shattering that had come before, Aubrey disappeared.

Lauren was silent and still for several moments. Then she lifted her right hand. Staring at it, she traced the fingers of her left hand down her palm, wrist and forearm. "Wow, I'd forgotten."

"Lauren?" Raef asked, even though his gut told him her answer before she did.

She turned blue eyes to him. Her smile widened. "No, Kent, not Lauren. Or at least not *just* Lauren."

"Aubrey!"

She closed the few feet between them. "Yes, it's me." She lifted her right hand again, cupping his cheek. "You shaved just this morning, but you're already stubbly. All that dark, manly stubble. I like it. It's going to feel wonderful against Lauren's soft skin."

"Possession—it's, uh, dangerous." He sounded like an idiot, but her touch had his pulse jumping and his dick hardening.

Her hand went from his cheek to his neck. Her fingers were soft and delicate and so, so warm. They slid from there down the front of his sweatshirt, pausing over his nipple, where she used her nails, lightly, to caress him.

He inhaled sharply.

She smiled.

"For most people it is dangerous, but we're twins. We shared the same womb. It's different for us." As she spoke, Aubrey moved her hand to the waist of his jeans. There she paused again, and slipped her hand up under the edge of his sweatshirt, until her fingers touched the skin just beneath his belly button. There she used her fingernails again. Lightly she stroked naked flesh, following the waistline of his jeans.

"It's still not healthy. Not right." Raef was breathing so hard he sounded like he was running a damn marathon.

"This is where the part about promising to be open comes in." Her fingertips moved down until they found his erection, and then she traced the long, hard line of his cock—slowly—up and down. "Kent, you strike me as a man who keeps his promises," she whispered as she leaned into him. "Am I wrong?"

"No!" The word came out with a moan of desire. "But you're not alive. And you're not Lauren."

"Kent, just open yourself to me and let yourself feel it." She lifted her other hand and curled it around his broad shoulder.

"Feel what? All I can feel is you, and I'm fucking sure that's not right!"

She smiled. "Yes, feel me, but also let yourself feel hope—the hope that there is more to this life than what you've known, or even what you've believed yourself capable of." Then, before he could say anything, or move away, or second-guess what was happening, Aubrey kissed him.

She was sweet and soft, and so damn warm. Her mouth was open and inviting, and he could not say no. His arms went around her and his tongue met hers, touching, tasting, desiring, and as he moaned again and lost himself in the taste of her, he *felt* it—hope. It filled him to overflowing. He'd been right in the bedroom. It was better than pleasure and joy. It was a rare and wonderful thing that lit him from within.

Raef stopped kissing her long enough to look down

at her flushed, smiling face. "I don't care that you're dead. I don't care that this is Lauren's body. Right now—for this moment—I'm going to hope that somehow this is all going to turn out right. And I gotta have you, Aub. I gotta."

"Then I'm yours—for this moment." She gave him a little push and he sat back on the couch. Lauren had been wearing a pullover sweater the color of her eyes, and a pair of ass-hugging jeans. Still smiling at him, Aubrey pulled off the sweater and unzipped, then stepped out of, the jeans. She paused for a moment, looked down at herself and laughed softly. "French lace from Muse at Utica Square. Sis, I knew I could count on you for the sexy specialty lingerie." Her eyes found Raef again. "Do you like it?" Aubrey touched her nipple through the pink lace.

How the hell could pink lace be so damn sexy?

Raef nodded and swallowed. His mouth felt dry. "Yeah," he said gruffly. "I like it. A lot."

"And this?" Her hand moved caressingly down her softly rounded, womanly belly to the tiny triangle of pink lace that was the matching thong panty.

Raef thought his dick was going to explode. He nodded again. "Yeah, and that." Then he had her gasping as he moved quickly, reaching around her to cup her curvy ass in his hands, and pulling her forward so that he could press his lips against the blond triangle of curls he could see through the lace.

With a laugh that was definitely more breathless than she'd been before, Aubrey stepped back, just out of his reach. "Now it's your turn." She gestured at his clothes. "I want to look, too."

Raef didn't have to be asked twice. He peeled his

sweatshirt off and tossed it across the couch and, with a quick motion, stripped off his jeans and kicked them away.

Aubrey widened Lauren's eyes. "Commando? Always?"

"Always," he said. "Your turn." His eyes went from her bra to her panties.

"Well, it only seems fair," she said teasingly, reaching around to unhook the bra, and shimmying out of it. She took off the panties more slowly, letting him watch her glide them down her thighs and lift her gorgeous little feet up, one at a time, and step delicately from them.

"Will you come to me now?" Raef opened his arms to her. "Please."

"Yes, Kent. Yes, I will."

The wide leather couch became an erotic playground as Raef explored her body. Her nipples were tight under his tongue, and he loved how they filled his hands, but he stopped only briefly there—he had to taste her, he had to feel her against his mouth. He moved down to the damp blond curls between her legs. She opened her legs for him and he pressed his lips against her mound. Then his tongue found her clit, and she moaned his name as he teased it—back and forth. His mouth moved down, to the very center of her, and he guided her hand so that her fingers took the place of his tongue. He looked up at her and met her gaze. "Will you touch yourself for me like you did last night?"

"Yes," she whispered.

And then her whisper turned to gasps and moans as her slim fingers stroked herself, and his tongue teased and caressed along with it until he felt her thighs tense and her body tremble. She called his name out as she came and he pressed his mouth to her, tasting the waves of pleasure that washed through her body.

Aubrey surprised him then, by reaching down and pulling him up to her. She was laughing and flushed, and her hair was wild all around her shoulders. "Your turn. Again." She shifted her body so that she was on top of him, and then, with a mischievous grin, began moving down his body.

He didn't have to tell her. She already seemed to know his hot spots—those two places on his body that drove him mad. Her tongue found the first—his nipples—and he couldn't hold back the moan of pleasure. She glanced up. "Yeah, that's what I thought." Then she dipped her head and her tongue went back to work on his nipple, lightly and quickly, teasing him while she flicked the other one gently until it, too, was taut and ready for her tongue.

When she took his cock in her hand he had to grind his teeth together and try like hell to think of taxes so he didn't come. Her hand was as warm and teasing as her tongue, and she worked both of them together. Just when he knew he was going to explode, she stopped, pressed her breasts against his chest, and kissed him deeply, playing the same game with his tongue that she had with his nipples. In one motion, she shifted again, and straddled him. Tossing back her hair, she sank onto him, consuming him with her wet heat. While their gazes met and held she began moving up and down, sliding the length of him.

"Do you feel it? Do you feel me?" she asked him breathlessly.

"Yes, oh, God, yes." He did. He felt the heat of her body and the pleasure it was giving him, and he also felt her emotions—joy and pleasure and hope, most of all hope. His hands found her waist and he guided their tempo so that his reality narrowed to only her. He was looking in her eyes as his orgasm took him, an earthquake of feeling that shook the very foundations of his world. He cried her name, too—the name of a ghost, the name of a woman he couldn't hope to really have, but who had somehow breathed life into his battered soul.

When she collapsed on his chest he held her tightly, feeling her heartbeat against his, feeling the slickness of their sweat between them. She nuzzled his neck and kissed him and murmured something sleepily. He stroked her hair, loving the silky feel of it. She sighed then, and lifted herself just enough to look into his eyes.

"I have to go now," Aubrey said softly.

There was a terrible tightness in Raef's chest. "I know."

"Even though we're twins, this is hard for Lauren."

Raef started to draw away from her, trying to gently slide her aside. "I hope she isn't—"

Aubrey pressed her fingers against his lips. "Shhh, don't say it. Lauren isn't sorry. Lauren isn't upset. She's been here the whole time." Aubrey took his hand and put it over her heart. "She's just letting me drive, that's all."

"This isn't easy for me," Raef admitted, his voice hesitant.

"Me, either. But we're going to make it through to a happily ever after," Aubrey said.

"God, I hope so," he said.

She smiled. "Hope—I like that. Hold on to it, Kent."

Then Aubrey closed Lauren's eyes. Her body went limp in his arms. Raef felt a chill pass over him.

He didn't look. He didn't need to. He knew Aubrey was gone.

In his arms Lauren stirred and looked up at him, blinking groggily.

"Hi," he said, not sure what the hell to do and wishing Aubrey had at least waited to get dressed before she'd unpossessed her sister.

"Hi," she said.

Lauren didn't move out of his arms, but he could feel the tension in her body—her very naked body—because it was pressed against his very naked body.

"So," she said, "how do we make this not awkward?"

"I have no idea," he said honestly.

At that moment his cell phone, which was still in the front pocket of his discarded jeans, had the good sense to start vibrating.

10

"MIGHT BE THE office," he said, carefully pulling away from her, grabbing his jeans and the phone in one quick motion. The number was from After Moonrise, and, grateful for the reprieve, he punched the accept-call button. "Yeah, Preston, what do you have for me?" Raef spoke into the phone, keeping his back to Lauren while he pulled on his jeans.

"Got the results of the accidental-death search," Preston said.

"Hang on, I'm gonna put you on Speaker." Raef turned around to find Lauren in the process of pulling on his USAF sweatshirt.

"Let me get some paper first," she said when her head popped into view. She hurried back to his office and he numbly muttered something to Preston about waiting a second.

Actually, he didn't remember much of what he'd said to Preston. Raef was too busy staring at Lauren going and coming. His sweatshirt was huge on her, coming almost to mid shapely thigh, but somehow it was even sexier than the damn pink lace.

She sat on the couch, crossed her legs demurely, brushed back her hair and held the pencil expectantly. "Okay, I'm ready," she said.

He pressed the speaker button, thinking that he'd never look at that old sweatshirt the same way ever again.

"Let's hear it, Preston."

"So, I think there are two cases over the past twelve months that you'll be interested in." Preston's voice was as businesslike and efficient as he was. "One happened last January. Remember that bad snowstorm just before the long weekend?"

"Yeah, I do," Raef said. Lauren nodded agreement.

"On January 20, some local teenager, Charlie Padgett, took his daddy's Camaro for a joyride to Mohawk Park, along with a case of beer. The storm dumped six inches of snow in an hour. Police report said the kid got drunk and then stuck in the snow. He tried to walk out of the park and fell down and froze to death instead. It was ruled an accident."

"I'm hoping the tree connection is more than just the fact that Mohawk Park has trees," Raef said.

"Definitely. The kid's body was discovered by a tree-trimming team," Preston said.

"Is there anything in the report besides the tree trimmers being there for regular maintenance?" Lauren asked. "Were they there for a more specific reason?"

Into Preston's stunned silence Raef explained, "That's Lauren Wilcox. She's working her sister's case with me."

Preston cleared his throat. "Oh, well, okay. Yes, Miss Wilcox, the police report was thorough. TPD questioned the trimmers extensively. Apparently they were under the direction of a consulting arborist who was overseeing the cleanup after the storm."

"Did they list the tree doc's name?" Raef asked.

"Let me check." Preston paused while Raef heard the tapping sounds of a keyboard. "No, the report just says that they were under the direction of a city-hired arborist."

"What about the other death?" Raef asked while Lauren took notes.

"The other was in April. Caused by a frat-boy binge, complete with the kid choking on his own vomit, even though he was described by all of his friends as a non-drinking nerd. There's no direct arborist connection listed, just a coincidental tree connection. The body was found by the campus landscapers behind a very expensive pallet of saplings the university had spent lots of alumni money on to replace the trees that didn't make it through the last ice storm in February. I figured no one would spend so much money on a bunch of trees without consulting an arborist, so I thought you might be interested."

"Please tell me the university you're talking about is TU and not OSU-Tulsa or TCC," Raef said.

"As a matter of fact, it is," he said.

"Preston, you might have just served our killer to me on a silver platter. Take the rest of the day off."

"You know it's already an hour past quitting time, don't you?" Preston said.

Lauren hid her giggle with a cough.

"Right. I've been, uh, busy." Raef didn't meet Lauren's gaze. "So, what I meant to say was for you to take the morning off. Tomorrow. And good job."

"Thanks, boss," Preston said, with only a hint of sarcasm before disconnecting.

"It's Braggs," Lauren said.

"Good possibility it is," he agreed.

She tapped the paper she'd been taking notes on, frowning. "January, April, July." Lauren looked up at him. "If this is him, he's killing in three-month cycles. Raef, it's October."

"He's due," Raef said.

"So we're going to go apprehend him, right?" Lauren was already getting up and heading toward the pool of pink lace that was very near his feet. "I mean, we'll question him and see if he squirms?"

He sighed and grabbed her by his sweatshirt, lifting her up so that she wasn't bending over and showing way too much of her pretty little ass. "*We're* not. *I* am."

She frowned up at him. "I'm going with you."

"To confront the serial killer who murdered your twin sister, still has her soul trapped and is ready to murder again? No, you're not."

Instead of pulling away from him, Lauren pressed her hand against his chest. "I have to. It's logical."

"Putting you in danger isn't logical." Her touch was doing weird things to him, and he had to keep reminding himself that she was not Aubrey. *But, damn! She felt like her and looked like her and even if she wasn't Aubrey he really liked her and—* Raef shook his head, trying to clear his thoughts. "I'll check him out and tell you everything. You'll be in on all of it, but from a safe distance."

"There is no safe distance for me, Raef! I'm being drained just like Aubrey is being drained. We don't have time to mess around with this. The bottom line is that it's logical that I come with you because you'll know as soon as he sees me if he's the killer."

Raef stared down at her. She was right. If Braggs was the killer the sight of Lauren, looking so much like one of his murder victims, would evoke strong, negative emotions from him—emotions Raef's Gift would definitely be able to pick up.

He blew out a long breath of frustration. "You can come, but it has to be on my terms."

"Anything," she said, hugging him hard.

Raef let himself hold her and breathe in her scent. "Stay close to me. Stay quiet. And if bad shit starts going down you run like hell and call 9-1-1. Promise me."

"I promise," she said, and squeezed him tightly before letting him go.

"And I want my sweatshirt back, too," he said.

She had bent over to pick up her panties. She paused, straightened, and with a smile that had his heartbeat speeding up, Lauren pulled his sweatshirt over her head and tossed it at him. Then, very slowly, she said, "Be careful what you ask for, Raef."

He swallowed, muttered, "Thanks," and retreated into his bedroom as fast as his rubber legs could carry him.

THERE'D BEEN A MAJOR redo to the University of Tulsa's campus over the past couple of years. What had once been a nondescript entrance to a cluster of light-colored stone buildings mixed with modern stuff stuck in a kinda dicey part of town at Eleventh and Harvard had turned into a real university campus—complete with a swanky stone-and-wrought-iron perimeter fence and excellent landscaping.

Hell, they even had a fountain.

Raef was an ex-TU student. He hadn't graduated, but he liked to think that the several thousand dollars he'd paid in tuition during his three long years there had bought at least a few yards of the new fencing. Or maybe a portion of the fountain. Whatever. He still knew enough about the campus to pull into the main entrance at Tucker Drive and take a right to snake around to the bio building, Oliphant Hall. He parked in the west lot, shut off the car and turned to face Lauren.

"Okay, here's why we're here. We need Dr. Braggs's advice on how to save the big old elm in my front yard because we heard he's an expert on curing Dutch elm disease."

"There is no real cure for Dutch elm disease," she said.

He sighed. "Look at me. Do you think he'd think I know that?"

She raised her brows, and even though her eyes were tired and shaded, they sparkled at him. "Probably not."

"Exactly. So, if this is our guy you need to understand that his first sight of you will elicit some strong negative emotions. He'll be in turmoil, even if he looks totally calm to you. I'm going to ask for his business card—so I can reach him later about my elm, because right now we're in a hurry to get to a dinner date. You stay behind me. I'll be between you and him. You'll be near the door. We'll get in, and get out, and if I pick up negative emotions from him I will make a call to TPD. They'll take it from there."

"And I'm supposed to?"

"Play blonde. You can do that, right?"

Instead of getting pissed and narrowing her eyes at him, she blinked guilelessly and fell into a very good Okie accent. "Why, what do ya mean, sir? I'm simply standin' by my man like any well-trained woman would. Could ya please help him so that he's in a real good mood when he lets me fry him up some dinner while he 'reads'—" she air quoted "—the *Sports Illustrated* swimsuit issue?"

"Stop scaring me," he said, trying—unsuccessfully—to hide his smile.

"You lead and I'll follow," she said, obviously not trying to hide her smile.

"Hey," he said before she could get out of the car. "Remember that this isn't a game. If Braggs is our guy he's a killer."

Her blue eyes met his steadily. "I'll never forget that. Don't worry about me. Do your part. I'll be the silent bait and then I'll stay out of your way."

He started to tell her that she wasn't the damn bait, but she was already out of the car and standing on the sidewalk that led to the front entrance of Oliphant Hall.

Raef, you have lost your fucking mind, he told himself.

Lauren didn't stay on the sidewalk long. When he joined her she was crouched over some short greenish bushes inspecting their leaves.

"Azaleas," she said, before he could ask the question. "Sleeping ones, actually, which is what they're supposed to be doing this time of year. They're well tended—definitely in good shape. The groundskeepers know their business here."

"Ted Bundy had a girlfriend who said he was a good

guy—and all the while he was slaughtering young coeds."

"Who?"

"How old are you?"

"Twenty-seven. What does that have to do with—"

"Never mind," he interrupted, feeling old and worried and insane, all at the same time. "Just keep in mind not everything is how it looks. And do exactly what I tell you to do."

"Okay, I got it." Then she touched his arm. "If it's Braggs and he's arrested, what happens then?"

"Well, I'll let the police know about the psychic entrapment, and that we believe he's taken his victims' souls to the Land of the Dead. They'll bring in a shaman who specializes in soul retrieval."

"Right away?"

He hated that she sounded so scared. "Yeah, I'll make sure of it." *And if they don't move fast enough, I'll Track the bastard to the Land of the Dead and kick his ass myself,* Raef added silently.

"Then Aub will go free?"

"That's the plan," Raef said, his stomach suddenly feeling not so good.

Lauren looked out across the campus, shivered and whispered, "Yes, that's what has to happen, no matter what it does to me."

"Lauren," he said, sounding sharper than he'd meant to because of the worry for her that spiked in his twisting gut. "You won't be drained anymore. You'll be able to—"

"I know," she interrupted him, back to her steady, no-nonsense self. "It'll be okay. Aub and I will be okay."

Lauren took her hand from his arm and started walking briskly down the sidewalk.

He didn't have a clue what the hell to say to her. All he could do was try to wade through the conflicting emotions this damn case was making him feel while he caught up with her as Lauren followed the sidewalk around the light sandstone building. Together, they turned to their left to walk beneath white pylons that gave way to a very ordinary-looking glass door.

Raef had taken classes in Oliphant Hall—more than a decade ago, but the smell had stayed the same. "Books and formaldehyde mixed with testosterone and stress. I'll never forget that smell," he said.

"It was the same at OU. I think it's a common higher-education smell. Well, minus the formaldehyde."

A petite girl with big blue eyes and straight, well-maintained blond hair was coming toward them. She had a ridiculously thick anatomy-and-physiology tome clutched against her chest and an it's-midterm-and-I-gotta-study frown creasing her otherwise lineless forehead.

"Excuse me." Raef smiled at her. "Do you know where we can find Dr. Braggs?"

The girl blinked as if coming up through layers of essay test hell, and pointed at the ceiling. "He's probably still in the dissection lab on the third floor—room 303."

"Do you know if he has a class right now?" Lauren asked.

"No," said the college coed. "Lab is done for the day."

"Thank you," Lauren said.

The girl smiled, nodded vaguely and hurried on her way from the building.

Raef called on the recesses of his college experience and accessed a few brain bytes that he hadn't killed with alcohol poisoning. "Over here." He led Lauren a little way down the wide hallway to an industrial-looking metal door that had been painted the same unpleasant yellow as the rest of the first floor. "It's the stairwell that leads up to the third floor. If I remember correctly, and don't quote me because halfway through my freshman year I changed my major from Environmental Science to Beerology, this is how we get up to the third-floor classrooms."

"You went here?" Lauren asked as they climbed the stairs.

"For almost three years this is where I matriculated."

"Which means you didn't graduate," she said.

"Not even close," he agreed. "College and I didn't agree."

"Makes sense to me. OU and I had a fundamental disagreement, as well."

"Which was?" he asked, realizing he was actually interested in her answer.

"Well, they thought their students needed to attend class. Even if said students could *not* attend class and just show up for tests and still make decent grades." Lauren shrugged. "OU and I agreed to disagree."

"You agreed to leave and they agreed to let you?"

Her smile was sly. "No, I agreed to let Mother endow a chair in the botany department, and OU agreed to give me a BS." Her smile turned into a giggle. "A BS! It still makes me laugh. That's exactly what it was—bullshit."

"What about Aubrey?" He couldn't seem to stop himself from asking.

Her gaze met his. He tried to read her eyes and found

all he could decipher was weariness and a healthy dose of cynicism.

"Aub graduated with honors—*without* Mother bribing anyone. She has always been the smart one."

"And which one are you?"

"I'm the pragmatic one. Which one are you?" she fired back at him.

"I don't have a twin."

"Let's pretend like you do."

"All right. I'd be the grumpy one," he said.

As he grabbed the metal handle of the door to the third-floor hallway, she said, "Really? My guess is you'd be the lonely one."

11

THE SMELL HIT him right away. It had been bad enough on the ground floor. Up here in the dimmer, cooler third-floor hallway it was downright disgusting.

Lauren wrinkled her nose. "Eesh, what is that?"

He glanced at her. "You were a botany major but you didn't take any labs?"

She rolled her eyes at him. "I told you—I *took* a bunch of classes. I just didn't *attend* many of them. So, what's the smell?"

"Death," he said. "Formaldehyde only preserves bodies for so long. It never completely covers the scent of decay."

Lauren looked horrified. "There are dead bodies up here?"

"Yep. Humans, animals and probably a bunch of bugs, too."

She shuddered. "No wonder I never went to class."

"Stay close," he said.

"Don't worry about that. I'm not going anywhere." She wrapped her arm through his.

Raef moved forward with Lauren practically stuck

to his side, trying not to think about how good she felt and how badly he wanted to keep her safe.

The classrooms were clearly labeled and in numerical order, with odd numbers to the left and even on their right. Room 303 was only a few yards from the stairwell exit.

"Ready?" he asked her.

She unwrapped her arm from around his and lifted her chin. "Ready."

Speaking quietly, he said, "This isn't going to take long. Remember, let him see you, but then I'll move between the two of you. Stay behind me."

"And close to the door," she whispered back. "I remember. Let's just get this over with."

He nodded tightly, and pulled the door open by the cold, metallic handle. Only half of the fluorescent bulbs in the classroom were on and very little light managed its way through the high, rectangular windows. Black lab tables were clustered in pods. The smell was bad, but the tables and the aluminum lab chairs—which looked ironically like bar stools—were spotless. The wall closest to them was decorated with large feline physiology posters that were almost as gruesome as the stuff that was floating in huge jars on the shelves that lined two of the other walls. The place was so dim and creepy that at first Raef didn't think anyone was in the room. Then, from the head of the classroom, a man cleared his throat and said, "May I be of some assistance to you?"

"Dr. Braggs?" Raef asked in his best nice-guy voice.

The professor pulled off his glasses and rubbed the bridge of his nose with the back of his hand, which was covered in a latex glove.

"Yes, I am Dr. Braggs. How may I help you?"

"Well, if ya have a sec I'd like to ask you 'bout a tree," Raef said, adding a healthy dose of Okie and country-ing up his words.

Braggs blew out a little sigh. "I'm a bit busy setting up tomorrow's lab. But I can talk while I work."

"Hey, great! That'd be great," Raef said, and started moving toward the front of the room, staying ahead of Lauren.

"All right, then. Ask away." Braggs put his glasses back on and bent over the large metal tray that was mounded with something Raef couldn't quite make out. He studied Braggs as he approached him.

Had Raef not been so accustomed to the many faces of evil, he would have automatically discounted Braggs. The guy was absolutely average. His height was average—his balding was average—even the slight paunch he was working on was completely average. He appeared as harmless as Raef's dorky tenth-grade math teacher.

But Raef had spent ten years with the OSI in the air force, and he'd been involved in the apprehension of men who looked like Mr. Rogers, even after they'd strapped explosives to women and babies and intimidated them into going into restaurants to blow themselves up, along with innocent civilians, just to make a pseudo-religious point. It'd been tough to learn to separate the seen from the unseen, but he'd damn well figured it out—lives had depended on him. He'd been good at his OSI job then, and that military experience had helped him become one of the best psychic murder investigators in the U.S. of A.

So, Raef looked past what his eyes could see, reached

out and tested the invisible energy around him. Nothing. He felt nothing. Not even the slight hum of irritation Braggs should have been feeling at being interrupted.

"I'm Buddy Chapman," Raef began when they were within handshaking distance of Braggs, "and this is my wife—"

But Raef didn't get a chance to finish his introduction. Lauren, who had been following just a little behind him, had stopped like she'd run into a glass wall. Her eyes were wide, staring at the tray Braggs was working on, and her voice was unusually loud. "You're cutting up a cat!"

Braggs looked up, pulled off his glasses again, his average brown eyes blinking like he was having trouble focusing on Lauren. "Young woman, I am dissecting the internal organs of a feline specimen for tomorrow's nursing students to identify in their anatomy and physiology midterm," he said patronizingly. "I realize this might appear unsavory to an outsider, but I hope you will try to realize that this creature died for the greater good of science." He hesitated and blinked again. Then, as if his vision had finally cleared, his eyes widened. He smiled at Lauren. "You look familiar. Are you a graduate of TU?"

It was when Braggs smiled that the bedlam of emotions hit Raef. Braggs's expression never changed— never wavered from the benign dismissiveness and slight curiosity he was showing Lauren—but inside the *real* Braggs was a seething cesspool of hatred and rage, lust and fear, all mixed with the most disturbing wash of greed and violence Raef had ever felt.

"Graduate of TU? My wife?" Even though Raef was being battered by emotions, Raef forced himself to keep his tone normal, his voice jovial and as mildly patronizing as Braggs's charade. "No, sir. My little woman here married me right outta high school. She went straight to the college of havin' babies, if you know what I mean." As Raef spoke he kept his eyes on Braggs, moving one more step forward, and positioning himself directly in front of the professor, who was on the opposite side of the dissection table, and between him and Lauren. "Hey, I gotta apologize. We shouldn't have barged in here on ya. I just got a question about the big elm in my front yard. It's lookin' sickly and I hear you're a damn good tree doctor."

"Well, thank you," Braggs said, sounding calm and cordial, even though Raef could feel that he roiled with hatred and a deep, desperate need for violence. "I truly do not mind that you and your lovely wife have sought me out."

"Yeah, but you got your work to do, and the wife, she's a little squeamish." Raef tried to chuckle, but only managed to clear his throat. "How 'bout you give me your card and I call and set up an appointment proper?"

"Whatever you wish, Mr. Chapman. I have cards here in my desk, and I do see that your wife is looking rather faint."

Braggs opened the top drawer of the dissection table, and Raef took the opportunity to glance back at Lauren saying, "Honey, you go on back to the car and the kids. I'll get Dr. Braggs's info and meet you—"

"Raef! Watch out!" Lauren screamed, eyes wide and terrified.

Raef lunged to the side, reaching for the concealed Glock he kept in his side holster, but Braggs was already over the table and on him, striking with superhuman speed at his arm with a dissection blade that was so sharp it slit through Raef's sweater and sliced a long, deep path down his arm from bicep to wrist, causing him to drop the gun. It skittered across the slick floor as if it had been paved with ice.

"Lauren, go! Now!" Raef couldn't even look at her. All of his attention was focused on Braggs, who had suddenly morphed from average Joe Blow to a slashing, cutting machine.

Raef grunted with effort as he dodged the guy's blows. His body was taking too damn long to respond. *No, it's not me. It's Braggs. He's abnormally fast—abnormally strong.* Braggs struck again. Raef couldn't be quick enough. This time the blade sliced a red line across his chest, but Raef's adrenaline was pumping so hard he only felt the warm wetness of his blood. The pain would come later—if he lived until later. *Gotta buy Lauren time to get out of here—to get help.*

Braggs slashed again, ripping a line of blooming scarlet down the inside of Raef's thigh. As Raef staggered, Braggs rushed around him.

"No!" Raef snarled, reaching out and catching the edge of his lab coat and pulling him back. "You're not getting her unless you go through me."

Braggs laughed. Raef thought it was the most terrible sound he'd ever heard. "She's as dead as you are." His words were filled with venom. His face was twisted with anger. "I won't go after her until you bleed out. She can run as far as she wants. I'll find her. I'll kill her. I'll drain her. Just like I did her sister."

Raef didn't see her coming. Neither did Braggs. But suddenly Lauren was there, behind the professor. She swung the long metal pipe she was holding in both hands like a baseball bat, connecting with the back of Braggs's head as she yelled, "Like hell you will!"

Braggs dropped to the floor where he lay utterly motionless.

Lauren was actually descending on him, pipe raised, to hit him again when Raef caught her in his arms. "Stop—he's unconscious. We got him. We got him."

Lauren hugged him hard and then abruptly pushed away from him, her trembling hands hovering over his bleeding knife wounds. "He cut you. Oh, God, Raef. You're bleeding so much."

"I'm gonna be okay." He wanted to touch her face— to hold and reassure her—but she was right. He was bleeding. A lot. "Lauren, I'm going to cuff Braggs. You call 9-1-1." Stifling a painful groan, Raef crouched over Braggs and took out his handcuffs.

"I can't. I tried, but there's no reception up here. At all." Lauren's breath caught on a sob. "Raef, God, the blood!"

"I'm okay," Raef repeated, trying to sound calm even though he could already feel that he was getting light-headed. He managed to roll Braggs over and cuff him. "Here's what you need to do. Go outside. Call 9-1-1. Get help." He staggered over to where his Glock had slid to a stop against the classroom wall. When he bent to retrieve it his legs gave way so he sat beside the gun, and started to unbuckle the belt to his jeans.

"I'm not going without you." Lauren rushed to his side and was trying to take his hand, obviously thinking she could tug him to his feet.

"Lauren," he said, speaking as quickly and clearly as possible as he cinched the belt around his thigh. "I'm six foot four. I weigh two hundred and thirty-five pounds.

You can't even drag me out of here. I've got a tourniquet on this leg wound. The rest will wait. *If* you get your very shapely little butt outside and call 9-1-1. Understand?"

"Yes. Sorry." She wiped tears from her face, leaving bloody smears across her cheeks. "I'm going right now." She hesitated only long enough to lean down and kiss his forehead. "Don't you dare die on me."

"Not planning on it," he muttered as she turned and started to hurry away.

It was then that Braggs sat up.

His entire face had changed. His eyes were larger, darker and sunken into his head. Blood flowed freely from the cut in the back of his scalp—it ran down his neck and seemed to cloak him in crimson. Raef had no idea how it could be, but the professor looked as if he'd lost half his body weight in a matter of minutes. He'd become almost skeletal and looked more reptilian than human.

"You have both been very inconvenient. I will take particular pleasure in draining you." Braggs drew a deep breath, and with that inhalation Raef could feel the surge of siphoned violence and hatred that filled him, and as it did Lauren dropped to her knees with a terrible moan of agony.

"Lauren!" Raef shouted.

Lauren's gaze met Raef's. "He's draining Aubrey now!" she gasped.

"I've never had twins before," Braggs said. "It's like a two-for-one special." He lifted his arms and snapped the handcuffs as if they were a child's plastic toy, spread his arms and embraced the flood of terror and pain that cascaded into him.

The raw sound of agony that escaped from Lauren sliced through Raef. "He's killing us," she sobbed.

"No, he fucking is not." Raef lifted his Glock and, in one smooth, quick movement, shot Braggs between his eyes, blowing away the entire top of his head.

Even though the world was going oddly gray around the edges, Raef could hear Lauren whimpering not far away from him. "Hey, it's okay. The bastard's dead. It's over. Just don't look at him—it's not a pretty sight."

When Lauren didn't respond, Raef dragged himself over to her, thinking she must be in shock. "Lauren, honey, you gotta pull it together and get me some help. I know I look indestructible, but—" His words cut off as he reached her. She was in a fetal position, her arms wrapped around herself. Her face was absolutely colorless, her eyes blank, open and staring. "Lauren!" With a trembling hand he felt for a pulse. It was weak, but there. "Lauren, damn it! Don't do this! He's dead. He can't hurt you or Aubrey anymore."

The air above Lauren shimmered as Aubrey tried to materialize. Raef could only catch fleeting glimpses of her silhouette.

"Aubrey, what's happening? I got the guy—I killed him!"

Like her spirit, her voice was a weak, whispering shadow of itself, and all Raef heard before Aubrey faded away was, *"You killed his body. It's his soul that's draining us. Save us, Kent...."*

"Fuck! I'm a moron!" He closed his eyes against the pounding in his head. "Okay, yeah, I can do this. I Track murderers. Just because the asshole's dead doesn't mean I can't Track him." Raef drew a deep breath and reached out with his Gift.

Nothing.

The only negative emotions left in the room were his own. There was no murder trail. The murderer was dead.

"Save us, Kent..." seemed to hover in the blood-scented air around him.

"How?" Raef shouted. "How the hell do I save you? I can't Track a dead guy!"

The realization hit him and Kent's eyes opened. "I can't Track a dead guy, but I have Tracked a dead girl. I found Aubrey before—I can find her again. And when I find her, I find the bastard that killed her."

Raef only had a moment to feel the relief of his discovery when the world pitched and rolled, and suddenly he was on his back lying beside Lauren's motionless body.

"Hang on, Lauren! I'm not going to die on you!" he tried to shout, but the words came out as barely a whisper. He was losing strength fast…fading fast.…

Lauren was going to die. He was going to die. Aubrey was going to cease to exist—they all would. He was going to fail. He was going to die.…

So this was it? Time to quit—to give up? He tried to sit, to do something, anything, but his body wasn't obeying him, wasn't working. He knew it because his fucking mind wasn't just working—it was working with bizarre clarity.

Raef might have smiled, but he couldn't be sure because his face had gone numb.

To hell with this Negative Nancy bullshit, Raef growled silently to himself. *If I have to go to the Land of the Dead, being almost dead has gotta be a plus. So all right. Let's really get this thing done.*

Raef closed his eyes and focused on his breathing while he tried to recall what he'd done the night he'd Tracked Aubrey—the night she'd materialized and *felt* with him. What had that damn book said about soul retrieval and the Land of the Dead?

As his body continued to get weaker, Raef's mind became sharper and sharper. Snippets of the book he'd breezed through that night came back to him.

> …enter the Land of the Dead without protection and experience, and you risk becoming lost, too…

"Too late," Raef mumbled, and then he continued to recall.

Begin by lighting a candle.

Well, he didn't have a candle, but he did have the memory of a light that he'd never forget—Aubrey's shimmering thread of joy. What was next? What were the rest of those damn directions?

They came to him along with another surge of dizziness.

Once you have Tracked the soul to the Land of the Dead, your psychic Gift will cease to work. You must use mortal guile and your own wisdom to retrieve the lost one.

"That's right. That part seemed like good news then. Now I'm not so sure about my level of guile, let alone wisdom." Raef's voice sounded weird, like it wasn't really attached to his body. Hell, he felt weird, like *he* wasn't really attached to his body.

"Probably more good news for where I'm going." Then Raef shut his mouth and, after one last look at Lauren, closed his eyes.

He thought of Aubrey. Her laughter and her joy. The way she made him feel. No, not just hot and hard and sexy. Aubrey made him *feel*. Ironically, a dead girl had breathed life into a whole world of emotions he'd believed had been irrevocably lost to him because he'd spent most of a lifetime dealing with death and destruction.

And she called him Kent. No one but Aubrey had called him Kent since his Gift had been discovered.

Raef held the light of Aubrey in his mind and in his

heart, and with every bit of his skill as a psychic, he reached with his Gift, seeking, searching....

He found her more easily than he'd expected to, even though Aubrey's light wasn't a glowing, ribbonlike trail anymore. All that was left of the shimmering thread of joy he'd glimpsed before was a single, thin beam of light the color of champagne gone flat. The dimness of Aubrey's light scared him so deeply that it severed the tie that remained with his body, and Raef felt his spirit shoot away from the cold classroom. He didn't waste time worrying about how the hell he was going to get back. He didn't hesitate. Instead, he rushed after Aubrey's fading light, Tracking her with a speed and ease he'd never before experienced, which was good and bad. It was good because it was like he'd been fired from a cannon straight and sure into the Land of the Dead. It was bad because it was like he'd been fired from a cannon straight and sure into the Land of the Dead— and had less than a heartbeat to prepare himself for the experience.

Though I don't know how the hell anyone could be prepared for this shit, Raef told himself as he drifted to a halt, watching Aubrey's fading light disappear into the seething caldron of misery below him.

The sound of it hit him first. Voices drifting up to him were an awful mixture of sobs and screams and pleadings. He tried to make out single words, but it was difficult. It was like he had landed in the middle of an amphitheater that was hosting a chaotic symphony of hopelessness. He stared, trying to find the source of the voices. It was tough to get a good look at what was below him because a thick fog drifted over everything. Raef made himself drop closer to the land, and pockets of fog parted to reveal a landscape of utter desolation. It was like the Mojave mixed with the Arctic mixed with a nuclear wasteland. Almost totally devoid of color, the land lacked anything that was growing or sheltering, and all over the place was littered with what Raef at first thought were bizarrely shaped stones, jutting up from the bleak, drought-cracked ground. It wasn't until one of the stones moved that he realized they weren't rocks at all—they were bodies that had become grotesquely fused to the land. A shoulder jutted, an eyeless head was frozen, faceup, an arm protruded.

And even more awful, Raef watched as one of the fused bodies opened its mouth and shrieked.

Raef shuddered with revulsion. The bodies still had life in them, even though they lacked color or animation or expression, and they had actually become part of the land.

Aubrey? Oh, God, is one of them Aubrey? And Lauren? Is that how Braggs has them trapped—not by his own force, but by the force of this terrible place?

Almost in a panic, Raef reached out again for her slim beam of light, but he found nothing—felt nothing. He couldn't Track her at all.

Then he remembered—the book had said when he reached the Land of the Dead his Gift wouldn't work, that he'd have to use his brains and his wits. *So think!* he ordered himself. He'd Tracked Aubrey here—it was just when he actually arrived that his Gift had gone.

He stared around him, trying to clear his thoughts. Okay, maybe he should just start going from body to body and calling her name.

No. That felt wrong, and he didn't have time to waste searching aimlessly. *Think! Use some of that fucking wisdom both girls believe you have!* He stared around him. What a colorless, hopeless place. There was not one green thing—not one bit of sunlight or blue sky or even the familiar brown of a winter-nude tree.

Wait, he thought. *I might have something. Aubrey has color! Her spirit, even though it's trapped here and being drained, has enough color left in it to leave a trail for me.*

He didn't need to search the pathetic, colorless people who had utterly given up and had no more light about them at all. He just needed to search for light—any light.

Raef shifted his attention from the horrible, fused figures and began drifting. As he did he searched, sweeping his gaze back and forth, peering through fog and darkness, until off to his right a slight flicker of something like a candle caught in a great wind pulled at the edge of his sight. Raef redirected himself until he was hovering over the spot he was sure he'd seen the glimmer of color.

The damned fog was everywhere and he made himself drop down, closer to the ground itself. When he got lower the fog parted and the land beneath him fell away, leaving Raef staring down at a huge pit that was filled with a sewerlike, vitreous liquid that roiled and churned. With a shudder of disgust, Raef saw that people were bobbing around in the liquid, frantically trying to stay afloat. The people appeared to be as colorless as the bodies fused to the land, but as he watched, light fluttered across the face of one of the swimmers—right before she was engulfed in a wave and her head went under—only to reappear with a gasp and a terrible scream of agony a moment later.

It was the voice he recognized before he recognized her pale, terrified face.

"Lauren!" he shouted, commanding himself to go even lower—to go down to her.

"Raef! He's here! He—" Lauren's head went under again.

"Hang on! I'm coming!" Raef reached into the oil-slick water, feeling through the cold, dark liquid for her, but his search was suddenly stopped as something hard caught him in his gut and hurled him into the air and away from the pit.

He gasped with shock as pain lashed through him, blurring his vision. Raef blinked hard. When his focus finally came back he was looking down at a creature that was circling the top lip of the pit. Lizardlike, its body stretched all the way around the circumference of the pit. It had multiple tails that whipped in agitation at Raef. It opened its fang-lined maw to hiss at him—a sound that made the fluid in the pit churn even more crazily and had the swimmers, whose lights were now barely visible, crying out and struggling even harder to stay afloat.

"Stop!" Raef shouted at the creature. *"You'll drown them all!"*

The lizard thing opened its horrible mouth again and familiar laughter drifted across the liquid pit and up to Raef. *"Yessss,"* it hissed. *"I will drown them, but slowly, after I have bled everything I can from them. Are you here to join them? Your scarlet light will make a nice addition to my collection."*

Raef met the creature's dark eyes—eyes Raef recognized as easily as he had the laughter and the voice.

Raef looked from the Braggs creature to the pit, and

saw Lauren's head go under again. The sight worked like a goad on him and his answer rang clear and strong through the sounds of misery around him. *"I didn't come to join them, but I'll take their place. You can have me and my light, just let the twins go."*

"No, Raef!" Lauren shouted. The Braggs creature reached into the pit and swirled the liquid with a claw, and Lauren's head was engulfed in another oily wave.

"Look!" Raef felt foolish, but he waved his arms like he was trying to flag the attention of a charging bull. *"You don't want her. She's almost used up. I'm not."*

The Braggs creature paused, drawing his claw from the liquid. His dark eyes met Raef's gaze. *Hatred,* Raef thought. *I don't need my Gift to know that Braggs is hatred become tangible.*

Braggs's soulless laughter drifted around him again. *"No,"* he said. *"I will not trade with you. Between us there is that little matter of the fact that you killed my body. That will be inconvenient for me until I can find another to take its place."*

I need my fucking Glock right now, Raef thought.

"And if I remember correctly, back in the mortal realm your body is very busy dying. Soon you will be just another lost soul here. Who knows, you might accidentally stumble into my pit."

"Hey, it doesn't have to be like this. Maybe we can make a deal." Even though he felt like he was grasping at straws, Raef spoke quickly. At least while he talked Braggs was more focused on him than on pushing under the heads in the pit and slowly, slowly, while he spoke, Raef drifted closer and closer to Lauren. *"You say you need a new body. Take mine. I'll trade it for the twins."*

Braggs's laughter was a hiss. *"No, your body is dying."*

"I'm tougher than you think. Afghanistan couldn't kill me. I'll bet you didn't, either. That Glock makes one hell of a roar. Paramedics are probably on their way to TU right now."

"Perhaps. We could wait and see. If you drop to the land—you have died. If not—maybe you'll live. Maybe we'll trade then."

"No, Kent!" Aubrey's voice was weak. He could see that her mouth was barely above the churning liquid. *"You can't trade with him! He'll cheat you. You have to beat him. Remember what I taught you! That's all you need to—"*

Braggs snarled, and one of his tails snaked out and forced Aubrey's head under the liquid. Raef wanted to go to her—wanted to kick Braggs's ass and pull her and Lauren out of there—but Braggs was so fucking big that he covered the entire lip of the pit. Raef glanced down at himself, hoping for just an instant that he might have materialized in this realm as something other than his all too human, and all too vulnerable, body.

Sadly, he had not been turned into a knight in shining armor. He was just himself, albeit a less substantial version of himself.

The creature of hatred continued to circle the pit, watching him warily, tails writhing, jaws snapping. *"Why not come even closer? Let's fight for the twins."*

Raef wanted to—he wanted to so damn bad! But he wasn't an utter moron. Until he'd brought out the Glock, Braggs had been beating him. Actually, Braggs had probably killed him.

"Fight for the twins? If I'm gonna come down there

*to kick your scaly ass, I want more than just two women
if I win."* Raef stalled as Braggs taunted him, hissing
insults while his tentacled tail tortured the struggling
souls in the pit.

Think! Raef ordered himself again. *Listen to Aubrey!
Remember what she taught me.*

What the hell had she taught him? She'd made him
feel. She'd taught him that instead of holding on to suspicion and negativity, he could feel joy and laughter.
She'd reminded him that there was pleasure to be had
in life.

She'd taught him to have hope.

Hope was exactly what was missing in the Land of
the Dead!

As the understanding came to him, Raef felt the truth
of it swell within him—and joy and laughter, happiness
and pleasure and hope filled his floating spirit, warm-
ing him like a hearth fire.

"What are you doing?" Braggs snarled. He'd turned
all of his attention from the pit to Raef.

Raef looked down at himself and blinked in amaze-
ment at what he saw. From the middle of his chest light
glowed scarlet and orange, yellow and white, like an
otherworldly flame. *"I—I don't know. My Gift's not
supposed to work here."*

He hadn't realized he'd spoken aloud until Aubrey, obviously using the last reserves of her strength,
shouted up at him. *"It's not your Gift—it's you. It's who
you really are, so you brought it with you."*

"Silence, bitch! It is time for you to cease to exist!"
Braggs pressed a clawed foot against Aubrey's head,
holding her under the liquid.

"No, Braggs. It's time for you to cease to exist!" Act-

ing on instinct Raef reached within himself and found the Gift that was truly his—the joy and pleasure and hope that Aubrey had awakened in his life. And, like he was the starting shortstop back in middle school— back when he'd been an unlikely hero for anyone who was weaker than himself—Raef threw the ball of luminous emotions directly into Braggs's face.

Blinded, the creature shrieked and began lunging and snapping and biting so violently that it attacked itself— tearing huge hunks from his own flesh, which seemed to goad him on, making Braggs writhe and shriek and bite himself even more desperately.

With no hesitation, Raef rushed down, slipping past the creature that, blinded by hope, was destroying itself. He found Lauren first and held out his hand to her. *"Grab my hand!"* he shouted over Braggs's panicked roars.

Lauren grasped his hand, but as he began pulling her up she shook her head and resisted. *"No, I won't go without Aubrey."*

"I'll come back for her. I'll come back for as many as I can," he said.

"No. I'm not leaving without her—not without the rest of them."

"Lauren, we don't have time for this. I don't know what the hell is happening back in Tulsa with my body. You're alive. You're the only one here who I am one hundred percent sure is alive."

"If you believe that, we're all doomed," Lauren said.

"Damn it! I'm just being logical. I can't pull you all out. No damn way I'm strong enough. I'm gonna lose everyone that way. I have to—" His words cut off as Raef realized what he was doing. It wasn't force or logic

that had blinded Braggs and caused the creature to turn on itself. It was hope and joy, pleasure and laughter. He met Lauren's eyes and smiled. *"You're right, girl. We're all going home today. Find her. I know you can do it, and I've got you until you do."*

Lauren's smile was almost as brilliant as the beam of light that shot through Raef's body, sizzling with heat and hope, speeding down into Lauren, lifting her as it lifted Raef. As Lauren's body slid from the slimy pit, the ray of light extended down and Raef watched as a hand reached from under the surface, grabbing on to it. Aubrey's head broke the surface. She gasped and coughed, but she held tight to the ribbon of light, which passed through her and snagged another fading swimmer—a teenager. Lifting, Raef saw another swimmer grab the life light, and another and another until he had all of them free of the pit and of the creature of hatred as it completely self-destructed.

Raef's ribbon of light whipped up and up, carrying a whole trail of spirits, bright and glistening, all with colors of their own. Laughter filled the air, along with luminous light as the spirits Raef had freed floated around him, causing the bleak sky over the Land of the Dead to shimmer and shine, rainbowlike. And then, with a bright flash, each of the spirits began spinning off, reminding Raef of shooting stars, until he was left there hovering with Lauren and Aubrey.

"You did it!" Lauren cried. She was still holding tight to his hand, which she lifted to her lips, kissing his palm softly. *"Thank you, Raef. Thank you so much."*

He started to respond. To tell Lauren that she'd had a whole hell of a lot to do with the saving part, but before he could speak her eyes widened in surprise, then she gasped and disappeared.

"Lauren? What the hell?"

"She's not dead, Kent," Aubrey said, drifting to him. *"She went back to the mortal realm, back to her body."* She smiled, and even though joy sparkled like champagne all around her, tears filled and then spilled over her eyes. *"You'll go back soon, too."*

"I don't want to go back." He reached for her. *"Not without you."*

Aubrey wrapped her arms around him. *"I wish I'd met you before,"* she whispered to him.

"I can feel you," he said, holding tightly to her.

"It's our souls. They know each other. Maybe they always will." Aubrey kissed him then and Raef's spirit trembled at her touch. *"I never doubted that you would save us,"* Aubrey said against his lips. *"Never."*

"I didn't save you—you saved me. Because of you I learned to laugh again. To feel again. To hope again. Without you I wouldn't have been able to—"

Raef didn't get to finish. He didn't even get to say goodbye. His words were cut off as pain sliced through him and his spirit was ripped from Aubrey's arms, returning to his body with a terrible jolt of agony.

"That's it! We got him back! Hang in there, man, we're almost at St. John's."

Raef blinked up at the EMT who was putting the paddles back in the slots on the crash cart. There were tubes in his nose and arms and he felt like his chest was on fire.

"Aubrey," Raef tried to shout, but the name was barely audible. The EMT bent over him, putting pressure on his chest wound, and Raef repeated weakly, "Aubrey."

"She's fine. Just shaken up and a little shocky. The cops are bringing her in behind us."

"No," Raef whispered. "She's dead." Then he closed his eyes and the world went black.

RAEF CAME TO SLOWLY. At first he didn't know where he was, and his immediate thought was that he was really going to have to lay off the single malt. He was getting too damn old for two hangovers in as many days. He felt like utter hell. Shit, his chest hurt! Not even eighteen-year-old Macallan was worth this. He must have had more to drink than he'd had that night he'd gotten so shitfaced that he'd forgotten Aubrey was dead and…

Aubrey. His eyes opened as his thoughts caught up to her name and he remembered. *I'm not dead, but she is.*

He must have made some kind of noise because Lauren lifted her head from where she'd been resting it on the side of his hospital bed. "You're awake! Finally," she said with relief.

He tried to smile. "Are you okay?" His voice sounded gruff and his throat hurt like hell, but at least he didn't sound all whispery and weak.

"Yeah, we are." Lauren was much more successful with her smile. She beamed joy at him, and Raef could almost see it glistening in the air around her.

Which was bullshit. Raef couldn't feel positive emotions, or at least he couldn't feel them anymore. That ability had died with a dead girl.

The thought of Aubrey, and all that he'd lost with her, made his heart hurt like hell. Raef turned his head. He couldn't look at Lauren just then. Honestly, he might not ever be able to look at her again.

"Hey," Lauren said softly, touching his cheek familiarly and gently guiding his head toward her. "Kent, please don't turn away from me."

"Don't call me that." He didn't want to hurt her feelings. He really did like Lauren, really did care about her, but there was no damn way he was going to be able to handle her calling him Kent.

"Why not? I always have," she said.

"Bullshit—that was Aubrey. You've always called me Raef," he said, not sure if he wanted to cry or smash his fist into something.

"Yeah, well, we decided when we joined that we liked you as Kent best. So it's Kent you're going to be from now on," she said.

Raef blinked at her, utterly confused. "Pain meds. That has to be what's going on. You aren't making one damn bit of sense."

Lauren smiled into his eyes. "You are on pain meds, but that's not what's going on. What's going on is that we're both here—Lauren and Aubrey—together, forever."

Raef felt a rush of hope that he tried to squelch. "No, that's not possible. It can't be."

"Why not? We were never whole without each other. It only makes sense that we share one body since it seems like we share one soul."

"Aubrey?"

"Absolutely. And Lauren."

Raef looked into her shining blue eyes and saw her there—saw both of them there, and then he *felt*. An emotion flooded through his body that was so intense—

so incredible—that he suddenly found it hard to catch his breath.

"What's wrong?" She was on her feet, reaching for the nurse's call button, when Raef intercepted her hand.

"It's not bad," he assured her. "It's just a feeling like nothing I've ever felt before."

His soul mate let out a long breath of relief and gently cupped his face in her hands. Before she kissed him she whispered, "That's the one last feeling I had to teach you, Kent—love…."

* * * * *

HAUNTED

Gena Showalter

To she-just-gets-hotter P.C. Cast—
aka Miss P.C. Snowater-Cole—
for the phone calls, the emails and the laughs.
I had so much fun playing in your sandbox!
And of course, I love you!

To my editor Margo Lipschultz
for the keen insight and kind assurance!

To my agent Deidre Knight,
for always being in my corner!

To Jill Monroe,
for bouncing ideas and making me laugh
with her stories of dog vomit. (But if you baby
talk just one more time…I'll still love you, sigh.)

prologue

THE WOMAN LAY naked atop a cold slab of metal, her wrists cuffed above her head, her legs shackled apart. Frigid air that smelled of blood and disinfectant had turned her skin into a layer of ice over muscle too weak to even tremble. Determination to escape had drained out of her after the thousandth attempt, though the tears she'd shed forever ago were still crystallized on her cheeks.

This was it for her, she thought. The last day of her life. Sadly, there would be no changing course. The ship had already sailed and the storm had already begun.

She hadn't asked for this, certainly hadn't wanted it, but she'd gotten it. Now all she could do was fight. And she would. With every ounce of her strength, she would.

A muffled mewling sound echoed somewhere beyond her.

Though she was bound too tightly to twist and look, she knew her replacement had just woken up and realized she was locked inside a dog cage, only a metal slab and another female's shame visible. She knew—because she had once been locked inside that cage herself.

She had been forced to watch as the psycho who'd stunned her and stuffed her inside of his car had finished off the *other* woman who'd been on this slab. The one before her, now dead, killed in the most horrendous way.

"Do yourself a favor and shut up," she told the girl. Now wasn't a time for gentleness. "It's better to remain silent than to give him what he wants—and he wants you to cry. He wants you to scream and beg and tell him how badly it hurts."

The mewls increased in volume.

"Or continue doing that and make him the happiest murderer in the world," she added with a grumble.

The thump of booted footsteps suddenly filled the room. Her heartbeat spiked into a too hard, too fast beat. One second passed, two, before the hinges on the room's only door groaned. Sickness churned in her stomach.

He was here.

Was she really going to do this?

"Good morning, my lovelies." Such a smug tone, layered with threads of glee and malicious intent. "How are we feeling today?"

Yeah. She was.

Cries emerged from the cage as she said, "I'm feeling like it'd be fun to do a role reversal with you. What do you think? You on this bed, me with a low IQ, a tiny penis and—stop me if I'm wrong—big-time mommy issues."

A hiss of breath slithered in her direction. "You will never mention my mother again, do you hear me?" Anger had replaced the smugness, knives and other toys clanging together as he searched for the instrument he desired.

"If by 'never mention again' you mean 'never stop talking about it,' then, yeah, I heard. So, why don't you pretend I'm your therapist and this is a free-of-charge session?"

"Enough!"

Hardly. "Tell me. Did Mommy Dearest not breast-feed you? Or did she breast-feed you far too long?"

A heavy silence crawled through the small enclosure.

Dig the knife deeper—he soon will. "Come on, you can trust me. I'll keep everything on the down low, and only bring up your deep, dark secrets on my blog. Well, and maybe my Twitter feed. Oh, and Facebook. Possibly a video diary on YouTube. Other than that, my lips are sealed."

The metal crashed together with more force. At last he found what he wanted—an eight-inch serrated blade. Holding it up so that the silver gleamed in the too bright overhead light, he turned to face her, a half grin, half scowl lifting the corners of his lips.

"Darling," he said to the other captive, pretending to ignore her. He couldn't hide the clenching of his teeth. "You'll want to pay special attention to what happens next because if you displease me, you'll experience it yourself."

The cries became muffled whimpers, the cage rattling as the female tried to slink through the bars.

Never again will I give him that kind of satisfaction. "Oh, goodness, oh, no," she said, mocking him. "The psycho killer has a knife. Someone cue the spooky music and my terrified screaming."

His narrowed gaze landed on her, and he waved the blade back and forth, back and forth. "Have you not yet realized the beast you provoke?"

"Uh, hello. Obviously I have. He's as tiny as the rest of you, which is why I'm grinning."

He popped his jaw. He wasn't an ugly man, was actually quite beautiful, with golden curls, eyes of the sweetest honey and features as innocent and guileless as a child's.

Such a cruel, cruel mask.

When she'd first woken up in that cage she'd thought he was here to save her. A notion quickly disabused as he hauled her out, cut away her clothing and laughed with chilling delight.

"I can make this painless…or excruciatingly painful. Watch yourself," he snapped.

"Did I hurt your feelings?" she said. "Bad prisoner. Bad, bad, bad prisoner."

Steps slow and measured, he approached her. "Think you're so brave? Well, let's see what I can do to change your mind, shall we? I know you can't see her, but the girl in the cage is—drumroll, please—your only real friend. You remember her, don't you? Of course you do. She's the pretty one."

The first spark of heat ignited in her chest as she craned her neck to try to peer into the cage, but again, as tightly bound as she was, she was unable to contort herself as needed. She saw only the wall of pictures. Photos he'd taken of the other females he'd violated.

Tomorrow, her image would join them.

"You're lying, trying to hurt me because you're a miserable little runt whose heart has rotted and you can't find any other way to get to me."

Hatred flared in his eyes, creating deep, dark pits of evil. "You think so? Well, why don't you ask the girl and find out whether or not I spoke true."

Her fingers curled into fists. He wasn't lying. Was he? A liar would not appear so satisfied. Would he? "Say something," she commanded the girl.

Silence.

His smug chuckle resounded between them. "My deepest apologies, but she'll not be saying anything. She's mouthy, your friend. You know she is. I'm afraid I was forced to cut out her tongue."

Another spark of heat, this one containing fiery strands of rage. Growing…growing… Her friend *was* mouthy, and this man was vile enough to take her—and just cruel enough to stop her from ever speaking again. Anything to add to the torment he'd already unleashed.

How dare he abduct her friend! How dare he force such a precious girl to endure the horrors he'd visited upon her! Growing…growing…

"You sick, disgusting…argh!" she rasped, jerking at her cuffs. No description was foul enough. "I'll end you. You'll never be able to hurt her again. Just wait… I'll…end…you." *Don't cry. Don't you dare cry.* But she was having trouble catching her breath, forming words.

With his free hand, he stroked along her brow, his touch gentle, almost tender. "You've always thought yourself stronger than you really are. It's your biggest flaw. One I'll enjoy culling from you."

She tried to bite him.

He laughed. "I can't wait to show my newest plaything pictures of our time together. Think she'll be jealous?"

The rage spread through the rest of her, burning, blistering, causing any hint of tears to evaporate. "You can kill me, but I'm staying here, I promise you." There was her voice, stronger than before, dripping with determination.

He quirked an eyebrow in mock fear. "Oh, scary. And just how will you manage that, hmm?"

"I'll find a way. There's *always* a way, and good *always* overcomes evil."

"So certain," he said, and tsked under his tongue. "I've heard a strong spirit can prove victorious against anything, even death, but, darling, as I've tried and tried and tried to tell you, you aren't very strong."

"We'll find out." An accepted fact in their world: there was indeed an afterlife. Some people moved on to a better place. Some, to a worse place. But she wasn't going anywhere until her friend was safe.

"Well, I hope you're right. Just think, if you remain here on earth, we can be together again." He raised the blade, grinned—and plunged the metal deep.

1

Oklahoma City, Oklahoma

SIG-SAUER: EIGHT HUNDRED dollars.

Case of bullets: thirty dollars.

Shooting your neighbor in the face for going through your trash after you'd already warned him there would be consequences if he ever dared to do it again: price-less.

And I'll do it, too, Detective Levi Reid vowed as he polished the gun in question. *My stuff is my stuff. Even my trash!*

He'd moved into the King's Landing apartment complex three weeks ago, but he still wasn't sure why. Or how. Fine, he knew how. He didn't like it, and would never admit the truth to anyone but himself, but every day he experienced some sort of blackout. He would snap out of it missing anywhere from five minutes to five hours. Or, in the case of this apartment, seven days.

Honestly, here's what he knew about the events leading up to such a major loss: he'd followed a suspicious-looking guy to the building's back entrance.

The end. He'd next woken up inside this very room, all of his things surrounding him. He had no idea when he'd packed his stuff, given his home of six years to a stranger or rented this spacious though run-down two-bedroom hellhole totally *not* suitable for a king.

His coworkers hadn't come looking for him because he was currently on a forced leave of absence. He didn't have a girlfriend and had already canceled all of his "mandatory" appointments with the shrink. So, he'd decided to stay put, just in case another blackout struck and he came to someplace worse.

First he'd fumed about his total lack of control—and there were holes in his walls to prove it. Then he'd sunk into a (manly) depression. Manly: no crying or whining, just staring stoically—if not sexily—into the darkness. Now he pondered. He should have manned up and moved somewhere better, but some part of him had actually grown to like it here, despite everything.

Situated at the edge of downtown Oklahoma City, his new home gave him an up close and personal view of the homeless who littered the streets, the prostitutes who constantly hunted prey and the dealers who made back-alley sales day and night. He'd come to this area countless times while on the job, and it had always given him the creeps. (Again, in a manly way.) And okay, okay. The building wasn't as bad as he remembered. Someone had fixed it up, made it habitable.

His neighbors weren't so bad, either, he supposed. They had their quirks, but who didn't?

The guy in 211 skulked around every corner as if a serial killer had his number—and that number was up. Any time Levi heard a suspicious noise and decided to check the halls, the guy glued himself to Levi's side, crying and begging Levi to help but refusing to answer any questions or share any details.

The girl in 123 liked to tiptoe up and down the halls at all hours of the day and night, stopping to attempt to X-ray vision her way past every door she encountered. Any time Levi walked past *her,* her attention would swing to him and she would say something spine-chilling like, "I miss my baby. Will you be my baby?" Or, his favorite, "What will you do when you're dead? Dead, dead, dead, you're so dead."

The guy in 409 was Mr. Dumpster Diver.

As of last week, a redheaded stunner and her pretty blonde roommate had moved in. They might be as weird as the rest of them, but he was thinking about asking the redhead out. He wasn't a fan of dating, but he sure did like getting laid.

Right now he sat at his kitchen table, his SIG in pieces and mixed with his cleaning supplies. He greased the gun's rails, put the slide on, removed the slide and wiped off the rails, each action automatic. He'd done this a thousand times before, and now found the act calming.

Calm, something he was supposed to maintain. Apparently, if you were on the job and attacked an alleged serial killer who liked to store body parts in his freezer, you'd be told you had "temper issues" and needed to take time to "think and rest."

What he really needed was a distraction. So, okay, fine. No more thinking about asking Red out. He'd just do it. Hopefully, she was into rough-looking homicide detectives who were possessive of their stuff but trying to learn to share. Also, Levi wasn't interested in one-night stands and actually expected commitment. And despite popular opinion, he did know how to smile.

A hard knock at his door brought his head snapping up. Probably just another neighbor here to ask to hide from Johnny Law or to tell him the end was near. "Go away. No one's here."

Another knock, this one harder, more insistent. "I won't bite," she said. "At least, not more than a few times."

He liked her voice. Soft and sweet, yet determined. Still, an intelligent person didn't offer to nibble on strangers.

Motions swift, he put his gun back together and shoved it in the back of his running shorts. The weight created big-time sag, never a good thing but especially not when he was shirtless. His uninvited guest would probably get a peek at his goods, but by the time he finished with her that wouldn't be the worst of her worries. She needed to learn the consequences of this kind of behavior.

But…then he glanced through the peephole and spied the redhead's roommate, the pretty blonde. Teaching her a lesson took a backseat to getting rid of her. Last time he'd seen her, she'd made him feel a tide of guilt and shame. Why, he didn't know. Didn't care. He just didn't want to deal with her.

The moment he opened the door, however, urgency took a backseat to concern. She was highlighted by flickering overhead light, chewing on her nails and shifting nervously from one foot to the other. Crimson specks marred her cheeks and splattered her hands. Blood?

Frowning, he opened the door wider. "Are you okay, ma'am?"

Eyes of ocean-blue narrowed on him, her gaze becoming a laser that sliced through flesh. She stopped chewing and shifting at least, and no feelings of guilt or shame rose to the surface. "Ma'am? Did you just call me ma'am?"

"Yes, ma'am. Are you okay?"

"Wow, that hurts!" she said, ignoring his question a second time. "Just how old do you think I am?"

A minefield of a query, and one he was better off disregarding. He motioned to her stained hands with a tilt of his chin, even as he reached for the handle of his gun. "Let's try this again. Are you hurt?" He scanned the walkway. Empty. No suspicious shadows, marks or noises. "Is someone following you? Bothering you?"

"Why would you—" She glanced down, chuckled and wiggled her fingers at him. "This is paint. I'm a painter."

Paint. No mortal danger, then. His concern faded, and the surliness resurfaced. "Then what are you doing here?" Okay, so he probably should have pretended to be nice. She'd tell her friend he was a tool, and the friend would tell him she'd rather date a dishrag when he finally asked her out.

"As I was saying," she continued blithely. "My amazing art does not contain…" A shudder of revulsion shook her. "You know."

What? Blood? Probably. So many people had an aversion to the stuff, but he'd never had such qualms. "'You know'?" he parroted.

"Yeah. The elixir of life."

You're kidding me. "And the elixir of life is?" Levi

was having what he suspected was fun for the first time since his suspension. The girl was brave enough to knock on a stranger's door and demand he open up, but she couldn't say a certain five-letter word? How cute was that?

She ran her tongue over her teeth and whispered, "Fine. I can do this. It's *B-L-O-O-D*." Another shudder shook her.

Would it be rude to laugh at her? She'd actually spelled the word rather than said it.

His stance softened, and he allowed his arm to fall to his side. "So you're an artist, huh?"

"An *amazing* artist."

"I don't know about amazing," he said, "but you're definitely modest." And she was more than cute, he realized. She was short and curvy, her face something you might find on a little girl's favorite doll, with big blue eyes, a button nose and heart-shaped lips. She was utterly adorable.

"By the way," he added, "being called 'sir' would be a reason to have a hissy. Ma'am's all good. I say that to everyone with—" his gaze automatically dropped to give her a once-over, but he got caught on her breasts, which were straining the fabric of her pajama top. He managed to jerk his attention back up and choke out "—estrogen." Girl was *stacked*.

"Good point," she said, tossing that tumble of pale hair over one shoulder, "but I assure you, I'm all woman."

Noticed. Believe me. Rather than voice the sentiment aloud—and risk finding his testicles in his throat—he gave her a single nod of affirmation. "No argument here."

A relieved breath left her. "Thank you for not telling me I need to double-check my woman card."

"A double check isn't necessary." *Are you...flirting?*

"Well, isn't the big, strong he-man sweet?"

"Yes, ma'am, he is."

He wasn't the type to flirt, but yeah. Yeah, he was flirting, and she was flirting back.

He'd planned to ask the redhead out, not really wanting anything to do with the blonde and all that guilt and shame she'd caused, but now, with the emotions out of the way, he changed his mind. He wanted this one.

In female-speak, that meant he wanted to get to know her better. In male-speak, he wanted her in his bed, like, now.

She was young, probably in her mid-twenties, with that cascade of wavy blond hair, blond brows and blond lashes, those delicate doll features and the fair skin of someone who preferred to hiss at the sun rather than to bask in it. And she was—

Familiar. He knew her, he realized. Somehow, some-way, he knew her. Finally, an explanation as to why he'd felt what he'd felt when she'd first moved in, and yet he had no idea when or where they would have met.

"You're staring," she said, chewing on her bottom lip.

A nervous habit, definitely. One that made him think she was slightly...broken.

A protective instinct he usually only experienced on the job sprang to life. Annnd, yes, there was the guilt and the shame again.

Why? Why would he feel this way about her?

Well, no matter the answer, Red was back in the running. Levi didn't date the broken. Ever. He protected, he avenged, but he didn't fix. How could he? He couldn't keep his own life on track. Besides that, he didn't like feeling this way.

"Seriously. What?" she demanded.

"Just wondering if we've met before." Even as he asked, his arms felt heavier, the muscles tense, as if memory had been stored there and he was now reliving his time with her. But…that would mean he'd held her. That wasn't something he would forget.

Her nose scrunched up endearingly. "Is that a line? Because that sounds like a line."

"Actually it's a question—" *can't date her, can't date her, really can't date her, even though you dig her straightforwardness* "—and an answer would be nice."

"Oh." Was that disappointment in her tone? "Well, the only answer I can give you is no. I would remember someone with your particular…attitude." Her gaze raked over him, and the little tease shuddered as if they were discussing *B-L-O-O-D.* "And for your information, I'm entirely lacking in modesty about my paintings because there's no need for it. I'm an incredible artist. Incredible!"

Confidence was more of a turn-on than straightforwardness, and she possessed more than most. There was no way she could be the broken girl he'd imagined her. Right? And guilt and shame weren't that bad. *Right?*

"Never said you weren't incredible. And what's wrong with my attitude?"

"It kind of sucks, but I'm sure you're told something similar all the time." Up her hand went, her nail back in her mouth, her teeth nibbling. "I, uh, smell coffee," she said, a sudden tremble in her voice, "and yes, I'd love some. Thanks."

She darted around him and breezed inside, a waft

of cinnamon and turpentine accompanying her. As he watched, momentarily speechless, she stalked to his kitchen.

His brain eventually chugged out of the station. Who did she think she was? His home was his sanctuary and strangers were never allowed. Not even hot ones.

To be honest, this girl was the first person other than himself to ever step inside the apartment. His partner was avoiding him, and his family was…well, he had no idea where. At eighteen, he'd left home and had never looked back. His parents had died when he was six, and none of his relatives had wanted him, so he'd hopped from one foster family to another until the age of thirteen, when a depressed housewife and her emotionally abusive husband had adopted him. Good times.

So, yeah, call him paranoid, call him domineering and selfish and rude, but what was his was his, and he never shared.

But you're learning to share, remember?

Not anymore!

He would kick her out after scolding her for her daring—and, as a courtesy, he wouldn't shoot her in her pretty face—and then they could discuss going to dinner, maybe a movie.

He would have the blonde or no one, he decided.

But he took one look at her and found himself rooted in place. Her motions were stiff, jerky, as she gathered the supplies she needed. A cup, the sugar, a spoon. As many interrogations as he'd conducted over the years, he knew when someone wanted to say something but hadn't yet worked up the courage. His new neighbor was desperate to confess a secret; she just needed a little push.

Take control of the situation. "Hey, lady. You need to get something straight."

"'Lady' is just as bad as 'ma'am.' I'm Harper," she called over her shoulder.

Harper. The name didn't quite fit her.

He closed the distance, checking the living room to make sure he'd cleaned up after himself. Besides the shirt and pants he'd draped over the side of his couch, he had, thankfully, done a little picking up. As for his furniture, the dark leather of his couch and love seat were scuffed but of high quality, his coffee table as polished as his gun, and his rug threadbare only where he liked to pace. The floorboards creaked with his every step, but then, creaks, groans and moans as wood settled and hinges dropped were the standard sound track, blending with chatter that could be heard through the ultrathin walls.

"Listen up," he said.

"Okay, I've waited long enough for you to offer," the woman—Harper—interjected. "What's your name?"

"Levi. Now why are you here?" He gripped the counter to stop himself from shaking her. Shaking was bad. Very, very bad. Or so his captain was always saying.

Clutching *his* cup, sipping *his* coffee, she turned to face him. Only, rather than spilling her reasons, she grimaced and gasped out, "What *is* this crap? Because honestly? It tastes like motor oil."

So he liked his joe strong. So what? "Maybe it *is* motor oil."

"Oh, well, in that case, it's actually pretty good." She took another sip, sighed as though content. "Definitely grade-A motor oil." Her gaze slipped past him. "You know, your place is so much bigger than mine, with much better lighting. Who'd you have to sleep with to get it?"

She's as weird as the rest of them. "Who says I had to go all the way?" *Apparently, I am, too.*

A laugh bubbled from her, and she choked on the coffee. "Dude. Do you know what you just implied?"

"Uh, yeah. That's why I said it." Now, then. He'd allowed her to dominate the conversation long enough. He needed to move this along before she gave another one of those laughs. *Gorgeous.*

He sidestepped the counter, moving closer to her, closer still, the fragrance of cinnamon thickening the air between them, the turpentine fading. He claimed the cup, set it aside and crowded her personal space, forcing her to back up until she ran into the cabinets.

She peered up at him, those ocean-water eyes haunted…and, oh, so haunting. Just then, she reminded him of a fairy with a broken wing.

Broken. There was that word again.

Muscles…tensing again…

In his experience, everyone had secrets. Clearly Harper was no exception. He recalled the day she moved in. She'd kept her eyes downcast, the long length of those pale lashes unable to mask the shadows underneath. There'd been a hollowness to her cheeks that had since filled out, and a stiffening of her spine every time someone had neared her. And wow, he'd noticed a lot considering he hadn't allowed himself to watch her.

"You have five seconds to start talking," he said more harshly than he'd intended. There was no reason to break her other wing, but dang, his instincts to protect those weaker than himself were taking over, every part of him rebelling at the thought that someone had hurt her. "Why. Are. You. Here?"

She gulped, and her trembling increased. "Can't a girl get to know a guy before she begs him for a favor?"

"No." Evasion never worked with him. "Are you in some kind of trouble?"

Color darkened her cheeks, even as the rest of her blanched to chalk-white. "Not exactly, no." Softer voice, danger hidden by silken threads of…fear? Yeah, definitely fear. No longer was her gaze able to meet his.

More gently he said, "Explain 'not exactly.'"

And there went her nails, smashing into her teeth. "Word on the street is, you're a detective with the OKCPD."

"I am." No reason to mention his forced leave of absence.

Those ocean-water blues finally returned to him, so lovely in their purity his breath actually snagged in his throat. "What kind of cop are you?"

"A detective, as we've already established."

"Like there's a difference. A badge is a badge, right? But I meant, are you the good kind or the bad kind? Do you care about justice, no matter the cost, or do you just like closing a case?"

He pressed his tongue into the roof of his mouth and reminded himself that he was a calm, rational being (with a gun) and she probably hadn't meant to insult him and his coworkers.

"Harper." A swift rebuke, her name uttered as though it was a curse. He should have called her "ma'am" again, but since he'd teased her about how he'd gotten the apartment, formalities were out. "You're seconds away from being arrested for public intoxication, because only a drunk person would say something like that."

A relieved sigh left her. "The good kind, then. Otherwise, you'd try and convince me of just how good you are, rather than taking offense."

"Harper."

She swallowed. "Okay, fine. I told you I'm a painter, right?"

"An *incredible* painter."

Her chin lifted, those haunting secrets in her eyes momentarily replaced by affront. "Well, I am," she said, having to speak around her fingers. "Anyway, I, uh, hmm. I knew this would be hard, but wow, this is worse than the time I had to tell Stacy DeMarko her butt did, in fact, look fat in those jeans."

I am not amused. He wrapped his fingers around her wrist and pulled her hand away from her mouth.

The contact jolted her, and she gasped. It jolted him, too. Her skin was unbelievably soft, decadently warm, something out of a fantasy. Her pulse hammered erratically, every pound caressing him. He let her go, stepped away.

"Last chance, Harper. Just say what you came to say. That's the only way to get what you need."

She rubbed at the elegant length of her neck, the picture of feminine delicacy, and whispered, "I'm painting something…from memory, I think, and…the problem is…I don't really remember, but it's there, in my head, the horrible image, I mean, and…and…I think I witnessed a murder."

2

Aurora Harper, named after Sleeping freaking Beauty—and if anyone dared call her by the awful name they'd soon get a personal introduction to the razor in her boot—sat "calmly" on her neighbor's couch. He was peering at her, silent, waiting for her to answer his latest question.

Her tongue felt thick and unruly, unusable, and there was a lump growing in her throat, making it difficult for her to swallow. She hated talking about this, hated *thinking* about it, and would have given anything to slink away unnoticed, soon forgotten.

Thing was, Levi would not be forgetting her. After her grim announcement, he'd gone stiff and jarringly quiet, then had ushered her into his living room, gently pushed her onto the couch cushions and pulled a chair directly in front of her. He'd spent the next half hour drilling her for information.

She'd had no idea what to expect from him, had known only that he was the most rugged-looking man she'd ever seen. Oh, yeah, and every time she'd glanced in his direction he'd made her heart pound with an urge

to fight him or to jump into his arms and hold on forever—she wasn't yet sure which.

He had wide shoulders, muscled forearms and the
hard, ridged stomach of an underwear model. Dressed
as he was in black jogging shorts, she could see that he
had scarred knees and calves. He was barefoot and his
toes were strangely cute.

She forced her gaze up. Black hair shagged around
a face honed in the violence of a boxing ring, or perhaps even the down-and-dirty streets, with still more
scars crisscrossing on his forehead, his cheeks sharp
and skirting the edge of lethal, and his nose slightly
crooked from one too many breaks. A shadow of a beard
covered his jaw.

He was just as bronzed up top as he was below,
and she would guess his ancestry Egyptian. His eyes,
though…they were the lightest green, emeralds plucked
from a collector's greatest treasure. Long black lashes
framed those jewels, almost feminine in their prettiness.

Not the only thing pretty about him, she thought then.
His lips were lush and pink, the kind her best friend
and roommate Lana would "kill to have…all over me."

And, okay, enough of *that.* Harper wasn't here for
a date, wasn't sure she'd ever date again. The past few
weeks, she could not tolerate even the thought of being
touched. Maybe because every time she closed her eyes
she felt phantom hands whisking over her, heard the
laugh of a madman who enjoyed inflicting pain, and
smelled the coppery tang of blood deep in her nostrils.

She could have written off the sensations as an overactive imagination, except…sometimes she fell asleep
in one room and woke up in another. Sometimes she
would be in her kitchen, or in her studio room paint-

ing, or anywhere, really, and would blink and find herself standing in a neighborhood she didn't recognize.

The blackouts freaked her out, filled her with soul-
shuddering panic, and each time she realized she was
someplace new, her mind would paint her surroundings with blood, fill her ears with screams…such pain-
drenched screams.

The only explanation that fit was that she'd witnessed
a murder, but had suppressed the details. Suppressed
until she painted, that is, the blurred images of horrors no one should ever have to bear taking shape and
emerging unbidden. Either that, or crazy had razed the
edges of her brain and she needed to be locked away
for her own safety.

"Honey, I asked you a question and you need to answer it."

The harshness of Levi's voice jerked her out of her
mind. Guess he was done calling her by her name and
even the old-lady "ma'am," and was now resorting to
endearments that sounded more like curses.

"No," she said, just to pick at him. "Not 'honey.' I
told you. I'm Harper."

One black brow arched into his hairline, and for a
moment he appeared amused with her rather than ac-
cusatory. "Is that a first or last name?"

"Does it matter?"

"Yeah."

She popped her jaw, finding strength in the familiar-
ity of an irritation she'd never been able to shake. Her
mother had named her after a fairy-tale princess and
had expected Harper to mimic her namesake. Years of
training in manners and deportment, followed by years
of competing in a pageant circuit she'd despised, had

nearly drained the fighting spirit out of her. Nearly. "Well, I'm not telling you the rest of my name." He'd laugh; he'd tease her.

He shrugged those beautifully wide shoulders. "Easy enough to find out. A few calls, and boom." He paused, clearly waiting for her to jump in.

"I will never willingly volunteer it, so you'll just have to make those calls."

A gleam of challenge entered those green, green eyes. "So be it." He rested his elbows on his knees and leaned closer to her, the scents of minty toothpaste and pungent gun oil intensifying. Scents she really, really liked, if the flutter of her pulse points was any indication. "Let's backtrack a bit. Tell me again what you think you're painting."

This was the third time he'd demanded that information, and she'd watched enough cop shows to know he was testing her, looking for any mistakes between her first and subsequent telling. If he found them, he could write her off as a liar.

"Shouldn't you be taking notes?" she said, stalling.

"No."

"You'll forget—"

"I never forget."

"Anything?"

"Not anything like this."

How intriguing. "Really, because that's—"

"Talk," he barked.

His intensity gave her the strength to obey. "Okay." She closed her eyes and forced the painting to the front of her mind. "There's a cold metal slab, stainless steel, I think, and it's splattered with dried b-blood. There are shackles at the top and bottom, holding a woman's wrists and ankles, and those are also splattered. There are holes on the slab and floor…drains, I think, and they're splattered, as well. There's a man. He's clutching a knife over the woman's abdomen." Every word caused her heart rate to quicken and little beads of sweat to dot her skin. Sweat, yet her blood had thickened with ice.

"Describe the man."

"I can't." Her lashes fluttered open as a shudder rocked her. Nausea rolled through her stomach, a common occurrence these days. "I haven't yet painted his face." Wasn't sure she wanted to see it. Even the thought of him made her want to hide under her covers and cry.

"What *have* you painted of him?"

"His lower body. His arms. Some of his chest."

"And he's wearing…?"

Good question. She'd been so focused on what was happening in the picture that she hadn't paid any attention to the little details her mind had somehow caught. "A white button-up shirt and dark slacks."

"Possibly a businessman, then. Gloves?"

"No."

"Is he pale, tan, black, what?"

"Tan, though not as tan as you."

"Okay, now describe the woman."

"I can't," she repeated, a mere whisper. She flattened a hand over her stomach, hoping to ward off even a little of the sickness. "Not her face, I mean. She's naked, and her skin is pale."

"Does she have any birthmarks or scars?"

Harper licked her lips, pictured the female and shook her head. "If she does, I haven't added them yet."

His gaze sharpened on her, more intense than before and kind of, well, terrifying. This was not a guy to anger, or taunt, or even to play with. He would retaliate, no question. "How much of her have you painted?"

"All but the head."

"Is she a brunette, blonde or redhead?"

"How would I—"

His pointed gaze explained for him.

"Oh. Uh, I don't actually know. The bottom half of her is blocked by the man's torso."

"Is she alive or dead in the painting?"

"Dead, I think." And probably happy to have escaped the pain.

Silence once again permeated the room, thick and oppressive, reminding her of exactly why she hadn't wanted to come here. She'd known he would doubt her—as she sometimes doubted herself—or suspect her of playing a part in the murder.

Lana believed the woman was indeed real and Harper had stumbled upon the scene. As an employee of the Oklahoma City branch of After Moonrise, a company specializing in grisly murders and the spirits those murders sometimes left behind, she ought to know. But her belief stemmed not from the painting, but from the fact that there were two weeks neither Harper nor Lana could account for. Harper could have been trapped with the man and his victim, and somehow, miraculously, have managed to escape.

Her friend had showed the painting to her coworkers, but they hadn't taken the case. Lana had even begged—which, in her case, meant she'd cracked heads around—and they'd finally given in and said they would look into it, but so far, they'd discovered nothing. *If* they'd even tried. Lana was doing everything she could on her own, but as someone used to dealing with spirits rather than bodies, this wasn't her area of expertise.

So, when Lana heard a detective was living in their building, she had insisted Harper nut up and speak out.

This tormend you, she'd said in a Lithuanian accent that came and went with her moods. When she was happy, she sounded as American as Harper. When she was scared or angry, hello, the accent appeared, as thick as if she'd just stepped off the plane. So often now, she was sad, and at the time she'd been filled with so much sorrow over what Harper might have endured that her teeth had chattered. *Let man help you. That girl...she deserve peace, rest. Please.*

I can't. He'll suspect me of hurting her.

Maybe at first, but then he see the trut.... Please, do for her, for you, for...me.

Given the fact that Lana had spent every night of the past few weeks sobbing for the pain *Harper* suffered over the entire ordeal, well, Harper had been willing to do anything her friend asked, no matter the consequences to herself.

"Harper." The curt bark of Levi's voice jolted her out of her thoughts. "You with me?"

"Well, I am now," she grumbled. "Do you have an inside voice?"

His lips twitched at the corners, hinting at an amusement he'd so rarely shown. That humor transformed his entire face. Those emerald eyes twinkled, little lines forming at the corners. His mouth softened, and his skin seemed to glow.

"Have you ever painted anything like this before?" he asked.

"No. I love painting people, but not like this. Never like this. Why does that matter?"

"Once, and it's plausible you stumbled upon some kind of scene. Twice, and it's more plausible your mind manufactured everything."

Okay, that made sense. "Well, it was only once. And just so you know, I can't see the dead, so it wasn't a bunch of spirits putting on a show for me, either." She wasn't like Lana, who had always had the ability to see into that other realm.

"I'll need to view your new painting, as well as a sample of your usual work," Levi said.

"All right. The new one isn't done, though. Obviously."

His head tilted to the side, his study of her intensifying. "When did you begin painting it?"

"About two weeks ago." She tried not to squirm or wring her fingers under such a probing stare—until she realized that his probing stare was a good thing. Criminals would not stand a chance against this man's strength and ferocity. If her painting were a depiction of a real-life event, Levi would find out the identity of the man responsible and punish him. "Little by little, I've been filling in the details."

Another bout of silence before he sighed. "Let's switch gears for a minute. Forgetting the fact that you've never before painted anything like this, what makes you think this is a memory?"

Bottom line, she wasn't ready for a stranger to know about her blackouts and to, perhaps, use them against her, yet neither was she ready to lie to a man who could have kicked her out but hadn't. He'd listened to her, had asked her questions and truly seemed interested in helping her.

So, she said, "I'm struck by moments of absolute terror," and gazed down at her feet. Her pink snakeskin boots were one of her favorite possessions. She'd had to sell four paintings to buy them, as well as live off peanut butter and jelly for a month, but she'd never regretted the choice. So pretty. "Moments I can almost feel the shackles around *my* wrists and *my* ankles."

"Delusions hold that same power," he pointed out.

Don't act surprised, you knew it would come to this. And better this than the other avenue he could have taken: blame. "Well, I hope it *is* a delusion," she whispered.

"Me, too, Miss…Harper?"

"Just Harper." She would *not* be tricked into revealing her full name, thank you.

"Had to try," he said with a shrug. "What if you discover you were the one on that table, that you somehow escaped but repressed what happened?"

"Impossible. I was only gone—" She pressed her lips together, stopping her hasty confession before it could fully emerge. "I would have had bruises at some point, and I haven't."

He sat there a moment, silent again, before nodding as if he'd just made a decision. He pushed to his feet and stuck a finger in her face. "Stay there. Do not move. I'll get dressed and we'll walk to your apartment together. Nod if you understand."

"And there's that lovely attitude again," she muttered.

"Nod."

Oh, very well. She nodded.

"Good. Disobey, and I'll cuff you faster than you

can say, 'I'm sorry, Levi, that was the dumbest thing I ever did.'" Without waiting for her reply—because he clearly didn't expect her to have one—he turned on his heel and headed for the hall.

"Uh, just thought you should know that your gun is showing," she called.

Just before he disappeared around a corner, she thought she heard him say, "Honey, you're lucky you're only seeing the butt of it."

She wasn't *that* bad. Was she?

Harper waited. The click of a closing door never sounded. Well, she wouldn't let that stop her; she stood with every intention of walking around his place and checking out his things.

Maybe she *was* that bad.

"I told you not to move," Levi called with more than a hint of annoyance.

He'd heard the quiet swish of her clothes? "Tell me you don't talk to your girlfriend with that tone." The moment her words registered in her head, she groaned. Basically, she'd just asked him to marry her and have a million babies.

"No girlfriend." A tension-ripened pause. "You?"

"Nope, no girlfriend, either." The jest served a dual purpose. One, lightening the mood, and two, discovering whether or not he cared to know her lack-of-boyfriend status. If he pushed for more info, he might just be as fascinated by her as she was by him.

And she was, wasn't she? Fascinated by this rough-and-gruff detective with the jewel-toned eyes. *Thought you weren't interested in dating anyone.* She wasn't. Right? She hadn't taken one look at a grumpy cop and changed her mind, *right?*

"Boyfriend?" Levi barked out, and she nearly grinned.

You're in trouble, girl. "Nope, no boyfriend."

She scanned his walls. There were no photographs, no artwork, nothing hanging anywhere to inform her of his tastes so that she could peel back the curtain surrounding his life and reveal the man he was with others, when he was relaxed. Did he ever relax, though? Probably not. Judging by his perma-frown, it would take a miracle.

"Your decorating…did you decide to go with Minimal Chic?"

Stomping footsteps echoed, and then he was there, in front of her again, tall and dark and ruggedly delicious, an erotic dream come to life in a black T and black slacks.

She'd bet his gun was still at his back. He was a warrior, a protector. A danger. Sweet heaven, but she had to paint him, she decided. He wasn't handsome in the classic sense, but, oh, he was so much *more*. He was interesting.

She'd always favored interesting.

"We're not discussing my decorating," he said.

"You mean your *lack* of decorating."

"Whatever. Lead the way."

"So you can stare at my butt?" Sometimes her tongue got the better of her, and now was definitely one of those times. There was no way he could respond to that without—

"Exactly."

—making her sigh dreamily.

She was in *big* trouble. "I'm not interested in dating anyone, just so we're clear."

He glared down at her. "Good, because I was thinking about asking out your friend."

Oh, ouch. Yet wasn't that always the case? Men slobbered all over Lana like babies who'd just found fuzzy candy on the floor.

"Good!" she said with a huff. "Rude isn't my type." She turned, giving him her back, and marched out.

"But then I met you and changed my mind," she thought she heard him grumble from behind her.

3

HARPER WAS UTTERLY baffled when Levi gave her painting a once-over, asked a single question, then turned
and left her apartment. He did this *after* she'd overcome
her urge to vomit and placed the wretched canvas—
though perfectly painted—in the heart of her living
room, just for his benefit. Sure he'd paused to eye Lana,
as any man with a pulse would have done—and even
some without, surely—but he hadn't so much as called
out a token "Don't leave town." Or even a very necessary "I'm on the case, no worries."

The door slammed ominously behind him, echoing
throughout the somewhat dilapidated two-bedroom
apartment with plush furnishings Lana had restored
with loving care, a hobby of hers. *Their* decorating style
was Match Smatch. Every piece was an odd color and
shape, and nothing harmonized.

Levi's question played through her mind. "You said
there was blood. Where is it?"

The answer was simple. Seeing the blood on the canvas freaked her out, so every morning, after her sub-

conscious mind forced her to add it back, she erased it, leaving the walls pristine and clean.

"That has to be a record for you," Lana said, her Lithuanian accent nonexistent because her darker emotions weren't yet engaged.

Harper purposely kept her back to the gruesome scene of torture and death she had created and kept her gaze on her friend. "I have no idea what you mean."

Had the painting disgusted Detective Snarls? Was he even then searching for his handcuffs, intending to take Harper into lockup? No. No way. He would have dragged her with him, not allowing her out of his sight. He wasn't the type to cross his fingers and hope she stayed put. Even when he'd left her alone in his living room, he'd kept his bedroom door open so that he could hear her movements.

"I've seen you scare off a man within an hour of meeting you, but five minutes? You must have done something *really* special to this one."

Harper snorted. "Wasn't like I asked him to meet my parents or anything." And, bonus, she never would. Three days after her fourteenth birthday, her dad had taken off and never looked back. After that, Mommy Manners had forced her to become even more involved in pageants, and Harper had eventually cracked, poisonous words she still regretted spilling out. Though she'd tried to make amends, her mother hadn't spoken to her in years. "But you know, he could have had the decency to invite himself to breakfast." They had details to hammer out, right? "I mean, he wants to ask you out. Shouldn't he try to butter me up or something, so I'll put in a good word for him?"

"Uh, no, no, he not be asking me out."

"He said he would."

"Well, he lied or changed his mind because that man has a jones for a hot blonde with a taste for destroying fairy-tale princess."

Hope fluttered through her, causing her heart to skip a beat. "First, the taste is justified. Sleeping Beauty sucks. Evil showed up and instead of fighting she took a nap."

"Is that reason enough for you to buy figurines of her likeness just to smash when you're angry?"

"Yeah. And second," she continued, "there's just no way you're right about the cop wanting me. But go ahead and tell me why you think so, beginning once again with how smoking hot you think I am and ending with how you think he's willing to drop to his knees and beg me to go out with him, and don't leave out a single detail."

Lana rolled her eyes. The bold shadow she wore gave those eyes an exotic, smoky look, extending all the way to her temples in glittery points. "You are hot. He will beg. You will say no—and don't try to deny it. I noticed your antiman campaign. I will call you stupid. You will paint a mustache on my face while I sleep. I will carve the legs out from under your bed. We will laugh. The end. Now, tell. Will he help you or not? Because I will hurt him if not."

Okay, so it wasn't the story she'd hoped for but it was true nonetheless. "I might have you hurt him, anyway. After I'm done with him, of course." He was surly with a capital *S-U-R-L-Y,* glaring at her when she'd entered his apartment after he'd clearly invited her in—with his eyes. "He needs someone to turn his frown upside down. By hanging him out of a window by his ankles."

"Just say a word, and it is done."

Oh, how she adored Lethal Lana.

They'd met in junior school, when Lana's family moved to the States, and their instant connection had changed the very fabric of Harper's life. Harper, the "lady" of her mother's dreams, had been fascinated by Milana Buineviciute, the wild child of her mother's nightmares.

A (now reformed) smoker, drinker and full-time cusser who never backed down from a fight, Lana had taught Harper how to get down and dirty with brass knuckles and steel-toed boots. Harper had taught Lana to channel the jagged edges of her emotions into art, and the exchange had bonded them.

They balanced each other, even in looks. Lana's hair was naturally dark, almost jet, but she'd bleached the straight-as-a-board strands and then dyed them neon red, a color that complemented her cream-and-rose complexion perfectly. Her features were bold, aggressive, and yet her green eyes were always at half-mast, a sultry invitation to peel away her clothing and have your wicked way with her. Or so Harper had gathered from any man who'd ever looked at her.

Even as fatigued as Lana currently appeared, and had, for these past few weeks, with bruises marring the delicate tissue under her eyes, her lips chapped from constantly being chewed, and the weight she'd dropped from her already slender frame, the girl was a showstopper.

"Maybe we should move," Harper said. "We'll just pack my precious valuables and your crap and—"

"No!" Lana shouted, then repeated softly, "No. I stay here."

A relieved breath escaped her.

After Harper had snapped out of her first blackout and seen what she'd painted, she had walked the streets trying to reason things out. Lost in her thoughts, she'd unknowingly entered the worst part of town. She'd ended up in front of this building, and a desire to live here had instantly consumed her. She'd raced home to tell Lana, and Lana had paled, burst into tears for no reason. Well, there had been a reason, but she still refused to say.

Eventually Harper managed to talk her friend into subletting their place and moving here. But where Harper had thrived, Lana had declined all the more. And yet, she couldn't be dragged out with a tank.

Harper felt guilty about that, she did, but she had no idea what to do.

"By the way, we are not done talking about the cop," Lana said, calm now and rubbing her hands together with glee. "I saw the way you looked at him so I must ask. By 'done with him' did you mean you will hurt him when you jump into his arms and beg him to marry you?"

Harper rolled her eyes, and it was then that she noticed the black shadow creeping along the walls of the living room. Dread poured through her veins, hot and as slick as oil. She knew that shadow, had battled it each time a blackout descended, and knew it would crawl down the walls, consume the entire room and try to swallow her whole.

"I'm sorry, but I have to go," she muttered, grabbing her purse and stalking into the hallway outside their apartment, overly warm air enveloping her. The darkness would catch up to her, but that wouldn't stop her from running.

The floor whined with her every step, other apartment doors slammed closed and the overhead light flickered on and off, on and off. Creepy, yes, but it suited her new frame of mind.

Lana, in her long-sleeved top and pajama pants with a tool belt painted around the waist, stayed close at her heels. "You okay?"

"I will be." *I hope.* Only Harper was able to see the shadows, and she could guess why. Either she was halfway down the road to crazy or she was already standing at the edge, waving goodbye to the life she'd once lived.

She quickened her pace. As always, a pretty young girl stood in front of one of the doors, trying to peer inside an apartment that was not her own. Black hair fell in silky waves to her shoulders. Usually when Harper passed her, the girl remained quiet and unaware, her attention locked on whatever she saw through the obstruction. This time, her head whipped in Harper's direction and violet eyes more otherworldly than human pierced her to her soul.

"Such a naughty girl," said the teenager in a voice chilled by lack of emotion. "You should have known better."

Surprised, Harper stumbled over her own foot.

Lana flipped the girl off and said, *"Tu mane uzknisai."* She waited for Harper—who knew she'd just told the girl how ticked she was—to straighten up before hurrying on.

"What'd I do?" Harper demanded of the girl, looking over her shoulder. She hadn't had a serious boyfriend in over a year and hadn't been on a date in months, even before her whole "no touching" rule. There'd been no naughtiness in her life. None. Well, not until today, when she'd eaten Levi up with her eyes. "Were you listening through the cop's walls while I was with him, you little—"

"I never should teach you to fight." Lana motioned her forward. "She clearly out of mind. Pay no attention or she drag you into her insane."

Another full-on appearance of her accent, proving Lana was as affected by the girl's taunt as Harper. For that reason, she let the subject drop. Until Harper solved the painting mystery, Lana had enough to deal with—whatever "enough" entailed.

A few minutes later, they were outside, the pulsing heart of Oklahoma coming into view. Tall structures with chrome and glass on every floor knifed toward a baby-blue sky with no hint of clouds. Thick green trees with curling branches lined the river walk and overly crowded sidewalks. Sidewalks far more crowded than usual, in fact. On the streets, cars of every color whizzed past, the speed limit clearly a suggestion not to be heeded.

There was a deep chill in the November air, yet Harper remained unfazed. "So, anyway," she said, getting them back on track, "if you hate the apartment so much, why do you want to stay?" She asked even though the very idea of leaving made her quake. She asked even though she'd asked before and Lana had not answered.

"I don't hate the place. I belong there."

That was something, at least. "But—"

"Give me another but, and I smack yours!"

Harper laughed, she just couldn't help herself.

A man and woman walking toward them jumped,

as though startled by the sound of her voice. The pair gave her a strange look before passing her. So she was in her winter pj's, like Lana. So the heck what!

"So where we go?" Lana asked.

After a moment's thought, a heavy sigh left her. "Let's go to the place that started us on this journey. Maybe if I figure out what happened to me, I'll stop hearing screams of pain in every single one of my dreams."

REMAINING IN THE SHADOWS, Levi kept pace behind the two females. What a striking pair they made. The tall redhead and the petite blonde, both feminine beyond imagining. Nearly every guy that passed them stared at the redhead, dismissing Harper as if she just couldn't compare.

Idiots, he thought. There was a delicacy to Harper, a fragility, yet when she opened her mouth you discovered just how much of a ballbuster she was. The contrast was exhilarating.

But those blue, blue eyes of hers—those haunted eyes with their secrets and pain and a thousand questions waiting to be answered—continued to, well, *haunt* him. As much as they would have turned him off any other woman, and should have turned him off her, he wanted her more with every second that passed. The shame and guilt were completely gone, and now, every time he caught sight of her, an urge to protect her rose up, one stronger than before, nearly overwhelming him.

A man had to touch a woman to protect her, and he really wanted to touch Harper again. That softness... that heat...

Figure out her mystery first.

He'd walked into her apartment, and for a second he'd seen crumbling walls, even a rat racing across his feet. But then in a snap, he'd seen freshly painted walls of bright yellow and blue, colorful furniture and every surface scrubbed clean. The momentary hallucination had freaked him out, but he'd said nothing. Then, after viewing her painting, a gruesome thing to be sure and exactly as she'd described it—a man standing over a bound, battered and naked female, a knife in his hand—he'd needed a moment to collect himself. Part of him had wanted to gather Harper close and make sure she was kept safe, even from the past. The other part of him had wanted to shake her for not coming to him sooner.

If what she'd painted hadn't sprung from an overactive imagination, the only way to have witnessed such a scene was to have been in the room with the killer. A room like that wouldn't have windows. So, discarding the overactive imagination argument for the time being—something he would do until proven otherwise—she had either aided and abetted the killer or had been captured herself and had somehow managed to escape. Levi doubted the first. Harper's aversion to blood was real; no one could fake the draining of color from their face. And that, of course, left the second option....

Actually, there was a third possibility, he realized. She could have been captured and killed.

Death wasn't the end of life. He knew that beyond any doubt. Knew spirits existed eternally. Only problem was, he'd never developed the ability to see the spirits in the unseen realm, and at thirty-four, he doubted he ever would.

He'd been told only specifically gifted people could

see into the invisible world around them. He'd also heard that with specific exercises, the gift could be developed over time, but he'd never tried any of them. Now he kinda regretted that. Two of his coworkers possessed the ability and they always uncovered answers pertaining to the worst of cases, even those deemed unsolvable, when no one else could.

Levi could have used some of that uncovering now.

He'd get his answers soon enough, though. He always did. And yeah, he should be on the phone, finding out what he could about Harper and her past, as well as her roommate's past, but he'd heard the pair stomping and chattering down the hall and he'd decided to follow them instead. He was glad he had.

A few interesting tidbits he'd already picked up. They loved each other, were comfortable together. They talked and laughed, teased each other good-naturedly. Yet ninety percent of the people who passed them eyed them as if they were certifiable, even the males drooling over Lana. And as beautiful as the redhead was, and as fragile as Harper appeared, not a single male approached them.

Of the remaining ten percent, well, five percent eyed them with amusement, but the other five eyed them with fear. That same remaining five-and-five eyed *him* with sheer terror. He was used to people turning away from him, or outright running from him, as if he were a mass murderer with a blood vendetta or something. But usually those people were criminals, and he'd just caught them committing heinous crimes.

Finally the two women stopped in front of an art gallery, their happy moods draining and leaving only grim expectation. The place was small but open, with big glass windows staring into an elegant space with columns and hanging lights.

Harper flattened her hand on one of the panes. "I was here, I remember that much."

"Yes, and you sold bazillion paintings that night."

The accent…Czech, maybe.

"And you…"

"Left early on arm of some loser." Guilt saturated the redhead's tone.

"Yes, and I failed to come home."

Neither female knew he was here, listening. The fact that they were searching for answers ruled out the possibility of an overactive imagination entirely. Yeah, people could convince themselves of the strangest things and actually think they were real, but they usually couldn't get someone else to agree with them.

The hand on the pane, so delicate and tiny in comparison to his, fluttered to Harper's neck. She closed her eyes and breathed deeply, seeming to ponder the fate of the world before a slow smile curled her lips, lighting her expression with a mix of pride and sadness. "I was so happy by the end of the show, my nervousness gone. My first genuine presentation was a raging success, more so than I could ever have dreamed, even as amazingly talented as I am, and every painting sold."

Yeah, there was no way this woman could have aided a murderer. He knew criminals, had dealt with them on a daily basis for years, and yeah, some of them were good actors, well able to mask the monster within, but that smile…that sadness…combined with her physical reactions, there was just no way this was an act.

If he was wrong, he'd shoot *himself* in the face.

He was going to find out the truth. He was going to help her.

"What next? You remember?"

He watched as a tremor rocked the curve of Harper's spine, spiraling into her limbs. Nearly knocked her off her feet. "I...I..." She wrapped her arms around her middle, skin turning a light shade of green.

"You do not do this now," the redhead rushed to add. "We come back later."

"No," Levi said, stepping from the shadows, "you won't. You do this now, Harper." As sick as she currently appeared, she might not work up the nerve to return.

In unison, both women spun to face him. Harper reacted first. With a face bathed in panic and a mouth hanging open to unleash a scream, she jacked up her knee—and nailed him in the balls.

4

DESERVED THIS, LEVI thought. He never should have snuck up on Harper. He'd known better. Women were more unstable than C-4.

What? They were.

Silence permeated the tension-filled space between Levi and Harper as he struggled to find his breath and forget the fact that his testicles would probably need to be surgically removed from his throat. Even the crickets were too uncomfortable to laugh about what had just happened.

Harper's eyes were wide, her hand now over her mouth, and the friend was—doubled over laughing, he realized as the haze of pain gradually faded. Okay, so *she* wasn't too uncomfortable. Suddenly he was glad he hadn't gotten around to asking her out. *So not my type.*

Harper, on the other hand... His fairy with the broken wing and secrets in her ocean eyes had a nasty flight-or-fight response. It wasn't such a wonderful thing when he was on the wrong end of her knee, sure, but it'd be white-hot sexy when he wasn't, he was certain.

Still. Lesson learned. Never again would he underestimate her. But next time—and considering the amount of time they would have to spend together, working this case, there would be a next time—if given a choice, he would much rather chase her. Then, at least, he'd get to tackle like the good ole days when he'd played for OU.

Finally oxygen passed through his nostrils, filled his lungs. He smelled car exhaust and sunshine and…cinnamon. Her. He liked the smell of her.

Her hand fell away from her mouth. "I'm not going to apologize," she said, chin lifting. With the morning sun stroking her exposed skin, flushing her cheeks to a deep rose, she practically sparkled with vitality. "You scared me, and I reacted. Deal with it."

"You don't need to apologize. I do." He rubbed the back of his neck, grunted out a quick "Sorry" and left it at that. It was more than he'd given anyone in years, and you know, it hadn't left the bleeding, gaping wound that he'd expected.

The stiffness drained from her, and she worked up a beautiful grin that lit her entire face. It was genuine, with no hint of sadness, and she looked as if she'd swallowed the sun. Her hand fluttered just over her heart as she said, "Wow. Never has a more poetic apology been spoken. I'm all warm and tingly inside."

His body reacted to her words—warm and tingly—heating, tensing. He really had to get this attraction thing under control. He didn't mind wanting her, liked it, in fact, but he did mind the growing intensity of that wanting. "So you disappeared from this place?"

"I think." The grin was the next to drain away, followed by that gorgeous light. "Maybe."

"Maybe?"

"I just remember bits and pieces."

He heard the frustration and anger in her tone and sympathized. Levi knew he'd attacked the serial killer, but didn't know what he'd done or what had provoked him. He had flashes of flying fists, could even hear grunts of pain, but that was it. And for a man who prized his memory, having never forgotten a locker combination or even a file number, that irked.

"Ever talked to the owner of the gallery, asked questions? Ever talked to anyone who was there the night you're speaking of and might know?"

"No, but—"

"I have," the redhead said.

He arched a brow at her, a silent demand for her to continue.

Harper waved a hand between them. "Levi, meet Lana. Lana, meet Levi."

"You are so pleased to meet me, I know. Now, no one knew or saw anything," Lana said, the accent vanishing with an obvious, concentrated effort. Her hand had fluttered to her neck, where her fingers tapped against her pulse, seeming to mimic the cadence of her voice.

"I need the names of the people you talked to, and anyone else you remember being there."

As she rattled off the names, he read the hours of operation listed on the gallery's window. It was eight in the morning, and the place wouldn't open for another hour. He checked the door. Locked. He knocked, just in case someone was in back doing inventory or something. No one answered.

"Shouldn't you be writing down these names and numbers?" Lana asked.

"No," he said without looking at her.

"Apparently, he remembers things," Harper said drily.

He rattled off every name, every number, and both women gaped at him. With two fingers, he helped Harper close her mouth. "Anything else either of you want to share before I start looking into this?"

Harper gave a little gasp, as though surprised by his agreement to help—or by his touch—and shook her head, but Lana shifted nervously from one foot to the other. Suddenly suspicious, he homed his gaze in on her. She licked her lips, narrowed her eyes, shifted from one foot to the other. He remained silent, waiting for her to crack. They always cracked.

Determination filled those green eyes. "Nope, nothing," she said.

Oh, she knew something, and he *would* find out what it was. But not here, and not now. He'd dig up some details about her, Harper, the art gallery, the owner, the people who had attended Harper's gala, and go from there. The more armed he was with information, the better chance he'd have of intimidating Lana and forcing her to talk.

He only hoped Harper was safe with her.

Has been so far, he told himself. "I'll swing by this evening," he told Harper, crowding her backward and forcing her to stop against the building. Their gazes were locked, the air charged between them. For a moment, her breath hitched in her throat.

He leaned down, careful not to touch her a second time—would she gasp if he did?—and whispered straight into her ear, "Consider this your first and only warning. Next time your knee goes near my balls, I'll retaliate. But don't worry…I think you'll like it."

WHEN THE ELEVATOR DINGED and opened up to the OKCPD bull pen, Levi tensed and he wasn't sure why. He recognized the sights: guys in button-ups and slacks, guys in uniforms, cubbies and desks, computers, criminals cuffed to chairs, papers all over the walls. He recognized the sounds: heavy footfalls, the clack of high heels and the stomp of boots, inane chatter, angry shouting, fingers tapping keyboards, phones ringing. And the smells: coffee, aftershave, soap, unwashed bodies, perfume, sugar.

He just wasn't sure he belonged here anymore. He felt disconnected, separated, and wasn't sure it had anything to do with his suspension. So…why?

Your neighbors' crazy is rubbing off on you, that's all.

Small comfort. He maneuvered around the cubbies, throngs of people headed in every direction, each too busy to pay him any attention. He reached his partner's office and rasped his knuckles against the already open door. Vince sat behind his desk, head bent over a file. His gaze flicked up, landed on him, but quickly returned to whatever he was reading. His features were pale, drawn, and lines of tension branched from his eyes. Though he was only thirty-four, he appeared fifty and unable to care for himself, his cheeks hollowed, his sandy hair disheveled and his white shirt coffee-stained.

"Ignoring me still?" Levi asked. Vince had yet to forgive him for attacking the suspect and placing himself in the line of fire.

A reel of memory suddenly played, startling him. He and Vince had stormed into a small basement room. The perp had raised his arms, seemingly accepting of his arrest, and smiled. Smiled, smug and proud of all he'd done to his victims—and silently promising to do it all over again if ever he was released.

Levi had worked too many gruesome crime scenes because of the man, the last one enough to turn even *his* iron stomach. A young female had been staged, her lifeless, bruised and battered body pinned to a billboard for all of Oklahoma's downtown commuters to see as they hurried to work.

That smile had razed the jagged edges of his already shaky composure, a desire to protect the rest of Oklahoma's females rising up inside him. A desire he hadn't been able to fight. He'd rushed forward, busted the guy around—and gotten busted around himself.

In the present, he experienced a pang in his side. His kidney must have taken a couple shots.

"Come on, Vince," he said, and was once again ignored.

Detective Charles Bright stalked down the hall, spotted him and did a double take. "Levi?" His gaze roved the area just over Levi's shoulder before returning. "What are you doing here?"

He watched as Vince finally glanced up. Jaw clenched tight, he gritted, "What do you think I'm doing here, Bright? Working. Maybe you should do the same."

Talking through him. "Real mature," Levi said, flipping him off.

Bright waved Vince off, then led Levi to the office at the end of the hall. He closed and locked the door, and motioned for Levi to sit as he claimed the chair behind a desk scattered with papers.

Levi had always liked Bright. Guy had dark skin and eyes and kept his head shaved to a glossy sheen. He was a laugher, truly cared about the victims he fought to protect and would work himself to death to solve a case.

"I can't believe Vince is so mad he refuses to speak to me."

A soft, sad smile greeted his words. "Had you put him in danger, he'd be over it and you'd be forgiven. But you put yourself in danger, and that's harder to forget. He loved—loves—you like a brother."

"He better still love me." Vince was all the family he had.

"He does. Give him time. He'll come around."

Levi understood the need for time, he did, but his balls were sore and he wasn't exactly in the best of moods, so he decided to forget Vince for now. "Listen, I'm not actually here to beg my partner's forgiveness. My neighbor thinks she witnessed a murder and I promised to help her find out the truth. I can't access any databases, so I need your help."

Bright frowned, instantly intrigued. "Your neighbor?"

"Yeah. I don't know if I told you but I moved into an apartment building downtown, close to Brick Town. She just moved in, too."

"Her name?"

"Harper."

"And the rest?"

"Just a minute." Levi shifted to dig in his back pocket. He withdrew the driver's license he'd slipped from her purse when he'd backed her into the building. After reading the text, a laugh bubbled from him. "Aurora Harper." How freaking adorable. Aurora fit her in a way Harper did not.

Fingers clicking on the keyboard, Bright was silent

for a long while. He would stop and read, then type again, then stop and read again, then type again. With every pause, his frown deepened. The wait for answers nearly drove Levi to pace, punch a wall, *something*.

"Okay, here's what I know," Bright finally said, propping his elbows on his desk. "Your Aurora—"

"Harper. She prefers Harper, and she isn't mine." He paid no attention to the fact that having her referred to as "his" affected his body just as strongly as her nearness had. Heat and tingling and want…so much want.

The denial earned him a swift grin. "All right. Well, Ms. Harper is twenty-seven. Five foot two. One hundred and ten pounds. She's gotten three tickets for speeding, one for parking illegally, and was in a car accident two years ago, but it wasn't her fault and she walked away with only a few bruises."

Silence.

"That's it?" Levi demanded. "That's what had you frowning?"

Bright drew in a deep breath, slowly released it. He settled back in his chair and folded his arms over his middle. "Milana Buineviciute, her roommate, works for After Moonrise and has the ability to see and communicate with the dead. Ms. Buineviciute reported her missing five weeks ago."

Milana Bonnie Wee Cutie. Now there was a name. Five weeks ago. Early October. She'd been in the apartment for a week, so that left four weeks unaccounted for. And the After Moonrise thing wasn't a point in her favor.

A few times, an After Moonrise agent had helped the OKCPD with a case. And for each of those few times, Levi had had to deal with a wealth of irritation.

A.M. came in with their fancy equipment and superior attitudes and simply took over, acting as if the detectives couldn't find their way out of a paper bag. But his favorite? They'd called him a "norm," as if it were a four-letter word.

Wait. It was. Whatever! It had ticked him off.

"Inquiries were made, and it was discovered that Harper was last seen at Carmel Art Gallery, on October fifth around midnight." Bright paused, flicked his tongue over an incisor. "That gallery certainly has been popping up on our radar a lot lately. Seems your boy Cory Topper bought a few paintings there. Only came to light a few days ago, since the sales were made under the table. We didn't think to tell you because you're, uh, off the case."

His stomach clenched. Topper. The serial killer who'd kept pieces of his victims in his freezer. The lunatic who'd tortured women in his basement. The psychopath who'd left a dead body on a billboard. The smug little ant whom Levi was now suspended for brutalizing.

To find out there was a connection between Topper, a dirtbag scum with evil in his veins, and Harper, a delicate, fragile little thing with knees of iron…he didn't like that. At all. But to learn that she'd been missing, to now know beyond any doubt that something *had* happened to her, was even worse.

He brought her painting to the forefront of his mind. The male Harper was bringing to life certainly fit Topper's body type, he realized now. Average height, slim build, deceptively gentle-looking hands.

"Where was Harper found?" he rasped. "When? And where had she been?"

"Oh, hmm." Bright glanced at the screen. "She

wasn't found. At least, nothing has been entered into the system."

"I don't understand. What do you mean?"

"The case is still open."

Irritation laced with anger flooded him, and he popped his jaw. Why hadn't Lana reported her as found? Why hadn't Harper come forward? Fear that Topper would find her again? But then, that would mean she remembered him, if he was truly the one responsible, and it was clear that she didn't.

Levi replayed his new memory of the night he'd come face-to-face with Topper. Topper had been standing beside…what? All he could picture were rivers of blood. Lots and lots of blood, flowing this way and that way and all around. Had there been any secret rooms? Someplace Harper could have been stashed, bound and helpless, forced to watch? Someplace she could have accidently stumbled upon and hidden?

A cage flashed through his mind.

A cage?

"Was there a cage in Topper's home?" he asked. "Actually, don't tell me. Just give me the crime scene photos." He'd never seen them.

"You know I can't do that," Bright said sternly.

"All I want is a glance at them." He could compare them with Harper's painting.

A sigh met his words. "I've always been a sucker. I'll see what I can do."

"Thanks. So how's our man Topper doing?"

Bright rolled his shoulders, easing tension. "He recovered from the injuries you gave him and is now locked up without bail, awaiting trial. We managed to find evidence of his crimes *after* his arrest."

Meaning, everything they'd found the day they'd arrested him had been thrown out because of Levi and they'd needed something new. And thanks be to God, they'd gotten it. Levi had read what had been fed to the media and knew there was more, but he wasn't going to ask. Yet.

Don't make everything a battle, son, his dad told him once. He didn't remember this on his own. He'd seen a home video of the two of them together. *You do, and you'll never win 'em all.*

"You got anything else on Harper?" he asked.

"A bit." Bright gave the computer screen another read. "The night of her disappearance, the art showing had wound down and only the owner remained in the building when she left, but he claims he was counting receipts in the back room and heard nothing unusual."

"Any connection between Topper and the owner?"

"Not that we've found."

"Are there *any* suspects in Harper's case? An ex-boyfriend with an ax to grind? A neighbor with a record? A stepdad with a grudge?"

"Oh…no, but I'll be sure and…close things now, and I suppose there's no real reason to press charges for withholding information."

Why the hesitation?

Bright cleared his throat and said, "Why don't you bring your Harper in? To me, only to me," he added in a rush, "and *I'll* question her about what happened."

"What do you know?" Levi demanded.

"What do you mean?"

"You're acting weird, hesitating to say certain things."

The detective pinched the bridge of his nose. "I'm

telling you everything I can, Levi. Given that you're on a leave of absence, in fact, I'm telling you more than I should, and could even lose my own job over this." Bright's scolding tone lacked anger but was filled with understanding. "Now, what about bringing her in? I'll make sure she's protected while she's here."

No one was better at interrogation than Bright, and he'd be as gentle as possible, but... "Questioning her right now won't do any good. She doesn't remember. Whatever happened—" and it had to be bad for her to have repressed it as deeply as she had "—she's painting the image of a murdered woman."

Another frown tugged at the corners of Bright's mouth. "A woman? Describe the woman you're talking about. Could she—" a pause, a shifting in his seat "—be Harper?"

"No. You know I can't see the dead." His stomach clenched as he once again brought the painting front and center and saw the pale skin of the woman, the delicacy of her bone structure. "There are similarities, granted, but no. And I can't tell you much more because Harper hasn't yet painted the face."

Bright worried two fingers over his stubbled chin. "Bottom line, there's a chance she saw the guy torture someone else."

"Yeah."

There was a whoosh of air as Bright straightened in his seat. "I want to see the painting. If we are, in fact, dealing with Topper, I want every piece of evidence I can gather. Yeah, he's going away for life, will probably be put to death, but maybe this is the way we'll find the bodies of his other victims."

If there was anything left of them. Levi had no idea

why Topper had deviated from his usual M.O. and bound that woman—with all her parts—to that billboard. He had no idea why he'd kept mementos of some but not others. But really, did Levi *want* to know the twisted reasons of a psycho? "I'll take a picture and email it to you."

"Good, for starters."

"And I'll want a copy of the missing-person's report."

"Fair is fair, but I'm only giving you a glimpse of it." A few clicks and the papers began printing. "You can't take it with you. And don't dare ask if I'll do the same with the crime scene photos. That's a bigger deal, and you know it."

Disappointment struck him, but he said, "All right. Understood."

Bright held out the paper, and Levi scanned the contents. He didn't try to sort things out; he simply memorized every detail for later. When he finished, he stood. "Thanks for everything. I appreciate it."

"Anytime. And keep me updated on what you learn about Harper, okay? I'll work a few angles from this end."

Meaning, legitimate ends. He nodded and trudged to his partner's office, only to find that Vince had left. Whatever. They'd talk eventually. Next time, he wouldn't let Vince ignore him.

Now to dig through the report, and question Lana. That guilt he'd glimpsed at the gallery…she knew something more. Had she helped the abductor? But why report Harper missing? To hide her own actions? And yet, he doubted that was her motive. Genuine affection existed between the pair. Although, a lot of people could be bought, whether they loved someone or not.

Great. He was talking himself into believing in Lana's culpability, then talking himself out of it. Well, he wasn't going to wait until Lana cracked. Tonight, he was going to crack her open…himself…and…darkness… so much darkness…closing in….

No, he nearly roared. Ice crystallized in his veins, while sweat beaded over his skin. Breath boiled in his lungs.

Right there in the bull pen of the OKCPD, a shroud of black fell over his mind, slowly at first, stealing his thoughts one by one. He tensed, hating this feeling, knowing what happened…next—how he would lose… hours…perhaps days—but what he didn't know was *why* this kept happening or what—

Black…

Nothingness…

Empty…

5

Not again, Harper thought, panic rising as she peered down at her paint-splattered hands. She clutched a paintbrush, the tip drip...drip...dripping crimson onto her bare feet. Sickness bloomed in the pit of her stomach like a poisonous flower, its pollen drifting through the rest of her, sticking and growing until her blood was ice and her skin fire, her breath jagged and burning as it rasped against her lungs.

Before she looked up and faced the reality of what she had created, she spun and checked her surroundings. She stood inside her apartment's studio. Her shoulders sagged with relief. Okay. She could deal with anything else. Right?

Her gaze took in other details. The clock on her wall flashed 12:01—no, 12:02. The dark of the night seeped through the five-inch crack in the red, orange and yellow curtains Lana had made, and the scent of rain saturated the air, a roll of thunder booming.

Once upon a time, she had loved storms. Had loved the smells and the drop in temperature, the feel of raindrops against her skin. But lately they reminded her too much of Lana's tears, and even the tears *she* sometimes wanted to shed. Now that love was dead. *As dead as the girl you're painting.*

Ugh. The sickness intensified. So…she must have blacked out. Last thing she remembered was sitting on the couch, talking to Lana, waiting for Levi to come over, praying he'd learned something, *fearing* he'd learned something. Then…nothing.

Lightning suddenly struck, blazing the sky with gold and—a scream lodged in her throat, her heart pounding uncontrollably. A girl stood on the balcony outside her window, staring in at her with violet eyes. Other details registered. A fall of black hair, the wistful features of a young woman ready to fall in love, happy with her life yet somehow miserable at the same time.

How long had she stood there, watching? Had she noticed the scene unfolding on the canvas? As the questions filled Harper's mind, anger filled her chest. The peeping had to stop. Now.

Harper dropped her brush, heard the plop of it against the plastic covering she kept over the floor and stomped to the window.

By the time she had the pane lifted, the girl was gone.

Cool, moist air wafted inside the room, carrying the scents of floral spices and freshly cut grass; both failed to calm her, only ratcheted her anger higher. Harper pressed her tongue against the roof of her mouth as she snapped the pane back in place and threw the lock. She closed the curtains, being sure to hook the edges and prevent even the smallest fissure from forming, then she stood there for several minutes, knowing she was stalling, knowing she needed to turn, to face the truth one more time. Maybe this time would be the last. Maybe this time she had finished the painting, and all the answers would slide into place.

Maybe.

But hopefully not.

As much as she wanted to know, she *didn't* want to know.

"I can do this," she muttered. Slowly, so slowly, she turned on her heel. Deep breath in, deep breath out, she lifted her gaze.

And there it was, her painting. The overhead light seemed to spotlight the entire canvas, and…oh, no, no, no! She hadn't finished it, hadn't given the man a face, but she *had* finished the woman.

Lana was the woman on that slab, a bloody blade poised over her heart.

Lana. *Her* Lana.

No, no. *No!* That wasn't possible. Couldn't be possible. Lana would have told her if she'd been in that nightmare situation and somehow managed to escape. Lana was alive, and like Harper, Lana had never come home with injuries.

How would you know? You black out, lose track of time. What if her injuries healed during one of those blackouts, huh? No, no, no, she thought again. Panic… rising…

Maybe she was mistaken. Maybe the woman only looked like Lana. But black hair bleached and colored red cascaded over slender shoulders—and how many women had hair like that? Long black lashes cast shadows over hollowed cheeks. A perfectly sloped nose, lips red and raw, chewed from worry.

Though Harper had painted over all the cuts and

bruises, though the woman's skin was smooth and creamy, blood spilled from her neck, her wrists, her stomach, her legs, her feet. Blood splattered the walls, pooled on the floor.

Blood.

Lana's blood.

Lana's. Blood.

If this truly were Lana—no, no, no, it couldn't be… just couldn't—how could Harper have known what happened to her? Lana hadn't told her. Or…what if she *had* told her, but Harper had repressed the memory, as she'd first feared?

Harper raced to the bathroom and dry heaved, thoughts batting through her mind one after the other. Every time Lana viewed the painting, she paled and clutched her stomach. The first time, she had actually vomited. Could she have repressed the memories, too, after confessing? Could something inside her recognize the pain she had endured?

With shaky hands, Harper brushed her teeth, splashed water on her face. "You have to confront her," she told her reflection. "Have to learn the truth. For both of you."

Determined, she stalked down the hallway. She'd forgotten to turn off the hall lights again—either that, or she'd turned them on during her blackout.

She stood in front of Lana's bedroom door. Her hand shook with more intensity as she wrapped her fingers around the knob and twisted. As the hall light spilled across the bed and the woman lying in the center, enveloped by a familiar rainbow-colored comforter, her red hair tangled over her pillow, her eyes closed in the sweet retreat of slumber, relief filled Harper to the point of bursting.

Whatever happened, she survived.

Did she really want to awaken Lana to a nightmare?

Harper gulped, the heavy question weighing her down. No. No, she didn't. The truth could wait until morning.

As quietly as she was able, she closed the door, checked every other door and window in the apartment. Levi had said he would get in touch with her yesterday evening, but he hadn't and now she was done waiting for him. She'd waited all day, in fact, and hadn't even received a hastily scribbled "Can't make it" note under her door. Well, he would now have to deal with the consequences of breaking his word.

She stomped out of the apartment, locked up after herself, double-checked the lock, triple-checked the lock, then padded to Levi's and—dang it! She'd forgotten to pull on a pair of sneaks. Someone had spilled a soda, so the carpet was cold and wet. Shivers were soon raking the length of her spine, intensifying when a clap of thunder boomed.

A hard rap at his door, shifting from one increasingly irritated and sticky foot to the other while glancing around to make sure no one tried to sneak up on her. When she spotted the freaky girl with the violet eyes gliding toward her, *dry* black hair floating back in a breeze Harper couldn't feel, her own bare feet seeming to lift off the ground, panic threatened to engulf her. How had the girl gone from outside to in so quickly, without getting wet?

"Such a naughty girl." In a voice as eerie as the rest

of her, the teenager added, "You should have been nicer to him. He loved you, loved you so much."

Could she be… Was she a spirit, maybe? Harper had never possessed the ability to see into that other realm, but this was just too weird to be natural.

And, to be honest, she wanted no part of it. "Levi." Another rap, this one harder, yet still Levi failed to respond. "Levi, it's Harper! Open up."

The girl was coming closer and closer…. Harper tried the knob. It twisted easily. She darted into the apartment, quickly barricading herself inside. One minute passed, two, but the girl never misted through the door as Harper had been half convinced she would, never so much as knocked.

Still trembling, she peeked through the peephole but found the hallway empty. As the panic left her, common sense piped up. Lana could see the dead. Lana had always been able to see the dead. She knew the difference between living and un-living at a single glance, and she would always tell Harper when she spotted a spirit. Not once since they'd moved into this building had she pointed one out.

Tomorrow, Harper was doing a little research of her own, and maybe she would try to speak to an expert on those who developed a latent ability to see into the spirit realm—and find out if it were possible for someone to *lose* the ability. She wouldn't speak with Lana's coworkers, though. If Lana was having trouble, she didn't want anyone else to know it. But then, who did that leave?

"Levi, it's Harper," she called. "Are you here?"

Silence.

No, not silence. Another crack of thunder boomed,

practically splitting the air in half. She yelped, her heart hammering against her ribs.

"Levi!"

Again, silence.

Why would he leave his place unlocked? That wasn't very coplike. And why wasn't he here? He'd said he was girlfriend free. Unless…maybe, while looking into Harper's story, he'd met a woman and stayed the night at her place.

Why that thought irritated her so much, she wasn't sure. She liked the look of him, yeah, but her life was a mess and she was pretty sure she'd already decided not to pursue anything with him, so— *Oh, why are you trying to fight it? You like more than the look of him. You like his strength and his intensity and that take-charge attitude of his. He makes you feel safe—when he's not sneaking up on you—and that's something you don't get from anyone else. You'll never know if something more could grow between you unless you try.*

Well, well. An intelligent line of thought, bypassing her qualms. That's how badly she wanted him, she supposed.

And he wanted her, too, which was an unusual occurrence, really. Most guys went for Lana and never changed their minds. But would Levi be okay with dating Harper, considering the trouble she was bringing to his door?

"Levi," she called again. "This is your last chance to announce your presence before I start nosing around your place. If you shoot me after I've given you this warning, I'll be very upset."

Again, silence.

"All right, then." No way was she going back into

that hall. Sighing, she flipped the light switch, chasing away the darkness and illuminating his living room.

She walked forward, intending to wash her feet in his bathroom—only to stop short.

He was here.

He was sitting on his couch.

And he was staring at the wall with a blank expression on his face.

Concerned, Harper approached him. "Levi?" She bent down and waved a hand in front of his face, but he gave no reaction.

He wore the same clothes he'd changed into the first time she'd been here. Black T-shirt, black slacks. A quick check of his pulse proved his heartbeat was strong and steady, but his skin was chilled. Alarmingly chilled. His pupils were unresponsive to the light, his ears somehow unaware of the now-constant roll of thunder.

Harper reached out, intending to pat his cheek to gauge his responsiveness to a more direct touch. He reacted with reflexes as swift as the lightning outside, grabbing her by the wrist and stilling her.

He blinked. A moment later, his gaze locked with hers. Awareness hit her with the force of a jackhammer. He smoldered with rumpled sex appeal.

"Harper?" Her name was little more than a growl.

"Yes."

"What are you doing here?"

"I needed to talk—"

"Never mind. Talk later." He jerked, and she landed in his lap.

6

ONE MOMENT LEVI was trapped in a world of black and helplessness, and the next Harper was spotlighted in front of him, all that he saw, all that he wanted to see. Like an angel, her pale hair had seemed to form a halo around her, her concerned gaze so gentle it caressed him. She had been his only anchor to the world, a tether that would not allow him to slip away.

He'd remembered going to the station, speaking to Bright. Remembered finding out Harper had been reported missing, and her roommate had failed to tell the police she'd returned home. He'd had every intention of interrogating Lana, but then the darkness had come for him, right there in the station. And now he was… somewhere else, and Harper was with him….

"Levi?" she said.

Had he called her and asked her to come over? Dragged her here? He *hated* not knowing.

Frowning, he glanced around. He was inside his apartment, the lights switched on, bright enough to make his eyes water, though he couldn't remember how he'd gotten here. He was sitting on his couch, and Harper was in his lap.

He liked that she was in his lap.

Was she truly here, though? Was she real? Was she healthy, whole, *alive?* Unharmed by a murderer? He had to know…and he had to taste her, he thought, the need consuming him in an instant. She would keep the darkness at bay. She would keep him in the here and now. And he would protect her, he vowed.

He pressed his lips into hers.

The moment of contact, she gasped, and the moment her mouth opened, he took full advantage, kissing her as if she possessed everything necessary for his survival.

Maybe she did.

No one would hurt this woman. Not ever again. He wouldn't allow it.

At first she was stiff, but as his tongue rolled against hers, she melted against him, her hands making their way into his hair. Nails dug into his scalp. Her legs straddled him, those lethal knees pushing into the back of the couch.

How sweet she tasted, like an aged wine, heady and something to savor. He forced himself to gentle, sipping from her for as long as his control would allow, then he drank deeply, already addicted and needing more. He wasn't sure he'd ever get enough, but, oh, he would try. He would take everything she had to give, and still demand more.

He didn't like the circumstances that had brought them together, but he was glad they *had* been brought together, that something good could come of something so ugly.

"Harper."

"Yes?"

He meant to say something, but once again he got caught up in kissing her and couldn't remember what it was. Him, a man who could memorize any number at any time, now so forgetful. But what better thing to concentrate on? Her moans of approval blended with the rough rasp of his breaths; they strained against each other, his need for her deepening, spiraling, threatening to burst from his skin.

And she was with him all the way—until his hands began to roam down her back, circle around her hips and slip up…up…toward her breasts. She gave another gasp, this one laced with fear. She jerked away from him, stumbling into his coffee table, tripping to the side, falling, then crab-walking away from him until her back hit the far wall.

Fear…that fear permeated the cloud of desire in his mind. "Harper," he said in a voice still affected by smoky desire. "What's wrong?"

"I'm not ready," she said with a tremble in her voice. "I can't. I can't, and you can't make me. Please don't make me."

I'm not ready. The words echoed through his mind, and he froze. *I can't, and you can't make me. Please don't make me.* Had someone once forced her? His hands curled into fists. No. He didn't want to believe it, was sick at the thought. This had to be about the painting. A lone female, bound to a cold slab of metal, naked, tools of torture hanging on the walls.

"Harper," he said. She was breathing too heavily, would probably pass out if she failed to calm.

He'd once looked at her and thought her somehow broken. Now he knew beyond a doubt. She was—but she was so much more. She had stalked into the apartment of a man she'd never before met and asked for help. She'd had the strength to patch herself up, to hunt for answers.

"Harper," he repeated as he stood.

A little mewl left her.

One step, two, he approached her, his steps unhurried, as nonthreatening as possible. He held his hands in front of his body, palms out. "I'm not going to make you do anything, okay?"

Another mewl.

"You're here with me, with Levi, and you're safe." Before, he'd told himself he would leave her alone if she was broken in any way, that he was too weighed down with his own concerns to help someone else recover. Now he knew there was no way he could stay out of her life. Not just because he wanted more of her, more of everything she had to offer, but because he hated seeing her like this. He wanted his smiling, teasing Harper back.

When he reached her, he crouched down, careful not to touch her. "Harper, sweetheart. Can you hear me?"

A tear rolled down her cheek.

A sharp pang in his chest had him biting his tongue to stop a curse from forming. Slowly, so slowly, he extended his hand to brush the hair from her brow. He wasn't sure what he expected, but what he got wasn't it. She erupted into a blaze of motion and fury.

"No!" Her fist struck him in the eye.

A surprising amount of pain exploded through his head, considering her tiny size, but still he remained immobile. He'd been hit enough times in his life that being smacked with a semi probably wouldn't have fazed him.

But she wasn't done, and next did her best to rain a world of hurt on him. He let her. By the fifth punch, his adrenaline was so high he hardly felt a thing, anyway. It was only when she began to kick and to twist, trying to claw her way out through the wall, that he reached out to stop her.

He caught himself just before contact. If he touched her too soon, her terror and desperation would only be driven higher and he'd have a whole new set of injuries to contend with. He would have to wait this out. Shouldn't be too much longer now. Her motions were slowing…slowing….

Finally, the fight left her entirely. She collapsed on the floor, sobbing, breaking his heart into so many pieces he wasn't sure he'd ever be able to glue them back together.

He said gently, "Harper, sweetheart?"

"Levi?" she asked with a sniffle.

Thank God! Springing into motion, he scooped her up and cradled her against his chest. She allowed this, her head burrowing into the hollow of his neck. He could feel the wetness of her tears, and wanted to howl.

He carried her to the couch and eased himself down, still holding her close. Several minutes ticked by in silence. He'd dealt with victims of abuse before, but never this up close and personal. So, because he wasn't exactly sure of what to do, he went with his instincts and massaged the back of her neck, played with the ends of her hair, traced his fingers along the ridges of her spine.

"Tell me what happened," he said.

She drew in a deep, shuddering breath, released it. "I don't know. One minute I was kissing you, and the next I was on the floor, crying. That happens sometimes. Not that I've kissed a lot of guys," she babbled. "Even the most casual of touches can set me off. Lana and I don't even high-five anymore."

He frowned. "So…you have blackouts?"

A heavy pause. Then a whispered, "Yes."

That little ball of information did more than land in his yard. It shattered his window. She had blackouts, just like him. A strange coincidence. Far too strange. His Spidey senses were suddenly tingling.

"Did I do something to you?" she asked, hesitant. "Say something I shouldn't have?"

"We kissed, only kissed, and you jumped to the floor. That's all, I promise. I never even made it to second base," he said with as teasing a tone as he could muster. *But I will. I will help you, and we will do more, all.* "And just so you know, I have blackouts, too."

She jerked upright, twisting to fully meet his gaze. "What! Really? You're not just saying that to— Oh, my goodness! What happened to your face?" she ended, horrified.

He could only imagine what he looked like. The beginning of a black eye, surely, as well as a swollen cheek and busted lip. A lip that ached as it twitched at the corners. How could she amuse him in the worst of situations?

"What's wrong with it?" He placed his hands on the couch, off her body. Just in case. He didn't want a repeat of the Episode; he just wanted her, but he was willing to wait.

"Everything! You look hideous!"

Won't grin. But man, he liked her honesty. "You should see yourself."

Her eyes were red, swollen, and her skin spotted with

pink. Strands of pale hair were stuck to her cheeks, saturated from her tears. "What's wrong with me?"

"Nothing." She was the most exquisite creature he'd ever beheld.

The thought made him cringe. He so was not a poet.

"You're *that* disgusted by me?" she squeaked.

He rolled his eyes. "You're hot. I'm hooked. And if what just happened didn't scare me away, nothing will."

Her features softened. "So what *did* just happen to you?"

"I got into a fight," he said, unwilling to say more if she couldn't remember.

"When? With who?"

He loved that, even though her hands were probably throbbing, she refused to consider herself.

"I promise you," she continued, "I'll *ruin* him. Me and Lana, we have a system."

He donned his best "I'm a cop and you're in trouble" expression. "What system?"

"Oh, uh. Hmm. Never mind about that."

As if he'd really arrest her for defending him. A body-cavity search, maybe. A stint with the cuffs, definitely. But anything behind bars? Probably not. "So how long have you been having those blackouts?"

"I don't want to talk about it," she muttered.

"Do it, anyway."

"No."

Stubborn. "Here's how this is gonna work. You're gonna show me yours, and I'm gonna show you mine."

A calculating gleam entered her eyes. "I do want to see yours, so…okay. Yes." She nodded. "They started just before I moved here."

His frown returned. "Same for me."

"So you really do have blackouts?"

"I do."

A thousand different emotions played over her features. "I can't believe… You're the first person… Levi, do you know what this means?" she asked, adjusting herself on his lap, once again straddling him.

"No." Only the memory of what had happened the last time they'd been in this position kept his hands at his sides.

"I'm not alone! Do you know how thrilling that is? I mean, no, not thrilling, that would be a terrible thing to feel." Her nose scrunched as she struggled to experience what she deemed appropriate. "I'm sorry you've had to deal with something like that. It's terrible. *But I'm not alone!*"

"Me, either." And he was as thrilled as she was, he realized. For the first time since his parents' death, there was someone who understood him.

"What do you think this means?"

"I don't know. Does Lana have them, too?"

"No. I asked."

But had the secret-keeping Miss Bonnie Wee Cutie told the truth? He *had* to interrogate that woman.

"That's what was wrong with you when I first got here, I bet," she suddenly exclaimed. "You were in the middle of a blackout, weren't you?"

"Yeah."

"Do you know what time or where you were when it began?"

"It hit a short while after I left you. I had just talked to my friend at the station, was walking to the elevator to leave, and that's the last thing I remember."

She toyed with his shirt, twisting the material. "I

can fill in a bit of the missing time. I came over around midnight to speak with you, but you didn't answer. The door was unlocked, by the way. When I came in, you were sitting on your couch, staring into the darkness, unaware of anything around you."

Relief cascaded through him. He'd always wondered—fine, feared—what he'd done while lost to the darkness, and sitting on his couch hadn't made the list. "What did you want to speak with me about?"

Her hand flattened over his heart, her nails almost cutting past his shirt. "Well…the blackout here wasn't the only one I experienced today. One second I was waiting for you, the next I was in front of my painting. I'd filled in a few more details."

He was gripping her by the waist, holding on to her as if she would slip away at any moment, before he even realized he'd moved. "Tell me."

"I… The girl I'm painting…it's Lana."

Lana? Impossible. But…the secretiveness, the trepidation, the odd behavior, reporting her friend missing but never reporting her found…yeah, the pieces could fit. "Where's the painting now?"

"My apartment."

He would study it—in a bit. "So, you think she was abducted, tortured and somehow escaped," he said, a statement, not a question.

"Yes. I mean, I know I told you the girl in the painting was dead, but I had to be mistaken about that."

"And?"

"And I think I went looking for her…saw her trapped, hurt."

Poor darling. "Have you recalled anything from the scene itself?"

"No." The rapid puffs of her breath were the only sound in the room. "I'm stumbling on one fact, though. Like me, Lana wasn't ever found with injuries."

There was that, wasn't there. "Maybe she healed during one of your blackouts."

Her shoulders drooped. "Maybe."

"There's one way to find out what happened to her," he said.

She sighed. "I know. I don't like it, but I know."

7

THOUGH HARPER KNEW Levi expected to return to her apartment that very second, shake Lana awake and treat her to an intense interrogation, and though Harper needed to hug her friend and cry with her and promise to make everything better, her emotions were still raw, the fear of sinking into another black hole a living entity inside her. She wanted to stay here, inside Levi's apartment, safe from the sorrow that awaited her for just a little longer.

He just smelled so good, heat radiating off him in continuous waves, wrapping around her. One of his hands caressed her back, and the other stroked the side of her leg. Both soothed her, despite the fact that she usually hated being touched, and all too soon her eyelids grew heavy. She yawned.

"Can we postpone?" she asked. "Just until morning. Please."

"Begging doesn't work with me. This needs to be done, Harper."

"I know, but I'm not at my best and I want to be at my best when we do this. *Pleeease.*"

A pause. A sigh. "Begging didn't used to work," he grumbled, and he stayed put.

A soft chuckle escaped her. "Don't beat yourself up. I'm irresistible."

He said something to her, but he sounded far away. She tried to respond, she really did, but...

...floated away...into another darkness, though this one offered comfort rather than terror. Maybe because she could still smell the musk of Levi's scent, could still feel the warm pulse of him, not just at her side but all over.

When the weight finally lifted from her eyelids, she blinked awake. A frown formed as she cataloged her surroundings. She was inside a strange apartment, stretched out on an unfamiliar couch. The overhead light was on, sunlight streaming through a dark curtain.

Morning had arrived, she realized. The last thing she remembered was talking to Levi, and agreeing to speak with Lana.

She sat up—or rather, tried to. Strong arms were banded around her, holding her in an intractable grip. Panic sparked to life while she attempted to orient herself. Warm breath trekked over her neck. A man's breath. A man who was aroused.

Had she blacked out, left Levi and gone home with a stranger? Bile burned a path up her throat as she struggled against that vise grip.

A growl rumbled from the man. "I've got you," a raspy voice said. "Be still."

A raspy voice she recognized.

Levi. Frowning, she glanced down, spied the bronze of his skin and the light dusting of dark hair. Drank in the strength of his fingers, and the thin scars that criss-crossed his wrists.

As quickly as it had formed, the panic left. Relief danced through her. But…this made no sense. They weren't inside his apartment. The furnishings were different. Before, there'd been no artwork on the walls. Now portraits of animals playing poker…and golf… and baseball filled the walls. Walls that had gone from white to pale blue in a single night.

"Levi," she said.

"Harper," he replied, his tone letting her know her name was a curse.

"You awake?"

"I'm talking, aren't I?"

Growling, more like. "Not a morning person, huh?"

"Not a morning, afternoon or evening person. You'll just have to deal with it because, this time, you're to blame. You stood up three times, and once even made it to the hallway outside."

Sleepwalking. The number-one reason she'd become a fan of insomnia. "I don't remember any of that," she admitted.

His arms tightened around her for several seconds before he sat up, dragging her with him. Sadly, he severed contact and she found herself mourning the loss of his strength and his heat. How unlike her. But then, with his confession about his own blackouts, his determination to help her, Levi had busted through her instinctive safeguards, making her as comfortable with him as she was with herself.

"So where are we?" she asked, smoothing her hair from her cheeks.

"Where else? My apartment."

She blinked over at him, confused. "And you decided to do a little redecorating while I was sleeping?"

"What are you talking about?" Frowning, he stood and padded to the kitchen, where he stumbled around as he gathered supplies for coffee. His shirt and pants were wrinkled. Sometime during the night he'd removed his shoes and socks and now his feet were bare. "You fell asleep, I helped you get comfortable, got comfortable myself and was out soon afterward."

"But your walls." She waved her hand over the portraits.

He glanced over his shoulder to examine them. "Yeah. What about them?"

She looked at his face, intending to gauge his reaction to her next words, but she got caught on another thought trail. The swelling had gone down in his eye and cheek, and his skin was only slightly discolored. Last night, he'd been black-and-blue. The split in his lip had already scabbed over.

"You heal quickly," she announced.

"Harper," he said on a sigh. "The walls."

Right. The walls. "Yesterday they were naked."

He froze, his hand raised to pour in the grounds. Slowly he set everything down and turned toward her. "You're sure?"

"Yes. I always study a person's walls."

His brows knitted. Suddenly he looked as confused as she felt. "Why?"

"Art. Why else? You can learn so much about a person that way."

He shook his head, as if dislodging a pesky thought. "And mine were…naked, you said."

"Yes. And a different color!"

His gaze swept over each of the portraits a second time, lingering, taking in every detail. "I recognize every piece, recognize the color. That's how they've looked since I moved in."

Her stomach bottomed out, the implications almost too much to take in. "One of us is mistaken."

"Or both of us are right and something weird is going on." He rubbed the back of his neck. "Forget the coffee. Let's shower, and go chat with Lana."

"Shower...together?"

"Well, not now," he grumbled. "You can use the guest bathroom if you want."

"I do. Thank you." Though she was tempted...

As he stalked out of the kitchen and into his bedroom, Harper lumbered to her feet.

She found the guest bathroom easily enough, only to discover a still-packaged toothbrush, a fresh tube of toothpaste and every feminine product known to man. Or woman.

As hard and gruff a guy as Levi was, he sure was prepared for female guests—something Harper wasn't sure she appreciated. Was he a player?

It wasn't like Harper had any type of claim on him, especially considering she'd just denied him, but still. He'd held her all night long. Before that, he'd kissed her. So...*she had a claim on him.*

Yeah, she'd first thought to keep things purely professional between them. But guess what? She'd just changed her mind. For sure this time. If he'd wanted to enjoy his bachelorhood, he should not have invited her to happy shower time. He should have kept his lips and hands to himself. He should have refused to snuggle her and keep her safe.

When she stepped out of the stall, dripping wet and wishing she'd looked for a towel before making use of the water, she found a small pile of clothes resting beside the sink. A T-shirt and a pair of sweatpants—neither of which belonged to her.

That Levi, she thought, unsure whether she wanted to grin or slap him. She'd locked the door, but he'd come in, anyway. At least the clothes belonged to him rather than another woman.

By the time she finished rolling the soft material at her wrists, waist and ankles, he was in the living room, waiting for her. He eyed her up and down, nodded his approval despite the fact that her hair was wet and the bulk of the clothing made her look as if she'd gained twenty pounds since they'd last seen each other.

While her heart drummed erratically, she gave him the same perusal. He wore another black shirt and pair of black slacks, but he somehow looked more delicious than ever. So unfair.

As he ushered her into the hallway, she said, "So those tampons in your guest bathroom…"

"They aren't mine, that's for sure," he said, locking his door.

"I know that. Moron! So whose are they?"

"You're not gonna like the answer."

"Tell me, anyway."

"They belonged to my ex, and I failed to throw them out." He escorted Harper down the hall and up the stairs to her apartment.

"Why would that make me angry?"

"You might think I kept them because I still had feelings for her. I don't. You might think I meant to let your roommate use them, since I'd planned to date her.

You might think I'm obsessive about keeping what's mine…and you'd be right, and the knowledge might scare you away."

She locked on to one thought. He'd first wanted Lana. "Why did you kiss me if you wanted to date my roommate?" she gritted out. Oh, he'd mentioned his desire to hook up with Lana before, but they'd just met and she'd just irritated him and that could have been a taunt. This wasn't.

"See?"

"Answer me."

"I didn't say I *still* wanted to date her."

"But she was your first choice."

"A choice made in a moment of insanity."

"So?"

"So, you're going to throw it in my face the whole time we're together, aren't you?"

The whole time we're together. That was relationship talk, and it was the only thing that mollified her. "Yeah," she said. "I am."

"I probably shouldn't admit this, either, but that's kinda hot."

And he was hooked on her, she remembered him saying. Well, okay, then. She wouldn't punish him *too* badly.

"Lana," she called when she was inside their place, hoping to give her friend time to wake up, dress or whatever she needed. "Lana!"

Silence.

"Wait here," she said, and went to Lana's bedroom. Inside, she flipped on the light. The bed was empty, the covers askew. The closet was empty, as well, no clothes remaining.

As she flattened her hands over her stomach to ward off an oncoming ache, she felt rather than saw Levi come up behind her.

"What's wrong?" he asked.

"She's gone." And she'd left in a hurry. Some of her things were on the floor—a shoe, a pair of panties and a brush—as if they had fallen out of a hastily thrown-together bag.

Levi brushed past her and searched every inch of the room. She stood there, numb, as she watched. Why had Lana left her? And she *had* left her.

"What are you doing?" she asked when Levi crouched on the floor and traced his fingertips over the carpet fibers.

"Checking for foul play." He went through the entire space from top to bottom before ushering her to the dresser and motioning to a wrinkled piece of paper. "Read it, but don't touch it, okay? I want it dusted for fingerprints. And tell me if it's her writing and if she sounds normal."

Harper's eyes watered as she glanced down. She had to wipe them three times before she could make out the words.

Please do not be mad, Harper. Your painting…I do not know why you paint me. I was not there, I swear to you. Nothing was done to me, and I witness nothing done to anyone else. I do not know what it means, but this has scared me. I will take off for a while. I must figure some things out. Don't worry about me, okay? I will be fine. And so will you. Your detective will take care of you now. I am sorry I couldn't. I love you more than anything on this earth and nothing will ever change that.

    P.S. I know I told you the OKC branch of A.M. did not wish to take your case, but that was a lie. I do not want them involved in this, no matter what. Promise me. Instead, I want you to go to Tulsa and visit the A.M. offices there. I called, and they expect you. They will take you seriously. Go to them, please, you and your detective both. What if you've seen into future?

Harper could see the tearstains on the paper, knew Lana had cried while she'd written this. "She definitely wrote this, and not under duress, but I don't understand it," she whispered.

What if Lana was right and she had seen into the future? What if Lana would one day suffer atrocities at some madman's hands? What if—

"I can see where your thoughts derailed, and you need to get back on the right track. *What if* can be two of the cruelest words ever created if you let them."

True. They lit a fire under fear while proving nothing, stopping nothing. And they could be wrong, her worry pointless. "If the painting is a glimpse of the future, why am I missing so much of my life in the here and now? Why am I having blackouts, but Lana's not?"

"Maybe she is. Maybe she lied. Why would she not want you to visit After Moonrise here in Oklahoma City?"

Lied…lied… Lana could have lied to her. Always they'd shared everything. Money, clothes, cars, food, sorrows and pains, joys and rewards. Brutal Honesty had been their motto.

Do I look fat in these jeans?

As a rhino.

What if my date tries to kiss me?

He won't. Not with that garlic breath.

"Maybe she didn't want her coworkers involved in my potential crazy," Harper said. Maybe. So many maybes.

Levi's hands settled on her shoulders. "I'll ask one of my friends to track her, watch her, guard her. She'll be kept safe, I promise you."

He hadn't said "and question her" but she heard the words in his tone. No matter how much Harper hated the way things were playing out, an interrogation needed to happen now more than ever. "Thank you. She's my best friend. I love her no matter what, same way she loves me, and I want her safe."

"She will be."

Emotion clogged Harper's throat, and her chin trembled.

"What are your plans today?" he asked.

"I want to paint the killer's face." She *had* to paint it. No longer would she resist.

Even thinking about him caused a flicker of rage to erupt inside her. If he had—or would—hurt the girl in the painting, then he had hurt other women, and would doubtless hurt many more. He had to be stopped.

"Okay. All right. I'll give you a few hours, but then we're taking Lana's advice and heading to Tulsa. We'll take your painting, whatever shape it's in, and let them have a look, tell them what's been going on. I want to hear what they have to say."

"O-okay." Maybe they could explain the blackouts, too. Because…no matter how wonderful it was to know she wasn't alone in her suffering, it was bizarre that both she and Levi were experiencing them, that they'd started at the same time. "You don't have to work?"

Guilt filled his eyes, quickly masked. "Not today. Why don't you get started? I'll make that call about Lana, gather a few things from my apartment and come back. I don't want you alone today."

"Okay," she repeated, peering down at the note. Why had Lana taken off without some kind of a confrontation? Running wasn't like her. In fact, Lana had never backed down from a challenge, any challenge. And where had she gone? Like Harper, she was without any family. They only had each other. Now she was out there, alone, scared.

Strong hands cupped her face. "Harper. Look at me."

A tear trekked down her cheek as she obeyed.

"Everything's going to be all right," he said gently. He wiped the tear away with the pad of his thumb.

"I don't like the uncertainty. I don't like that every time I get a question answered, a thousand more pop up. And I *hate* being afraid."

He kissed the tip of her nose. "I won't let anything happen to you, either. You have my word." He didn't wait for her reply, didn't ask permission, but lowered his head the rest of the way and claimed her mouth.

Without any hesitation, she wound her arms around him, holding on tight, allowing him to consume her bit by bit. Glad for him, glad for this, shocked by her need to touch and be touched, but more so by her lack of panic. This was real, and this was necessary. This was everything she hadn't known she'd needed. If any man could protect a woman from harm—from unseen forces, even—it was this one. He knew his power, his authority, and he wasn't afraid to wield it.

When he pulled away, lines of tension branched from his eyes. He opened his mouth to say something, thought better of it and stomped out of the apartment. Through the wooden door she heard him growl, "Lock this."

On shaky legs she followed his trail. Even her fingers shook as she flipped the lock.

"Good girl," he said, his footsteps sounding a moment later.

She rested her forehead against the door. That man... oh, that man. The kiss hadn't panicked her, but now the thought of losing him did. In a very short time, she'd come to depend on him...to need him. And maybe he needed her, too. He could have washed his hands of her. After all, this wasn't his problem. But he hadn't. He'd immediately taken up the reins of control, arranging their next steps. A good thing. She wasn't sure she would have had the strength to visit After Moonrise without him.

You're wasting time. Buck up and get to work. For Lana. She had to save Lana—so that she could yell at her for daring to abandon her.

With a sigh, Harper marched into her bedroom.

8

LEVI MERGED ONTO the highway. First he'd had Harper in his apartment, now his car. He'd allowed her to borrow his clothes—which she'd changed out of, and he kind of wished she hadn't. Letting someone else play with his toys should have put him on edge, but he was strangely settled. This felt right. He liked having her near, within reach, surrounded by his things.

"Did you reach your friend?" she asked. She chewed on her nail, watching as cars and buildings whizzed past. "Is he going to track down Lana?"

"Yep."

"You trust him? He's decent at what he does?"

"Yep."

"Well, that's good enough for me, I guess."

Her grumbling tone told him she reeeally wanted him to elaborate, but how could he elaborate, when the details were sparse? Why did he trust Bright? Instinct. How long had he known the guy? Years. What kind of cases had he solved? Complicated.

Half an hour of silence followed that little interaction before Levi could stand it no longer and asked, "Were you able to paint the guy's face?" He'd hoped she would open up on her own, and he wouldn't have to press. He wanted her to be comfortable with him, but he was also tired of waiting.

"No," she said, and he caught the taunt in her tone. He'd given little, so she would give even less.

This woman really cranked his chain. "Why not?"

"Blocked."

"Is there anything I can do to help?" He purposely didn't mention Topper because he didn't want to increase her worry for her friend. Not unless absolutely necessary.

"Yes," she said, and he could feel her gaze on him, as if she were judging his reaction. "You could pretend you know how to have a conversation and, I don't know, stop barking out one-word answers anytime I ask a question."

Won't grin. "Sure."

"Argh!" She leaned over and punched him in the arm. "You're a hard nut to crack, you know that?"

"Yes."

That earned him another punch. "Well, despite your sparkling wit, I'm going to let you stay with me tonight. I paint in my sleep, but fear somehow finds me and wakes me up, stopping me from finishing. If you're there, I'll feel safe and I'll continue painting until it's done. I know it."

Safe. Good. "Consider me there." Over the years, with as many victims as he'd dealt with, he'd learned a thing or two about fear. You absolutely could not meditate, or feed upon, thoughts that scared you. You had to cast them away, and force yourself to focus on something else. He would be her something else…his hands…his lips… He'd move slowly, take a little at a time, demand a little at a time, until she was ready.

Then he'd take all. Everything.

She must have sensed the direction of his thoughts because she said, "Now then, about the kiss."

"Yeah. What about it?" He wanted more, and if she expected him to enter some kind of friend zone, they'd have a problem.

"This is gonna tick you off."

"Say it, anyway."

"I know we've only kissed, like, once, but you're staying the night tonight, and…well…"

"And, well, you want me to keep my hands to myself." It was better than the total rejection he'd anticipated from her, and something he could work around.

"Not at all," she said, surprising him. "You can get handsy if you want…maybe…if you go slow. But I don't want you seeing another woman while we're… you know, involved."

Wait, wait, wait. She was demanding exclusivity from him? Giving him exactly what he wanted from her? He gave a mock sigh. "If you insist…"

"I do."

He liked knowing she was as possessive as he was. "Then I guess I can—"

"Oh, just forget it!" she huffed. "I'm not dog food, you know. I don't want a man who's this resistant. I don't have to throw myself at anyone, so you can just—"

"You're not throwing yourself at anyone. You're with me, and there will be no other men for you." Anger with himself—shouldn't have teased her over such an important subject—morphed into anger with any other man who'd try to hook up with her.

"You're sure?" she said in a snippy tone.

"Very. You?"

From the corner of his eye, he saw her flick her hair over one shoulder. "Kind of."

Really won't grin. She was sure all right, but her mean streak had kicked in.

Now to figure out what was happening to the world around them.

Finally they made it into Tulsa. Here, the trees were thicker and there were a few more hills. There were buildings of brownstone and stucco, brick and siding, some tall, some short, some thin, some wide. The sky created an eerie backdrop, a long expanse of dark gray layered with fat, rain-heavy clouds.

After Moonrise came into view. Eight stories high, with smoked-glass windows and a waterfall in front, it was one of the city's classier structures. The front doors were arched, all about the welcome.

He parked in one of the only empty slots, got out and moved to the other side of the car to help Harper. Clutching the sheet-covered painting in her hands, she gifted him with a soft smile of thanks. He couldn't stop himself from smoothing a strand of hair from her cameo face and luxuriating in the perfection of her silky skin.

She leaned into his touch, her eyelids dipping to half-mast—but not before he caught a glimpse of apprehension. Not directed at him, but at the coming meeting, he was sure. He knew she expected to be told she had predicted her best friend's death, knew part of her also expected to be told there would be nothing she could do to stop that death from occurring. He knew because he'd battled the same thoughts.

"Let me ask you a question," he said. "When you

first came to my apartment, what would you have done if I'd kicked you out without listening to you?"

Her brow furrowed as she gave serious consideration to her response. "I guess I would have annoyed you so badly you would have done anything to get rid of me. Even listen."

Exactly what he would have guessed. "How would you have annoyed me?"

A shrug of those delicate shoulders as she said, "By knocking incessantly on your door, following you around like a puppy and ultimately shoving the painting in your face."

"That would have taken balls of steel."

"And I polish mine every night. So what?"

Again, exactly what he would have guessed. "So," he said, trying not to grin, "I just wanted to remind you that you do, indeed, have them." He linked their fingers, confiscated the painting with his free hand and dragged her to the entrance.

As they strode across the pavement, he heard her praying under her breath. "Lord, give me the strength to hear what I need to hear and to do what I need to do. Thank You."

A bell rang as they stepped from outside to in. Soft music played in the background. The temperature rose considerably, from misty and cold to dry and bone-meltingly hot. Incense saturated the air, sweet and spicy at the same time, somehow pleasing and repugnant at once. His nostrils burned, but he endured the sensation as a necessary evil.

He scanned the area, taking in every detail at once. There was a reception desk, a long table with coffee and other refreshments, and a waiting room with big, comfortable-looking chairs.

Six people—four males and two females—reclined in those chairs, but only the little dark-haired girl perched on her mom's lap paid Harper and him any attention. She smiled and waved, and Levi waved back, charmed. The mom looked over at him, frowned and gently admonished the girl to behave and mind her own business.

The lady at the reception desk alternated between answering the phone and typing into her computer. In her mid-fifties, with hair dyed the darkest of jet, skin aged from sun exposure and features that were lovely nonetheless, she glanced up at his and Harper's approach—

—and screamed.

Her hand fluttered over her heart, and she jumped to her feet. "What are you doing here?"

He was used to alarming people with his gruff appearance and no-nonsense demeanor, but screams and accusations at minute one, when he wasn't waving a gun? Yeah, that was a first.

"It's okay, Mommy," he heard the little girl say. "He's not gonna hurt anyone. He just looks scary."

"My name is Detective Reid, OKCPD," he said loudly, hopefully calming the people in the waiting room who'd begun to mutter in distress. He lowered his voice and added, "Milana Bonnie Wee Cutie should have called to tell you we were coming. We have a few questions for whoever's in charge of…" Just how did you explain the weird things happening to Harper? And to him, for that matter.

"Lana works for the OKC branch," Harper blurted

out. At least she kept her hands at her sides, opting not to chew on her nails.

The receptionist exhaled with relief and said, "Okay, yes. Yes. I—I remember getting her call. I just wasn't expecting—" she waved her hand up and down to encompass Levi's big body "—this."

This. "What's wrong with *this?*" he growled.

"You're not a little blonde with a Napoleon complex, are you?" she snapped. "I was told to expect a little blonde with a Napoleon complex."

"Okay, taking over now," Harper muttered. "Here's the deal. I might be painting the future, and Lana thought you could help me. And besides that, other things have us freaked out, like the fact that Levi's apartment changed its furnishings in a single night, but he didn't do the changing and it still looks the same to him. This agency specializes in the paranormal, right? Well, there's nothing normal about anything that's happened to us lately, and I want answers. Like, yesterday."

The lady glanced between them, her color high but gradually lightening. "Just…stay where you are." Never taking her gaze off them, she bent down and picked up the phone.

A whispered conversation took place, and Levi thought he heard "I don't know" about a thousand times. Finally, she replaced the phone in its cradle and said, "Agent Peterson will be right out."

A few seconds later, a big man with a big scowl stomped from the elevator. A smaller man holding a stack of files raced behind him, desperate to catch up.

"Headed out, Mr. Raef?" the receptionist called.

"Yeah." Mr. Raef stopped, gave Levi a once-over, and glared. The smaller man rammed into Mr. Raef's back, dropping his papers, but the guy hardly seemed to notice. "What are you doing here? What do you want?"

"He isn't as evil as he looks," the receptionist said.

"You're sure?" the man demanded, taking a menacing step in Levi's direction. "My woman is waiting for me, and even the thought of being late makes me killing mad, so if any killing needs to be done…"

Levi rolled his eyes and wished he still had his badge.

"Ms. Peterson is taking— Ah, there she is," the receptionist said with relief as a woman stalked out of a second elevator. She was of average height—meaning Levi towered over her and she towered over Harper— and average weight. Meaning Levi could snap her spine with a single twist of his giant man-hands.

Peterson had short hair dyed pink and lacquered into tiny spikes. Her eyes were brown and rimmed by eyelashes she'd also dyed pink. She wore a dog collar, had brass knuckles tattooed on her fingers and was clad in a plaid shirt with ruffles and baggy black pants tucked into combat boots. She stopped abruptly when she spotted them and flashed her teeth in a scowl.

"What are you doing here?" she demanded.

Seriously. Could no one treat him like a human being? "We're friends of Lana's."

"Lana?" Mr. Raef cursed under his breath. "They're all yours, Peterson," he said with a mean-sounding chuckle, and exited the building, the other man scurrying behind him.

Peterson ran her tongue over her teeth. "Lana didn't say you looked like…this."

"Hey! What's that supposed to mean?" Harper snapped.

Levi swallowed a laugh and put his hands on her

shoulders, holding her in place. He had a feeling she
was seconds away from leaping on Peterson like an injured wolverine interested in a last meal.

Peterson's gaze danced between them before she
nodded. "All right, fine. I'm choosing to believe you
are who you say you are. So don't just stand there. This
way." She motioned to the elevator with a sweep of her
hand. "Fifth floor."

On the walk to the office, he counted three gasps,
two weird looks and one murderous glare, but other
than that, he was ignored.

"I'm telling you, I'll be fine," Peterson said as she
closed the door, sealing herself inside with him and
Harper. Levi had no idea who she'd been talking to,
since everyone had beat feet out of the hallway, but
whatever. He just wanted to get this over with.

They each took their seats, and he carefully leaned
the painting against his leg.

The office itself was normal, with white walls, brown
carpet, a desk, a computer, a phone system and papers
scattered everywhere. Even the portrait hanging over
the desk was something you'd find in any other estab-
lishment: pink rosebuds surrounded by green foliage.

Peterson leaned back in her swivel chair, crossed her
arms over her middle and said, "All right. Why don't
you tell me why you're here. That wasn't a question or
a suggestion, by the way. Lana was vague, and I don't
have a lot of time."

"Why don't you tell me your qualifications first,"
Levi replied, his voice wielding a sharp edge.

One of her brows shot into her hairline. "Qualifications for what?"

"For dealing with a situation like ours," Harper said.

Her nerves must have kicked back into gear, because the tip of her nail found its way into her mouth. "Besides the obvious, of course."

Peterson drummed her fingers together, but replied, "Well, I can see into the spirit realm and I'm usually given the cases dealing with people no one else wants to deal with. It's my sparkling personality. I can put anyone at ease. What else, what else. I've solved murders gone cold, helped lost souls figure out why they're still here, and aided families who've just lost a loved one."

"Are you trying to tell me Lana is...dead?"

"Do you think she is?" Peterson countered. Great, they'd been stuck with the paranormal equivalent of a shrink.

"She isn't. And you're not the one we need," Levi said. "Let's go." He reached for Harper, intending to stand. "We'll knock on every door in the building until we find someone who can actually help us."

"What do you need, then?" Peterson asked, seemingly unconcerned by his threat. "Exactly. Lana mentioned a few details, but I want to hear everything from your point of view."

He relaxed, willing to take a moment to test her out, and nodded to Harper. "Tell her."

She explained about her blackouts, the changes in Levi's apartment, about the painting she usually only worked on while she was sleeping and the fact that she'd just filled in Lana's face. As she spoke, Peterson finally softened, her features radiating something akin to sympathy.

"Let me see the painting," she ordered.

"Can you help us?" Levi asked.

"Maybe."

For now, that was enough. Levi lifted the canvas from its perch on the floor, keeping the back to Harper despite the fact that a sheet draped the front. A long while passed in silence as Peterson studied the thing from top to bottom. She would stare, then write a note, stare, then write another note. Finally she returned to her reclined position and sighed.

"I've spoken to Lana hundreds of times, but I never pictured her like *that*."

"What do you want to know about the painting?" Harper asked as he re-covered the source of her nightmares and lowered it to the floor. Shifting nervously, Harper licked her lips. "Did I paint the future?"

A decisive "No" cut through the tension. "Definitely not."

"You're sure?" she asked, relief already dripping from her.

"Didn't you catch that 'definitely'?"

Defensive, Harper said, "But how could I not have painted the future when what you saw hasn't happened...to my knowledge?" she added reluctantly.

"Well, how do you know I'm actually sitting here in the room with you?"

Her brow furrowed in confusion. "Uh, I just do."

"Bingo. I just know, too. It's my job, and I'm very good at my job."

That time, Harper accepted what she'd been told and fell against the back of her chair. "Thank you. Thank you so much."

Though he hated to ruin that relief, Levi couldn't let the facts slide. "What else could it be? Like she said, what's in the painting hasn't happened yet. Lana claims she hasn't lost days of her life, not like we have, and

Harper never saw any injuries on her. Are you saying the painting is a figment of Harper's imagination?" He knew it wasn't.

"No, that's not what I'm saying, but thank you for putting words in my mouth," Peterson retorted. She massaged the back of her neck, murmured something that sounded like, "I have my temper under control, I have my freaking temper under control," and said loudly, "Look. Did the two of you recently move into an apartment building near Oklahoma City's Brick Town?"

"Yes," he replied with a frown. "Both of us. How did you know that? Lana?"

"I told you. Lana was in a hurry and left out quite a few details. But I want to look around both of your apartments before I tell you what's percolating in my brain. And don't try to talk me into telling you now, 'cause it's not gonna happen. I need to do a little research before I turn your worlds upside down, so do yourselves a solid and go home. You'll see me sometime tomorrow—and you'll probably wish you hadn't."

9

BACK AT KING'S Landing, Harper fixed a late lunch while
Levi made some calls. He'd already packed his bag,
and now planned to spend the rest of the day and all
of the night with her. She could have put him in Lana's room—a sharp ache lanced through her chest—but
she wanted him with her, as close as possible. And he
seemed to want to stay with her, so she wasn't going to
allow fear about tomorrow and Peterson's dire predic-
tion to interfere.

And why think about the negative, when she could
think about Levi and the things he would try to do to
her tonight? Oh, she knew beyond a doubt he would
try something; he wouldn't be able to help himself, and
a shiver of anticipation nearly rocked her off her feet.

How she'd gone from never wanting to be touched
to wanting to be devoured by one specific man, she
would never know.

The sounds of popping and hissing echoed, drawing
her attention to the stove. Levi didn't yet know it, but
they were having breakfast for dinner. Lana had been
the last one to go to the store, and she'd purchased only

her favorite foods. Regular bacon, turkey bacon, thickly cut bacon, thinly sliced bacon and eggs.

"Well," Levi said, sitting down at the counter. "Lana hasn't reported to work, used a credit card to get a room anywhere or withdrawn any large sums of money. My friend Bright is checking your old home."

"Why would she be there? We sublet it to move here."

A curious gleam filled his eyes. "Is that what she told you? Because I hate to be the one to bust your best friend, but no one else has moved in."

No way. Just no way. "I'm telling you, the house was sublet."

"Bright checked just this morning. It's her name on the lease. The only change that had been made recently was your name being taken off."

Harper's blood went cold as she fixed Levi a plate. "But…" If that were true, Lana had lied to her. Again. "She couldn't afford to pay the full rent there *and* half the rent here."

A pause. Then, "Why did you move here, princess?"

A distraction. She knew the question was meant as a distraction from the wave of betrayal sweeping through her, and yet she grabbed on to it with a kung fu grip. "We—" Wait. *Princess,* he'd said.

He knew her first name.

She swung around to face him, teeth bared in a scowl and the fork she'd planned to give him stretched out like a blade.

He was grinning from ear to ear, the jerk. Oh, yeah, he knew.

"Don't you dare call me—"

"Aurora? Or Sleeping Beauty?"

"I will *gut* you."

His laugh boomed through the room. "Why? I like it. It's cute."

"It's humiliating!" she said with a stomp of her foot.

"It's adorable."

"It's *precious*." She sneered disgustedly. "What, do you want me to call you my very own Prince Charming?"

His laugh cut off, and his smile vanished in an instant. "Do it, and I'll shoot you. No guy on earth will convict me of a crime, either. They'll all say I did my civic duty."

"Just so we understand each other." Pretending to consider a weighty issue, she tapped a finger against her chin. "But you certainly have come to my rescue, haven't you?" she couldn't help but add. "All you lack is the white horse."

He was the one to scowl this time, and she was the one to laugh.

"So what's with the portrait of the nail and the portrait of the limp noodles with spikes?" he asked, changing the subject. He'd obviously been nosing around her home as she'd nosed around his. "Every other picture is of you or Lana or the two of you together and quite… *amazing,* I believe is the word you used, and don't get me wrong, the nail is cool, too. The details are awesome. I can see the scratches and the rust. But the noodles? It sucks. Sorry."

"I'm surprised you noticed."

"What, did you expect me to notice something else?"

"No. I just wasn't sure if you would see my apartment the way I see yours. But anyway, the nail and the thornbush, not limp noodles with spikes. Lana and I decided to paint each other. Only, we were to paint the other's inner self rather than outward. I painted the nail, and she painted the thornbush. We laugh every time we look at those." But she wasn't laughing now. *Oh, Lana. What's going on with you?*

She placed Levi's food in front of him, and settled beside him with her own.

"Thanks for the meal, princess. It smells good. But, uh, I don't think a thousand men could polish off all this bacon."

"One manly man could. After all, Lana always did. Now eat it," she quipped, ignoring his use of the hated endearment. Otherwise, she'd have to brain him with the frying pan, and she wasn't sure how much more abuse he could take from her without bolting.

"Sir, yes, sir," he teased with a salute. "But while I do, you need to tell me why you guys moved here. You never said."

She released the sigh that had been bottled up inside her. "Because I couldn't *not* move here. I saw the place, was drawn to it and felt as if I was finally home. How about you?"

"I'm not sure." He popped a piece of bacon in his mouth, chewed, swallowed. "I just woke up in my apartment one morning, all my things unpacked. I freaked, made some calls and found out I'd sold my place and moved."

"All during a blackout?"

"Yeah."

Understanding his pain, she patted his hand. "Has anything this weird ever happened to you before?" She tried to take a bite of her own food, but her stomach felt knotted and heavy. Guess she wasn't man enough.

"No. You?"

"Never."

He took another bite of bacon, followed by a healthy mouthful of eggs. Obviously he had no problem with his appetite. "Maybe the rest of the tenants are blacking out, too. Maybe it's something in the building. Like mold."

Ugh. Now she *really* couldn't eat, she thought, and pushed her plate away. "You're the cop. I'll let you check."

"Actually, I'm the detective."

"Like there's a difference."

He glared at her, but there was only amusement in his tone when he said, "I'll show you the difference later."

Later. The word echoed through her mind, followed by *in bed,* an addition that was all her own. She shifted nervously—and horror of horrors she chewed on her fingernail. It was the worst habit of all time, but now hardly seemed like the time to quit. What if, while he was showing her, she had another blackout? What if she—

"Hey, don't worry about it," he said, knowing exactly where her head had gone. "I'm prepared to deal with any type of freak-out this time."

"How?" *You can't think negatively, remember?*

He snorted. "Like I'll tell you and ruin the surprise."

His tone was teasing, engaging, and she wondered how she had ever considered him grumpy. He was a cream puff.

When he popped the last bite of food into his mouth, she pushed her plate in his direction. "I cooked, you clean."

"I'm not sure I like that rule," he said, but he stood, gathered the dishes. "What will you be doing?"

"Making a few calls of my own." First up, her old

landlord. If Lana had wanted to keep the house, Harper would not have protested. She would have worked harder to sell her paintings to help pay the two rents. The thought of leaving this building unsettled her more with every hour that passed, yes, but she also wanted her best friend happy.

"Shout if you need me," Levi said.

"Will do." Harper headed to her bedroom. She turned the hall corner and—

Unleashed a blood-chilling scream!

Someone loomed just in front of her.

Acting on instinct, Harper kicked the intruder in the stomach. A girl—the dark-haired girl who liked to spy—hunched over, trying to make friends with oxygen. But Harper's instincts were still raging, and she punched the girl in the jaw, sending her smashing into the wall and sagging to the floor.

Footsteps pounded, and then Levi was there, right beside her with his gun drawn. He shouldered her behind him, using his big body as a shield.

"What are you doing here?" he demanded of the girl. Before she had time to answer, not that she could have formed the words, he stepped on her chest to hold her down, crouched and patted her down with his free hand. "You're lucky you're not packing." He holstered his gun and removed his foot, though he did his best to remain in front of Harper.

The girl's expression smoothed out, becoming as serene as if she'd just woken up from a peaceful nap. "He always keeps his promises," she said. "I hope you know that."

"Who?" Levi snapped.

"He wants her," she replied as if he hadn't spoken.

"Wants his naughty girl. He'll have her, too. He always does."

Harper, whose heartbeat had yet to calm, pushed forward to glare down at her, ready to start giving another beat down to finally get some answers. "You better start talking in English or I'll—"

The girl vanished, on the floor one moment, gone the next. Harper gasped. Levi lost his balance and stumbled forward.

"What just happened?" she rasped out.

"Don't know," he growled. "That ever happened to you before?"

"Never." Surely the girl hadn't…couldn't be… Had to be a trick of the light, she told herself. An illusion. Surely. *An illusion you and Levi shared?* "A…spirit, maybe?" But…how could that be?

"I've never been able to see spirits."

"Me, either."

He stood, his scowl only growing darker. "Pack a bag. We're not staying here tonight."

"Okay." Harper rushed to obey, trying not to think about what had just happened while only throwing the necessities into a duffel. A duffel that turned out to be twice the size of Levi's. He didn't complain, though, just took it from her after gathering his own and escorted her to his car. He locked her in and returned to the apartment, only to stalk out a few minutes later with her painting and supplies.

"Thank you."

"Welcome."

He lapsed into silence and drove to a nice hotel across town. But every mile farther away from King's Landing caused an ache to intensify inside her. The need to go back bloomed…and spread…and consumed. He must have felt it, too, because his knuckles were white on the wheel.

Clearly his willpower was superior, because he managed to procure a room and maneuver Harper inside of it, even though she attempted to pull from his hold several times. He threw their bags on the floor, marched into the bathroom and started the shower. Then he was in front of her, backing her up, shutting her inside with him.

Steam enveloped him, creating a dreamlike haze. "What are you doing?" she rasped. The need to return to the apartment took a sudden nosedive as nervousness blended with excitement.

"What do you think I'm doing?"

"Seducing me."

"Smart girl."

Her nail found its way to her mouth. "'Kay."

"We'll figure all of this out," he promised, forcing her hand to her side.

"'Kay," she repeated.

"And just so you know," he said, the corners of his mouth twitching, "a cop would fine you for your insults now and kiss you later. A detective will fine you now, kiss you now, then do a little detecting to find his way to all his favorite parts."

"'Kay" was said with a tremble this time. The nervousness was taking over, dominating.

He arched a brow. "That's all you've got to say?"

He wouldn't like the thoughts tumbling through her mind. Or maybe he would. He reminded her of Lana, all honesty, no tact. He'd be glad she'd put her fears out there—so that he could put them under his feet, where they belonged. "Well, I'm thinking that this is a big step, and trying *not* to think about the freak-out I had last time. I'm thinking we just had the scare of a lifetime, and probably need a nap instead of sex."

"Big steps, big rewards. Freak-out, meet solution. Me. And for two committed people like us, there's nothing better than sex after the scare of a lifetime," he said, a layer of desperation entering his voice. "We're alive. Let's prove it. *I need to prove it.*"

In that moment she realized this wasn't *just* about desire. Her scream had scared him. He'd expected to find her hurt, or worse. Then, when the girl had vanished, he'd realized he couldn't protect Harper from that kind of unseen force. Now he needed to assure himself that she was here, that she was okay, and deepen the connection between them so that she wouldn't somehow slip away.

"Harper." He gave her a little shake. "Pay attention to me. Class is in session."

"'Kay," she said. She was right about his reasoning. She knew she was right—because, when she looked deeply enough, the same need swirled inside of her.

His hands fell away from her. "If you'd rather wait, we'll wait. I won't pressure you."

She placed her palm on his chest, just over his heart. The hard, fast rhythm proved just how desperately her answer mattered. "I don't want to wait." He was right, too. They needed to prove it. "I'm into you, this. I just hope—"

"Nope, no worries," he said, and the force of his relief was almost tangible. "I told you. I know how to handle you now."

"And that is? You can tell me. Honest. I won't tell anyone else."

"Nah. I'd rather show you." He cupped her cheeks and kissed her, a gentle kiss of comfort and exploration…that soon intensified, becoming something far better. Something passionate.

Soon she was clinging to him, kissing him back with everything she had, rubbing against him, moaning. He stripped her and then himself, and even then the kiss never stopped, their tongues dancing together, tasting, giving, taking, rolling.

"You're beautiful, Harper," he said softly. "The most beautiful woman I've ever seen."

Must have this man.

"Get it yet?" he asked. "I'm not allowing myself to push you for anything, but I'll work you until *you* have to have more."

"I'm past the point of needing an explanation. Do something!"

Chuckling, he picked her up and set her in the tub. Warm water rained against her bare skin, and she loved the dual sensation of the gentle patter of liquid and the harder kneading of his rough hands. He concentrated on her back at first, going up and down, then moving lower, giving her time to get used to each touch before conquering someplace new.

Any time a negative emotion would try to intrude and she would stiffen, Levi would slow down and concentrate on revving her back up. It wasn't long before her body was so sensitized her mind ceased to matter.

"I'm ready," she said. Her hands tangled in Levi's wet hair, her nails scouring his scalp.

He tugged from her hold, peered down at her, breathing harshly as he searched her face. And, oh, *he* was the most beautiful man *she'd* ever seen. Rugged, powerful, determined.

"What are you doing?" she asked.

He waited, just waited, and realization finally dawned. He expected her to direct him—and so, that's exactly what she did. She led his mouth to the places she wanted him, and she wanted him everywhere.

He moved far more slowly than before, but the more she moaned, the more she arched into him, the more fervently he worked her, as if the tether of his control was in danger of snapping. Her desire ramped up and up and up, until her blood was molten in her veins, until her limbs shook and she was arching and writhing toward him—exploding from the pressure as pleasure consumed her.

Straightening, shaking, he said with a half smile, "That was fast."

"You complaining?"

"Rejoicing. I've never been closer to death by heart attack."

A laugh bubbled at the back of her throat. Humor with sex. How unexpected. But she really, really liked it.

"Sure you're ready?" he asked.

More than ready. On fire. "You don't know, Detective Hottie?"

"Just making sure, princess."

"Did you bring protection?"

He nodded, left the shower and returned with a condom already sheathing the long, thick length of him. He didn't waste any time, but picked her up, growled, "Wrap your legs around me," and thrust deep the second she obeyed.

A strangled cry left her. He filled her perfectly and, oh, did her pleasure spark back to life. He pounded hard and fast, and reclaimed her mouth just as savagely.

"Good?" he demanded, and she knew he wasn't talking about the sensations rioting through her but the thoughts in her mind.

Even so, the answer was the same. "Amazing."

Faster…faster…harder…harder…until they were both moaning and groaning. He held her waist in such a strong grip, she knew she would have bruises tomorrow. Bruises she would savor, because they would remind her of this moment, of his total possession.

"Harper," he shouted, climaxing.

"Levi!" She was right there with him, crying out his name, enfolding him in her arms.

For a long while, he remained just as he was, his head resting on her shoulder, the rough pants of his breath trekking over her skin, his heartbeat drumming against her own. She could have fallen asleep just like that, because, despite everything that had happened, everything that would probably happen, she was suddenly more content than she'd ever been, but cool droplets of water began to splash on her, rousing her.

"Shower…turn off," she begged, then blushed when she realized she'd sounded like a caveman.

"Only if we can do this again in the bed," he replied, leaning back to turn the knob.

"Only if you're about a thousand degrees."

"Cold, baby?"

"Beyond."

"Well, what my princess desires, my princess receives. I'll heat you up."

Dirty little turd. "Well, the prince has just made the princess desire a nap. Alone."

"Is that so?" He set her on her feet, only to dig his shoulder into her stomach and hoist her up fireman-style.

"Levi! Put me down right now!"

"Why? I'm the prince's evil twin, who tricked the princess into going to bed with him, and now I've decided to hold you for ransom. And as I'm a stone-cold baddie, you're gonna need to do something to keep me from pillaging your people before that ransom is paid."

He carried her to the bed, and she laughed the entire way.

10

LEVI SNUGGLED HARPER in his arms, sated in a way he'd never been before. She was such fun, her laughter a study and gift of music. With only a smile she lit him up on the inside, shining a spotlight into hidden places. She fit him, her passion a match for his own, her cries for more an aphrodisiac, her kneading hands a revelation.

As long as he'd kept them both on the edge of pleasure, their minds had been too wrapped up in what was happening at the moment to delve into the dark, dangerous territory of past and future. He'd been right. That was exactly what she'd needed to relax and let go.

Afterward, exhausted from hours of learning her body, he'd noticed the haunted look had disappeared from her eyes. Those baby blues had crinkled at the corners as she smiled and teased him about his insatiability, color had been high in her cheeks, and her lips had been red and swollen from where he'd bitten and sucked.

Now, though, in the silence of the night, enveloped by shadows, Harper asleep and breathing deeply, evenly, he couldn't stay *out* of those dark, dangerous places. The two of them had been living in a building with a spirit of the dead. How could they not have known? How had he developed the ability to see into the spirit realm, when everyone he knew who possessed it had developed it before puberty or worked hard to spark it to life? How had Harper?

Harper. His pretty princess. He felt as if he would lose her at any moment, felt helpless as a baby. As if she would simply float away, never to be seen or heard from again. He'd willingly fight her demons for her, but a fist and even a gun could not stop an unseen force, could they?

Despite what he'd said in Peterson's office, Lana was probably dead. The painting probably wasn't the future, but the past. Harper had probably stumbled upon her friend's torture and slaying.

Probably. How he hated the word, but he hesitated to think in absolutes without more proof.

Lana's death had probably occurred while Harper was missing. And Lana's undead status would also explain the lack of bruises on her body, why Harper had never noticed any injuries and how Lana had taken off and hidden so expertly.

And, really, Harper's entire disappearance could be explained by the blackouts—meaning, she had never been abducted. She could have remained in a fugue state, unable to deal with what was happening, from the time she'd found Lana on that table to the time Lana reappeared in her life.

Lana's spirit would have repressed what had happened, too, continuing on as if everything was business as usual.

A few niggling questions remained, however. Why had Harper's blackouts continued? To allow her to slowly come to grips with what had happened? And then there was the timing of everything—Levi's own blackouts, his appearance here, the fact that *he* could see Lana. Harper seeing her was understandable. The two were bonded. But him? No. Unless…he was somehow bonded to Harper and saw what she saw.

Also, Lana had reported Harper missing, only to go missing herself? Talk about a major coincidence. And yet, that would explain why Lana had never returned to the station and reported Harper as found.

So many questions, new and old, and Peterson might have all the answers. That look of abject sympathy as Harper had spoken of her painting…that promise to do a little digging, spoken in a tone of dread and suspicion…

Peterson clearly suspected something terrible.

Harper mumbled something incoherent and began twisting out of his embrace. Dread worked through him as he loosened his hold. She sat up, stayed still for a moment, stood. Between one sexual marathon and the next, he'd had her place her painting and supplies in the proper places, mimicking the setup of her studio.

"Harper," he whispered, but there was no response.

Silent, she padded to the table with the brushes and paints. A soft light cascaded over the entire area, allowing him to watch her. With fluid motions she mixed colors, dipped the tips of the brushes and began to paint.

Levi sat up and scrubbed a hand down his face. He stood, nearly tripped as he shoved his legs into his underwear and closed the distance between them. Rather than study the canvas, he studied her face. Her eyes were closed, the length of her lashes casting shadows over her cheeks.

Her expression was scrunched, her skin pale as milk.

Protective instincts rose to the surface, and he had to fight the urge to shake her awake, to make her stop. He hated that a horrible image of blood and pain held her captive, but more than anything else they needed to see the killer's face.

She worked for hours. Several times she would stop and a tear would trickle down her cheek. He could tell she was trying to jerk herself out of sleep because her breathing would change, becoming choppy, ragged.

He would say, "Keep going, sweetheart. I'm here. Levi's here," and she would rally and continue.

He wanted this thing done, wanted its horrors out there, so that they could know what to fight, where to go, what to do. Maybe they'd luck out and get to tell Peterson to suck it.

Finally Harper's arms fell to her sides and her paintbrush dropped to the floor with a thump. Still she stood there with her eyes closed. He dared a look at the canvas—and nearly roared with shock and rage and fear.

She had painted the killer, and it was Topper as he'd feared. She'd also added more blood. Blood on the walls, on the floor, on the slab. On the man—and on the woman.

On Harper.

She'd painted over Lana's face and added her own. Oh, the woman still had Lana's dark red hair, but that face as delicate as a cameo was Harper's all the way.

Without thought, he swooped her into his arms and stalked to the bed to gently lay her across the covers. He did not want her to see that thing. Wasn't sure what it meant—wasn't sure he wanted to know what it meant.

And he'd thought himself helpless before.

She's not a spirit, he assured himself. He could touch

her, could feel the warmth and softness of her skin, smell the sweetness of her scent. *She's alive. Well.*

She stretched her arms over her head, arched her back. Her eyelids fluttered open, closed, fluttered open again. She drew in a deep breath, only to go still. Her gaze homed in on him.

"I painted," she said, her tone dripping with anxiety.

Unable to form any words, he nodded.

"Let me see."

He held her down. Her wide gaze, still on his face, searched and searched. He opened his mouth to speak, but no words emerged.

She stiffened. "I finished it."

Another nod.

"It's bad."

Yet another nod.

"Really bad."

Finally he managed to find his voice. "If you want to see it, you can see it, but I want you to remember a few things. Okay? You're here. You're real. And I've got you. I'll never let you go."

Her lips parted as she fought for breath and jerked upright. Her gaze drove past him, straight to the canvas. Horror cascaded over her expression.

"That's…"

"Yeah."

Slowly she stood. One step, two, she approached it. Her arm stretched out and she traced a fingertip through the blood dripping down the woman's leg. Crimson stained her soft, white skin. "I can't… That can't… There's just no way…"

"You're here," he repeated, staying close. "You're real."

"I would remember if something like this happened to me!"

Maybe she had done more than stumble upon Lana. Maybe she had been forced to endure a little torture of her own, but she had escaped.

Topper was now locked away, he reminded himself. She couldn't be hurt again.

"We'll go see my friend Bright." Levi's words were croaked. "He'll test your DNA against what we found in the killer's house." Topper had gotten sloppy there at the end, when he'd left that female on the billboard, and that's how they'd snagged him.

He'd stopped abducting women at night, with no one around to see as he stunned them and stuffed them into the trunk of his car. His last victim had rarely left home, and never at night, but Topper, who lived in the same neighborhood, had seen her, wanted her and had gone in to get her.

Eyes wider than before, Harper swung around to face him. "You know who he is? You already found him?"

"Yes." *And I nearly split his spine in two with my fist.* "He's in prison and can't harm anyone else."

"I…I want to talk to him," she said, shocking him.

"No," he growled, then more calmly repeated, "No. He's not allowed to have visitors right now."

"Try again." Scowling, she slammed her hands on her hips. "That might have worked on someone else, but I happen to be a *Law & Order* fan, and I know my rights according to Hollywood and television."

Stupid TV, ruining everything. Levi could put in a request with Topper's attorney, and if Topper approved it, yeah, Harper could visit him. And as much as Topper liked the ladies, he'd say yes. "We aren't bringing you to Topper's attention."

She mouthed the name, shuddered, then shook her head, obviously forcing her determination to rise. "He's locked up. What can he do to me?"

Uh, only annihilate her mentally. No biggie, though, right? Questioning evil had never brought anyone satisfaction. Evil lied. Evil taunted. A person would be better served keeping their eyes on the road ahead, running the race of life.

"He can make you cry, and if you think I'll sit back and watch that, those multiple climaxes I gave you killed your brain cells."

"I don't care. I want to talk to him," she reiterated.

"Have I ever told you I prefer soft, malleable women?" he said, as mean as a honey badger. This was too important to him. He couldn't cave.

"I. Don't. Care."

His eyes narrowed to tiny slits as he leaned into her. "You want to bring yourself to the attention of a killer who might have friends on the outside? A guy who would be willing to pay someone to hurt you just to send him the pictures? Yeah, that kind of thing has happened before."

Finally he spotted a crack in her stubborn facade. But still she said, "I don't want to, no, but I *have* to. Knowledge is power, and right now I'm pretty much without power. He's got it all."

"Lies are weakness, and lies are all you'll get from him."

"I have to try."

"If I refuse to help you?" he said on a ragged breath.

"If you refuse to help me," she replied, stepping into

his personal space, peering up at him with anger and determination, "I will work around you. I'm tired of wondering. I want the truth, once and for all. I want Lana protected."

"Peterson said the painting wasn't of the future. Maybe Lana doesn't need protection."

"And Peterson knows everything? Her word is law?"

Good point. "All right," he said. "I'll put in a request to see him."

11

HARPER WAS ON edge as she and Levi trekked through the halls of King's Landing.

She expected Peeping Thomasina to pop through the walls and scream "boo," but the girl never showed. In fact, all of the residents were strangely quiet.

Maybe they sensed Harper's mood. Fury and fear burned deep in her gut, desperate for a release that would not be pretty. Or, heck, maybe they were frightened of Levi. His gun was drawn and at his side, at the ready.

Unlocking her door proved difficult, because she refused to place the painting on the floor. She wanted it in her hands or in her studio, and nowhere else would do. Right now it was her only link to what had happened, what would happen or what could happen.

Before she could enter, Levi shoved past her. "I'll check things—"

"You're not leaving me—" She drew up beside him.

"Out," he finished.

"Alone," she finished at the same time. And then they stopped abruptly at the sight that greeted them.

Peterson, as well as a man Harper had never met, lounged comfortably on the couch.

The After Moonrise employee had her now-blue hair pinned into two knots that looked very much like horns. She wore a dark blue corset, a spiked dog collar and black pantalets that ended just below her knees, where blue-and-white-striped socks stretched to black ballerina slippers.

The man next to her had sandy hair and brown eyes. He was tanned and slightly weathered, as if he'd spent most of his life outdoors. But what struck Harper most was the fact that he bore the same hard look as Levi, as if he'd seen the worst the world had to offer and nothing could ever affect him again.

"Breaking and entering. Very professional," Levi muttered, shutting and locking the door behind him.

"It served its purpose. I'm sure you've broken into many houses in the line of duty." Peterson's gaze fell to the painting. "Did you finish it?"

"First," Levi said, stepping in front of Harper, "who's the guy?"

"Are you always this suspicious? This is my associate, Mark Harrowitz."

Harrowitz nodded.

Gaze shrewd, Peterson added, "I never enter a strange home alone. I'm sure you understand. He's just here to ensure you two don't try to murder me."

Oh, that was all? Harper's heart drummed in her chest as she moved to Levi's side. "And you call *us* suspicious?"

A smile devoid of humor flashed. "Now that the gang's all here, can we continue?" Her brows arched,

Peterson motioned to Levi's weapon with a tilt of her chin. "*Without* the threat of death?"

"Fine." Levi sheathed his gun *after* moving in front of Harper.

She liked the fact that he wanted to protect her, she did, but she didn't like that he placed himself in danger to do it. They'd be having a chat about that later. Of course, knowing him, he'd kiss her to distract her or vow only to do what he thought was right no matter what.

"Okay, so. The painting." Harper stepped around him and spun the canvas, allowing Peterson to view the horrific scene from top to bottom. "It's finished, yes."

Peterson studied the scene for a long while. Finally, she nodded. Harper took that as her signal to place the thing on its easel, out of the room, out of sight, then rejoined the group in the living room.

Levi had taken the seat across from Peterson and motioned her over. The moment she was within reach, he tugged her beside him, so that she practically reclined across his lap. A protest was not forthcoming. She liked where she was, and needed his strength.

"So what do you have for us?" he demanded. His tone lacked any kind of emotion, but there was no doubt he expected total compliance.

"You're not going to like it," Peterson warned.

Harper raised her chin. "Tell us, anyway."

Silence. A nod, a sigh. Peterson leaned over and dug into the black case resting at her feet. She withdrew several sheets of paper, several newspaper clippings, a DVD and a laptop. "Did you wonder why the receptionist and I had a meltdown at the sight of you?"

"No. Straight-up rudeness," Harper said at the same

time Levi said, "Yeah," and squeezed her in a bid for less attitude.

"Well, I apologize for that," Peterson said. "We just don't get many people like you in our offices."

"What does *that* mean?" Harper huffed. She was too uneasy to be nice.

Harrowitz stiffened, as if he expected Harper to launch across the coffee table and attack. He was very astute. No one talked badly about Levi's rough, gruff exterior but her!

Peterson placed her hand on his wrist, soothing him. "Before we get to that, let me ask you a few more questions."

"No, we—" Harper tried to protest. She wanted answers of her own.

"Have you noticed anything weird about this apartment building?" Peterson asked, plowing ahead.

Levi popped his jaw. "Last night a girl appeared in Harper's hallway and then vanished before our eyes. Clearly, she was a spirit."

Fine. They'd do this Peterson's way. "On more than one occasion that same girl has told me that I was a naughty girl, and that he would be coming for me, but not who 'he' is or what 'he' wants, or why she thinks I'm so naughty."

Peterson and Harrowitz shared a look that wrecked what remained of Harper's nerves. Never had she been so stressed, so unsure, and these people were taking time to communicate silently with each other. How frustrating!

"One more question. Someone other than you lives here," Peterson said, head tilting to the side. "I found some of her things. Who is she?"

"Lana. The one who works for After Moonrise here in OKC."

Peterson nodded to Harrowitz, who began typing on his PDA. Several minutes ticked by in silence, and Harper thought she would scream before he finished. At last, Harrowitz showed Peterson the screen.

After reading it, she said, "All right, then. We'll start with you, Levi." Peterson opened her laptop, inserted a disc, did some typing of her own and turned the screen.

Tense, Harper watched the screen. A local reporter appeared, a woman in her late fifties, distinguished with her hair in a slick bob, her makeup perfectly applied and her expression somber.

"It's a sad day for Oklahomans," the woman said. "One of our finest was killed in the line of duty today while trying to apprehend Cory Topper, the suspected Billboard Butcher. Allegedly, Topper stabbed the detective in the chest and thigh, and he was rushed to the nearest hospital where he was pronounced dead upon arrival." She kept talking, but Harper had trouble hearing her.

Levi's picture flashed over the screen, a younger version of the man she knew, serious, rough-and-tumble, wearing an army uniform. The date of his birth glowed underneath—as did the date of his death.

His death.

Eyes wide, she swung around to study him. His jaw was clenched, his skin pale.

"No," he said, shaking his head. "No. I would remember *dying*. I would have some indication that I'm no longer…human." The last word emerged broken.

"Not always," Peterson replied gently. "Sometimes the memory is buried because the reality is too painful to face. That leaves a big, black hole that needs to be filled. My guess is, things have happened to you lately and you have no way to explain them. You have gaps in your memory. And when you would find yourself on the right path, answers finally within reach, you'd lose more time. That was your mind shutting down as a way of protecting itself."

Another shake of his head. "I spoke to one of my co-workers just yesterday. In person, no less. He saw me, heard me, answered my questions."

"I'm sure he did. I'm also sure he can communicate with spirits, and that's why you successfully conversed with him."

He drew in a sharp breath, his nostrils flaring. "He can, but that doesn't mean anything. He would have told me."

"No. He wouldn't have wanted to be the one to break the bad news to you."

For a moment, stars winked through Harper's line of sight. "But I can touch Levi," she whispered. "And we crashed in a hotel last night, even talked to the clerk to get the room. Then Levi drove me here. In a car!"

"Either the clerk can see spirits and humored you, which isn't likely considering most of us work for After Moonrise or in law enforcement, or you convinced yourself of what you wanted to believe. And you didn't drive here, I promise you. Both of you expected to ride in a car, and so you both constructed a scene. If you talked it over, you'd probably discover you invented different makes and models."

No. Impossible. "You're wrong about this. I cooked, he ate."

"Another lie you told yourself."

"Then why did you tell him to put down his gun?" she demanded, her voice rising. Levi had yet to react to any of this. "If he's a spirit, he couldn't have shot you."

"If he'd pulled the trigger, he would have expected something to happen. When nothing did, he would have gotten angry, probably attacked me, and Harrowitz here would have had a problem with that. Now, I know you have more questions, but I'm afraid I'm not finished yet."

With a sad smile, Peterson typed something into the laptop and the screen changed once again. The same reporter was speaking, though her hair was styled differently and she wore a different top. Obviously this news feed was from a different day. She talked about the identities of some of Topper's victims, and how the most recent to be killed was—

Her.

Aurora Harper.

No. No, no, no.

The stars returned, thicker, more numerous, threatening to expand and consume her entire mind. *I'm not... I can't be...* "No!" she shouted, jumping to her feet. Dizziness swam through her mind, and she swayed.

Harrowitz jumped to his feet, too. His hands were fisted, his eyes slitted in warning.

Pale and a bit unsteady, Peterson unfolded more slowly. "You need to calm down, Harper. Your negative energy is painful to us, and Harrowitz here can make *you* hurt in turn. If he does, you may be forced into leaving this world for good, before you finish whatever you stayed here to finish."

She wasn't dead, she couldn't possibly be dead, but she would deal with that in a minute. "My friend. I painted her face before I painted mine. Is she... She can't be... Tell me she's alive!"

"She's alive," Peterson assured her, palms out in a gesture of innocence. "You painted yourself, your circumstance. I'm not sure why you first painted her face. All I know is your Lana can see the dead like Levi's coworker. That's why she was able to live here with you."

See the dead.

The phrase reverberated through her mind. *See the dead.*

Dead.

She wasn't, Harper thought again. She couldn't be. Lana would have told her.

Lana, so sad sometimes, crying and sobbing, keeping so many secrets. Lana, so guilty sometimes, so desperate for Harper to figure out what had happened to her. Lana, who had stopped touching her, even in the simplest of ways.

But that was because of Harper's aversion to physical contact. Right?

Learning the truth is the only way you'll ever find peace, Lana had said. As if she had already known the truth herself.

Harper...could suddenly see the walls of a basement room, photos of pain and blood all around her, staring down at her. Tools hung from a board by the only door. Knives of every size, saws, hammers, spiked boards, razors and gags.

Gags laced with drugs meant to keep you awake, to keep you lucid while...while...

"No," she croaked, shaking her head violently. She fell back into Levi's lap. Still he gave no reaction. Was he in shock?

"You can touch Levi and he can touch you because you're *part of the same world,* existing on the same plane. You will not be able to touch humans, however. Here." Peterson extended a shaky hand. "Try me. I'll prove it."

Harrowitz sat down and grabbed her arm. He shook his head.

Peterson dropped her arm, sighed. "Oh, yeah. No touching the dead."

Dead, she'd so casually stated. Dead.

"You were the last to die, Harper," Peterson said. "Levi busted in on Topper just after he'd killed you. He saw your mutilated body and reacted. That's why he attacked Topper. That's why he missed the blade Topper still held."

Harper felt a strong, warm band around her waist. The contact was too much, not enough; she couldn't breathe, could barely sit still, wanted to stay, wanted to leave. Was falling…tumbling down an endless void. And yet, somehow that strong, warm band kept her steady.

Merciless, Peterson continued, "Everyone in this building is a spirit. Certain spirits are drawn here, and we don't know why. Maybe like calls to like. All I know is that the OKC branch of After Moonrise bought it, and monitors it to the best of their ability, and as long as you're here, keeping to yourselves, they're happy."

"No," she said, shaking her head.

Peterson pressed on. "I'm guessing that's why Lana sent you to me, rather than to her own firm. She didn't want them involved in your afterlife any more than they already were. Yes, they know you're here. I checked. But they like that you're here and unaware of what happened. You're not out there causing any trouble. If that changes, they could decide to force you to move on."

"No," Harper repeated.

And still Peterson kept talking. "It's not all bad. This is supposed to be a fresh start for you, a chance to finally live right, to fix mistakes or tragedies before letting go of the ghosts of the past, to have the brightest future possible."

"No!"

"If I were you, I'd make the most of it. Too many people in your situation lose sight of what matters and sink back into old patterns and habits or even fail to act upon the new opportunity they've been given. They spiral into depression. They become angry—and their anger can ruin innocent lives."

"No," she said yet again, even though Peterson spoke with such certainty, as if Harper really was part of that world, as if everything she mentioned was fact and there was no reason to debate.

A soft sigh filled the room. "If you want to know more about what happened to you, read the papers and clippings I brought. And honestly? I suggest that you do. You're each here for a purpose, and I don't care what the OKC branch thinks. You're better off knowing. Think about it. You might be able to move on."

Move on. And lose Levi.

Lose Lana.

Lose *herself*.

It was too much to take in. Harper ripped from Levi's hold—Levi was the strong band, she realized distantly—and flew out of the room. She couldn't remember pausing to open the door, only knew that she was inside her apartment one moment and in the hall the next.

"Harper," she heard Levi shout. His first word in so long, she wanted to stop, to throw herself at him, but she couldn't.

I'm sorry, she thought. He'd been told the same thing, yet she wasn't comforting him. He deserved comfort, but she couldn't deal with this. Couldn't accept the fact that she had been tortured and murdered, that her life was over, that she would never again hug Lana, that she had lost everything. So she ran, just ran, with no destination in mind—yet somehow she appeared at the art gallery...without ever leaving the apartment building.

Sickness churned in her stomach. Another blackout, surely, she told herself.

It was daylight, too bright, and people walked along the sidewalks. Everyone ignored her. Cars sped on the road, fumes in the air, and she wanted to run from here, too, but didn't allow herself. Through the window she saw the owner showing someone a painting in back.

She would talk to him, she decided. He, who couldn't see the dead, would talk back to her. They would have a conversation, and that would be that. Yes. Simple. Easy. She would prove Peterson wrong—or right.

No, not right.

Lifting her chin, Harper entered the shop.

12

LEVI SEARCHED FOR several hours, but found no sign of Harper. She needed time to come to grips with what she'd learned, he got that—he was struggling with what *he'd* learned—but she was vulnerable right now, not paying attention to her surroundings. Someone could—

She's a spirit. Who can hurt her?

Yeah. There was that.

She was a spirit. Like him.

Him. Dead. Killed. Murdered by the same man who'd murdered Harper. How? *How?*

Peterson and her bodyguard were gone by the time he returned to Harper's apartment. Harper wasn't there, either. He fell heavily on her couch, put his elbows on his knees and his head in his hands. Dead. Killed. The words kept popping up, echoing through his brain. Dead. Killed.

He thought back. At first, he saw only a veil of black. He pushed through that veil with every bit of his strength, determination riding him hard. A wave of trepidation slammed through him, but he refused to back off. He had to know the truth.

Images began to flash through his mind, foggy at first but quickly solidifying.

A drive to Topper's house… *Gonna escort that psychopath to a cell where he'll rot until death comes knocking.…*

Levi and Vince had squealed to a stop, other detectives and patrolmen exiting their own cars. Red and blue lights flashed all around. They'd followed DNA evidence, had a warrant for Topper's arrest. Adrenaline and excitement were high, practically saturating the air. They were about to close the most gruesome case they'd ever worked and save countless lives.

Vince was the one to kick in the front door, and Levi was the first one inside the house. They searched the place from top to bottom and finally found a hidden door to the basement.

Opening it brought a wealth of smells he instantly recognized. Blood, chemicals, death. They heard screams, a buzz saw, sobs, laughter.

In an instant, Levi's mind went blank, the veil falling back over his memories. Gritting his teeth, he once again pushed through it. The trepidation increased, but he continued to surge forward. He saw himself, gun drawn. He pounded down rickety stairs to discover Topper had been busy cutting up a body—a body he now recognized as Harper's. No wonder he'd felt guilt and shame when he'd seen her at King's Landing.

He'd been too late. Hadn't saved her.

Pale hair spread out over the table, though it appeared red, soaked as it was with her blood. Though she was dead, her blue eyes were open, haunted, pained, sad, furious and fixed on something far away. Her lips were parted, having already expelled her last breath.

Then and now, sickness churned inside his stomach. The things she had suffered…the agony she had endured…

Another female—the screamer, the sobber—occupied a small dog cage, the sides covered with a black tarp to prevent her from looking at anything but Harper. Topper was laughing, holding up the limbs he'd removed to show his newest victim what would happen to her if she displeased him.

That woman… That poor woman…

Men rushed in from behind Levi, pushing him forward. Thoughts scrambled through his head, but he couldn't decipher them just then. All he knew was that he took one accidental step toward the guy and couldn't stop himself from purposely taking another and another. He'd spurred into motion, sheathed his gun instead of emptying his clip, wanting up close and personal vengeance. He threw himself into Topper. The limb tumbled to the floor. Levi punched…punched…

Topper had excellent reflexes and immediately made use of the blade in his hand. A blade he'd used on Harper. As enraged as Levi was, he failed to safeguard himself. Felt a sharp sting in his side, followed swiftly by a sharp sting in his thigh. Just boom, boom, and his blood went cold, seeping out of him at an alarming rate. Topper had punctured a kidney and severed a major artery.

He remembered his coworkers rushing over to pull him and Topper apart. He remembered the fade of their voices. The concern. He remembered looking into his partner's eyes, holding his hand, the world going black.

But he did not recall waking up in the hospital. Did not recall recovering from his wounds. He just remembered…what? The conversation he'd had with his captain had never really happened. He'd never been put on a leave of absence. He'd never left the station, too upset to go home, never driven downtown, spotted a suspicious-looking guy—

Wait. He *had* wandered downtown, *had* spotted a suspicious-looking guy. A spirit, he knew now. He'd entered King's Landing and blacked out, coming to in his new apartment. He hadn't made any calls about his old home. He'd simply convinced himself he'd sold it and moved on.

Now Levi laughed bitterly. No wonder Vince always refused to talk to him. Vince couldn't see him, couldn't hear him. No wonder Bright had been so surprised to find him back at the precinct. No wonder Bright had been so evasive about Harper's case. He'd known she was dead but hadn't wanted to share the news with Levi, who was also dead but unaware.

A clatter of voices penetrated his thoughts. The clack of keyboards, the pound of shoes.

Levi's head whipped up. No longer was he sitting on Harper's couch in Harper's living room. He was at the precinct. All around him were men and women going about their day, escorting suspects to processing, to interrogation or to a cell. Detectives sat at desks, reading files, researching a lead. The scent of coffee filled the air.

He straightened with a jolt. How had he whisked from one place to the other, in only a second of time? A spiritual ability?

Probably.

Not taking time to reason out why he'd come, he stalked to Bright's office. The door was closed, but why should that stop him now? Hesitant, he stepped *through* the wood. A sensation of cold washed through him, but that was it. No resistance. One second he was in the hall, the next he was in the office.

Proof, such stunning proof, of his new status.

And there was Bright, typing away.

"I'm dead," Levi announced rawly.

Bright's head jerked up, his hand reaching for the gun stashed in the top desk drawer. The moment he realized it was Levi, he relaxed. A sad gleam entered his eyes. "Yes."

"You knew."

"Yes."

"Why didn't you tell me?"

One dark brow arched. "Have you ever had to tell a spirit something he didn't want to hear? The results aren't pretty. You would have flipped out, and very bad things would have happened."

Peterson had mentioned chaos. Levi was upset right now, and had been for a while, yet so far hadn't caused any trouble. Maybe it was just a matter of controlling his actions, of pushing through his feelings.

"Sit down." Bright waved to the only chair. "I'm guessing you're here for answers, yes? What do you want to know?"

He obeyed, saying, "What happened to Vince after…" He cleared his throat. "After I left?"

The sadness intensified. "He still blames himself for not protecting you. Thinks he should have shot Topper before you reached the guy. No one can pull him out of his depression, which is why Captain has him in mandatory counseling."

Poor Vince. "Is there anything I can do to help him?"

"I'll tell him I talked to you. Maybe that'll help."

"Yes," he croaked out. "Tell him I'm sorry, that he did nothing wrong, and I miss him. Tell him I met a woman. Someone special."

"Your Harper."

"Yeah."

"About time." Bright reached out to trace his fingertip over the picture of his wife resting on the side of his desk. "We held a funeral for you. A real hero's send-off. Everyone showed up. You would have been proud."

Yes, but had he deserved that kind of send-off? "Did you tell me the truth about Topper?"

A wary sigh. "Yes. He lives. He's in lockup right now and awaiting trial for what he did to all those women, what he did to you."

Good. "I'm paying him a visit." Yes, he'd promised Harper and he would take her to see Topper. But Levi wanted to be the first, to smooth the way. "Can he see into the other world?"

"His file says no, but sometimes people lie about that, not wanting to be labeled a weirdo."

Levi ran his tongue over his teeth. He'd learn the truth soon enough. "You mentioned bad things happen when spirits are mad. How?"

Bright leaned back in his chair, folded his arms over his middle. "So you want to hurt Topper, do you? Plan to haunt him a wee bit?"

He wasn't sure what he planned to do. To cover his bases, he said, "Don't ask, don't tell."

"That's military, about sexual orientation."

"Semantics."

Fingers lifted and fell, drumming against Bright's hands, creating a symphony of sound. "I'm sure you already know this, but I'll tell you, anyway. There are good spirits and bad spirits out there."

Well, yeah, he got that. Now. But there was knowing and then there was *knowing*. "And how can I tell the difference?"

"Their fruit."

Uh, what? "Come again."

"You'll always know by the fruit they produce. An orange tree won't grow lemons."

"Meaning?"

"Meaning, haters say and do hateful things. Lovers say and do lovely things."

Okay. That made sense. The girl with the X-ray vision was a hater, no question.

"I don't recommend you visit the prison," Bright said. "Other spirits will be there, and you don't want to bring yourself to their attention, believe me. They could follow you, and if they follow you, they could run into your girl. But I could have Topper brought here for another round of questioning...."

Levi sat up straighter. "You're a good man, Bright."

"I know. Now if we could convince my wife. She's asked for a divorce and—and that's not your problem, is it." Another sigh left him. "So how's your Harper holding up? Does she know about the spirit thing yet?"

"Yeah. We found out together. She took off, and I haven't seen her since." Where was she? What was she doing?

"She'll be back, don't worry. I've seen enough spirits to know that when they find out, they think they want to be alone, but really, they need someone there with them, supporting them, letting them know they're still loved."

Loved? He didn't... He couldn't... He barely knew

her, he thought. Oh, he liked her more than he'd ever liked another. Craved her, even. Wanted her with him, wanted to protect her from every bad thing. Wanted to hold her, and assure her that he would help her through this every step of the way. And he wanted *her* to hold *him,* to know she would be with him every step of the way.

She fit him in so many ways, and in bed, he couldn't get enough of her. Her taste was a drug, her body the missing puzzle piece to his own. But love?

He'd been in love a few times in his life. Once with Kelly Roose, the prettiest girl in his third-grade class. Once with Shannon Halbert, his high school sweetheart and the girl who'd taken his virginity. All three minutes of it. And once with Donna Chang, the woman he'd wanted to marry, the woman he'd dated for two years—the woman who cheated on him because he wasn't "meeting her emotional needs."

He didn't think every girl he met would cheat on him. He knew better. He didn't even think Harper would cheat on him. She had the same possessive streak he did, if not to a stronger degree. But to fall in love now, while things were so uncertain, while he could move on—or whatever spirits did—at any minute…not just no but *I'd rather die again* no.

"Another question," he said. "Where do spirits go when they move on?"

Bright worked his jaw. "Some go up, some go down."

See? What if he and Harper moved on at different times? "Why do they go? Because they accomplished whatever had kept them around in the first place?"

"Yes. The good ones fulfill their purpose and go up, and the bad ones destroy something, or try to destroy something, and get sucked down. Some know what they need to do right off. Others have to figure it out. Others purposely don't find out because they either can't handle the truth or don't want to leave."

"So they can stay?"

"For the length of a human lifetime, yes. Despite what books and movies claim, I've never met anyone who stayed longer than that." A layer of strain entered his voice. "My wife left me because I still see Sally Wells. Sally was my high school girlfriend who died of cancer soon after we graduated. She comes to see me at least once a week, and won't leave my side on our anniversary." The strain increased. "She throws a tantrum if I forget to buy her a present."

Levi wasn't sure how he felt about haunting his friends for the rest of their natural lives—like he was clearly doing to Bright, he realized. "I'm sorry. If I meet anyone halfway decent, maybe I can set your Sally up on a blind date."

A booming laugh filled the room. "Levi the matchmaker. Classic!"

"Any word on Harper's friend, Lana?"

"Yeah." Bright leaned forward to tap away at the keyboard. "Her credit cards were stolen and used this morning. Some homeless guy bought cigarettes first, then half an hour later bought some beer. He was taken into custody, but he swears he found the cards on the street and that he hasn't seen Lana. We showed him a photo and nada. Still, I've got someone watching her home. We'll catch her."

The phone on the desk rang. He held up his finger for a moment of silence, and lifted the receiver. He listened, frowned. "I'll be right there." Reaching for his gun, he stood. Checked the clip.

Levi stood, as well. "I'll let you get to work." He would not allow himself to return to the station. This was it. This was goodbye.

Or not.

"No," Bright said with a shake of his head. "You'll come with me. Your girl's art gallery was just torn to shreds."

13

HORRIFIED, HARPER PEERED at her surroundings. She hadn't meant to hurt the first—and now only—person to give her a break into the art world, and she hadn't meant to destroy the building, but she'd walked in, tried to talk to him, tried to touch him, and like Peterson had predicted, she had failed. Clifford Rigsby had gone about his day, showing patrons his current pieces, then closing up for lunch.

Frustration had risen inside her, but she'd kept herself under control by repeating, "This is a dream. I'll wake up. And if not, there's some other answer to what's going on." But then Cliff had entered his office. His secret office. It wasn't the one he used for public business dealings; obviously it was meant only for his private use.

He had a portrait of Harper hanging on the wall. In it, she was splayed on the same metal slab *she'd* painted, naked, cut and bleeding.

A bright light flashed in her mind but quickly faded—and as it faded, a gruesome scene took its place.

"Say cheese," her captor said. He was blond and

handsome, with a smile any dentist would be proud of, and he was holding a camera, the lens directed at her.

Cold, hurting, trembling, hating the very fabric of his evil being, she scowled at him. "You will pay for this."

His chuckle reverberated through the room. "Such a naughty girl. But don't worry, you'll learn the proper way to address your new master soon enough, I promise you."

Another flash of bright light. This time it faded and she found herself back inside Cliff's private office. Her limbs trembled. For a moment, she had trouble catching her breath. Except, she was dead, wasn't she, and had no need to breathe.

Dead.

Dead.

She really was dead. She'd truly been tortured by a monster, killed by his blade. Peterson had tried to tell her, but Harper had fought the realization. Had fought the truth. Maybe because accepting her death meant accepting what had happened to her—what her mind had been trying to remind her of for weeks.

The room spun…spun…and other portraits came into view. Other women, each in a similar position to Harper, lying flat on a cold slab of metal, with similar wounds decorating their bodies. One fact became excruciatingly clear: Cliff and Topper knew each other.

Perhaps they were friends, if demons hiding in human skin were even capable of friendship. If so, Cliff had served her to Topper on a silver platter.

Another flash of light. Another scene crystallized.

Suddenly Harper was in the center of the gallery, dressed in an ice-blue cocktail dress with thin straps and a Tinkerbell skirt. On her feet were clear heels with jewels encrusted on ties that wound up her calves. Her hair flowed down her back, curling at the ends, though the sides were elaborately twisted at her crown. Usually she got ready in thirty minutes or less, brushing her hair, throwing on a little mascara and lip gloss and pulling a T-shirt and jeans from a drawer. Today she'd taken two hours, wanting to look her best to properly represent her (amazing) art.

After the last customer left, Cliff took her into his office where they celebrated her success with a glass of champagne. They'd talked and laughed as she'd sipped, but the moment she'd finished, he'd yawned and practically shoved her toward the front door.

"Go on home," he said. "You've outdone yourself and made me a ton of money. Now I want to count my cash."

She chuckled, not insulted in the least. This was too wonderful a day. People had loved her paintings. They'd stared at them, felt happy things, sad things, some even moved to tears. Not one painting had been left behind.

"Well, don't forget to count mine," she replied.

"No worries. Your check will be cut tomorrow."

Her chest swelled with satisfaction. "Thank you, Cliff. Thank you so much."

He waved her away. "Go on. Get."

The bell tinkled as she left the gallery. Smiling, she dug her keys out of her purse. Her car was parked a block away, in the closest available lot. The moon was high, luminous and so beautiful she could barely take her eyes off it as she walked. But then she tripped and nearly fell, which would have ruined her knees and her dress, so she forced her gaze to remain ahead.

And yet, she soon tripped a second time as a wave of dizziness crashed through her. Her smile fading, she stopped to lean against a building. What was wrong with her? In and out she breathed, thinking the sensation would pass. But, of course, it only grew worse.

Practically blinded because of the spinning, spinning, *spinning* world, she opened her purse to pat inside for her phone. The moment her fingers wrapped around the case, a sharp sting buzzed in the back of her neck, electricity flowing throughout her entire body.

Her muscles knotted, becoming unusable. Her back bowed, her bones vibrating, just as unusable. Even her jaw locked up, trapping her scream in her throat. *Dying,* she thought. *I'm dying.*

When the vibrations stopped, her knees collapsed. Trembling arms banded around her before she hit the ground, and suddenly she was floating. Relief cascaded through her. Someone had noticed her, was taking her to the hospital.

Something creaked.

No. Wrong, she realized. Someone was stuffing her inside a small, dark space. The air was stuffy, with old perfume caught in some of the pockets. She blinked, trying to orient herself. A blond man, his face blurred by the haze of her vision, stood above her. There was a streak of white; his teeth, maybe. Was he smiling?

"We are going to have so much fun, you and I."

More creaking, then a loud whoosh. A click. There was only dark, no hint of light. No fresh air.

Yet another flash of light, and Harper was back inside the gallery, Cliff eating a sandwich as he plugged away at his computer. Fury rose inside her. Fury like she'd never before known. The champagne…he must have drugged her.

Fury…growing…growing…

The walls around her began to shake. One of the paintings fell to the ground with a loud crash. Frowning, Cliff set his sandwich down and glanced around.

He'd known what would happen to her, but he hadn't cared. Had probably enjoyed every minute of her torture through the photographs Topper had taken.

Growing...

The walls shook a little more. Two more paintings fell.

Cliff pushed to his feet.

As long as Topper kept his mouth shut, Cliff would probably never be caught. And why would Topper betray his buddy when that buddy could continue hurting women, taking pictures, painting pictures and sending them his way?

Growing...growing...

The entire building rocked on its foundation. Cliff gripped the edge of his desk, a fine sheen of sweat dotting his brow. Harper longed to grab the paintings and beat him with them. But she couldn't touch him, and she couldn't touch the paintings, because she was dead. Dead.

Dead!

One of the paintings flew from the wall and smacked him in the back of the head. A grunt parted his lips. He dove for the floor and crawled under his desk.

Harper's eyes widened as another painting flew at him, crashing into the desk and cracking in two. *What are you doing? Stop. You shouldn't destroy the evidence. You have to show Levi. He'll tell his detective friends and Cliff will get what's coming to him.* But it was too late. The shaking never stopped, and the artwork never stopped flying. Around and around each piece twirled before hurtling itself at Cliff. The door rattled, too, before ripping from its hinges and slamming into the far wall.

Harper stood in the center of the turmoil, completely unaffected. She could hear Cliff's sobs, but that only angered her further.

A flash.

Suddenly she was the one crying, begging for Topper to stop. But her cries only spurred him on. Mercy was not something he possessed.

"Harper!"

Something hard slapped against her cheek, causing her head to twist to the side. She blinked rapidly and found herself back inside Cliff's office, a scowling Levi in front of her. His hand was raised, as if he meant to slap her (again?) out of her hysteria.

"Levi!" Relief swept through her, and her knees buckled.

He caught her, holding her up. "You have to calm down, sweetheart. Okay? Yes? I don't want you to destroy the entire building. You could hurt innocents and go... Just calm down, okay?"

Yes, she could calm down...would calm down.... Anger would not get the better of her.

At last the building stilled.

"Good, that's good." He hugged her close. "Are you okay?"

Tears burned the backs of her eyes. "He...he... drugged me. Set me up. *Gave* me to Topper."

Levi pulled away to peer down into her eyes, but he didn't release her. A good thing, because she needed the strength of his arms. "He was working with Topper?"

A nod as she motioned to the paintings on the floor, the tears spilling out, trickling down.

Levi bent down, taking her with him, and lifted one half of a painting, dug around—the things on Cliff's desk had shattered and scattered across the floor, too—and found the other half.

The moment he put the halves together, his nostrils flared. "They were accomplices," he said, emotionless.

One of her tears landed on the top of his hand. His gaze lifted. Seeing her upset, he straightened. "You remembered," he said.

All she could manage was a nod.

"I'm sorry," he added. "So sorry for everything you had to endure."

Somehow, she found her voice. "And you…did you remember?"

"Yeah."

Part of her wanted to slink away in embarrassment. He'd seen her there at the end, at her weakest, her worst. Part of her loved that he'd thought to come to her rescue, that he'd reacted on instinct. And yet… "I wish you had survived."

His hold tightened. "I'm not one of those people who believes everything happens for a good reason. I actually think that's stupid. No. But I do believe the bad stuff can be worked to our favor."

"How can *this* be worked to our favor?"

"Sweetheart, you just unearthed a very bad man. I'd say we're on the right track."

He was…right, she realized. She twisted, eyeing the man in question. Cliff had crawled out from under the desk, his eyes red and watery. He rushed around the office, trying to gather the paintings. To save them or hide them, she wasn't sure.

"Without you," Levi said, "he would have squeaked by without anyone knowing the part he played."

"How do we let the police know?"

"Detective Bright, the one I have looking for Lana, is almost here."

Pounding footsteps sounded.

"Scratch that. He's here."

Two firemen rushed inside the room.

"Or not," Levi said with a sigh.

The two firemen spotted Cliff, paying no attention to Harper or Levi—and even misting through them to get to Cliff. She felt the heat of their bodies and gasped.

"Are you all right, sir?" one of them asked.

"Yes, yes," Cliff said with a tremor.

"Anyone else in the building with you?"

"No, I'm alone. What about the rest of the gallery? Show me." He spread his arms, blocking the firemen from stepping deeper into the office. "What happened? An earthquake?"

"No!" Harper screamed, reaching out to stop him.

Levi stopped *her*. "It's okay. Let them go."

The firemen once again walked through them, and she once again experienced that strange wave of heat. The pair explained that Cliff's building was the only one that had been affected by…whatever had happened, and they'd be looking into it.

"But…but…" she sputtered.

"My guy will be here," Levi reminded her. "Let's wait at the front door and show him what you found. The man who betrayed you will be arrested before the day is over, you have my word."

14

LEVI HAD LIED. Clifford Rigsby wasn't arrested by the end of the day. He was arrested by the end of the hour.

Later that day, Harper sat in on her first interrogation, though no one but Levi and the detective asking the questions knew she was there. Her nerves were frayed as she listened to Cliff claim the portraits had been mailed to him anonymously. As if! Topper wasn't a painter—Levi told her there had been no art supplies in his home—but Cliff was, which was why he'd first opened the gallery.

If he got away with escorting women to their slaughter...

The walls of the interrogation room began to shake, and Levi squeezed her hand. She forced her mind to blank. He'd tried to talk her out of coming, but she had insisted and so he had insisted on coming with her in an effort to keep her calm.

"If they were gifts, why didn't you turn them in?" Bright asked, casting Harper a dark frown. He was a handsome black man, and he'd stood at the gallery's entrance, pretending to look the building over as Levi told him what she'd learned before going in to check things out.

He'd left with Cliff, who'd been cuffed and crying.

She and Levi hadn't needed to enter the police car with the men. They'd thought about the station and simply appeared there. The swiftness of the location switch had startled her, but the need to see Cliff behind bars had overwhelmed everything else.

Now she released Levi to pace as Cliff answered. "I didn't know they were real," he said. "I didn't!"

Bright arched a brow, looking curious rather than suspicious. "You don't watch the news?"

"No."

"But you do know the paintings are real now, when we haven't told you anything of the sort? When we've only asked you how they came to be in your possession?"

She stopped, standing behind Cliff, unsure what she wanted to do. Levi came up behind her and wrapped his arms around her waist.

"I know this is hard," he whispered, "but you have to maintain control of yourself. Otherwise, you'll have to leave. Bright has to do his job."

"All right." With tears of frustration burning her eyes, she rested her head against him. The mint of his scent enveloped her. His heat comforted her.

Cliff stuttered for a bit, but managed to collect himself with a few deep breaths. "I heard about Cory Topper on the news. Heard what he'd done to those women. I *guessed* they were real."

"You said you didn't watch the news."

"I misunderstood the question."

"So why didn't you come forward the moment you

realized what you had?" the detective asked, as calm as ever.

More stuttering. "Well, I, uh, well."

"Bright's got him now," Levi whispered.

Bright glanced up at them and gave an almost imperceptible shake of his head—a gesture for silence.

Levi lowered his voice and said, "Come on. We're distracting him. He's got this. You know that. Let's go home."

So badly she wanted to witness Cliff's end, but if she stayed, she would eventually speak up. She wouldn't be able to help herself. She would distract Bright far more than she'd already done and possibly cause him to screw up the interrogation. And if Cliff got away because of *her*...

"Okay," she said on a wispy catch of breath.

"I want a lawyer," Cliff growled. "I know my rights. I'm not saying another thing until—"

He did say another thing, but she didn't hear it. One moment she was in the mirrored room with him, the next she was standing in her living room—just because she wanted to be there. It was as easy as that. There was no dizziness, no recovery period.

"That's a nice little perk," she said, pretending she wasn't freaked out.

Levi, who was still behind her, placed his hands on her shoulders and spun her around. There was a grave cast to his face, a seriousness, a somberness she'd never seen before. Made sense, though. He'd just learned that he was dead, but she hadn't been there for him. Had focused only on herself. Guilt filled her.

"I know you're upset," he said.

She cupped his cheeks, scraped her thumb against his stubble. "I'm not the only one."

"What happened to us was terrible."

"Yes."

"But we're here, and we're together."

Together. Yes. "Kiss me, Levi."

He swooped in, pressed his lips to hers and thrust his tongue into her mouth.

They kissed for minutes, hours, days even, tasting each other, relearning each other, comforting each other. They were here, and while the rest of the world might consider them dead, they were alive to each other. That was enough.

As passion flowed through her veins, consumed her, it was difficult for her to believe that her life had ended, that she was no more. She was on fire, aching for Levi's total possession. How much more real could a woman get?

He tugged at her shirt. She tugged at his. He removed her pants, and she removed his. Underwear was the next thing to go. And when they were both naked, he picked her up and carried her to the bedroom.

Looking down at her, he grinned. "If this is the end to a crappy day, I'm all for crappy days." With that, he tossed her on the bed.

She bounced once, twice, and on the second descent, he was there, pressing her down into the mattress, pinning her with his muscled weight. The heat of him had intensified, delighting her in every way. His skin was a study of masculinity, rough in some places, smooth in others, with patches of dark hair on his chest and legs.

"You feel so good," he praised. "I don't think I ever want to let you go."

"Then don't." Just then he was her anchor. And she so desperately needed that anchor. She was afraid of floating away and never returning, of losing him, and losing herself.

"Grab the headboard."

"Why?"

"Because King Levi said so."

Unable to stop her own grin, she obeyed. The moment her fingers curled around the iron railing, he bent his head and laved her body from top to bottom. He bit, he sucked, he licked, ratcheting up her already inflamed desire. His tongue was like a stroke of fiery silk, tantalizing her, making her gasp and pant and beg for more... then plead with him to stop and finish her.

"Levi! If you want me to start beating you, keep doing what you're doing."

A warm chuckle, his breath tickling over her in the most decadent caress.

"I'm serious." She released the iron and waved a fist at him.

He playfully nipped at her fingers. "Back on the railing, princess."

So commanding. So wonderfully carnal with her. "Fine." She tried for reluctant, but merely came across as snippy. "But you had better do everything in your power to make this princess happy or you'll lose your head."

He gave another of those sexy chuckles. "You can't behead a king. Now do as you've been told before things get ugly and I have to summon my guard. He may look exactly like me, but he isn't as nice as I am."

Moaning, she obeyed him. The moment she did so, he returned to his play. Only, his hands were rougher, his mouth more insistent. He worked her over, worked her just right, so that she was arching into him, following his every move, desperate, so desperate for completion.

"Levi!" she shouted. "Enough! You have to… If you don't…"

"I'm a king, remember?" The strain in his voice delighted her. He'd break soon. He wouldn't be able to help himself. "I do what I want, when I want."

"Well, I do damage to—"

"He's coming for you," a familiar voice said from beside the bed. "Oh, uh, never mind."

"What the—" Harper hurried to cover herself. Levi jumped up, clearly intending to murder the black-haired girl who'd been haunting them all over again, but she vanished just before he reached her.

He stood there for a moment, silent and naked, and clearly floundering about what to do. "I want to chase her, but I don't want to leave you."

An unexpected laugh bubbled from Harper's throat. Levi spun around and glared at her.

"You think this is funny?" he demanded.

Unable to speak through her giggles, she nodded. And, oh, the amusement felt as good as his touch. As dark as the day had been, she hadn't expected to find excitement, arousal, fulfillment, acceptance, comfort or humor—much less all of those things at the same time.

With a mock scowl, he stalked back to the bed. "Well, I'll make you sorry for that. If I can't tackle her, I'll have to make do with you."

She laughed all the harder. He pounced.

The air whooshed from her lungs. Without any more preliminaries, he claimed his woman. Her laughter was cut off, becoming a low groan of pleasure. She wrapped her legs around him, wrapped one arm around his waist and one around his neck, all while arching her hips to meet his next thrust.

His lips returned to hers, and, oh, this kiss was so much better than any that had come before. The passion was rawer, the need sharper. His hands were everywhere, all over her, no place left untouched.

"Harper," he growled. "Yeah, just like that."

They strained together and breathed together and panted together, and his pace increased, faster and faster and faster, until the entire bed was shaking, until she was groaning as the pleasure split her in two and he was roaring with satisfaction.

He collapsed on her and rolled to the side, dragging her with him. She found herself sprawled across his chest as he fought to breathe.

"That was…that was…"

"Worth dying for?" she said, then wished she could snatch the words back. "Sorry. Too soon for that kind of—"

"Yeah," he said, sounding confident. "Worth dying for."

Darling man. As replete as she was, sleep tugged at her. She resisted with all her might, suddenly afraid that sleeping would be the thing that pulled her out of this world—out of Levi's arms.

It didn't before, she reminded herself and relaxed. "So what's next?" she asked through a yawn.

"Tomorrow we'll return to the station and find out what else Bright learned from Cliff."

"And then visit Topper," she said, a statement, not a question.

Levi sighed. "I knew you'd want to do that."

"Yeah, because I told you so. I need to know why I painted Lana's hair... I..." A bright flash in her mind, a memory tearing free of the darkness. Suddenly she was lying on that metal slab, cold, so very cold. She could hear a woman crying a few feet away, could hear metal rattling.

The cage. The woman trapped in the cage. A woman who was next in line for the table...which meant Harper had to die. Room had to be made; a new toy had to be played with.

"Well...I know you can't see her, but the girl in the cage is—drumroll, please—your only real friend. You remember her, don't you? Of course you do. She's the pretty one."

Harper had tried to look, but she had failed. *"You're lying, trying to hurt me because you're a miserable little runt whose heart has rotted and you can't find any other way to get to me."*

"You think so? Well, why don't you ask the girl and find out whether or not I spoke true."

"Say something," she had commanded the girl.

Such terrible silence had filled the room.

Ultimately a chuckle had broken through that silence, and it was far more terrible. *"My deepest apologies, but she'll not be saying anything. She's mouthy, your friend. You know she is. I'm afraid I was forced to cut out her tongue."*

Hearing that, Harper's fury had gotten the better of her. She'd thrown taunts at Topper, and he'd retaliated with taunts of his own—followed by a brutal stabbing that had finally stolen her life.

The pain...oh, the pain... She'd endured so much,

those last few minutes should have been more of the same. But she had felt the sting all the way to her spine, had felt her blood leaving her, pooling around her. Had noticed her eyesight dimming. Any second now and she would—

"Aurora Harper!" Levi shouted. "You pay attention to me right now."

Using his voice as a lifeline, she tugged herself back to the present. She blinked into focus, saw him looming over her, knew she was on the bed and swallowed bile. "He threatened Lana," she croaked. "He said she was next."

Levi brushed his fingers over her brow. "She wasn't in the cage, sweetheart. I promise you."

"But what if Cliff wasn't the only person helping him? What if Lana is still a target? She's in danger, Levi. I feel it. Deep down, I know it."

15

AGAINST LEVI'S BETTER judgment, he decided to phone
Bright later that evening and set up a meeting with
Topper before he'd had a chance to check things out.
What he quickly learned? All the times he'd thought
he called the man he'd actually popped in and out of
Bright's office (and home). His mind had simply re-
worked the details.

This time, Bright had been home, alone, in bed. The
man had nearly had a heart attack when Levi shook
him awake.

With a few conditions tacked on, Bright had done
him a solid and arranged for Topper to be brought into
the station early the next morning for questioning about
Clifford. At least, that was the official statement. Levi
and Harper were testing Topper to discover whether or
not he could see the dead. If he could…the real interrogation would begin.

Levi and Harper didn't get much sleep. They arrived
at the station hours early, and waited in the interview
room. Within thirty minutes of their arrival, Peterson
and Harrowitz entered the room behind the two-way

window. He couldn't see them, but he could *feel* Harrowitz, some kind of energy pulsing off him. If either Levi or Harper became upset, they were to leave the room. If they failed to leave, Harrowitz was to vaporize them before they could harm anyone in the building.

Levi was not happy about the threat to Harper, and was determined to keep her calm no matter the course of action he had to take. Already she was shaking, pacing and mumbling about everything that could go wrong. He reached out, latched on to the base of her neck and tugged her into his side.

"Don't talk like that. Why invite trouble? Why worry when everything could go right?"

"I don't like the word *could*."

"Because you're looking at it through negative glasses. Try positive."

A pause, a sigh. "You're right. I'm sorry," she said, and up went her finger to her mouth. "I know better."

He breathed in the cinnamon of her scent. All night he'd held her in his arms. They'd talked, shared things about their pasts. He'd told her about waking up one day to discover his parents were gone forever and he had no place to live, the nightmare of some of his foster families and how the military had given him a purpose, a goal for the future.

She'd told him about the formal gowns her mother made her wear to dinner to practice for her pageants, even when her friends were over, as if every evening at their house was a high-society party. She'd told him about the many classes in deportment she'd had to take, the singing lessons and the bird training—because yes, her mother had wanted her to sing Disney songs while a bird perched on her finger—and about how Lana had taught her how to laugh and stand up for herself.

He'd promised to send Lana a thank-you card. He'd also promised to protect the girl with his (after)life. And he would. Somehow, someway, he was going to end Cory Topper's reign of terror once and for all.

"So…everyone's pretty locked on the no-killing-him idea?" she asked.

How wistful she sounded. He almost laughed. When a delicate-looking female talked about the destruction of evil, it was odd—and maybe kind of wonderful. "Yeah. Pretty locked. Otherwise, I'd be all over him the moment he stepped through the door."

"Darn."

See? She couldn't even cuss properly. "If I have to behave, you have to behave."

"Deal. I guess."

The door opened and a chained Topper finally shuffled inside, his orange jumpsuit so bright it was almost blinding. Tensing, Levi looked him over. The chains stretched from between his wrists, which were in front of him, to his ankles, which were only allowed a few inches of movement at a time.

Harper straightened with a jolt. Levi had been with victims facing their attacker for the first time before. He knew it could be traumatic and cathartic all at once. But he himself was a victim just then. In more ways than one. Yes, Topper had killed him, but that hardly seemed to matter in light of what Harper had suffered.

What were you supposed to do when you faced your *girlfriend's* killer?

End him…

"You know the drill, Topper. Sit down facing the window. I'll be back in a bit."

Bright met Levi's gaze, gave a stiff nod and closed the door, leaving Topper inside.

End him now. He's trapped…

The chains rattled as Topper obeyed, easing into one of only two chairs in the room. A small table stretched out in front of him. His bound wrists remained in his lap as he peered around the room. His gaze swept over Harper, then Levi, without pause.

Levi forced his arms to drop to his sides, severing contact with Harper. It was taking every ounce of his control to behave, as he'd promised Harper. *Not here. Not now.*

Not ever, he thought next, surprising himself. Not just because he would have destroyed something, and could possibly move on to a not so wonderful place, but also because he was…had been…a cop. He wouldn't take the law into his own hands. He just wouldn't. He'd done that before, reacting on emotions, and he'd gotten himself killed. Plus, doing so now would make him no better than the people he'd locked away.

Yes, Topper deserved to suffer. Yes, Topper was evil incarnate. And yes, giving in to the urge to end him would be easy. *Resisting* would be difficult. But he would do it, Levi decided. Topper had earned a punishment, and he would just have to live with it.

His fellow inmates wouldn't treat him well. He was blond and as handsome as a movie star, tanned, with a straight, white smile. He was the kind of man women dreamed of dating. But his eyes…his eyes gave him away. They were bottomless pits of wicked.

Bright had certainly nailed it with his fruit comment. Topper produced pretty disgusting fruit.

"He can't see you, sweetheart, and that means he can't hear you. You'll get no answers here. We should go." *Before I forget my good intentions and get us into trouble.* "Bright will find out if he's working with anyone else."

"The abuse wasn't sexual, you know," she said, her voice trembling. As though in a trance, she wrapped her arms around her middle. "As much as he loved dominating, humiliating and hurting, that would have fit his personality."

A small blessing, considering everything else she'd endured, but one that relieved him. Last night, he'd tried to replace her memory of being bound and helpless with one of being bound and pleasured. A subtle transition, yes, but he hadn't wanted her scared of anything ever again.

"So why did he take us?" she asked. "Why did he do what he did?"

"Maybe he's impotent, and was lashing out. Maybe he's just a twisted, warped little man who enjoys other people's pain. There could be a thousand different reasons, but none of them matter. He did it."

"Well, I think...I think he has mommy issues."

The cop in him switched on. "I know you think there's someone else involved. Did he ever bring another person into his, uh, workshop?" He'd almost said little shop of horrors, but had caught himself just in time.

"No. He took pictures, though. Lots and lots of pictures." Steps slow and measured, Harper moved in front of her tormentor.

Topper continued his study of the room.

"Look at me," she commanded.

His head fell back, and he closed his eyes. In and out he breathed, deep and even, as if savoring something sweet. The corners of his lips lifted into a smug smile, then he straightened, lashing fluttering apart, gaze suddenly alert.

"Well, well," he said in a smooth voice. "Who do we have here, hmm?"

Harper straightened. Levi rushed to her side.

After another deep breath, Topper laughed with apparent glee. "I think my favorite little blonde, Aurora Harper, has finally found me. I can't see you but I can smell the hint of turpentine you carry on your skin."

A tremor moved through her, her hands clenching and unclenching.

A hard knock sounded on the window.

Levi wrapped an arm around her waist. "Calm down, okay?" He wasn't sure whether the words were for her—or himself.

"You stayed here, after all," Topper said, then gave another laugh. "I should have known you'd keep your word. Where are you, darling? Give me a hint."

Her muscles knotted, as if she was preparing to launch over the table and choke the life out of him. Levi tightened his hold. A second later, he felt fingers of electricity stroke through the entire room. Topper didn't seem to notice, but Harper released another gasp.

The hairs on the back of his neck stood on end, as did the hairs on his arms and legs. His skin suddenly felt sensitized, his nerve endings raw.

"Harrowitz," he muttered. "And my guess is, that was just a warning."

Harper licked her lips, squared her shoulders. "I'm

fine," she said, and he caught the threads of her determination.

"I liked you best, you know," Topper whispered, as though sharing a scandalous secret. "I saw you and I just had to have you. Had to add you to my collection. And I'm so glad I did. Your screams…" He closed his eyes again, smiling softly. "Beautiful. A true symphony. And your skin, so smooth and perfect…at first."

Okay. That was it. *Levi's* resolve cracked. This was evil in its purest form, the worst of the worst, the devil made manifest. "Come on, princess," he said, tugging her away. "We're not going to stoop to his level."

"Your scent is fading," Topper said with a pout. "Are you leaving me? But, darling, there's so much more I have to tell you."

Levi gritted his teeth when Harper pulled from his grip.

"Let him talk," she said. "He might reveal something useful."

"Or he might lie and confuse things that much more."

Topper frowned, sniffed. "And what's the scent mingled with yours, hmm? Mint, I think." Another sniff. "Oh, yes. Mint. I remember a certain detective carrying that scent on his skin just prior to his untimely demise. Detective Reid, is that you? Have you decided to join us?"

Levi curled his hands into fists. *Control yourself.*

Harper swiped out her arm, attempting to punch Topper in the nose, driving cartilage into his brain. Her fist simply misted through him, causing no damage.

He shivered, and his grin widened. "Whatever you did, I liked it. Do it again."

Levi's fists tightened so forcefully his knuckles could have ripped through his skin. *Control.*

Another knock on the window, another graze of those electric fingers. A second warning. Probably the last.

Topper said, "You've pleased me so much, I'll tell you a little truth, Harper darling. I'm glad you succeeded. I *want* you to kill me. There's a chance I'll end up just like you. If that happens, if I stick around, we can be together again...for eternity."

Harper backed away. Levi continued to struggle with his rage.

"But even if you decide not to deliver my killing blow, I'll be happy," Topper continued blithely. "I have someone on the outside. Someone other than Clifford. And yes, I know you caught him. The guards bragged about it on the drive over, and to be honest, I confess I'm glad he's going away. He's the reason I'm here. He loves his art, his statements, you know, which is why he left that woman out in the open, for the world to see. I tried to warn him, but he wouldn't listen." He leaned forward, whispering, "He's changed his name, but he was a foster child in my mother's house. That's how we met."

A pause. Both Harper and Levi stiffened. He wasn't done, had more to tell.

"Speaking of childhood friends, don't think I've forgotten about yours. The sweet and spicy Milana."

Harper's hand fluttered to her throat.

"Oh, yes. I know her name and I also know where she is. My...person on the outside has kept tabs on her. If you kill me, maybe I'll become a spirit, maybe I won't. But what's certain? My friend will ensure the same fate befalls your Lana. Death."

16

Doomed if I do, doomed if I don't, Harper thought.
Alive, Topper was a threat to Lana. Dead, Topper was
a threat to Lana.

Lana. Who had yet to be found.

Lana. Whom Harper had to protect at any cost.

At last Harper knew why she hadn't moved on. Not
for vengeance but for her friend's security. Yet, how
was she going to ensure it?

A shudder moved through Harper. Just then she
stood on the roof of the police station, peering down at
the parking lot, where Topper was being shoved into a
van. The sun was bright, the sky a maze of dark blue
and white. Wind blew around her, trees dancing, bushes
shaking, but she felt nothing. A sign of her existence in
another realm, perhaps.

There was only the barest amount of railing to prevent a person from tumbling to the ground. Not that she
cared. She wasn't sure what would happen if she fell,
but it wasn't like she'd die, so…

Levi suddenly materialized beside her.

"About time," she said. After Topper's threat to Lana,

Bright had stomped into the interrogation room to try to pry the name of the "person on the outside" from him. Peterson and Harrowitz had been waiting out in the hall, and had commanded her and Levi to come out.

Harper and Levi had looked at each other in shock as their feet had begun to move one in front of the other, of their own accord, toward the waiting duo. But the moment the door had shut behind her, the tug had loosened and Harper had grabbed Levi's hand, flipped her gaze to the ceiling, indicating the roof, and disappeared. No way had she wanted to stick around and see what else the pair would force her to do.

What she did know—they were scary. Scarier than even Peeping Thomasina, that was for sure.

"We've gotta work on your fight-or-flight reaction," he said wryly. "I stuck around to hear what they had to say."

She forced herself to turn away from the van, now motoring toward the gated exit, and face Levi. Breath caught in her throat. In the sunlight, his skin was… alive. She could see lightning strikes just beneath the surface, the crackle of electricity, a storm of vitality.

"What?" he asked with a frown.

"Nothing," she muttered. Everything. He was so beautiful. That rough face had come to mean so much to her. Protection, safety, humor, passion…the very hope keeping her on her feet and trudging ahead. "Bright will fail. Topper won't reveal the name of the person helping him."

"No, probably not." Levi cupped her cheeks. "This is going to be okay, though."

"I don't see how," she replied. "But I did figure out why I'm here."

"I know, sweetheart. You're here to save your friend. That's why I'm here, too."

Her brow scrunched with confusion. "I don't understand. You knew Lana?"

"No. But I saw what he'd done to you. I was so disgusted with myself for not getting there sooner. Ten minutes, and we could have saved you. I could have saved you from such a terrible fate. Saved myself from guilt and shame."

"I'm not sure I would have wanted to be saved," she muttered. "Not after everything he put me through."

"You would have. You would have found a reservoir of strength, the same way you found one that let you pick yourself up and continue on." He kissed her, gentle at first, then harder, the act spinning into a decadent tasting.

When he lifted his head, she sighed. "What are we going to do?" she asked.

"Did you tell her?" Peterson asked from behind them.

Harper glanced to the side and saw Peterson and Harrowitz in the doorway leading from inside. The wind whipped Peterson's newly green hair from its ponytail, strands slapping at her cheeks. Harrowitz was his usual scowling self.

"Not yet," Levi said. He met Harper's curious gaze. "They want Topper to escape. Or rather, for Topper to think he's escaped. He will be tracked, monitored, and everyone he speaks to brought in for questioning."

"That's dangerous."

"Extremely."

"We won't be taking any extra chances," Peterson said. "He'll escape with the most recent inmate cuffed to his side. That'll be Harrowitz, by the way."

"Why would you do that?" Harper demanded.

"Because they want Lana safe and you happy. Oh, and for a price," Levi added with a roll of his eyes.

O-kay. "We don't have any money or even access to money." Her gaze slid between Peterson and Harrowitz. "You won't do it simply to prevent a criminal from killing other innocent women?"

The perky punk snorted. "Aren't you just an adorable little thing? I gave you one freebie, and told you about your current status. You won't get another. Besides, this entire operation is gonna be costly."

"So what's your price?"

"For as long as we're here, we have to work off our debt," Levi said.

"How?"

"By working for the agency," Peterson replied. "Harrowitz has grown to love you and isn't sure what he'd do without you."

Harrowitz didn't even blink.

"Fine." Peterson shrugged. "There are places humans can't access, but spirits can, things humans can't learn but spirits can. You'll be my eyes and ears, as needed."

A small price to pay for saving Lana from a madman. "Done."

"Good, because you start tonight. We'll be at your apartment at eight, and I'll fill you in. As for now, come down from there. I'm about to barf." Peterson went back inside, dragging Harrowitz with her. The door slammed behind them.

"What will they do with Topper once his other accomplice is captured?" Harper asked.

"Put him back in prison."

"Hardly seems harsh enough."

"He won't enjoy his time there, believe me."

Yeah, if there was one thing she'd learned, it was that you always reaped what you sowed. Topper had sown seeds of pain and death. His harvest would not be pleasant. Harper had sown seeds of love, wanting to protect Lana, and she had reaped a second chance. "Did Bright have any luck finding Lana? I'd feel better if I knew where she was."

"He has someone staked out at your old house, but so far she hasn't returned. Yesterday her credit cards were used by some random guy, but I have a suspicion those cards weren't stolen. I think she gave them away, hoping to throw us off her scent."

"Why do you think that?"

"As close as you two are, it's a safe bet she watched the same television programs you watched."

He was right. "Has Bright been inside the house?"

"Yeah. He didn't see her."

"Even still…you know what I'm going to say next, don't you?"

"Of course I do. You want to search for yourself. You know her better and you might notice something he missed."

"Exactly." She rattled off the address before picturing her old home. A modest one-story on the north side of town, close to a gym but closer to a doughnut shop, her favorite art supply store and Lana's favorite tool shop. Brown and red brick, with dark shutters over the windows, and the most incredible garden in back. Harper had often painted there, breathing in the perfume of the flowers.

Just as before, there was no sense of weightlessness, no change in temperature, but when she opened her eyes, she was in that backyard. A pang of homesickness instantly hit her. She was here, but not here. A part of this world again, but completely separate from it. The roses were in full bloom, the flowers around them a multitude of colors. A man-made pond sat off to the side, the water running through the rocks.

She was glad Lana had kept the place. There were a thousand memories here, most of them good. But even the bad, when they'd fought with each other or gotten their hearts broken by a man, were welcome. They'd become stronger here. They'd grown.

Harper turned on her heel and entered the house without even trying to open a door. Maybe she could have. Maybe she could have caused it to blow open with her emotions, because the wind seemed to kick up several notches as tears formed in her eyes. But she simply walked through the brick, the movement as natural as breathing used to be.

In the kitchen now, she studied the pots hanging from the racks, the cabinets, the counters. Lana had been here, and recently, she realized. There was a cup with leftover orange juice, Lana's favorite, sitting on the bottom of the sink along with a plate with crumbs around the edges.

"Where are you, girl?" she whispered. And where was Levi? He should be here by now.

A quick search of the rest of the house proved Lana wasn't currently there. Harper did her best to ignore the pictures on the wall. Pictures of her and Lana and all the fun they'd had together. Shopping for antiques, eating hot dogs at a carnival, on vacation in the Rockies.

In Lana's bedroom, she found tools scattered all over the floor but no project in sight. No chair or couch or table in need of repair. She found— A gasp lodged in her throat. She found a bloody bandage in the trash.

Blood.

Bile burned a path up her chest. Lana had been hurt. Why had Lana been hurt? Who had hurt her?

"Bright stopped me before I left," Levi said, suddenly beside her.

Her heart skipped a beat—or would have, if she still had one. What she felt was the residual effect of once being alive, she realized. Kinda like muscle memory.

She wanted to look at him, she did, but she couldn't tear her gaze away from the trash. Lana. Bleeding. Hurting.

Dying?

He added, "Traces of blood were found inside Clifford's secret office, and that blood matches Lana's. I'm sorry, princess, but there's no reason to panic, okay? There wasn't a body."

Clifford. More blood. Blood that matched Lana's. Not panic? Please! But before she could work up a good shout, she heard a floorboard creak. Lana, she thought, already running. Levi grabbed her by the arm and jerked her into his body. He placed a finger on her lips, hushing her.

He reached for a gun that he no longer carried, and probably couldn't carry, now that his mind had accepted his new reality, frowned, then shoved her behind him.

"For once, I *will* protect you," he growled.

17

"WHAT YOU DOING here?" Harper heard Lana shout. "Where Harper is? If she hurt, I kill! I kill you dead!"

She nearly fainted from relief. "No need to protect me from Lana." She sprang forward and wrapped her friend in her arms.

"Harper!" Lana hugged her back. "I so happy to see you."

"Me, too. I missed you, you overgrown pain in the butt."

"Missed you, too, my little garden gnome."

They laughed and hugged a thousand more times, and Harper breathed her friend in. Hints of sawdust, with an overlying fragrance of jasmine, Lana's favorite scent, wafted from her.

When they finally parted, Harper looked her friend over, checking for injuries but finding none. Lana had dyed her hair black, with no hint of red. Pretty, but... She frowned. Something was wrong. Something was... off, but what, she couldn't quite figure out.

Does it matter? Here was her friend, appearing healthy, whole and safe. And, for the first time in weeks, relaxed. There were no dark circles of exhaustion and guilt under her eyes, no hollows from grief in her cheeks.

"What have you been doing?" Harper demanded.

"Thinking." Lana nibbled on her bottom lip and shifted from one foot to the other. She wore a black top and baggy black pants, with combat boots on her feet. "Planning."

"Planning what? And why are you walking around in combat boots?" Lana believed high heels were a feminine staple, and constantly complained about Harper's refusal to decorate her feet as "the good Lord intended."

A shrug of one seemingly delicate shoulder. "I was going to come to you today." Gone was the heaviest part of her accent, her emotions now under control.

"Planning what?" she insisted.

"Just a minute, princess. How'd you sneak in and out without detection?" Levi demanded of Lana.

Her friend snorted. "As if I could not spot the guard dog out there. Child's play."

He was the next to snort. "Well, it wasn't smart to come to your own house to hide out."

Lana waved away his words. "So how you be?" she asked Harper, eyeing her up and down. Perhaps her emotions weren't quite under control yet.

"I'm good." Thanks to Levi. "Learned a lot these past few days, most of it disturbing, but I'm surprisingly good."

"Promise?"

"Promise. But what about you? You took off without a word and—"

"Unfair!" A stomp of Lana's foot. "I left a note and—"

"—I wasn't yet done with the painting. Now I am and—"

"—told you not to worry. I can take care of myself and I was so afraid my coworkers would turn on you if I stuck around, thinking you would hurt me—"

"—I know I wasn't predicting the future when I painted you, only giving voice to my own fears."

Silence.

"Holidays are gonna be fun," Levi muttered.

Harper tried not to smile. "Listen. I wasn't painting you, Lana. I was painting me."

Lana had been trying not to smile, as well, but now frowned, looking as sad as she had for the past few weeks. "You know, don't you? About yourself?"

Before Harper could reply, Levi came up behind her and cupped the back of her neck. He applied a bit of pressure, and she glanced over at him. Leaning down, he placed the gentlest of kisses on her lips. There was something in his gaze, a sadness that mirrored Lana's maybe, and that disturbed her.

"I'll leave you two alone, let you talk."

"Thank you," she said, wanting to ask him what thoughts danced through his head but knowing he wouldn't answer in front of an audience.

"Shout if you need me."

"I will."

He gave her another kiss, and Lana made gagging sounds. He flipped her off before he walked away.

Lana wiggled her eyebrows. "I knew he was into you, but wow, you worked superfast."

Heat bloomed in her cheeks, spreading all the way to her collarbone. "I really like him," she admitted.

"You should. He's sexy."

"And smart."

"And sexy."

"And protective."

"And sexy."

"And within hearing distance," he called from outside. "The window is open, and you two aren't exactly quiet."

The heat in her cheeks intensified, but then Lana laughed and she followed suit, and it felt so good to find humor in something, she just went with it. They laughed until they were doubled over. If she'd been alive, she might have peed herself.

When they finished, Lana led her to the couch and eased down. Harper sat beside her, suddenly curious about why she didn't ghost through the material. Or was she really hovering, her mind showing her only what she wanted to see?

Lana hooked a lock of hair behind her ears. "I'm sorry I lied to you. I just, I didn't know what else to do, and I know, that's no excuse. If I could go back... Anyway, seeing you every day, knowing you were dead, knowing what you were about to remember, knowing what you suffered was my fault...I was breaking down and I didn't want to be the cause of any more of your pain."

"It wasn't your fault. It was never your fault!"

"I left you at gallery to make hookup. I should have stayed put, should have walked to car with you."

"Cliff was working with the killer. He set me up, drugged me. And if they hadn't gotten me that night, they would have gotten me another. I'm glad you weren't there. If they'd taken you, too..." A shudder rocked her entire body.

"I know about Cliff," Lana whispered. Tears cascaded down her cheeks. "I went to gallery to talk to him."

"What!"

"I tell you what happened in a minute. Right now, you have to tell me what was done to you. The details were kept out of the news, and I have to know."

No, that wasn't information she would ever share with Lana. Her friend might want to know, perhaps hoping the details were not as bad as she imagined, but she didn't need to know. Knowing wouldn't help her, would only hurt and torment her. "I'm still in the process of remembering," she said, and that was the truth. She remembered most, but not all.

A barely perceptible nod. "When I discover you missing, I panic. That so was not like you. I went to police, but they say you were probably with someone. I say I know you better than that. They say give it twenty-four hours. So I wait, asking around the area but no one had seen or heard anything and Cliff…that slime! He said he thought he heard you mention going to bar to celebrate, which I thought was odd, but I now know he was sending police in the wrong direction."

Harper stayed quiet, sensing her friend needed to purge these details from her mind.

"And then you show up here, as if nothing is wrong, but I knew truth. I could tell what you were. Knew you'd died. I'm so sorry." The tears fell in earnest.

Lana had cried just like that when Harper came home all those weeks ago. She remembered that day. Lana had taken one look at her and burst into great big sobs. Her knees had collapsed, and Harper hadn't known what was wrong. All she'd known was that her friend had left with a man—she'd thought it was the next day after the gallery showing—and feared Lana had been raped.

But Lana had assured her that while the man had turned out to be a jerk, he hadn't harmed her.

"You have nothing to be sorry for," Harper said.

"Sometimes people don't know what they are, that they are d-dead, and you did not. I didn't want to be the one to tell you, could barely face the fact for myself. So I pretend all is normal, fine, and I know, I know, I shouldn't have. I should have told the truth then, too, but then you gravitate toward a building I'd had to watch many times in the past while on the job, and I knew you were close to answer, so I couldn't let you go without me."

"So you moved in with a bunch of spirits, inside a dump, knowing your coworkers could be watching your every move."

More nibbling on her bottom lip, another nod. "If they had thought you were a danger to me or anyone else, they would have tried to force you to move on. I didn't want them any more involved in your life than they already were, and so I left you and sent you to Tulsa. I thought answers would help you move on under your own steam, knew that leaving on your own would be far better for you, but I also couldn't stand to see you go. I am sorry," she said again.

"You are the craziest, sweetest friend anyone has ever had, you know that? I love you *so* much, and I forgive you for keeping secrets."

"Hold that thought," Lana said, shifting guiltily. "I have to tell you something else."

Harper moaned. Could she withstand something else? "What?"

Lana licked her lips. "Just that I...love you."

Oh. Well. Good. "But that stops today," Harper said sternly. She even wagged a finger in Lana's face. "Not the loving part, but the throwing away your life for me part. You did nothing wrong. You are *not* responsible for what happened to me, and you have to stop punishing yourself. And don't try to deny you were punishing yourself. I watch *Dr. Phil* so, of course, I know my psychology."

Lana peered down at her lap, where her fingers were wringing together. "Well, I have to tell you something else, too. It's about my future...."

"Don't worry. I won't let anything happen to you." She told her friend about Topper's threat. "We've got a plan to find his accomplice before the accomplice finds you."

Lana smiled and rubbed her hands together. "I hope he does send someone after me."

"You are not going to put yourself in danger, do you hear me?"

"You can't stop me."

"Can, too."

"Can't."

"Can."

Annnd the slap fight began. They smacked on each other's hands as if they were only three years old. But this was par for the course with them, and so familiar Harper was soon laughing again.

Levi appeared in the entryway, glaring down at them. "Seriously?" he said. "This is how two grown women conduct themselves?"

Harper stuck her tongue out at him.

His lips pursed. "You'll have to excuse us, Lana."

Bending down, he hefted Harper over his shoulder, so that she hung over him like a sack of potatoes.

"Wait," Lana said. "I have to tell—"

"No, you don't. Which way is your room, Harper?"

"I'll never tell!"

"That way," Lana the traitor said, pointing.

"Thank you," Levi replied.

"No need. I'll demand some sort of payment one day."

Harper tried not to giggle. This was almost…normal. Well, what a normal family would be like, anyway, she thought. Teasing one another, helping one another. And she knew that's what Levi was doing right now. Helping both her and Lana. They'd discussed some heavy topics, were both highly emotional right now and needed a break. This was his way of providing one without making it obvious.

I think I might love him.

Once inside the bedroom, he kicked the door shut with his foot and tossed Harper on the bed. Just as the couch had been solid, the bed was solid and she bounced up and down. She didn't have time to catch her breath, because he was on her by the time she hit the mattress the second time, pinning her down with his muscled weight.

Eyes of jade-green bore into her, past clothes, past skin, past bone and into the heart of her. "You're a good friend," he said, his tone gruff.

"So is she."

"Yeah, but you're the one who went to hell and back." She didn't have to tell him what had been done to her; he'd seen. He knew firsthand. "Make me forget," she whispered, "if only for a little while."

"I will." And, oh, did he.

18

At eight o'clock sharp, Levi, Harper and Lana strode into the King's Landing apartment, where Peterson and Harrowitz waited on the couch. Now that his spiritual eyes were open, so to speak, Levi could see the place as it really was. A death dungeon.

The furniture was dirty, ratty and not fit for the streets. Dilapidated boards had been pulled from the floor and there were holes in the ceiling. There was a window, but it was boarded up and spray-painted with gang signs. Yeah. *This* was the place he remembered raiding on the worst of his drug busts.

Malevolence practically dripped in the air, a darkness, a dankness that stuck to your skin, something you would never be able to wash off. Every so often, the walls rattled, the floor shook, dust pluming the air.

How could Peterson and Harrowitz stand to come here? How could Lana have stood to *live* here?

Lana. He'd listened to her conversation with Harper, and had fallen the rest of the way in love with Harper. Yeah. Love. He hadn't realized it, had even denied it, but he'd already been well on his way.

He loved the stubborn little baggage with all that he was. There was no denying so real a truth, not any longer. They were bonded in the most elemental of ways. He'd seen her abused body laid out on a slab. He'd died to avenge her. To protect others, yeah, that, too, but the bulk of his rage had stemmed from what had been done to her, so fragile-looking a female.

Then he'd met her and discovered the teasing smile and the sad frown, the confidence and the worries, the absolute love she had for those she trusted. He wanted to be the man she trusted, now and always.

And if they left this life, so be it. Everyone left at some point. He wasn't going to let the fear of losing her stop him from, well, living.

How did she feel about him? he wondered. Needing to touch her, he wound his arm around her. She rested her head on his shoulder, as she liked to do, her softness the perfect contrast to the hard line of his body.

"Who is this?" Lana demanded.

"The rescue squad. Glad you could finally make it," Peterson grumbled. She leaned forward to dig through a black case.

"Finally?" Harper snorted. "We're right on time."

Lana looked Peterson up and down, studying her as if she were under a microscope. When she spoke, however, she directed the words to Harper. "I thought you say 'that jerk Harrowitz' was man. He looks a little womanish to me."

Levi had to press his lips together to cut off his laugh.

Even Harrowitz experienced a twitch at the corner of his mouth, his first ever sign of amusement.

Peterson ran her tongue over her teeth. "Har, har. As if you don't recognize my voice, Lana Bo Bana. Good job with the painting," she said to Harper. "You took a face like Lana's and actually made it pretty."

"Will you two stop?" Harper said. "I'm currently in shock because Lana actually lived here for several weeks, without dying from some flesh-eating bacteria." She must see the truth, as well.

"I know! You *so* owe me."

"So, Lana," Peterson said, looking the girl over. "Why didn't you tell me you had been—"

"Enough chitchat," Levi interjected. He knew what Peterson was going to say. Had figured it out back at the house, and that was the real reason he'd left the two girls alone. But Lana hadn't confessed what had happened to her, and he wasn't going to spill for her. At least, not yet.

Harper had claimed to want nothing to do with secrets, but when Lana had tried to admit the truth, she'd stopped her.

After Topper was taken care of, Levi would tell her. Harper deserved to know the truth, but he didn't want her distracted by it right now. He just wanted her safe.

"Why are we here, Peterson?" he added. "To discuss our feelings or the case you've got for us?"

Peterson blinked rapidly, as if trying to jump-start her brain. Harrowitz finally took things into his own hands and grabbed several sheets of paper from the case, placing them in her lap.

"Okay, yes, well," she said, and there was that sad smile again, coming out to play. Bingo. She'd just figured it out. "Well, that girl, the one who popped in and out of here and told you some guy was coming for you? She was Topper's first victim."

Breath caught in Harper's throat as her hand fluttered over her heart, where sympathy had to be welling. While she had a viper's tongue, she had a cotton-candy heart.

Knowing the case as he did, Levi said, "Gloria Topper," pieces suddenly fitting together. "His sister." He'd seen pictures of her. Should have realized the truth before now, but his faulty memory hadn't let him.

"Yes. Though no one linked him to the crime until the OKPD busted into his home and found pieces of her remains. A few years ago, she disappeared from her college campus. Since her death she's freaked out several humans," Peterson said, "caused trouble in the city, destroyed an entire building." Her gaze pinned Harper in place as she spoke that last one. "A few days ago, someone spotted her, followed her here and asked After Moonrise to intervene. OKC was all set to act, but I interceded and took over. I'm sweet like that."

"You want us to help you get rid of her," Harper said. "To force her to move on."

"Yes, again."

"No," Harper said, not really surprising him. "I don't care who she's related to, she was hurt. Of course she's had a hard time adjusting."

Uh-oh. Harper had just decided to protect another female.

Peterson rolled her eyes. "This girl is causing trouble, *hurting* people, threatening people. She must be stopped. If you can't—"

The entire building shook, the dust suddenly so thick Peterson and Harrowitz had to cough to breathe.

"If you want our help with the brother, you'll help us with the sister," Peterson said when she calmed. "Because, if we don't send her packing, someone else will, and we deserve the bonus, no one else. Callous of me? Maybe. But unlike you, I still have bills to pay, and I *am* doing the world a favor. Besides, she'll be better off with the memory of her suffering no longer tormenting her."

Okay, now, that ticked Levi off. Basically, she'd just said Gloria Topper would be better off dead-dead, as though she didn't deserve a second chance. And maybe she didn't. What did Levi know? He couldn't see to the heart of the girl, didn't know her thoughts or emotions. But he wasn't going to be the one who made the decision about her fate.

"You know what?" he said. "Thanks for your help, but no, thanks. We've got this. We'll handle Gloria on our own."

Peterson looked him over for a long while, then sighed. "She's not as innocent as you think. She—"

"Is protected by us," Lana snapped. "End of story."

Harper raised her chin. "Yeah. What she said."

"Fine." Another sigh. "We'll—"

The building shook again, this time so forcefully Peterson was thrown into Harrowitz's lap. Levi would have laughed, considering he, Harper and Lana were able to remain exactly as they were, but as the two struggled to right themselves, Gloria whisked into the room. Her hair flew wildly behind her, and her arms were spread wide. A shrill scream erupted from her.

Eyes as dark as the night, she flew over Peterson and Harrowitz, the hem of her dress seeming to envelop them in a black cloud. Next, Peterson was the one to scream. Harrowitz grunted, as if in pain.

Levi tried to step forward, intending to pull the girl off the humans. Only, she held out her hand, somehow locking him in place. His boots seemed to be glued to the floor. Frowning, he tugged one leg, then the other, using all of his strength. No luck. He budged not an inch.

"What did you do to me?" he demanded.

"He comes, he comes, he comes." Her laugh was as evil as her eyes. "There's nothing you can do to stop him. I won't let you. Mommy did special things with her foster boys and ignored her real son. He became my baby, and I love my baby. I give him what he wants, whatever he wants. And he wants the girl."

Topper? Oh…no. *No.* But there was no denying the truth. The sister they'd been trying to defend was the "person on the outside" working with Topper. Had been the one to spy on Harper and Lana, to relay the information to Topper.

She'd taken her second chance and flushed it down the toilet.

"Gloria," Harper said, her voice as gentle as a summer rain. "Listen to me. You don't want to do this."

"He comes, he comes, and he'll be happy. Finally happy."

Determined, Harper tried again. "Gloria. I know he hurt you. He hurt me, too, but we don't have to be afraid of him any longer. We don't have to do what he wants. We can stop him. We can—"

Peterson slid to the floor, out from under that dress. Her body writhed, her hands flat on her ears, her eyes squeezed shut. Her skin was devoid of color.

Harrowitz rolled on top of her, and Levi couldn't tell whether he did it to guard her or because he had no control of his actions. His body was bowed as tight as a rubber band.

"Harper," Lana said, her tone layered with foreboding.

"Gloria," Harper pleaded. "Please, listen to me."

"Harper," Lana said again.

"Quiet!" Gloria demanded, and though Lana's mouth moved, no more words escaped. "I've been around a lot longer than you and I've picked up a few tricks. You will do what I say. You will wait here, and you will give yourself to my baby. You will do whatever he desires."

Tears pooled in Harper's eyes. Levi knew what was wrong. She didn't want to fight one of Topper's victims, even one as disturbed as Gloria, but they were going to have to. Otherwise, Gloria would destroy everyone in this room.

Gloria glanced toward the door, smiled serenely. "He's on his way. So close, finally so close."

Levi tugged at his legs all the harder. When that failed, he bent down to untie his boots. "What do you mean, on his way?"

"He's like you. He's like me. The guards couldn't stop him. I wouldn't let them. He killed himself, and now he comes."

No way. Just no way. Topper…a spirit, a bad, bad spirit…on his way here…but even with the laces undone, Levi couldn't force his feet to move. Frustrated, he tangled a hand through his hair. He had to break free. Had to get control of this situation.

Harper wrapped her arms around her middle. "If…if you're telling the truth, and he comes to this apartment, I can promise you he'll never leave it. I won't let him."

"You will do what he says!" Gloria screeched. "You will."

"I won't."

"You will. I'll make you." Gloria lurched forward, colliding with Harper. Because the two existed on the same plane, they were solid to each other. Gloria could not envelop her as she'd done the humans and the two ended up fighting like alley cats, Gloria clawing, scratching and ripping at Harper's hair while Harper punched like a man.

Levi glanced over at Peterson and Harrowitz. They were no longer writhing, but they were no longer lucid, either. They would be no help. His attention moved to Lana. She was trying to speak, but couldn't.

"Come on, princess," he urged. If Harper could subdue the girl—if the girl had lied about Topper—they might walk away from this.

If not, and Levi couldn't get free, Harper would have to face Topper all over again. And this time, Levi would have to watch every second of it. Helpless, useless.

Doomed.

19

BECAUSE OF LANA, Harper was not a dainty fighter. She was brass knuckles and knee-to-balls all the way, as poor Levi knew so well. She swung a fist and nailed Gloria in the nose. No blood poured, but the girl's head did twist to the side. She threw another punch and another and another, until the girl—clearly a novice, relying only on emotion—couldn't recover from the impact.

Gloria's legs buckled and she hit the ground. Harper leaped on top of her, threw a right, a left, another right, boom, boom, boom. The girl's brain had to be rattling against her skull. All the while, the building continued to shake, and she wasn't sure if Gloria was responsible—or her. Rage, so much rage, burned in her chest.

She had to get herself under control.

She wasn't like Topper, wasn't controlled by her baser urges. She could stop when she needed to stop. And she would.... Harper threw one last punch and lifted her arms in a gesture of innocence.

See? She'd stopped.

Gloria remained sagged on the floor, her eyes closed, her lips slack.

"Give me your shirt," Harper said to Levi.

At first, she got no reaction from him. She glanced up.

He gave her a slow, proud grin. "Good job, princess. I mean, uh, hoss. I'll never call you princess again, I swear." He tugged his shirt up by the collar, revealing the most mouthwatering chest and stomach ever to be created. Hard-won muscles, row after row of strength.

She rolled Gloria over and used the material to tie her arms behind her back.

"I still can't move," he said.

"What did she do to you?"

"Have *no* idea."

She straightened and walked to Lana, who had gone motionless, her eyes glazed over. A blackout? Harper waved her hand in front of her friend's face. Again, no reaction. "What's wrong with her?"

"Have to...send girl...away," Peterson said.

Harper's attention jerked to her. A pale, sweaty and shaky Harrowitz was stretched out beside her, gently stroking her cheek.

"Her evil...have to...get rid.... Move on...only way."

Move on. Of course. Someone would have to force Gloria to move up...or down. Probably down.

"Well, that won't be happening, because Daddy's home."

That voice! Dread washed through Harper as she spun toward the sound of it. Her eyes widened, and a tremor of fear swept through her. Gloria had told the truth. Topper had killed himself, and his spirit had remained on earth. She knew—because he'd just misted through the front door.

"Don't you dare go near her," Levi growled.

"What will you do if I do?" Topper grinned his smug smile as he surveyed the room, but his gaze quickly returned to Harper. "My sister has been so much more useful in death than in life. First she watched you, reporting your every move, and I must say, I was quite happy to hear you were with the cop. I mean, how thrilling will it be to tear the two of you apart? Then, of course, she disabled you." His gaze landed on Gloria, who had yet to awaken. He shrugged, unconcerned. "I told you we would be together again, little Harper."

Of course he remembered who and what he was in death, she thought. As wicked as he was, he loved the life he'd lived, had no regrets. There wasn't anything he'd wanted to forget or apologize for.

"Harper," Levi said.

Topper ignored him. His gaze remained on Harper as he reached out to play with a lock of Lana's hair. Lana gave no reaction. "This is going to be fun, don't you think, my darling?"

Fear bloomed in Harper's chest, joining what remained of the rage. *Must stop him.*

She stepped forward, only to stop as a realization formed. Topper could touch Lana. Could touch Lana as Gloria could touch Harper.

Lana was a spirit.

Lana had died, sometime between when she'd left their apartment and when they'd reunited. No wonder something had been off inside their old home. For the first time in weeks, Harper had been able to touch her, too.

Shock and grief joined the other emotions, but she brushed everything aside. They would get in the way, hinder her, and even delight Topper.

"You and me," she said to him. "Here and now."

"No!" Levi roared, jerking at legs that refused to obey him. "Why don't you try me? I'd love a chance to thank you for my current condition."

Again, Topper ignored him. "You think you can take me?"

"You don't have a Taser and I'm not drugged," Harper said. "I'm not restrained, either. So yeah, I think I can take you. You always thought more highly of yourself than you should have," she added, mimicking what he'd once told her. "A trait taught to you by your sister-mom?"

That wiped the amusement from his expression. "She was never my mother! My mother was beautiful and wonderful, and I was her very special boy. She loved me more than all the other boys, I don't care what my sister says."

Harper didn't waste another second. While he was distracted and emotional, she launched at him. The action was unexpected, and she was able to knock him back into the door. Air seemed to push from his lungs. Air…breath…as warm and fragrant as before, in that cold, bright room of horror.

Logically she knew he couldn't possibly be breathing, that her mind was simply playing tricks on her. But the memory trapped her for a moment, allowing Topper to grab her by the hair, swing her around and slam her into the wood. Stars winked before her eyes. He fit his body against hers, no gaps between them.

"Fight!" Levi called. "With everything you have, fight!"

"Fight. I like that idea," Topper said against her ear. *With everything you have….* She'd never gone looking for this battle, but it had been dropped on her, anyway. She *would* fight. And this time, she would win.

Harper elbowed him in the stomach. He hunched over. She spun around and kneed him in the chin. He flew backward, landing on his back.

She jumped on him, straddling his waist. "Not so cocky now, are you?" Punch, punch, punch. Each blow filled her with new strength, empowering her. How many times had she longed to do this? Countless. How many nights had she lain on that cold slab of metal and dreamed of doing this? Countless more.

He fought back, punching her and bucking to dislodge her, but she kept at him. Finally he managed to work his legs between them and shove her off. Before she could regain her footing, he crawled away—right in front of Levi.

"Much obliged. You just made my job easy." Levi bent over and punched, punched, punched, doing to Topper what Harper had done to Gloria.

From the corner of her eye, she saw Harrowitz crawl to Gloria. Saw Harrowitz place a hand just over Gloria's heart. Saw a bright light spark between them and leap to the floor, growing and tracing a line around Gloria's body. Gloria's now-writhing body. Flecks of black sparked from her. Harrowitz said something, but Harper couldn't make out the words. A moment later, Gloria's body was sucked through the floorboards, vanishing.

Harrowitz sagged onto the floor, even the light disappearing.

Harper rushed to his side. "Come on. You have to do that to Topper. Please!"

His eyelids were slitted, his eyes rolled back, revealing only the whites.

"Come on!" She tried to slap him across the face, but her hand went right through him.

Still, he blinked as if he'd felt something, sharply drew in a breath and frowned. "Do that again, and I'll return fire."

His voice…he'd never spoken before and now she knew why. He'd either been choked and his voice box broken, or he'd been slashed across the throat and hadn't healed right.

He dragged himself up and crawled to Topper.

She followed.

"Stop," he told Levi in that damaged voice. "You can move now, Levi, so move away from Topper."

"Can't." Punch, punch, punch. "Feels too good."

Understand that. "You have to stop, Levi," she said. She wanted this over. One way or another. "If you don't, this can't end."

Surprisingly, Levi obeyed *her*. He stopped. Teeth bared, he looked up and caught her gaze. She knew how hard that had been for him, and realized in that moment just how much she loved him. He'd do anything she asked, she realized. He wanted her safe, he wanted her happy. A woman couldn't ask for more than that.

Lana suddenly appeared at her side and kicked Topper in the teeth. One of them went flying like a piece of candy. "That for hurting my friend." Another kick, another lost tooth. "That for breaking my heart."

Levi grabbed the man's arms before he could retaliate, and Harrowitz was finally able to place his hand over Topper's heart. He glanced up at Lana to make sure she was done, and when she nodded, he closed his eyes to concentrate.

Harper grabbed her friend's hand, watching as the

same thing happened to Topper that had happened to
Gloria. A bright light sparked, forming a ring around
the body. Black flicked up. Topper writhed and kicked,
screamed and pleaded, and at one point, Harrowitz
looked ready to topple over, but in the end, Topper was
sucked under the floorboards, disappearing for good.

Harrowitz passed out.

Lana released a cry of relief.

Harper let her go and threw herself into Levi's waiting arms.

"It's over," he said, hugging her tight. "Finally over."

"I love you." She couldn't keep the words inside. If
he freaked, he freaked, but he would learn to—

"I love you, too. *So* much."

Thank the Lord! "Are we going to disappear, too?"
she asked, pulling back only enough to peer up into his
eyes. "We did what we stayed here to do. Well, most of
it." They hadn't protected Lana, but they had protected
others from Topper's evil.

They both stiffened, waiting, expectant, gazing
around the room.

"I told you," Peterson said, making her way to Harrowitz. She was the one to stroke his cheek this time,
surprising Harper with her gentleness. Clearly, the two
had feelings for each other. "Some people stick around
for years, even after they've done what they originally
set out to do. Or did I not tell you that? Whatever. The
stronger the spirit is, the happier the spirit is, and the
happier the spirit is, the more likely it is to stick around."

And Harper was happy. Happier than she'd ever
been. "Is Harrowitz gonna be all right?"

"Yeah. He just burned through all of his energy. All
he needs is time."

She was right. A short while later, he was working his way to his feet. He swayed and paled, and had to hold himself up with a hand on the wall, but he was back in control.

"Thank you," she said. They couldn't have done this without him.

He nodded.

Peterson helped him lumber out of the apartment, turning to look at Harper and Levi. "See you tomorrow?"

As Harper moaned, Levi slammed the door in the woman's face...but not quickly enough for Harper to miss the wink Peterson shot them over her shoulder.

And okay, with the immediate danger of losing her life and her love over with, and their audience gone, she had some business to take care of.

"You!" she said to Lana, spinning to face her friend. "You're dead."

Lana backed away guiltily. "Not my fault. I was poking around the gallery, trying to find out how Topper had gotten you. Cliff caught me. We fought. I was injured. He knocked me out."

Her poor Lana! "Where's your body?"

"I don't know. A ditch probably. When I came to, I knew immediately that I was dead and that he had done it, but not how."

"Why was there blood in the house, then?"

"Cliff was covering his tracks, is my guess," Levi said. "Planting evidence that would lead the cops in the wrong direction, just the way he gave a false lead when Harper disappeared after her showing."

Lana nodded. "Your man has to be right. That's what the bad guys do in the movies."

"Argh! I hate that you suffered like that." Harper threw herself into Lana's arms next. They hugged and cried, and then Levi joined them, hugging them both, as well.

"All this death," Lana said. "But Cliff will get what's coming to him."

"Sooner or later, people always do, don't they?" Harper said. "Look at Topper."

"And now, we're safe. We're happy," Levi said.

And they were one weird family, Harper thought, grinning. "So what do we do now?"

Lana clapped with enthusiasm. "Now we find me a date, of course. I need a happily ever after, too."

"Speaking of dates," Levi said. "I owe Bright a blind date for his undead stalker."

"Trolling for spirits, you two? Really?" Harper laughed.

"Maybe. I feel bad for everyone else, not having what we have." Levi leaned down to kiss her. "You are happy, right?"

"Very much so."

"Aw, how disgustingly sweet," Lana said, wiggling her brows. "Here's a thought. Maybe we could just share Levi."

"No," Harper and Levi shouted in unison.

"Okay, okay. Geez."

"Don't worry. I've already got the perfect guy in mind for you," Levi added. "He's in 409…."

* * * * *

The Darkest
CRAVING

CHAPTER ONE

New York City
Present day

JOSEPHINA AISLING PEERED down at the male splayed across the motel room bed. He was an immortal warrior, beautiful in a way no mortal could ever hope to be. Silky hair of jet, chestnut and flax spilled over the pillow, the multicolored strands forming a flawless tapestry, inviting the eye to linger a minute, then a minute more…sweet mercy, why not forever?

His name was Kane. He had long, boyish lashes, a strong nose and a stubborn chin. At six feet four, he was cut with the kind of muscle only earned on the bloodiest of battlefields. Though he wore stained and dirty pants, she knew a large butterfly tattoo dominated the right side of his hip, the ink thick and black, a little jagged. The tops of the wings stretched over the material and every so often tiny waves rippled through them, as though the insect struggled to lift from his skin—or burrow deeper.

Either was possible. The tattoo was a mark of absolute, utter evil, a visible sign of the demon contained inside Kane's body.

Demon…she shuddered. Rulers of hell. Liars, thieves. Murderers. They were darkness without any hint of light. They lured and tempted. They ruined, tortured and destroyed.

But Kane wasn't the demon.

Like all of her race, the mighty Fae, she had spent a good portion of her life studying Kane and his friends—the Lords of the Underworld. In fact, at the command of the Fae king, spies had spent countless centuries following the warriors, watching and reporting back. Scribes had then printed books with stories and pictures of what they'd witnessed. Mothers had bought those books and read them to their children. Then, when those children had grown up, they had made their own purchases, the need to know what happened next too strong to ignore.

The Lords of the Underworld had become the stars of the best and the worst soap opera in Séduire, the realm of the Fae.

Josephina always ate up every detail. Especially those about the ultra sexy Paris and the devastatingly lonely Torin. Kane, the beautiful tragedy, was a close third. She could probably recite his life history better than she could her own.

He was thousands of years old. He'd only had four serious girlfriends in his lifetime. Although, for a while, he'd had a string of meaningless one-night stands. He'd fought in bloody battle after bloody battle with his enemy, the Hunters. Three times, they'd managed to capture and torture him—and she'd waited, breathless, to hear of his escape.

Going back even further, to the beginning, he and his friends had stolen and opened Pandora's box, unleashing the demons from inside. The Greeks had been in power at the time, and they'd decided to punish the warriors by turning their bodies into receptacles for the very evil they'd freed. Kane carried Disaster. The others carried Promiscuity, Disease, Distrust, Violence, Death, Pain, Wrath, Doubt, Lies, Misery, Secrets and Defeat. Each creature came with a nearly debilitating curse.

Promiscuity had to sleep with a new woman every day or he weakened and died.

Disease couldn't touch another living creature without starting a plague.

Disaster caused catastrophes everywhere Kane went, a fact that sliced at Josephina's heart and resonated deep. Her entire life *was* a disaster.

"Don't touch me," he muttered, his voice a sharp, callous rasp. Powerful legs kicked the already battered sheets away. "Hands off. Stop. I said stop!"

Poor Kane. Another nightmare plagued him.

"No one's touching you," she assured him. "You're safe."

He calmed, and she released a relieved breath.

When she'd first stumbled upon him, he'd been chained to a dais in hell, his chest cavity split open, his ribs spread and exposed, his wrists and ankles hanging on by fraying tendons.

He'd looked like a slab of beef at the local butcher's.

I'll have a two-pound rump roast and a pound of ground chuck.

Gross. Just gross. I'm thoroughly disgusted with you. Over the years, she'd spent so much time alone, conversing with herself had become her only source of amusement…and sadly, companionship. *I would have ordered four pounds of pork loin.*

Despite his condition, finding him was the best thing to ever happen to her. He was her ticket to freedom. Or possibly…acceptance?

Princess Synda, her half sister and the Fae's *most bestest* female ever born, wasn't a Lord, but she carried the demon of Irresponsibility. Apparently, there had been more demons than naughty, box-stealing warriors, and the excess had been given to the inmates of Tartarus—an underground prison for immortals. Synda's first husband had been one of those inmates, and somehow, when the male had died, the demon had wormed its way inside her.

When the king of the Fae had learned of it, he'd launched a hunt for details about the cause—and the solution. So far, everyone had come up empty.

I could bring Kane to a meeting of the Fae High Court, show him off, let him answer any questions the congregation has, and my father might see me, really see me, for the first time in my life.

Her shoulders drooped. *No, I'm not ever going back.*

Josephina had always been, and would always be the royal whipping girl, there to receive the punishments Synda the Beloved was due.

Synda was always due.

Last week, in a fit of temper, the princess had burned to the ground the royal stables, and all of the animals trapped inside. Josephina's sentence? A ticket to the Never-ending—a portal leading into hell.

There, a day was like a thousand years and a thousand years like a day, so, for what had seemed like an endless eternity, she had fallen down, down, down a blackened pit. She had screamed, but no one had heard. Had begged for mercy, but no one had cared. Had cried, but had never found an anchor.

Then, she and another girl had landed in the center of hell.

How startling to realize she'd never actually been alone.

The girl had been a Phoenix, a race descended from the Greeks. Every full-blooded warrior possessed the ability to rise from the dead, time and time again, growing stronger after every resurrection—until the final death came, and there could be no more bodily restoration.

Kane began to thrash and moan again.

"I'm not going to let anything happen to you," she told him.

Again, he stilled.

If only the Phoenix had responded to her so well. When the girl had first seen her, hatred had lanced at her, hatred going far beyond what the children of the Titans—like Josephina—and the children of the Greeks usually felt for each other. But even still, the Phoenix hadn't tried to kill her, had instead allowed her to follow her through the cave, searching for the exit, without having to exert any of her own waning energy. Like Josephina, she'd just wanted out.

They had stumbled past crimson-splattered walls, inhaling the fetid stink of sulfur. Grunts and groans had reverberated in their ears, creating a terrible symphony their deprived senses hadn't been ready for. Then they'd stumbled upon the mutilated warrior. Josephina had recognized him, despite his condition, and stopped.

Awe had filled her. There, in front of her—her!—had been one of the infamous Lords of the Underworld. She hadn't known how she could help him, when she could barely help herself, but she'd been determined to try. Whatever proved necessary.

A lot had proven necessary.

She looked at him. "You were my first and only opportunity to achieve my new greatest desire," she admitted, "something I definitely couldn't do on my own. And as soon as you wake up, I'm going to need you to make good on your promise."

And then...

She sighed, quieted. She brushed her fingertips over his brow.

Even in his sleep, he flinched. "Don't," he snarled. "I'll *destroy* you, piece by piece. You and your entire family."

He wasn't bragging, wasn't issuing a hollow threat. He would ensure it happened, and he would probably smile the entire time.

Probably? Ha! He would. Typical Lord.

"Kane," she said, and again, he calmed. "I think maybe it's time to wake you up. My family is out there, and they want me back. While a thousand years passed for me inside that pit, only a day passed for them. Since I failed to return to Séduire, Fae soldiers are probably hunting me."

To add to her bowl of miserypuffs, *the Phoenix* was definitely hunting her, determined to enslave her and avenge the wrong Josephina had done her during their escape.

"Kane." She gently shook his shoulder. His skin was shockingly soft and exquisitely smooth, yet also feverishly hot, the muscles beneath as tight and firm as grenades. "I need you to open your eyes."

Long lashes flipped up, revealing gold-and-emerald irises glassed over and dulled. A second later, big masculine hands wrapped around her neck and tossed her to her back. The mattress bounced, even with her slight weight. She offered no resistance as Kane rolled on top of her, pinning her in place. He was heavy, his grip so tight she couldn't breathe in the rose scent she'd come to associate with him. An odd fragrance for a male, and one she didn't understand.

"Who are you?" he snarled. "Where are we?"

He's speaking directly to me. Me!

"Answer."

She tried to reply, couldn't.

He loosened his hold.

There. Better. Deep breath in. Out. "For starters, I'm your amazing and wonderful rescuer." Since receiving compliments had died with her mother, she'd decided to give them to herself at every opportunity. "Release me, and we'll work out the particulars."

"Who," he demanded, squeezing her tighter.

Black winked through her line of sight. Her lungs burned, desperate for air, but still she offered no resistance.

"Female." The pressure eased again. "Answer. Now."

"Caveman. Free. Now," she retorted as she sucked in oxygen.

Could you watch your mouth, please? You don't want to scare him away.

He jerked away from her to crouch at the end of the bed. His gaze remained on her, watching intently as she slowly sat up. A red flush colored his cheeks, and she wondered if he was embarrassed by his actions or simply struggling to hide the weakness still pumping through him.

"You have five seconds, female."

"Or what, warrior? You'll hurt me?"

"Yes." Determined. Assured.

Silly man. Would it be totally gauche of her to ask him to sign her T-shirt? "Don't you remember what you promised me?"

"I didn't promise you anything," he said, and though his tone was confident, his features darkened with confusion.

"You did. Think back to your last day in hell. It was you, me and a couple thousand of your worst enemies."

His brows drew together, and his eyes glazed with remembrance, comprehension…then horror. He shook his head, as though desperate to dislodge the thoughts now swirling through his mind. "You weren't serious. You couldn't have been serious."

"I was."

He popped his jaw, an action of frustrated aggression. "What's your name?"

"I think it's better if you don't know. That way, there's no emotional attachment and you can more easily do what I require."

"I never actually said I'd do it," he gritted out. "And why are you looking at me like that?"

"Like what?"

"Like I'm…a giant box of chocolates."

"I've heard of you," she said, and left it at that. Truth, without explanation.

"Hardly. If you'd heard anything about me, you'd be running away in fear."

Oh, really? "I know that during the many wars you've fought, your friends often left you behind, afraid you'd cause some kind of travesty for them. I know you often keep yourself shut away from the world, terrified of the same. And yet, still you've managed to slay thousands. Dare I say bazillions?"

He ran his tongue over perfect white teeth. "How do you know that?"

"Why don't we call it…gossip."

"Gossip isn't always right," he muttered. In seconds, he had swept his gaze through the small room and refocused on her.

She also happened to know that visual caress was a habit he'd developed through the years, one meant to take everything in. Entrances, exits, weapons that could be used against him—weapons he could use.

This time, all he would have seen was the peeling yellow wallpaper, the scarred nightstand with the chipped lamp. The sputtering air-conditioning unit. The brown shag carpet. The trash bin filled with bloody rags and emptied tubes of medicine she'd used on his abrasions.

"That day in hell," he began. "You told me what you wanted, and then you made the mistake of assuming I agreed."

That sounded like a refusal. *But…he can't refuse me. Not now.* "You gurgled your assent. Afterward, I did my part. Now you will do yours."

"No. I never asked for your help." His voice lashed like the sharpest of whips, striking at her, leaving an undeniable sting. "Never wanted it."

"You did, too! Your eyes begged me, and you can't deny it. You couldn't see your eyes, so you have no idea what they were doing."

A protracted pause. Then, quite calmly, he said, "I think that's the most illogical argument I've ever heard."

"No, it's the smartest, but your puny brain simply can't compute it."

"My eyes did not beg," he said, "and that's final."

"They did, too," she insisted. "And I did a terrible thing to get you out." Sadly, sending the Phoenix a note of apology wouldn't fix the problem.

As weak as Josephina had been in hell, she'd required help with Kane. Only, once she'd caught up to the Phoenix, still hacking her way to freedom, there'd been a slight problem. The girl had refused so vehemently—*rot in hell, Fae whore*—that Josephina had known there would be no hope of changing her mind. So, Josephina had used the ability she alone carried. A blessing in the right circumstances. A curse that had kept her locked in a world without physical contact. With only a touch, she'd stolen the strength right out of the Phoenix's body, reducing the girl to a boneless heap.

Yes, Josephina had draped the warrior woman over one shoulder and carried her out of hell, the same as she'd done for Kane, fighting demons along the way—a miracle considering she'd never fought a day in her life—eventually finding a way outside, but that wouldn't matter to the Phoenix. A crime had been committed, and a price had to be paid.

"I never asked you to do terrible things." His voice contained the darkest of warnings.

One she did not heed. "Maybe not audibly, but even still, I nearly broke my back saving you." She settled to her knees, shaking the mattress and nearly bouncing the weakened Kane to the floor. "You weigh, like, ten thousand pounds. But they're glorious pounds," she rushed to add. *Stop insulting the man!*

His slitted gaze tripped over every inch of her. The action lacked the stealth he'd used for the room, and yet, it was almost tactile, as if he'd touched her, too. Could he see the goose bumps now breaking over her skin?

"How did a girl like you manage such a feat?"

A girl like her. Did he sense her inferiority? She lifted her chin, saying, "An information exchange wasn't part of our bargain."

"For the last time, woman, there was no bargain."

Tremors of dread rocked her, overshadowing…whatever he'd previously made her feel. "If you don't do what you promised, I'll…I'll…"

"What?"

Suffer for the rest of my life. "What would it take to change your mind and make you do the right thing?"

His expression shuttered, hiding all of his thoughts. "What species are you?"

A question totally off topic, but okay, she could roll. Since the Fae were not a well-liked race, the men best known for their lack of honor in battle, as well as their insatiable need to sleep with anything that moved, and the women known for backstabbing and scandal—and okay, fine, their ability to sew a killer wardrobe—the knowledge might spur him into action.

"I'm half human, half Fae. See?" She pulled back the sides of her hair, drawing his attention to her ears and the points at the end.

His gaze locked on those points and narrowed. "Fae are descendants of Titans. Titans are children of fallen angels and humans. They are the current rulers of the lowest level of the skies." He shot out each fact as if it were a bullet.

Can't roll my eyes at a star. "Thank you for the history lesson."

He frowned. "That makes you…"

Evil in his eyes? An enemy?

He shook his head, refusing to finish the thought.

Then, his nose wrinkled, as if he'd just smelled something…not unpleasant, but not welcome, either. He inhaled sharply, and his frown deepened. "You look nothing like the girl who rescued me…*girls* who rescued me…no, just one," he said with another shake of his head, as if he were trying to make sense of things that had happened. "Her face and hair kept changing, and I recall each countenance, yet what I see now I didn't see then. But your scent…"

Was the same, yes. "I possessed the ability to switch my appearance."

One of his brows arched. "Possessed. Past tense."

Even in his compromised state, he'd caught her meaning. "Correct. I no longer have the ability." The strength—and capabilities—she borrowed from others could remain with her for as little time as an hour to as long as a few weeks. She had no control over the time frame. What she'd taken from the Phoenix had faded yesterday.

"You're lying. No one has an ability one day, but not the next."

"I never lie—except for the few times I do, in fact, lie, but it's never intentional, and I'm totally telling the truth right now." She raised her right hand. "Promise."

He pursed his lips. "How long have I been here?"

"Seven days."

"Seven days," he gasped out.

"Yes. We spent most of our time playing incompetent doctor and ungrateful patient."

A dark scowl contorted his features, and oh, it was a scary thing to behold. The books hadn't done him justice. "Seven days," he repeated.

"I didn't miscount, I assure you. I've been crossing off the seconds in the calendar in my heart."

He gave her the stink eye. "You have a smart mouth, don't you?"

She brightened. "You think so? Really?" It was the first compliment she'd received from someone other than herself since her mother had died, and she would cherish it. "Thank you. Would you say my mouth is extremely intelligent or just slightly above average?"

His jaw fell, as if he meant to reply, but no sound emerged from him. His eyelids were closing...opening...closing again, and his big body was swaying from side to side. He was about to go down, and if he hit the floor, she would never be able to lift him onto the bed.

Josephina surged forward, reaching for him with gloved hands. Though he teetered backward, he slapped her arms away, wanting no contact between them. Smart man. (As smart as he thought she was?) Down he fell, slamming into the carpet with a loud thud.

As she scrambled to her feet to rush to his side—and do what, she didn't know—the motel door burst open, shards of wood raining in every direction. A tall, thickly muscled warrior with dark hair stood in the center of the gaping hole, his features bathed in shadows. Menace lanced from him. Maybe because he gripped two daggers—and they were already stained with blood.

Another warrior moved in behind him, this one blond, with...*oh, someone save me*. Guts hung from his hair.

Her father's men had found her.

THROUGH THE
ZOMBIE GLASS

Where should I begin?

With travesty? Heartache?

No. I don't want to begin with where I am now.

I don't want to end that way, either.

We'll start with this. A truth. Everything around us is subject to change. Today is cold. Tomorrow, heat will come. Flowers bloom, then wither. Those we love, we can grow to hate. And life...life can be perfect one minute and in shambles the next. I learned that lesson the hard way when my parents and beloved little sister died in a car crash, shattering every corridor of my heart.

I've done my best to weld the pieces back together, but—*tick, tock*. Another change.

A change that cost me everything.

The respect of my friends. My new home. My purpose. My pride.

My boyfriend.

And it's my fault. I can blame no one else.

One mistake gave birth to a thousand others.

I knew there were monsters out there. Zombies. I knew they weren't the mindless beings movies and books portrayed them to be. They exist in spirit form, unseen to the ungifted eye. They're fast, determined and, at times, smart. They hunger for the source of life. *Our* spirits.

I know, I know. That's laughable, right? Invisible creatures determined to feast on humans from the inside out? Please. But it's true. I know, because I became an all-you-can-eat buffet—and offered my friends as dessert.

Now I'm not just fighting the zombies. I'm fighting to save the life I've grown to love.

I will succeed.

Tick, tock.

It's time.

BEGIN AT THE BEGINNING

A few months earlier

MORE AND MORE I'd been dreaming about the crash that killed my parents and younger sister. I relived the moments as our car flipped end over end. The sounds of metal crunching into pavement. The stillness when everything was over, and I was the only one awake... maybe the only one alive.

I'd struggled to free myself from the seat belt, desperate to help little Emma. Her head had been twisted at such an odd angle. My mother's cheek had been slashed open like a Christmas ham, and my father's body had been thrown out of the car. Panic had made me stupid, and I'd hit my head on a sharp piece of metal. Darkness had swallowed me whole.

But in my dreams, I watched my mother blink open her eyes. She was disoriented at first, moaning in pain and trying to make sense of the chaos around her.

Unlike me, she had no problem with her seat belt, freeing herself and turning, her gaze landing on Emma. Tears began to rain down her cheeks.

She looked at me and gasped, reaching out to place a trembling hand on my leg. A river of warmth seemed to rush through me, strengthening me.

"Alice," she shouted, shaking me. "Wake up—"

I jolted upright.

Panting, my body dotted with perspiration, I scanned my surroundings. I saw walls of ivory and gold, painted in swirling patterns. An antique dresser. A furry white rug on the floor. A mahogany nightstand, with a Tiffany lamp perched next to a photo of my boyfriend, Cole.

I was in my new bedroom, safe.

Alone.

My heart slammed against my ribs as though trying to burst free. I forced the dream to the back of my mind and moved to the edge of the bed to peer out the large bay window and find a sense of calm. Despite the gorgeousness of the view—a garden teeming with bright, lush flowers that somehow thrived in the cool October weather—my stomach twisted. Night was in full bloom, and so were the creepies.

Fog that had brewed on the horizon for hours had finally spilled over, gliding closer and closer to my window. The moon was round and full, set ablaze with orange and red, as if the surface had been wounded and was bleeding.

Anything was possible.

Zombies were out tonight.

My friends were out there, too, fighting the creatures without me. I hated myself for falling asleep at such a critical time. What if a slayer needed my help? Called me?

Who was I kidding? No one would call, no matter how badly I was needed.

I stood and paced the room, cursing the injuries that kept me tucked inside. So I'd been sliced from hip to hip a few weeks ago. So what? My stitches had been removed and the flesh was already scarring.

Maybe I should just arm up and head out. I'd rather save someone I love and risk another life-threatening injury than do nothing and stay out of harm's way. But…I didn't know where the group had gone, and more than that, if I did manage to track them down, Cole would freak. He would be distracted.

Distraction killed.

Dang it. I would do as I'd been told and wait.

Minutes stretched into hours as I continued to pace, a sense of unease growing sharper with every second that passed. Would everyone come back alive? We'd lost two slayers in the past month alone. None of us were prepared to lose another.

The hinges on my door squeaked.

Cole slipped inside the room and threw the lock, ensuring that no one would bust in on us. Relief plucked the claws right out of the unease, and I thrilled.

He was here. He was okay.

He was mine.

His gaze landed on me, and I shivered, waiting for a vision…hoping for one.

Since the day we'd met, we'd experienced a small glimpse of the future the first time our eyes locked on any given day. We'd seen ourselves making out, fighting zombies and even relaxing in a swing. Today, like almost every day since my stabbing, I experienced nothing but crushing disappointment.

Why had the visions stopped?

Deep down, I suspected one of us had built up some sort of emotional wall—and I knew it hadn't been me.

I was too entranced by him.

Always he threw off enough testosterone to draw the notice of every girl within a ten-mile radius. Though he was only seventeen years old, he seemed far older. He had major experience on the battlefield, had fought in the human/zombie war since he could walk. He had experience with girls, too. Maybe *too* much experience. He knew just what to say...how to touch...and we melted. I'd never met anyone like him. I doubted I ever would again.

He wore all black, like a phantom of the night. Inky hair stuck out in spikes, with leaves and twigs intertwined in the strands. He hadn't bothered to clean his face, so his cheeks were streaked with black paint, dirt and blood.

So. Danged. Hot.

Violet eyes almost otherworldly in their purity shuttered, becoming unreadable, even as his lips compressed into a hard, anguished line. I knew him, and knew this was his let's-just-burn-the-world-to-the-ground-and-call-it-good face.

"What are you doing out of bed, Ali?"

I ignored the question as well as the harshness of his tone, understanding that both sprang from a place of deep concern for me. "What's wrong?" I asked. "What happened out there?"

Silent, he disarmed, dropping daggers, guns, magazines of ammo and his personal favorite, a crossbow. He'd come to me first, I realized, not even bothering to stop at his house.

"Were you bitten?" I asked. Suffering? Zombie bites

left a burning toxin behind. Yes, we had an antidote, but the human body could take only so much before it broke down.

"I saw Haun," he finally responded.

Oh, no. "Cole, I'm so sorry." A while back, Haun had been killed by zombies. The fact that Cole had seen him again meant only one thing. Haun had risen from his grave as the enemy.

"I suspected it would happen, but I wasn't ready for the reality of it." Cole's shirt was the next to go.

The blade-sharp cut of his body always stole my breath, and now was no exception, regardless of the horror of our conversation. I drank him in—the delightfully wicked nipple ring, the sinewy chest and washboard abs covered with a plethora of tattoos. Every design, every word, meant something to him, from the names of the friends he'd lost in the war to the depiction of the grim reaper's scythe. Because that was what he was. A zombie killer.

He was total bad boy—the dangerous guy monsters feared finding in *their* closets.

And he was closing the distance between us. I buzzed with anticipation, expecting him to draw me into his arms. Instead, he bypassed me to fall onto the bed and cover his face with scabbed hands.

"I ashed him tonight. Ended him forever."

"I'm so sorry." I eased beside him and brushed my fingers over his thigh, offering what comfort I could. I knew he understood that he hadn't actually ashed Haun, or even the ghost of Haun. The creature he'd fought hadn't had Haun's memories or his personality. It had had his face and nothing more. His body had simply been a shell for unending hunger and malevolence.

"You had to do it," I added. "If you'd let him go, he would have come back for you and our friends, and he would have done his best to destroy us."

"I know, but that doesn't make it any easier." He released a shuddering sigh.

I looked him over more intently. He had angry cuts on his arms, chest and stomach. Zombies were spirits, the source of life—or afterlife in their case—and had to be fought by other spirits. That was why, to engage, we had to force ours out of our bodies, like a hand being pulled out of a glove. And yet, even though we left our bodies behind, frozen in place, the two were still connected. Whatever injury one received, the other received, as well.

I padded to the bathroom, wet several washrags and grabbed a tube of antibiotic cream.

"Tomorrow I start training again," I said as I tended him, distracting us both.

He glared up at me through lashes so thick and black he looked as if he wore eyeliner. "Tomorrow's Halloween. All of us have the day and night off. And by the way, I'm taking you to a costume party at the club. I'm thinking we'll stick with the whole battered and bruised theme and go as a naughty nurse and even naughtier patient."

My first outing in weeks would be a date with Cole. *Yes, please.* "I think you'll make a very sexy naughty nurse."

"I know," he said without missing a beat. "Just wait till you see my dress. Slutty doesn't even begin to describe. And you will, of course, require a sponge bath."

Don't laugh. "Promises, promises." I tsked, then tried to continue more seriously. "But I never mentioned hunting." Too many people would be out, and some would be dressed as zombies. At first glance, we might not be able to tell the real deal from the fake. "I only mentioned training. You *are* working out tomorrow morning, aren't you?" He always did.

He ignored my question, saying, "You're not ready."

"No, *you're* not ready for me to be ready, but it's happening whether you like it or not."

He scowled at me, dark and dangerous. "Is that so?"

"Yes." Not many people stood up to Cole Holland. Everyone at our school considered him a full-blown predator, more animal than human. Feral. Dangerous.

They weren't wrong.

Cole wouldn't hesitate to tear into someone—anyone—for the slightest offense. Except me. I could do what I wanted, say what I wanted, and he was charmed. Even when he was scowling. And it was strange, definitely something I wasn't used to—having power over someone else—but I'd be lying if I claimed not to like it.

"Two problems with your plan," he said. "One, you don't have a key to the gym. And two, there's a good chance your instructor will suddenly become unreachable."

Since *he* was my instructor, I took his words as the gentle threat they were and sighed.

When I'd first joined his group, he'd thrown me into the thick of battle without hesitation. I think he'd trusted his ability to protect me from any kind of threat more than he'd trusted my skills.

Then I'd proved myself and he'd backed off.

Then he'd accidentally stabbed me.

Yep. Him. He'd aimed for the zombie snarling and biting at him; I'd stepped in to help, and, with a single touch, ashed the only thing shielding my body from his strike. Cole had yet to forgive himself.

Maybe that was why he'd built a wall.

Maybe he needed a reminder of just how wily I could be.

"Cole," I said huskily, and his eyelids lowered to half-mast.

"Yes, Ali."

"This." A slow smile spread as I circled my hands around his ankles—and jerked. He slid off the bed and thumped to the floor.

"What the hell?"

I leaped on top of him, pinning his shoulders with my knees. The action caused the scar on my stomach to throb, but I masked my wince with another smile. "What are you going to do now, Mr. Holland?"

He watched me intently, amusement darkening his irises. "I think I'll just enjoy the view." He gripped me by the waist, squeezed just enough to make sure he had my full attention. "From this angle, I can see your—"

Choking back a laugh, I took a swing at him.

"Shorts," he finished, catching my hand just before impact. I wasn't given the chance to tug free. He rolled me over, stretched my arms over my head and held me down.

Tricky slayer.

"What are you going to do now, Miss Bell?"

Stay just like this and enjoy? I could smell the pine and soap of his scent. Could hear the rasp of our breath intermingling. Could feel the heat and hardness of his body pressing against me.

"What would you like me to do?" I met his gaze, and the air around us thickened, charged with electricity.

Would he touch me?

I wanted him to touch me.

"You're not ready for what I'd like you to do." He searched my face as he reached between us, his actions belying his words...*please, please*...until he slowly pushed the hem of my tee over my navel, revealing every inch of damaged flesh.

He looked me over, and my stomach quivered. Heck, all of me quivered. He crawled down, down, and kissed one edge of the wound, then the other, and a moan left me.

Please. More.

But a moment passed, then another, and he merely returned to his former position, driving me crazy with his nearness but never doing anything to relieve the tension spiraling inside me.

"One more week of rest," he said, his jaw clenched as if he'd had to force the words to leave his mouth. "Doctor's orders."

I shook my head. "I'll ask Bronx and Frosty to train me."

His eyes narrowed to tiny slits. "They'll say no. I'll make sure of it."

"At first, maybe." Definitely. Everyone always followed Cole's rules. Even other alpha males recognized a bigger, badder predator. "However, I have a secret weapon."

He arched a brow. "And what's that?"

"Sure you want to know?" I asked, rubbing my knees along his hips.

"Yes. Tell me." His tone had gone low, gruff.

My knees slid higher, higher still, and he went utterly motionless, waiting to see what I would do next.

I had two options. Try to seduce him into making out with me—*the way he's looking at me...I might actually succeed this time*—or prove I wasn't out for the count.

Sometimes I hated my priorities.

I planted my feet against his shoulders and pushed with all my might. He propelled backward, catching himself on his knees.

"With you? Distraction," I purred.

Laughing, he stayed where he was and lifted my leg to place a soft kiss on my ankle. "I must be seriously disturbed, because I like when you rough me up."

Heat spilled into my cheeks. "You make me sound like some kind of he-woman."

He laughed again, and oh, it was a beautiful sound. Lately, he'd been so somber. "I also like when you blush."

"Yes, well, I'll bug Frosty and Bronx until they say yes." Apparently my inquisitive personality was *not* charming to everyone. Go figure. "They'll be so irritated by their lack of fortitude, they'll throw me around like I'm a meat bag."

"So? You'll get a boo-boo I'll have to kiss and make better. Problem, meet solution."

I swallowed a laugh of my own and had to concentrate to adopt a stern expression. "I'll let you kiss me better—if the boo-boo is on my butt."

"Hmm. Kinky. This is a plan I can get behind... It's a very nice behind."

Tease! "Cole," I said with a pout. "You can't flirt with me like this and then do nothing about it."

"Oh, I'll do something about it." The gruff, wanting tone was back. His gaze locked on my mouth, heating with awareness. "Once you've been cleared."

So, seven more days of Cole's china-doll treatment? *Don't whimper.* "Mr. Ankh would have cleared me already if not for you and your protests." I sat up and shifted my fingers through the silk of his hair. "I'm better now. I swear!"

"No, you're finally on the road to better. But if you start training, that could slow your progress. Besides, you're mine, Ali-gator, and you're precious to me. I want you better. I *need* you better. And okay, yeah, I don't like the thought of my friends putting their hands on you."

Ali-gator? Really? I think I would have preferred something like, I don't know, cuddlecakes. Anything was better than a comparison to an overgrown lizard, right?

And had he just called me *his?*

See? Melting...

"Bronx is secretly into Reeve and Frosty is bat-crap crazy for Kat. They wouldn't try anything." And really, before Cole, no boy had *ever* tried anything with me. I had no idea what made me so irresistible to him.

"Don't care," he said, leaning forward to nuzzle my neck. "I will put my boys in the hospital if they come near you. I don't share my toys."

I had to swallow a snort. "If anyone else called me their toy, internal organs would spill."

"Agreed. Like I said, you're mine. And, Ali, I'd love to be called your anything, especially your toy. I *reeeally* want you to play with me."

Okay, I did snort. Hello, mixed signals. "I'd really like you to prove that, Cole Holland."

His response? A groan.

I sighed. There was nothing mixed about that, was

there? "Back to the pimp hand you're planning to throw around." I had no doubt he could put people in the hospital—he had before—but his friends? Never. I opened my mouth to tell him so, only to gasp. He'd just bitten the cord of my shoulder, and the most delicious lance of pleasure had shot through me. *"Cole."*

"Sorry. Couldn't help myself. Had to do a little proving."

"Don't stop," I breathed. "Not this time."

"Ali," he said with another groan. "You're killing me." He stood with me in his arms and gently laid me on the bed. He stretched out next to me but didn't pull me into his side.

I swallowed a shriek of frustration. I wasn't sure if he was punishing himself for what he'd done to me or if he really was afraid he would break me. All I knew was that I missed the feel and taste of him.

I rolled toward him and rested my head on his shoulder. His skin was warm and surprisingly soft as I traced a circle around the piercing in his nipple. *Bad Ali.*

Smart Ali. His heart kicked into a faster rhythm, delighting me.

Disappointed Ali. He remained just as he was, here but set apart from me.

"When you're better," he finally said.

His ability to resist me was *so* not flattering.

"I wouldn't be able to forgive myself if I caused you any more harm," he added, and I lost my ire.

His concern for me was *beyond* flattering.

"Look, I have to help you guys in some way, King Cole." The moment the nickname left my lips, I knew I'd made a mistake. He'd embrace that one a little too tightly. "Doing nothing is *destroying* me."

He pushed out a heavy breath. "All right. Okay. You can come to the gym tomorrow morning. We'll see how you handle things."

I kissed his jaw, the shadow-beard he sported tickling my lips. "I think it's cute that you thought I was asking for permission."

"Thank you, Cole," he grumbled. He cupped the back of my neck, tilting my head. My gaze met his. "I just want to take care of you."

"You will…just as long as you keep your swords to yourself."

His eyes darkened. "That's not funny."

"What? Too soon? My near-death experience and your part in it aren't something we can joke about yet?"

"Probably not ever."

I nipped playfully at his chin. "Okay." Taking mercy on him, I changed the subject. "Will you finally tell me what's been going on these past few weeks?" Boss's orders. Business wasn't to be discussed. "As you can see, if it's bad news, I can take it."

"Yeah. All right," he replied, his relief obvious. "To start, Kat and Frosty broke up again."

I made a mental note to contact her first thing in the morning.

"Also, Justin's sister is missing."

Justin Silverstone used to be a slayer. Then his twin sister, Jaclyn, had convinced him to switch sides and join Anima Industries; the Hazmats, we called them. They wanted to preserve the zombies for testing and studying and planned to one day use them as weapons, uncaring about the innocent lives that were lost along the way.

"She probably ran off, afraid we'd come after her,"

I said. She and her crew had helped bomb my grand-parents' home. I owed her.

Cole nodded. "Then there's my search. We need more slayers. I know there are kids out there as con-fused as you used to be, unsure why they see monsters no one else can see, and they have no idea what to do about it."

"Any possibles?"

"Not yet. But two slayers from Georgia came to help us out until we've rebuilt our team."

For a while, I'd thought the zombie problem existed only in my home state of Alabama. I'd since learned differently. There were zombies all over the world. Slay-ers, too.

"You should have shared this info long before now. You are such a pain, Coleslaw," I said. Better, but that nickname wasn't the winner, either.

"I know, but I'm *your* pain."

And just like that, my irritation drained away. How did he do it?

"Does Mr. Ankh know you're here?" Since my grandfather had died and my grandparents' house had been torched, Nana and I had moved in with Mr. Ankh and his daughter, Reeve.

Mr. Ankh—Dr. Ankh to everyone outside his cir-cle of trust—knew about the zombies and did all the medical work on the slayers. Reeve had no idea what was going on, and we were supposed to keep her in the dark. Or else. Her father wanted her to have as normal a life as possible.

What was normal, exactly?

"I gave Ankh's security the finger," Cole said with a twinge of pride. "He would feel the need to tell your grandmother, and I don't want to be kicked out and have to sneak back in. I just want to be with you."

"So you're planning to stay here all night and hold me, Coley Guacamole?" Ugh. I shouldn't have gone there. That one reeked.

He barked out a laugh. "I liked King Cole better."

"That's not actually a surprise."

"It just fits me so well."

"I'm sure you think so." I gave a gentle tug on his nipple ring.

"I doubt I'm the only one. And yes, I'm staying." He curled his fingers over mine, pried my grip loose and brought my knuckles to his mouth for a kiss. A second later, there was a flash of panic in his eyes. One I didn't understand and must have misread. Because he said, "Just so you know, you can call me anything you want—just as long as you always call me."

**A timeless seduction
A unique temptation
And a whole world of dark desires...**

From *New York Times* bestselling author

GENA SHOWALTER

And from debut author

KAIT BALLENGER

It all happens in AFTER DARK

Available wherever books are sold!

Be sure to connect with us at:

Harlequin.com/Newsletters
Facebook.com/HarlequinBooks
Twitter.com/HarlequinBooks

HARLEQUIN® HQN™
www.Harlequin.com

PHGHKB825

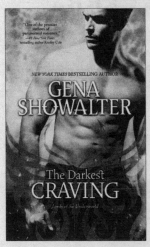

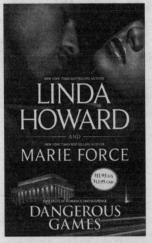

REQUEST YOUR FREE BOOKS!

2 FREE NOVELS FROM THE PARANORMAL ROMANCE COLLECTION PLUS 2 FREE GIFTS!

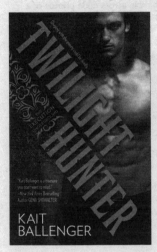